William Robinson

The diary of a samaritan

William Robinson

The diary of a samaritan

ISBN/EAN: 9783337125950

Printed in Europe, USA, Canada, Australia, Japan

Cover: Foto ©Andreas Hilbeck / pixelio.de

More available books at **www.hansebooks.com**

THE
LAND AND THE BOOK;

OR,

**BIBLICAL ILLUSTRATIONS DRAWN FROM THE MANNERS
AND CUSTOMS, THE SCENES AND SCENERY OF
THE HOLY LAND.**

By W. M. THOMSON, D.D.,

Twenty-five Years a Missionary of the A.B.C.F.M. in Syria and Palestine.

With two elaborate Maps of Palestine, an accurate Plan of Jerusalem, and *several hundred Engravings* representing the Scenery,
Topography, and Productions of the Holy Land, and the Cos-
tumes, Manners, and Habits of the People. Two elegant Large
12mo Volumes, Muslin, $3 50; Half Calf, $5 20.

The Land of the Bible is part of the Divine Revelation. It bears
testimony essential to faith, and gives *lessons* invaluable in exposition. Both have been written all over the fair face of Palestine,
and deeply graven there by the finger of God in characters of living
light. To collect this testimony and popularize these lessons for
the biblical student of every age and class is the prominent design
of this work. For *twenty-five years* the Author has been permitted
to read the Book by the light which the Land sheds upon it; and
he now hands over this friendly torch to those who have not been
thus favored. In this attempt the pencil has been employed to aid
the pen. A large number of pictorial illustrations are introduced,
many of them original, and all giving a genuine and true representation of things in the actual Holy Land of the present day. They
are not fancy sketches of imaginary scenes thrown in to embellish
the page, but pictures of living manners, studies of sacred topography, or exponents of interesting biblical allusions, which will add
greatly to the value of the work.

Published by HARPER & BROTHERS,
Franklin Square, New York.

HARPER & BROTHERS will send the above Work by Mail, postage paid, to any
part of the United States, on receipt of the Money.

☞ Every Number of Harper's Magazine contains from 20 to 50 pages—and from one third to one half more reading—than any other in the country.

HARPER'S MAGAZINE.

THE Publishers believe that the Ninenteen Volumes of HARPER'S MAGAZINE now issued contain a larger amount of valuable and attractive reading than will be found in any other periodical of the day. The best Serial Tales of the foremost Novelists of the time: LEVERS' "Maurice Tiernay," BULWER LYTTON's "My Novel," DICKENS's "Bleak House" and "Little Dorrit," THACKERAY's "Newcomes" aud "Virginians," have successively appeared in the Magazine simultaneously with their publication in England. The best Tales and Sketches from the Foreign Magazines have been carefully selected, and original contributions have been furnished by CHARLES READE, WILKIE COLLINS, Mrs. GASKELL, Miss MULOCH, and other prominent English writers.

The larger portion of the Magazine has, however, been devoted to articles upon American topics, furnished by American writers. Contributions have been welcomed from every section of the country; and in deciding upon their acceptance the Editors have aimed to be governed solely by the intrinsic merits of the articles, irrespective of their authorship. Care has been taken that the Magazine should never become the organ of any local clique in literature, or of any sectional party in politics.

At no period since the commencement of the Magazine have its literary and artistic resources been more ample and varied; and the Publishers refer to the contents of the Periodical for the past as the best guarantee for its future claims upon the patronage of the American public.

TERMS.—One Copy for One Year, $3 00; Two Copies for One Year, $5 00; Three or more Copies for One Year (each), $2 00; "Harper's Magazine" and "Harper's Weekly," One Year, $4 00. *And an Extra Copy, gratis, for every Club of* TEN SUBSCRIBERS.

Clergymen and Teachers supplied at TWO DOLLARS a year. The Semi-Annual Volumes bound in Cloth, $2 50 each. Muslin Covers, 25 cents each. The Postage upon HARPER'S MAGAZINE must be paid at the Office *where it is received.* The Postage is *Thirty-six Cents a year.*

HARPER & BROTHERS, Publishers, Franklin Square, New York.

THE

DIARY OF A SAMARITAN.

BY

A MEMBER OF THE HOWARD ASSOCIATION OF

NEW ORLEANS.

Non nobis solum nati sumus.

NEW YORK:

HARPER & BROTHERS, PUBLISHERS,

FRANKLIN SQUARE.

1860.

TO FRIENDS

TOO NUMEROUS TO NAME,

THIS WORK

Is Inscribed

IN GRATEFUL REMEMBRANCE OF MANY KINDNESSES
SHOWN TO

THE AUTHOR.

CONTENTS.

A 2

CHAPTER VIII.

CHAPTER IX.

CHAPTER X.

CHAPTER XI.

CHAPTER XII.

CHAPTER XIII.

CHAPTER XIV.

CHAPTER XV.

CHAPTER XVI.

CHAPTER XVII.

CHAPTER XVIII.

CHAPTER XIX.

CHAPTER XX.

CHAPTER XXI.

CHAPTER XXII.

CHAPTER XXIII.

CHAPTER XXIV.

CHAPTER XXV.

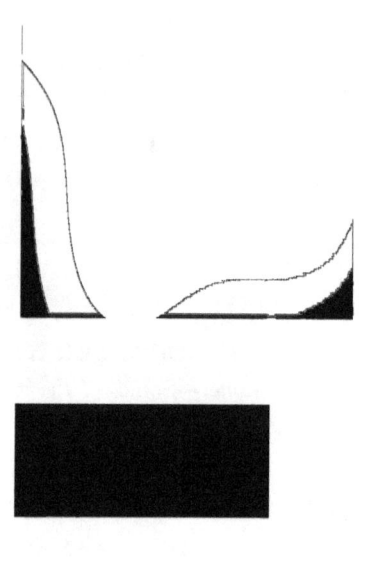

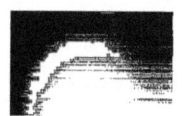

DIARY OF A SAMARITAN.

CHAPTER I.

Object of the Narrative.—The Happiness of the Rich and Poor, in Health and Sickness, contrasted.—Origin of the Samaritan and Young Men's Howard Associations.—Epidemic of 1839.—The Samaritans visit Mobile.—Their Welcome.—The Virtue of Quinine.—Condition and description of Patients.

OF the numerous contributors to the Howard Association of New Orleans for the relief of the destitute and sick during the memorable and fatal epidemic of 1853, none but those in the immediate field of its usefulness have had the satisfaction of being informed of the extent of good accomplished by their mite or largesse. I purpose to show, in an unconnected narrative, the rise, progress, and workings of that and other associations, and by detailing the labor of a member of one, to epitomize, as it were, the character of all.

In the selection from my notes of subjects to introduce the multitudinous duties performed, I have in several instances changed both date and locality, to avoid giving pain to any recipient of our charity, and to mislead the too inquisitive. The narrative makes no pretension to order or style; it is written *con amore*, for the subject matter in reminiscence, and *currente calamo*, as intervals of leisure permitted. As the object of the author is chiefly to uphold the virtue of charity in its fullest sense, he confidently hopes that any digressions or desultory remarks which appear to be latitudinarian in sentiment, or any opinions which might be distorted into a construction of encouragement to vice or immorality, will yield to a view of the whole work in a Hogarthian light. Some subjects treated of will doubtless shock the sensibilities of those unsophisticated in this world's misery and vice; yet, as no disease and no class are excluded from our services and charities, so nothing that concerns humanity is deemed by the author to be foreign to his notice.

Aside from offering this as a tribute of gratitude for the flattering sympathy which magnetically thrilled the American heart from ocean to ocean of its continent so soon as the distress was made known, the beautiful moral will ever present itself to the reader, who has made us his almoner, that charity is a virtue which meets its own reward. "It is twice blessed; it blesseth him who gives and him who receives." It will bring to mind, too, that mutual dependence is a necessity in man—that it is self-preservation—all animate creation, besides, having the unfailing assistance of instinct to guide each independently through existence.

It has been justly said that the adaptation and fitness of matter, organic and inorganic, is the completest evidence we have of a wise overruling Providence; that nothing is misplaced; and that there is a design in the most insignificant creations, without which the universe would be incomplete. With many who are surprised into gray hairs, the reflection comes that *le jeu ne vaut pas la chandelle*. Some have raised a proud head, canopied with happy earthly illusions—they have sunk to rest without the consciousness of the purpose of life. Others plod the path of usefulness humbly and perseveringly, without estimating the virtue of existence beyond the fulfillment of necessary duties; they, too, heedlessly— ay, necessarily heedless—glide into the vortex of eternity, fulfilling a design which they deem they are no party to, because they had no choice in it. When bless-

ed with health, an equal share of happiness is the fruit
of every life, of every condition.   The susceptibility of
enjoyment is finely graduated to the educated capacity
to enjoy.   With each and all, the same passions have
their play.   The laborer, who toils through life by the
sweat of his brow, and draws from the earth its grateful
essence—the miser, whose joy is the possession of dross
which the spendthrift delights to dissipate—the student,
forgetful of his own wants in his Utopian dreams for
the advancement of others—the seamstress at her ever-
plying needle, the wealthy merchant or professional, the
vulgar tippler or the Champagned debauchee—ay, and
to a no less extent than any, the falsely commiserated
slave, all have their proportioned share of hopes, anx-
ieties, and joys, when health, fancied or real, tingles
through their veins.

Change the scene.   Place them all on the threshold
of eternity, the pointed victims of a lingering or fatal
disease, and mark then the inequality of their condition.
To the rich and prosperous, disease or dissolution is refined to a comparative luxury.   The studious cares and
solicitude of friends—the ministering of loved ones to
soften the pillow to the afflicted head, or to ease the
aching heart—the mind untrammeled in its reflections
on, and preparations for, "immortal longings" by gloomy
forebodings of the future of dear ones left behind—all
tend to suffuse the departure of the spirit with a halo
of serene hope, satisfaction, and gratitude to its Maker.

Not so the poor and destitute.   Not so!   With joys
equal to the more prosperous while in health—without
envy and repinings at their lot—grateful, too, to God for
daily success to their toil—the closest approximators to
content—to such, the feeling of abjectness, the consciousness of helplessness, only comes on them when disease,
like a thief in the night, steals upon them.   Then, with
joy dispelled, anxiety is painful, and hope becomes sick-

ened. The reflections on a well-spent life, or the religiously educated assurance of a better, is no balm, no pal-
liative to the painful reflections which overpower them,
as they contemplate the cessation of their usefulness, and
the future of the unprovided ones who are to survive
them. Then comes the dreadful reality *that they are
poor!* Long-accumulated savings are soon spent for
medicines. Day by day the sum diminishes. The cherished articles of furniture or ornament—their household
gods—are sacrificed to sustain the life of their sick, or
to ward off the misery of starvation. The advent of
such intrusion, not counted on—not provided for—par-
alyzes reason, and strikes terror, with harrowing reflections. The maddened brain of the mother, as she
soothes the feverish brow of her sick or dying husband,
while children, languishing and helpless, cry to her in
burning accents of hunger or neglect, may be read in the
intense contraction of the brow—picturing, too, her re-
gardlessness of futurity, her disconsolateness, her despair,
and her desire for death as a blessing.

To such as these the members of the Howard Association have devoted themselves. They have been no
niggards of the fund placed at their bestowal; on the
other hand, they have donated large sums to other associations and to other communities. Every thing that
could induce hope, all appliances of comfort to the sick
or destitute, were actively and assiduously studied. Nature seemed to have endowed some of the members with
more than the allotted share of watchfulness. Every
success or benefit, aptly bestowed, stimulated them, by
the pleasure afforded, to increased exertion and to a
wider field of usefulness. When I add that no sacrifice
of time or comfort labored in the scales of choice, I do not
assert it from motives of self-laudation, or to be famous
for a virtue in the eyes of the world, but to express the
force of any passion where "increase of appetite grows

by what it feeds on." Their recompense is the certain and secret one of self-satisfaction, which the notice of the world or publicity of their acts tends to destroy. As Goethe justly remarks, "Virtues must be loved for their own sake or utterly renounced. They bring no reward unless they are practiced, like a dangerous secret, in utter privacy." In the following pages I shall avoid the mention of any living names, however important to the development of facts, and shall say as little as possible to expose myself to recognition. I count upon a conjecture occasionally unveiling the author, yet, as no one is aware of my undertaking, and as I court concealment, I trust that the curious will not sin against that politeness, delicately insinuated by Plutarch in his reply of the countryman who was asked what he so carefully concealed in his covered basket. *Quam vides velatam, quid inquiris in rem absconditam?* Freely anglicized, "Did I not wish to conceal, I should not have covered over."

He whose lot has been cast in a latitude unvisited by a periodical epidemic among strangers, or where, perhaps, in a lifetime, disease does not assume the aggravation of suffering characteristic of an epidemic, can have no conception of the earnest anxiety for the sick which possesses the acclimated of New Orleans on such occasions. While the sympathy of the former is apt to be chilled at the prospect of his own danger, the consciousness of security in the latter enables him to indulge in the exercise of benevolence to the highest degree of satisfaction.

Until the year 1837, it was the custom of the acclimated to direct their attention more particularly to the victims in their respective neighborhoods. In the epidemic of this year, the calls for relief having been much increased, owing to the large accession to the population since a previous one, the happy suggestion of greater

benefit from associations presented itself to the citizens,
whereby the duties performed would be more equally
divided, and the accident of neglect to any be prevented.
Hence sprung institutions whose fame, though ephemeral as the objects of their care are obscure, yet are constantly active in their benevolence.   Some are endowed
yearly by the state, and others enabled to fulfill their
design by fairs and contributions.   It has been no less
complimentary than flattering that similar institutions
have sprung up throughout the country, whose pro-
gramme for efficiency has been copied from the constitution and by-laws of our society.

The most prominent of associations were the SAMAR-
ITAN and the YOUNG MEN'S HOWARD *Society*.   The
former was composed of middle-aged men and old residents who had the greater confidence of the city authorities.   Funds were supplied by the latter to relieve the
distress throughout the city.   The number of Samaritans did not exceed thirty.   Many of these were incapable of very active duty, and confined themselves to
visiting the sick, engaging nurses for, and giving pecuniary relief to the poor.   They also supervised a body
of younger men, whom they admitted as assistants, whose
duties comprised those of the nurse in its most extended sense.   The *physique* of the latter enabled them to be
spendthrifts of the hours allotted to sleep, with impunity to health.

The other association, the *Young Men's Howard Society*,
was chiefly composed of clerks, who were unwilling to
be tasked out to a service to which they were so enthu-
siastically disposed.   This society depended for its out-
lays upon private contributions, and was the more active
in its labor and appliances of relief.   This assertion is
based upon the fact that they hunted up their sick, while
the Samaritans contented themselves with attending to
such only as applied for assistance through friends or
neighbors.

I had first fallen into the ranks of the Samaritans in the year 1839, as an assistant, anxious to balance the debt of gratitude I entertained toward others who had kindly and perseveringly delivered me through a prolonged attack of yellow fever in the previous epidemic; in remembrance of which, and more fully to designate the intent of these pages, I have denominated myself a *Samaritan*, without pretension or claim to the high character or professions associated with the name. To put the sincerity of the assistants to the test, we were placed as night-watchers and purveyors to the most destitute. Instead of being horrified at such service, the greater the misery, the more abject the individual, the more offensive the surroundings or the duties, the prouder were we of service. As business engagements did not require of us the attention of more than two or three hours of the day, these, and one or two hours after a meal, constituted our only respite from the sick-room. I have no notes of the extent of usefulness done by either society that year in New Orleans, and, upon diligent inquiry, I have failed to obtain any papers or minutes of proceedings, but retain notes of every thing in connection with both societies since.

By the middle of September, 1839, the epidemic had run its allotted course of severity, which rarely exceeds sixty days. Assistants had been daily reporting themselves for service without obtaining a case, and many ceased altogether from attending the rendezvous of the Samaritans. While thus hugging exemption from duties that well-nigh overmatched nature, we were suddenly called together to deliberate on means to subdue a like calamity to that we had passed through, which had set in later at Mobile. The fever was reported to be in its acme of virulence there. As much as we courted repose, the melancholy picture of unattended sick, of prostrated physicians, and of citizens paralyzed with fear,

calling for assistance, chid our conscience as if of unfin-
ished duty had we hesitated to fill the breach of their
affliction. What staggered some was the report that
the disease had the marked character of a pestilence,
and bore equally upon the acclimated and the stranger.
I remember distinctly, as of an occurrence of yesterday,
the meeting which took place in our office in the basement of the St. Charles Hotel. The attendance was full.
When we were called to order, over forty members and
assistants answered to their names. There was a few
moments only of suspense, not to explain the object of
the meeting, but for a suggestion of what action to take.
Each man waited upon the other. Without preliminary
remarks, a resolution was introduced that ten members,
accompanied by as many female nurses, with a physician, be at once dispatched with medical stores and other appliances known to be wanted. Silence gave the
willing response of every heart. There was no need of
putting the question. The only difficulty that arose
was how to select the ten members, as more volunteered
to go than were required. From the number who urged
their claims most pressingly, ten were drawn by lot, I
among them. It was the work of that night and the
next morning to make preparations for our departure.

We landed at Mobile early of the day succeeding.
Contrasted with the bustle and noise of New Orleans,
Mobile presents a Sunday-looking garb of repose along
its extended harbor; but on that morning it struck us,
as the boat touched the wharf, that Silence stood sentinel
with Death. Not a living soul came forward to make
the boat's fastenings—not a hackman to importune us
for baggage. There was only heard the faint surf mur-
murs from a swelling tide, and an occasional order from
the captain, whose voice seemed to shake all space with
its hoarseness.

Taking with us our personal traps, and leaving bulkier articles to be sent for, we scattered along the streets in the direction of the Mansion House. As we progressed, the sound of many footsteps attracted several faces to the windows, all of which appeared to be stamped with the mingled expression of surprise or pity for the ignorance or insanity of such a concourse walking, as it were, into the jaws of death. "Good God! massa," said a negro we encountered, " dey hab Yellow Jack here berry bad; better not stay long." This negro's words and other people's reflections were apparently identical.

The hotel entrance was invitingly open, but, instead of the obsequious or flattering Boniface to greet the advent of so many representatives of currency, we were kept waiting, after our ring at the door, full half an hour, before a half-roused darkey, of about fifteen years, slowly approached us from the rear, and then, as if cognizant of our wants, as slowly sauntered back to look after his master. Very shortly thereafter the surprised host installed us in convenient apartments. He had not been informed of the object of our visit, nor did we inform him, until we were seated at breakfast. We found him a man of noble impulses, who welcomed us directly to the hospitality and freedom of his house, while he detailed a vivid picture, from personal observation, of the misery around. Our physician, with several members, called upon the mayor at an early hour. Had a comet's tail suddenly whisked this functionary to celestial regions, he could not have shown more astonishment and delight than when we were before him to relieve his anxious cares for the population. An extraordinary meeting of the few councilmen was immediately convoked, and our services formally accepted. Conveyances were ordered to be at our service before the hotel, and the expense of our stay, and for provisioning the sick and destitute, assumed by the authorities. A physician of experience had been dispatched with us on the part of the Young Men's Howard Society. He was solicited to accept the appointment of physician to the City Hospital.

In a few hours the news of our arrival had spread rapidly throughout the city, and by noon calls upon us for immediate attendance thickened on us. The city was districted off agreeably to population, and two members appointed to each. As it was impossible for our physician to visit all the patients on notice, we were required, when the case was desperate, or called for palliatives in its incipient stage, to apply certain remedial agents, agreeably to the condition of the patient and the violence of the attack, and to make a note of the symptoms, or, as physicians say, a diagnosis. In all cases we were to visit our patients at least twice a day, and, where they were restless or watchful, to proportion accordingly our night attendance. We were required to serve the medicines to the patients with our own hands, and, in the absence of an efficient nurse, to do every thing promotive of his comfort or cleanliness. Our physician had stated hours to be seen; in the intervals he made calls on all urgent cases, leaving, in our absence, directions for farther treatment.

He had adopted, with the strongest faith in its efficacy, the use of quinine in his treatment of the fever. A physician at the Charity Hospital in New Orleans had recently resurrected this once celebrated agent, and restored the fame of its charming effects by his success. We were advised to give ten to twelve grains of the sulp. quin., if, as we generally found, the patient had taken a cathartic or emetic, and the fever was in its incipient stage. As rapidly as it subdues the fever—to all appearances on the following day removing the symptoms of danger—it nevertheless is a treacherous security unless the patient be closely watched. Relapses were frequent from its use long after convalescence had set in, owing to the prostration it causes to the nervous system. It has warm advocates and violent opponents. The latter argue that the blood requires a certain time to be rid of its poison, be the agents active or slow, and that, by checking the effort of nature to work it off in violent agitation of the blood, we invite a more precarious disease.

The greater part of our patients was of the most destitute class. Before 3 P.M. I had visited ten sick, several of whom were in the advanced stage of the disease, and all too poor to purchase medicines, much less provisions for their household. I hurriedly noted every thing that was wanted, and returned to the hotel, where I found my demand for provisions anticipated. Having received proper instructions from our physician for particular cases noted, and having filled the seats of the carriages with buckets of soup, loaves of bread, and cold meats, we were driven off with glad hearts. Our physician, who encountered us at several shanties where we had entered, shared our joy at the happy countenances of dirty chubbiness as they received the dainties put before them, and felt the good that was done when he witnessed the thankful and thoughtful smile of the sick mother for the considerate care of her offspring. The supplying of provisions was a daily duty, and punctually attended to by all the members. As the number of patients increased on us, causing this attention to engross too much of our time, we were authorized and did open accounts with neighboring grocers to supply a part of the necessary sustenance.

On that evening and night the entry of sick on our book amounted to over forty persons, applications being made by neighboring residents who had heard of our mission. Until after midnight we did not again assemble, and then not for relaxation or repose, but for refreshment. All of us passed the night with our pa-

tients.   Of the latter were two who had been given up
by their physician.   These we resolved to do our utmost
for, as an earnest of what we were capable.   Both were
in the last stage, and had been treated, or rather prostrated, with the strongest mercurial remedies.   To these
two members were detailed, who relieved each other alternately, watching and nursing them with all the appliances of comfort, and succeeded in saving the one who
had entered the first stage of black vomit.

At daylight the following day, each, in his respective
district, drove round to search for objects of his care.
Poor people and destitute sick are only thus known of;
for distress and misery hide themselves in dark holes
and obscure corners, as if sunlight and fresh air were a
mockery to them.   The part of the city allotted to me
was mostly suburban, and surrounded the gas-works.
Grocery-stores at the corners appeared to be the only
habitable places.   In them I made inquiries, for such as
I sought I thought to be their customers.   When the
daily provision of vegetables, bread, meat, or bottle of
spirits failed to be sent for, it was there the cause would
be conjectured.   In the course of that morning I was directed to places with from two to three sick in a room,
none of whom had been visited by a physician.   In some
places I found men, women, and children, the sick sharing the pillow of the well, on the floor, despondingly,
and in some instances drunkenly, waiting their turn to
be relieved by death from a threatened starvation.
Doubtless few of them knew why they lived.   If they
could give utterance to their sentiments, they would say
that necessity placed them here, and that they strive to
live to see the end of it.   As I entered their doors with
uncovered head, some looked wildly, others insultingly
at me.   When I told them that I came among them not
only to use my personal efforts to cure them, but to
make their minds easy by seeing to the comforts of their

household, some shed tears of welcome, while others, as
if I were the city undertaker, gruffly told me I could do
nothing for them, and should not. The latter, I have no
doubt, mistrusted the profession of a benevolence they
could not account for. This suspicion I dissipated by
an early return from the apothecary with medicines and
from the grocery with provisions. Having inquired
closely into their condition and duration of illness, I gave
them their respective doses, enjoining upon them necessary care and a judicious indulgence in their drinks. In
all families I hired an inmate or a neighbor to see that
simple directions in my absence were carried out. These
were generally to give the patients a hot mustard foot-
bath; to keep them well covered to induce perspiration;
then to place at intervals on the forehead a cloth saturated with cold water. All the experienced nurses
brought with us had been placed with the patients of
the first day. As I have often found those who make a
profession of nursing rather prone to adopt a treatment
of their own to the prejudice of the physician, I was not
sorry of the substitutes I had made; and I consider that
to the obedience of the latter to the simple instructions
given them by the physician and myself I owe the success of so many more cures than my associates. A few
days of attendance, and the constant visits of the physician, induced my patients to lean upon me confidently.
"When will you call again, doctor?" was the invariable
inquiry accompanying my departure as often in the day
as I would call. Indeed, they looked upon me as one
of them, and as if all that was done for them had been
prearranged by themselves. On many occasions, when
my orders were not to the letter fulfilled, my temper got
the better of my reason; but the lecturing I gave them,
instead of creating animadversion, appeared to me to
have the effect of drawing them still closer to me.

B

CHAPTER II.

Necessity of Watchfulness on the part of the Nurse.—Delusions of the Dying.—The Pains of Dying exaggerated.—The Widow and her Son.

THE yellow fever is a disease *sui generis*. When the crisis has been reached or passed, the patient enters upon a state so critical that what in other diseases are trifling imprudences are here fraught with most alarming consequences. The cravings of appetite are so sharp during convalescence, and the imagination so active in foretasting the pleasures which are to accompany indulgence, with a reinvigorated, and, I may almost say, a rejuvenated system, that the severest self-denial on the part of the patient is put to the test in the spare diet enjoined. Not only is it important to limit the ration of weak chicken or veal broth, and afterward gradually introduce food to the capacity of the invalid's strength for digestion, but a close watching is imperative to keep him from temptation. The smell of food, no less than the sight of it, will divide his desire between life and gratification. One minute's absence of the nurse from the room at an unseasonable time has been fatal to thousands. Convalescents have been known to use all manner of cunning to induce the nurse to "wink an opportunity;" to beg and implore as if their life was in the indulgence. The fatal mouthful has been sometimes obtained so surreptitiously from the leavings of the nurse's dinner or lunch, while her back is turned for a minute; the cup of coffee drained of its contents so quietly; the emptied plate or vessel shoved beyond the reach of the bedside so unsuspiciously, that no conjecture can reach the cause of a sudden relapse, until the patient confesses in his despair the manner he dared his fate. The force of medicine or palliatives is now rendered useless. Farther treatment is only torture. We see the spirit of him, whose recovery was a hope and a joy, or a professional pride, pass from view as a phantom whose course we can not arrest. Disappointment, mingled with more mortification than sympathy or sorrow, and sometimes expressive anger, are exhibited at the bedside by those who have so fondly and anxiously watched the patient for days and nights; so much so, that I have, in some instances, witnessed an abandonment by friends, who now scarcely commiserated or felt regret at the fatal result.

An invalid of yellow fever must be treated like a child. He must be kept entirely under control. It is a safe rule to follow, when the physician or nurse is confused by symptoms, to do for the patient precisely opposite to what the latter wishes or what he does. If he is thirsty, a piece of ice may safely be placed at intervals in his mouth, or, the better to allay the heated gums, inclosed in a piece of muslin. His excessive thirst must be restrained by spoonfuls of lemonade at long intervals. Should he throw off his covering, it will be found that his extremities are cold, and that the circulation must be equalized by a warm mustard bath and additional covering, for when he feels hot his skin is cold, and *vice versa*. He requires the unremitting aid of external topical applications and sponging. If he is disposed to *coma vigil*, or to be watchful, invite him to sleep by fanning, or by the frequent passage of a cologne-moistened cloth on the forehead and temples; if too much prone to sleep, enliven him with such subjects only as will not create excitement by inducing too much thoughtfulness. In a word, the deceitfulness of symptoms to the physician and patient is a characteristic feature of the yellow fever, creating desires and wishes in the patient almost always antagonist to his well-being. Even a few hours previous to death, when increased hemorrhage of the gums and mortification is indicated in the cold extremities, from the nails transparent of coagulated blood, and when the dent left upon the skin by the pressure of a finger, showing its impress some time afterward, marks an unmistakable prognosis, the patient does not interpret your sadness or silence into despair. For a while the eye brightens, the brow is expressive of thought, the intellect clear, the articulation only indistinct; and merely complaining of languor, with an absence of all pain, he can not realize, when circumstances force you to ask his dying requests, that his end is near. I have known patients to remain in this state for twenty-four hours, but generally then sustained by stimulants. The maddening conviction of dissolution only flashes upon him in one severe convulsion. The eye then becomes suddenly dimmed, the iris alternately and rapidly contracting and dilating; articulation is hurried; and, as evidence that all sensation is giving way, the eye wanders without recognition, the ear is closed to the most endearing epithets, he responds only to the wild imaginings of a fevered brain, restless the while in every limb. Life and death are in fearful contest. It is the last desperate struggle of vitality. The breast heaves with strangulatory efforts, the whole frame quivers under muscular excitement. By one paroxysm all is hushed, and nothing but decay and corruption lies before us.

The witness of such a scene naturally remarks, "How hard he died," from the painful sympathy which the apparent intense suffering creates in him. In a majority of instances, especially in the death of a yellow-fever subject, I believe it is a delusion that the dying man is conscious of any pain. It is a noted fact that the excitement of the brain from mental or physical causes, a disturbance to tranquil breathing from a convulsive effort, a fainting-fit, or a syncope, will paralyze sensation. The appearance of much suffering is shown in the effects of all these, yet the patient, on recovery, has no recollection of any. There is a point in pain which a body in health from a sudden accident may reach; beyond that the senses are numbed and do not sympathize. When the body is enfeebled by disease, the nervous system is more likely to be immediately unstrung, and the suffering is proportionately less, though more active in development. Muscular irritability in both cases is mistaken for sensibility. It is consolatory to think that the paroxysms which stifle the sense of speech, of hearing, and of seeing, should also so affect the brain and unsettle reason that our friend is insensible also to feeling. I have watched the bedside for hours with sympathizing friends whose anguish was poignant in the extreme at these manifestations of dissolution, accompanied with the haunting throes of the death-rattle, and with them prayed for a termination of this seeming, or implored the physician to smooth the way of death by administering a powerful opiate. It is a charity to all for such action on the part of the latter, though it is not generally adopted, on account of the prejudice that "while there is breath there is life," and that no man should be hastened from the earth except by the course of natural laws.

One morning, being accompanied by our physician on visits to my patients, he requested me to stop before No. — Dauphine Street, to meet an urgent call for his attendance. When we found the house by the description given, we noticed that the surroundings indicated the wealth and comfort of a tenant who could not claim our attention, as our mission was entirely to the poor and destitute. The few minutes we allowed ourselves to hesitate was ample time to attract the notice of a servant on the gallery, who hurried to us to say that this was the house we were looking for, and that his mistress had been anxiously waiting for us.

Intending only to enter and make our excuses, we alighted. After crossing a tastefully laid out garden, the door was opened to us, when we encountered the lady of the house in the hall. She greeted us warmly, and was about leading the way up stairs, when, seeing that the doctor held his position, she asked if he would not follow. He replied that his time was engrossed with the poor ; besides, it was uncourteous in him to interfere with the resident physicians, some of whom were yet practicing. On this information she approached, and, with a countenance expressive of some sudden calamity, and in a trembling voice, she told us that her physician was himself taken ill the day previous, and that she, unable to obtain another, had been since relying upon the prescriptions of a neighboring apothecary to save the life of her son. "So," said she, "do not refuse me, for I am poor too, though able to pay." The appeal, from being expostulatory, was irresistibly commanding. We were shown to the second floor. As we surmounted the stairway, a light southern breeze wafted to us, through the opened window, a rich perfume from a Madeira vine which shaded the upper gallery, while the cheerful chirping of some caged canaries indicated to us the studied cares of home beautifying. Upon entering the sick-chamber, every thing, though indistinct from obstruction to light from latticed shutters, completed our impression that we were in the house of one educated to a chaste taste and to the study of comfort.

Dr. —— approached the bed and lifted the musquito-bar to look at his patient. A young man of about twenty-four years was lying in a stupor threatening congestion. This was his third day. With difficulty he was aroused sufficiently to be aware of our presence.

He finally collected his thoughts sufficiently to respond to our questionings. Directions were left for immediate applications, and a promise given to stop at the house that evening, or sooner if sent for. Mrs. L. followed us to the door with almost servile acknowledgments; and, as if fearful of reply, and wishing to delay it if adverse to her hopes, waited until we were descending the steps, when she said,

"Doctor, do you think my son dangerously ill?"

"Always dangerous, madam, when sick of this disease; but I do not despair of him. His symptoms are not the worst; and, with his apparently strong constitution, it requires only close attention to secure his recovery."

"Thank you, doctor," was all she said, but in such a reliant tone as to impress us that the delicate sensitiveness of a refined mind was here afflicted by an imaginary ill which "forestalled its date of grief."

Until 3 P.M. I was around among my patients, busy in the purchase of medicines, instructing attendants and inmates in the procedure of external treatment by my own example, mixing and giving doses, drinks, and nourishment.

On joining my associates at the hotel, I found a table had been spread for us in a private room, well stocked with substantials and wines. Each recounted the increase of labor on his hands, with instances of extraordinary distress, which caused our stay at the table to be as melancholy and gloomy as at a funeral feast. Dr. H., after listening to the cases in charge of the different members, and noting such as required his immediate personal attention, left by himself in a gig. All of us followed to our respective districts.

What principally operated against our greater usefulness was the scarcity of cots and mattresses on sale in the city. Families in indigent or middling circumstances, from necessity or to economize room, huddle the younger members three to four in a bed. It was invariably so with all large families I visited; so that, when one child was sick, it was placed with its parents; when more succumbed, all sorts of expedients were resorted to by us to make them separately comfortable. The little parlor was turned into a dormitory; carpeting, folded as a substitute for a mattress, was laid upon the floor, on tables, or on planks resting on chairs, and a chair placed beside the sufferer for the convenience of placing his drinks or medicine. By a little exertion, we succeeded in making our sick more comfortable and better cared for than they would perhaps have been if they were the only ones ill in the city, and dependent upon their neighbors for attention.

As our sick increased, the facility to obtain female nurses diminished; I had, consequently, to employ male ones, and those black. In no time of his life does a darkey set such an estimate upon his importance and dignity as when intrusted with the care of sick "white folks." He sees the white, always so mindfully his superior by authoritative language and intellect, now subserviently imploring comforts and indulgences, and dependent upon his watchfulness for recovery. Negroes are so organized that they are capable of resisting sleep for successive nights. It is a noted fact on plantations, that after the severest labors of the day, the slaves sit round their fires at night, awake to every occasional remark, and are equal to their daily labor without closing their eyes or reposing. It is a remarkable fact, too, that they are superstitiously afraid to close their eyes when any one is threatened with death in their immediate neighborhood. The extent of this self-denial is carried so far, that I knew one, while the doctor and myself were in conversation, who allowed sleep to steal a march on him in a standing posture, visible in an absence of mind or stupor which required a shake to enable him to recover his thoughts, his eyes the meanwhile open and gazing on vacancy. These are physiological traits, to be accounted for, perhaps, by the contraction of brains or deficiency of mental vigor, but which all know to be common to the jaded horse and other animals which sleep standing in harness.

At seven o'clock I had visited again all my sick, and was occupied until two or three hours after with new patients.

On my return I drove to the door of Mrs. L. As I was expected, I passed in without an alarm at the door. In fact, after a first visit I never disturbed the family by arousing the servants from without, but merely apprised them of my presence by a tap at the chamber door. On this occasion I saw Mrs. L. sitting in the parlor, apparently in great despondency, for, without rising or uttering a word, she directed me to a chair.

"Oh, sir," she said, "I have been thinking how kind it was in you to give me hope, when every body that has called has caused me to despair. My son is my only link to earth; if I lose him I too must die. Indeed, I am afraid I am getting the fever—for—I feel—more exhausted than I ever did; my bones ache; and I feel myself so much disposed to sleep—yet when I try—I can not. Do feel my pulse."

The room being only lighted by the oblique rays of the hall lamp, it was too obscure for me to discover any symptoms from her countenance of what she feared. I took her hand, and, without counting three pulsations, I was satisfied that her system was penetrated by the poison, indicated on its advent by a hot, dry skin.

"You are," said I, "madam, certainly debilitated, and require repose. I now urge upon you, if you would be useful to your son to-morrow, or escape the dangerous consequence of neglecting yourself, that you retire to

B 2

bed immediately. In the mean time, permit me to order your servant to prepare a warm foot-bath, which
will much facilitate your rest; shortly I will return with
the doctor to see your son."

As she arose to follow my suggestion, she complained
of the continued aching of her limbs and of intolerable
thirst.

"I left my son asleep," she said, as we were passing
out of the room; "the prescriptions have been all followed. Come with me and see him before you leave."

Before she reached the stairway I saw that she totter-
ed. Divided between apprehension of alarming her and
desire to serve her, I permitted her to mount several
steps before I took her by the elbow and assisted her.
She insisted upon my entering her son's chamber. He
was sleeping soundly. I thought too soundly, but with
a handsome perspiration, and pulse of about 85. I assured her that he was doing well, and would require
nothing that the nurse could not give, and that she must
now look to herself; that, if there was necessity for her
presence, the servant would call her. She approached
her son, lifted the bar, and throwing it over her, she
knelt by the bedside, dropping her head upon his outstretched hand. This did not arouse him. She sobbed
for a few minutes, and then appeared composed, while
I caught whisperings of prayer, which were prolonged
ten or fifteen minutes. Again she kissed his hand, and
arising, pressed her lips to his brow; then, without addressing me a word, entered her chamber adjoining. I
turned toward the servant, and by the glimmer of the
taper on the mantle I saw the big tears coursing his
cheeks, which spoke volumes for him and in me for the
disconsolateness of the widow. But I am not to be
moved to tears; my province is to check them. I sent
her female servant to instantly prepare hot water, and
to mix in it a quantity of mustard. I gave her the nec-

essary directions to administer. In fear of inordinate delay, I went below and hurried the preparation. In the passage I remained while she underwent the foot-bath. Not a word passed her lips. After ordering the servants to be watchful in both rooms, and on no account to allow a visitor to the house, I set out to seek our physician. On my arrival at the hotel I encountered one of our female nurses. The doctor was not at home. Knowing the importance of immediate attention to, and a proper performance of certain offices in the management of this new case, I drove the nurse at once to the residence of Mrs. L. On my return I learned she had been vomiting considerably, and was what is termed a beautifully developed case. I gave her ten grains of sulp. quinine, leaving the nurse to attend to farther necessities.

As it was about the time I should make my nightly round of visits, I set out in the direction of my district. At some of the houses I found the doors ajar, the inmates careless of intruders, and perhaps fearing none, so long as a dreaded guest had stalked in; at others, loud knocking had to be resorted to to arouse the wearied ones within. I had four new cases. After giving foot-baths, applying cataplasms, seeing that the cups were replenished with drinks and placed within reach, I enjoined upon all to keep the covering well over them, as the night air was damp and chilly. All promised to obey my injunctions, and, in return, seemed to treat me as one of the family, by boldly expressing their wishes for me to attend to certain services for them.

A singular feature which manifests itself in this disease after the fever is broken is a weariness, akin to the sensation of sea-sickness, which, like the latter, makes the patient indifferent to all and every thing around him, regardless of the present and fearless of the future. This is more apparent in those afflicted with the congestive type. Such as these require to be watched closely. They are too lazy to stretch their hand for drink, how much soever they may want it, and even the effort of rolling a piece of ice in the mouth appears to be done with labor.

It was 3 A.M. when, without notice, I again entered the house of Mrs. L. The son was tranquil, but with mischievous symptoms of a typhoid character. The mother was asleep, suffused in perspiration, and with a reduced pulse. Dr. —— had seen them since I left, and approved of what I had done for her.

As I have before stated, we were organized exclusively for the benefit of the poor and destitute sick, who, in this latitude, are chiefly recent immigrants, and uneducated. I have noticed that the indifference to recovery is in inverse ratio to the intelligence of the patient. This is likely to be mistaken for resigned despair, heroism, or philosophy; but it is hopelessness. Unprovisioned for such a calamity, never having dreamed of the reality, they do not trouble themselves with thinking, but stare a future existence in the face with a welcome. To this apathy they owe their deliverance from a fatal result, even under all the disadvantages of neglect, privation, and imprudence; while those of superior intelligence, whose brains never cease to be agitated by apprehensions of the future, with the slightest departure from a prescribed course fall victims to their fears. Whenever I have perceived an intelligence superior to the mass— I know not why—my sympathies have been more enlisted, and my exertions to save more unremitting. Life to him has certain joys which gold can not purchase, and which the dark future does not promise to his sense. The enjoyment of distinction, and to make a name for himself, is strong in his many desires to cling to life. The man of equal industry, but without such incentives to live for, is readier to bow to the will of his Maker. The former is not worldly selfish; he desires life for its usefulness to others, not for parade. The latter frequently desires death for himself and his little household, that they may participate in the joys of a futurity which they have been taught they will partake of as a reward for virtue. With a healthier organization than the former, his disease is more manageable, because reflections which, ghost-like, actively flit before the former, do not shut out from him the sweet and indispensable restorative, sleep. It has been our invariable practice to dispossess the mind of the patient of apprehensions of death. Our countenances, as is the physician's, are schooled to conceal anxiety and doubt. We talk over the morrow or the future as if it were a certainty. We promise a stronger nourishment, a social julep at our wonted resort, a ride in the country, a visit from their shut-out friends, and sometimes we lose ourselves in irreverence by perpetrating a joke on their condition or by the relation of an anecdote. It is a hard service to inure one's self to, especially when adopted toward almost hopeless cases; yet, after witnessing its efficacy in the cheerfulness and hope it induces, we continue to practice it.

The ignorant poor are not so much consoled by words as by a freedom of thought of how or where they are to be supplied with relief and sustenance; satisfied on this point, they are resigned to whatever fate awaits them.

I reached the hotel shortly after leaving Mrs. L., where I found six or eight of my associates. They were awaiting a repast at that late hour, which was in preparation for them. At the table we recounted the day's adventures. Our work was progressing famously. It appears that our fearlessness in visiting the sick and with impunity, dispelled the prevalent terror as to the pestilential character of the epidemic, and, from our example, the young men of Mobile formed a society for similar duties as ours, calling themselves the "Can't Get Away Club;" an institution which continues to be the pride, and a feature of Mobile, from the incalculable benefits rendered.

A clergyman who stood high in the regards of the citizens, and who had solicited, through the mayor, the attendance of our physician and one of our nurses, was this day pronounced convalescent.

On the day following the attack of Mrs. L., which was the fourth day of her son's illness, I was accompanied on my early visit by the doctor, who informed me that he had no hopes of the latter, as the symptoms were encephalic and complicated. He was repeatedly calling for his mother as imploringly as a child. The attendant told us it had been thus for several hours, and that the distracting sounds kept her constantly restless and excited by his frequent cries of "Why don't you answer me, mother?" We were also informed that, upon his noticing the door between the apartments to be closed, and his order to open it not being obeyed, he had partly risen from the bed, and was with difficulty held therein, until his request had been complied with. We expostulated with him on his conduct, telling him of the danger to his mother from constant interruptions to repose; and we threatened that, unless he checked himself, we would remove her to another apartment, out of reach of his voice. This stilled him for the nonce.

The patients were more closely examined. The stomach of the son was extremely irritable, a slight pressure thereon causing acute pain. His head was hot, his skin cold and clammy. His strength was fast wasting. The doctor ordered appliances for relief, and gave him a soothing potion. While I was preparing and administered the prescriptions, the doctor remained in the room. Just as I had finished, the patient commenced to toss himself from side to side, and exclaimed, "Jack! harness the mare right off, as I must be at the Pavilion in fifteen minutes," followed by other expressions referring to his daily habits. Delirium or flightiness at that period of his sickness was an unmistakable *avant courier* of approaching dissolution.

Having closed the door between the rooms, we entered the apartment of the mother. The head of the bed intervened, concealing our entrance from her view. As we stole to the bedside, so as not to disturb her repose, we surprised her with her hands folded in prayerful position on her breast, as she murmured forth, "My poor son! may God bless and save you!"

When she recognized us, the doctor congratulated her upon the favorable symptoms—that her pulse was natural, and, having passed the first danger, her future safety was in her own keeping.

" A little patience, madam," he said, "a little self-denial in the gratification of your appetite for food or drinks, a quiet mind, and you will be well enough in a few days to sit beside your son."

Is such language a mockery of truth when its healing influence is certain?

" Then he is getting better, doctor?" she rejoined.

"Doing well—very well, madam."

" Thank God!" she responded, and lay with her eyes fixed on the tester of the bed, abstracted in thoughts perhaps of gratitude for the realization of her wishes. We never before had an opportunity of closely reading the character of the face before us. The features were amiable in their traits. Her large and prominent blue eyes were such as pictured ideality. Her forehead, unruffled by the lines of a severe or anxious existence, was gracefully arched, and stamped with intellect, while the mouth and chin developed a sweetness of disposition, which, as the possessor grows older, is the more distinctly expressive. When she spoke her sentiments were imaged in the play of features. In a few words, her face was a devotional one, such as is represented by the portrait of St. Cecilia.

At 10 o'clock that night I was again present. I encountered the servant on the step, who told me he was "just going for me;" that his master was out of his senses and unmanageable, calling again loudly for his mother, and striving to get from the bed. The nurse for the mother met me at the door with the remark that it was impossible for her patient to recover so long as she heard the moans and calls of her son. I approached the bedside of the latter. By the light of a candle I caught sight of his eyes protruding from their sockets, wild and bloody in their gaze as is that of an infuriated tiger. I knew that it does not well to provoke a thought in a patient such as this; so I was silent; but on handing him a lemonade, which he fancied more than any thing else, he seized with sudden force and strength the hand which clasped the glass, as if afraid I should take it away before he had finished the draught. Wondering at this, I asked if drink had not been freely given to him. I was answered that he refused, since my absence, to take any, but would occasionally allow pieces of ice to be put in his mouth.

Yellow-fever patients are sometimes troubled with the suspicion—and very difficult to dissipate—that a nurse or attendant, or even a friend, has a design upon their lives. They thus stubbornly refuse, without a reason, kind offices shown them. In New Orleans it was the custom among clerks who occupied *chambres garnies*, when conscious of approaching death from yellow fever or cholera, to make partition of their effects among their friends and distant relatives. As they commonly lived up to their salaries, the doctors and nurses could not be promised to be paid in cash unless they were cured, so that their bills were engaged to be paid in kind. The nurse, for instance, to have the watch, and the physician and undertaker to be paid from the sale of clothing, ornaments, or books. It can readily be imagined, under such circumstances, that when the effects left were valuable, a suspicion should arise in a patient that there was a designing interest in his death, as is unjustly mooted on the death of a rich man, from the physician generally charging his estate five times more than if a cure had been effected; but I can not conceive any cause for the suspicion, or for the conduct of the widow's son, especially in preferring the ministering of a stranger to that of his own servant.

While yet watching my patient I noticed his hand extended toward me, which I pressed. Then, gazing on me, he addressed me:

"Thank you, doctor, don't leave me; there have been robbers in this room, and they have been giving me fire to drink. See! they are now preparing to— See! there is one—keep him off—oh! look at him! See! see! see!" and he pointed toward his faithful servant, whose outline could be scarcely distinguished by him through the musquito bar.

With an impressive earnestness, the affected negro replied,

"This is me, massa—I ain't no robber."

I saturated a cloth in ice water, which he let me place upon his forehead for a few minutes, and with a wet handkerchief, sprinkled with cologne, passed over his face and neck, I soothed him and calmed his fears. The cataplasms gave him uneasiness; he pointed significantly to them to be taken off. The bedclothes were now arranged around him. A freshly-bolstered pillow being in readiness to put under his head, I raised him by leaning over him, and placing his clasped hands around my neck. Every thing was done to invite quiet and repose, and for a time promised well. He motioned for the candle, and, as I saw that he was not disposed for sleep, I

took it from the hearth and placed it on the mantle-
piece. He became busied in his own thoughts. At
length he remarked,

"Didn't you hear my mother vomit just now?"

"No," I replied; and I really did not, and thought it
imaginary on his part.

"I did," said he; "why don't you go and see her?"

I entered by the way of the corridor, and shut the
door quickly after me. I found his assertion too true.
She had just vomited an inordinate quantity of liquid.
I did nothing to check a farther disposition to it, as she
felt no pain; indeed, I would not assume the responsibility of her case, and awaited the physician. She acknowledged to me that she could not resist the indulgence, and had helped herself to more than the nurse
had allowed.

I was now invited by a servant to a repast that had
been prepared for me in the parlor. The dishes were
appetizing, but continued watchfulness and irregularity
of habit had made me dyspeptic, and the main sustenance I sought I found in stimulants. I threw myself
on the sofa, waiting to be disturbed by the least noise
overhead. Every twenty minutes I crept up stairs:
both patients remained quiet.

As I smoked a cigar, for the twofold purpose of gratification and relief from musquitoes, I had abundant leisure to note the admirable taste displayed in the furnish-
ing of the rooms. That charm of home attraction and
dispeller of ennui, the acquired taste for indulgence in
which is a blessing, a well-selected library, prominently
met the eye in the Gothic structure of the bookcase; a
piano, surmounted by a guitar, with a stand of sliding
shelves beside it stocked with well-thumbed music—engravings of a national character suspended from the
wall—each chair a luxurious lounge, with corresponding furniture tastefully chosen—all were in beautiful

keeping with the estimate we had formed of our patient's character.

It was now near to midnight, and, judging I could safely steal away on a rapid drive among my other patients, I jumped into my buggy at the door. After the ordinary incidents of visits which did not occupy long, I drove to the hotel. I was much surprised to find our office thronged with visitors, who, it appears, unable to sleep from thinking of the horrors around them, sought companionship to dispel their gloom. I threw myself, exhausted, on a sofa, and slept until daylight, awakening much refreshed. I was too much engaged on the next day to pay the usual visits to Mrs. L. and her son, but heard from the doctor of their condition.

At 10 P.M. I stopped at her house. The servant, who heard me enter, met me with the information that his mistress was much worse, and that the doctor, who had just left, had said his master was dying.

The musquito bar had been drawn from the bed, and there he lay in all the violent symptoms of dissolution. The black vomit curled involuntarily from his mouth to the pillow; a twitching at the corners of his mouth gave it a sardonic expression; his breath was quick, hot, and repulsive; as his breast heaved, he moaned; the eyes wandered in every direction he could turn his head, resting not a second on any thing; and, to complete the picture, his fingers were active in picking at the bed-clothes.

To all my inquiries he was silent. He seemed bent on combating the disease one moment, passing his hands as if for relief across his breast; at another, rolling on the side to avoid suffocation. He gratefully received the pieces of ice we placed in his mouth, and rapidly cracked and swallowed them. Again he repeated the cries of "Mother! mother!" at the same time endeavoring to rise from the bed; which effort, after we

had overpowered him, completely, as we thought, prostrated his remaining strength. "Here! here!" cried he,
pointing to his breast; "fire! fire! mother! oh, come to
me!" This continued cry gave me serious fears for her
and I left for her room. The constant interruption to
repose, and the disturbance of mind occasioned by these
poignant cries, had injuriously affected her. She said
she knew her son was dying, and that she did not wish
to survive him. She complained of great heat of the
stomach, which made itself evident shortly after in
retching. In a moment I was at the hotel, and returned
with the doctor. He gave his orders to the nurse, and
requested I would remain to see or assist in carrying
them out. Before he left I did not think it worth while
to ask his opinion of her. I read it in his countenance.

While the nurse was attending to matters which dispensed with my presence in the room, I descended to
the parlor, and, taking a book, hoped to relieve myself
from the saddening reflections which possessed me. My
eyes mechanically passed over pages without impressing
my mind with the subject. I had been thus engaged
when Mrs. L. sent the nurse to say she desired to see
me.

"As I am assured," she said, "that there is no hope
of my son's recovery, and as his end will be the immediate precursor of mine, I have called you particularly
now, while I am able to do so, to do farther acts of kindness, which shall receive my last acknowledgments. I
am told my son is insensible to any impressions. It will
please me much, though, if you will take this, his father's
gift, to him—" Here sobs and bitter tears, lasting many
minutes, prevented farther utterance. She had grasped
a book from her side as she spoke the last words, and
still held it in her hands. I saw that it was a small
edition of the Bible. She continued: "Take this book
to him; press it to his lips, as it has been often to mine,

in remembrance of the same act performed by him to his father, and cherished on that account. It was our promise to each other to sanctify the first act by the like performance to either of us under a similar misfortune."

It was a simple performance, and I rose to do her bidding. At first I attempted to arouse him by saying his mother had sent him the book for the expressed purpose. He turned his gaze toward me without answering, even in action, as I held the book before him. I then placed it in his hand and conveyed it to his lips. So soon as I did so he appreciated the object, and, pressing it to his lips, he increased his moans, with the cry of "Mother! mother! where are *you* when I am *dying?*" Again it was with the utmost force we could keep him in bed.

I returned to Mrs. L.; she had heard all; and upon being told that her son had performed the required act, she exclaimed, "It is all well now: my son is God's own child. Just reaching manhood too—to die! He was the favorite of his set, sir. We will leave this world together—oh yes, together!"

I thought there was an effort to shed tears. It would have been a relief; but she was trying to be resigned, and the anguish expressed in her countenance spoke of the combat going on within herself. Thus she lay for ten minutes in intense abstraction, the Bible pressed to her lips with both hands. In a quiet tone she said, "Another favor: with the last survivor, place this book in the coffin."

By her request, I read to her several psalms and hymns which she selected. She would frequently interrupt me before finishing a stanza, and repeat the line which struck her as applicable to her condition, and dwell upon each word with impressive eloquence. Then followed, in a subdued voice, the Lord's Prayer, the beauties of which are only known to those who have felt its embodiment of praise, and are themselves gratefully dependent. The rich and the poor, the fortunate and unfortunate, the easily contented and the woebegone, in their practice of religion articulate these same words. They are as comfortable to the mind of the dying as to the living; yet how different in meaning and expression are they respectively ejaculated! Its grateful essence of dependence brings all to a better knowledge of themselves. It is an epitome of faith, hope, charity, and praise. The universality of its application to the condition of man is an earnest of its divine origin. It is the embodiment of morality. In a word, it typifies the volume of Sacred Writ as well as it embraces the cardinal features of heathen worship and savage adoration.

She now expressed a desire to live, to do the same acts for another which I had done for her and hers. She thanked me in all language that can be used, unmindful that her very gratitude and appreciation of the service I had performed made me her debtor for the opportunity. As I arose to leave she gave me her hand and said, "Indeed, indeed, you should be blessed. An angel could do no more."

It occurred to me now to ask if she would not permit me to go for her clergyman, which before I feared to do, as it might confirm her in her presentiment, and render medical treatment powerless.

"Alas!" she said, "he and his family became terror-stricken, and long since left for the interior."

"Shall I not call in another? The form of a religion or profession of faith is too trifling a thing to except to, when all have the same object and purpose in view."

"No, no; stay you only, as my guardian angel, for yet a short while. I feel that this burning heat within will soon exhaust me. I hope so. I have made my peace with my God. Would you believe that I looked for all this? Yes, and just as it has happened. When my son was first taken sick, the whole of the painful reality—his now dying state, my prostration in this bed, a strange visitor, and a termination horrible to dwell on, all passed before me."

An infatuation similar to this is often met with in fever-patients. The reality seems to the sufferer a dream of earlier date. I saw that my presence incited her to too much conversation; and, as I could not be farther useful, and repose was all-important, I withdrew.

Again I approached the bedside of the son. His pulse was scarcely perceptible to the touch. He lay calm, and unmindful of any thing passing around him. From time to time he opened his mouth as a sign for the negro to give him more ice.

I descended to the parlor, and tried again to read. My thoughts still dwelt upon this picture, so different from others I was attending. I tried to sleep, expecting to be awoke when there was need of me. The mantle clock struck one; I thought it was at least three o'clock. So different wear the hours away when the heart is glad in its sympathies than when desponding of success. A thousand mournful memories arose before me as I lay down to court the "dewy-feathered sleep." Stimulants now to nerve me to my duties became a substitute for repose. Of a sudden I heard a shriek, startling to the hearers. It was one long, agonizing sound, which at its close was accompanied by a sound as of heavy bodies falling on the floor above me. In an instant I was on the spot. The horror of a more heart-rending scene than ever fancy painted shocked me, and riveted me to the floor as I stepped into the room.

It appeared that the servant of the son had left the room to procure more ice from a box at the end of the corridor. The patient had watched this opportunity, and the desire that had been uppermost in his mind for several days to see his mother was not lost sight of. With almost superhuman exertion he arose from his bed, and, supporting himself to the next room, before the nurse could intervene, he had fallen a corpse by his mother's bed, with his last breath crying "My mother! my mother!" As soon as she perceived her son, she raised herself in the bed and uttered the terrifying scream; then, as if in the act of catching, lost her equilibrium on the bed, and, bearing down the coverings with her, fell upon his lifeless body. I took no note of minutes; we were all nearly helpless from surprise. We took hold of the widow to lift her on the bed. She had just begun to be conscious of the reality, and, throwing aside our arms, she sobbed upon his brow in wild agony. In a short time she was gentle and yielding as we took her in our arms and lifted her in bed. While the nurse and I watched the mother, the corpse of the son was taken into the next room.

She lay perfectly tranquil, her eyes fixed on vacancy. Dreaming or insane? For either it was my prayer; for the realization of such a scene was enough to crush with avalanche force remaining vitality. We had no comfort in words to offer, but occupied ourselves in offering drinks, and in cooling her fevered brow. For a long time she moved not a limb or muscle; still fixed were those eyes, full of thoughtfulness. Her lips were compressed, and to resignation despair now seemed to succeed.

Suddenly her eyelids closed, and, lifting her hand to her forehead, as if recalling a dream, she exclaimed,

"Who's there? who's there?"

"It is I," we simultaneously replied; "do you not know me?"

As if begging for her life, and with the intonation noticed on her first appeal to the doctor to visit her son, she ejaculated at intervals, "For pity's sake, do not murder me! My son! my son! they are taking me away from you. Haste! haste! Ah! ah! ah! ah! you have come in time." Her arms wildly clasped a shadow, and, as her head rolled on her arm, I thought it was her last effort. Soon the dread precursor came in a continuous stream, followed by such violent convulsion of the whole frame as to shake the bedstead. Hastily replacing clean linen under her head, I saw my services were coming to an end. I directed the servants to wash the corpse of the son; assisted them in dressing it, closed the eyes, and tied a handkerchief under his chin. This did not take more than half an hour. I was about to depart on other duties deferred, when the nurse stopped me to say Mrs. L. desired one word with me.

"Don't leave me *now*," said she. "Oh! stay a little longer. I shall soon die."

I told her that I intended to apprise the neighbors of her situation, who would be glad, from their inquiries of her, to wait upon her.

"I do not want them. For charity's sake, *you* stay."

I drew a chair and sat by the bed. She drew my hand to her lips, saying, "God bless you, sir; a stranger, and so kind."

I was not as experienced then in mastering my feelings as I am now under such circumstances. Tears involuntarily gushed from me, and, on looking at the nurse, I found her equally affected.

The widow asked for the Bible. She looked at me as she placed it to her heart, and said, "This has been my comfort and happiness; be it so to you."

An indistinct muttering as she closed her eyes told me she was absorbed in prayer. Alternately her remarks were sensible and unmeaning. She told me that papers in her drawer would be called for by Lawyer ——. She begged me to take from her jewelry a memento of her. She thanked me over and over again; repeated

C

parts of a hymn I had read to her; and, just as day was heralding its advent by the gray tint on the horizon, her spirit gently and imperceptibly left its mortal tenement, wreathed in pleasant fancies, doubtless borne on the wings of hope and faith, in company with her son, to the happy future of a well-spent life.

It was the occupation of a few minutes to apprise the neighbors of the fatality. I hurried to the hotel, threw myself on a bed without undressing, and slept the sleep of the inebriate, unconscious of the outer world, and tossed in horrid dreams, the fruits of the scenes just passed through. Two hours after I awoke with a violent headache. With a memorandum and report of their deaths was buried temporarily the recollection of the incidents. The condition of others equally distressed engrossed anew my time and thoughts.

CHAPTER III.

The Confidence of the Sick.—The Sickness of a Family.—The Devotion of Ina.—The Death of little Georgy.

THE *modus operandi* of the Howard Association is imperfectly shown in the details of the preceding case of the widow and her son. I selected it the first, among others, to bring it in comparison with those of humbler life, which is more peculiarly our province. It will strike many that there is a vein of pretentiousness and egotism running through the opinions and conversations, which will have the effect to detract from the merit of the narrative, if they do not bring the veracity of the author into question; for true merit is modest to assert, and vaunts not superior virtue in its works. My aim, to place the practice of good works before the world, to drag to light their hidden pleasures for imitation, can

not be restrained by the fear of censure or ridicule.. I
claim no praise for what I have done. I should be less
than human if my sentiments were other than I expressed, albeit we blush at our amiable weaknesses. I have
curtailed the conversations of much that would be con-
strued into vanity. It is impossible, however, to escape
the affectation of it, unless I omit them altogether, and
destroy this character of all narratives. Family difficulties and oppressions of kindred, which slander gloats
over in refined circles, and for which redress is had,
without shame, to the courts of law, are submitted to by
the lower classes with dignified grace, and with more of
sorrow than indignation. When the physical infirmities
and temporary wants of families had been dispelled and
satisfied, they leaned upon me for condolence and advice for their sickness of heart or crushed feelings. The
lapse in morality or virtue which stained their hearth
was dwelt upon with a bitterness of anguish which expressed how strongly they despised the sin, how deeply
they pitied and lamented the sinner. Their recitals left
upon me no such impression that they considered their
characters reflected upon by the sins or misdeeds of a
relative, how much soever they might suffer from the
acts. As I deemed their confidence in their revelations
the mere tribute to and consequence of my services and
sympathy, how interesting soever the details might be
to the reader, where there is the least possibility of recognition, or where painful reflections would ensue to a
survivor or relative, I have kept their secrets as closely
locked in my breast as in a confessional.

A cottage house near the gas-works at Mobile was
the residence of a family consisting of man, wife, and
five children, the latter ranging in age from five to seventeen years. Being attended by a resident physician,
their demand upon us was for the necessaries of life.
The citizen who informed me of their condition told me

that all but one were prostrated by the fever, and from the long duration of it in the family their means had become exhausted, and that they would starve rather than beg. He thought they might be approached so that they would appreciate a kindness even from a stranger, without feeling the shame of dependence on charity. I thought so too, and started forth in search of them.

A small garden-patch between the house and sidewalk was divided by a walk, and planted with rose and other bushes, neglected of late, but no less an introduction to the endearment of home entertained by the inmates. The house contained four rooms, with a gallery in the rear, having cabinets on the sides. In a spacious yard a shed was erected, where the necessary utensils of cookery met the eye. The rooms of the house were respectively appropriated to a parlor, with eating-room in the rear, and two sleeping-apartments, all with doors opening to the rooms adjoining.

When I entered the parlor, the door of which was open, and with a gentle rap met with no response, I advanced to the adjoining front room, the door to which was partially open. With a gentle tap here, I received an invitation to enter, and I found myself before a bed where lay the mother with a girl of fourteen years, and near to them the father in a bed with the boy of five years. Two other children, both girls, occupied a small bedstead in the back room. The remaining child, a little girl of eight years, had just entered, bringing a pitcher of water.

As I made my bow, with a salutation of "I should be glad to have it in my power to be of use to you," the little girl, whose name was Ina, remarked that "perhaps I was the good gentleman Dr. —— said would call to see us."

The father looked at me, as if he saw in my youth or apparel nothing to indicate a sympathy for him; the

wife, disturbed by my entrance, and perhaps unwilling to
be seen to be afterward recognized as an object of charity, drew the coverlet of the bed close above the neck
of herself and daughter. None spoke or looked a welcome. I patted the little girl with the pitcher on the
head—a bright, healthy, and happy-looking child—as
though I depended upon her for assistance in furthering
my wishes. At that moment she was called by her
mother. She bounded to the bedside, flinging back a
smile to me. She listened to the whispered orders of
her mother; removed several articles from the room;
then brought a chair, with a smart grace, and placed it
before me. Having seated myself beside the mother, I
learned from her that her two daughters and husband
were first stricken with the fever, and had been convalescing for several days; that herself and the daughter
in the bed with her were pronounced out of danger, and
that her fears were only now for little Georgy, who was
in his third day of attack. From the commencement of
the fever among them, the well had nursed the sick;
but, since three days past, Ina, the youngest daughter,
was their sole reliance to run errands, and to prepare
their drinks and broths, and to attend generally in the
rooms. For an hour or so at a time a neighbor would
sit with them, who feared by too long attendance to con-
tract the same disease. I saw my visit was well timed.
Turning toward the father, I explained to him the objects and duties of our association; among others, that
an inviolable secrecy was enjoined upon us in our intercourse with applicants; and that, if he would permit me
to gratify his wishes, he would place me under obligations to him. He returned me no reply. A conflict, I
thought, was passing within him as he pondered on my
words. Perhaps I had awoke in him a sense of the desolateness of his condition. Seeing he continued silent,
I left him to his reflections, to take a survey of the pan-

try, or to inquire of Ina the necessaries required for their sustenance and comfort. The father heard me in conversation with her, and called to her in an authoritative tone to come to him. I followed, and explained the purport of my conversation with her. I told him I was determined to perform what I had promised, and what was enjoined upon me; that, 'where I found distress, I would relieve it, *nolens volens.*

"We want nothing, sir," he replied. "I have a physician, and can pay for my own medicines. I have friends, sir, and do not seek the charity of strangers. I thank you for your kind offer, but I choose not to trouble you."

This was said in a slow and determined voice, and I thought angrily. The eyes of all the sick were upon me, and no doubt looked for my immediate departure. I spoke of my acquaintance with their physician, and urged my claim to their notice on the strength of our mutual friendship; and told him that his family should want nothing, for an invisible hand would do for them all that was required, through the former. "Indeed, you are good, sir," said the mother. "Why don't you let the gentleman have his way?" To this he made no response. I left them, saying I should shortly return, allowing them sufficient time to hold a family consultation on the propriety of acceding to my request. Certain of the result, I drove in my gig to the hotel. I there found a nurse of some experience in a sick-room, though chiefly recommended herself to me on account of being known to the family. Taking her along with me, I left her in the parlor, while I softly opened the door of the bedroom and looked in, unobserved by any of them. All was silence; Ina was not there. Expecting to find her about the house, I walked to the rear, and thence beheld her under a shed in the yard, on her knees, bending over some half-expired embers, endeavoring to coax them to a flame. When she was apprised of my presence, she merely turned her head, bowed with a smile, and resumed her occupation. Her earnestness in her work impressed me with the opinion that she was proud and conceited with self-importance in having such a weighty charge upon her as now devolved from necessity. She the sole prop to her father and mother's comfort! It was a triumph, truly, in one of her years, to be able to administer to their wants, to be their only dependence. I questioned her as to the result of her family's deliberation on admitting me to visit them. " Pa told me," she said, "to do what you ordered." That was sufficient to satisfy me that I had overcome the objections I feared.

Perhaps the reader—free from the accident of poverty or the humiliation of dependence—will smile at my credulity, and think it a false delicacy, to be frowned down in a laboring man, to refuse the charity or free offerings of neighbors to relieve him. It is a mistaken notion. Many have died with starvation in sacrifice to their pride ; many more have rushed headlong, on the advent of adversity, into forgetful dissipation, rather than suffer the humiliation of dependence or the risk of refusal for assistance. The impulses of men are mental instincts, alike in poor and rich. They feel alike, notwithstanding the refinement (!) of education or position in society make them act differently. "A man's a man for a' that."

I now informed Ina that I had brought her one to assist her; that she had proved herself a worthy, good, and smart girl, but must work no more, or she too would fall sick.

She turned toward me, and, in a tone of mortified pride, she asked, " Who will make my pa and ma their tea ? Who will go for their medicines ? They will not take it from any body but me, and I won't let any one else wait on them." She now began to cry aloud, and was approaching the house, when I farther expostulated on the necessity of a more experienced person, and of one, too, whom she knew. When I pointed to her the nurse, she became appeased. I promised that she should yet have enough to do. I entered the house by the rear. The two eldest girls occupied this room. They kindly recognized me as I entered, and answered questions as to their condition. A bowl of broth and a glass of diluted ale on a table beside them evinced the progress of their convalescence. They seemed pleased at the interest I took in them by engaging the nurse. Our conversation was overheard by those in the next room. I began now to give instructions to the nurse in her duties. I particularly charged her to notice and guard the patients against any sudden change in the temperature.

It is a characteristic evidence of pure yellow fever, and the unmistakable criterion by which its attack is known, to be ushered in with a chill and pains in the limbs. During an epidemic, all fevers will assume the types of a yellow fever; but they have other predisposing causes than that which initiates the Simon pure into an organization full of health but a few hours before. The sudden change in the temperature provokes the latter, particularly in the evening, as the sun's rays leave the earth, when the thermometer falls sensibly. During the day perspiration oozes from every pore on the sunny side of the street, which the transition to the shady side arrests. To the acclimated, the periods of epidemic visitation are invigorating to the frame. While, in the Northern States, the oppressive heat of the day is succeeded by a close, enervating atmosphere of sleep-dispelling influence, in this latitude extra covering has to be kept near at hand, to protect the body from cold.

During this day and previous ones, the gentle breezes

from the southeast were succeeded by the sudden veer
of the wind at night from the opposite direction. It was
necessary to keep the door well closed during the latter,
as the draught upon unguarded frames was dangerous.
In doing so, where many are sick in the same chamber,
a disagreeable fetid odor, arising from the perspiration
of the sick, fills the room, to the prejudice of recovery.
This odor is also conclusive of the presence of pure yellow fever, and is familiar as such to every physician. To
prevent it being poisonous to the patient from reinhal-
ing it, to purify the atmosphere of it by insensible ventilation, fires are made in the rooms.

I set Ina about this, and in a few minutes the hearth
blazed with a correcting heat. This was done without
consulting the parents. Shortly afterward the nurse
brought in the hot water for foot-baths. I told the
nurse not to encourage a conversation, knowing the
propensity of her sex and some of her class, when so
employed, to be too communicative, and frequently upon
subjects dangerous to the quiet of the sick. She was
simply to do what was, with propriety, asked by them,
and to adhere closely to the physician's instructions and
prescriptions. The nurse and I gave the baths, which
completed the work of the night. The paraphernalia
of a member of the association are incomplete without
several useful adjuncts, and many instruments we made
it a point to have always near at hand.

Both man and wife essayed to draw me into conversation, especially the former, while I was busy in making
him comfortable, after having administered to him a
simple but indispensable application. I had now satisfied them that I was in earnest, and told them, if they
wished me to be useful, and to be pleased with my visits,
they should not talk unnecessarily to me or to each other. I promised that in a day or two, when all danger
would be passed, I would talk them to death. With a

press of the hand all round, a simultaneous "good-night" in answer to mine arose from both parents, and was echoed from the daughters in the next room.

Here was a triumph! What their feelings were I might guess; but mine were elation at the revolution I had caused in my favor and in their fate. My stay in the neighborhood detained me until after 10 o'clock.

It was on this night that the fatal results attended the widow and her son. The effects of that excitement had enervated me, and delayed my visit to my patients until 8 o'clock.

From day to day my occupations with the family were the same. As with others, so with them, the half hour, morning and evening, that I remained with them, was spent in chatting over their future, telling them the news, and listening to their repeated congratulations that they had escaped from a dreadful disease unscathed. The incidents of treatment, their respective remarks under appliances, now became a merry source of reference.

I had so far lost but five patients out of thirty-four; most of the sick were convalescing. On the morning of little Georgy's sixth day, when I confidently expected to find him complete the healthy circle, I was much surprised on seeing restlessness, with a hot skin. His mother said he had slept soundly all night, but he would not be prevailed upon to keep on the covering. The enema given to him had been effective, when I left him the night before, with the most promising results. A close observation alarmed me of the threatening danger.

With a family whose warm attachment to each other enlisted my anxiety for each, whose fervent piety exhibited itself in the morning and evening prayers read aloud by one of the oldest sisters and responded to by the others, to start a doubt with regard to the recovery of any one of them I knew would excite painful feelings to interfere with their recovery. In Georgy's critical condition, by the consent of the physician, I proposed to remove him to the adjoining parlor, under the excuse that he would be less disturbed and less disturbing. The mother's objections to losing sight of her child were with difficulty removed, and, as she afterward told me, with fatal presentiments. I procured a cot and mattress from the neighborhood. Entirely unconscious, or indifferent from lassitude, of what we were doing with him, he offered no resistance. I promised the mother that the door between the rooms should be left open so long as it was mutually beneficial. The physician found that his urine was suppressed, the most fatal symptom in this disease, as it is the most difficult to correct. It is a frequent attendant of relapse, yielding to no remedies that do not leave the patient under long convalescence. Some pronounce it to be caused by the excess of nourishment, and thereby overtaxing the secretory organs. I spent several hours in watching the result of appliances to correct the symptoms and subdue the pain. On the following night I found him rapidly expiring, unconscious of all around him.

Ina came into the room and interpreted his stupor into a healthy sleep. She kissed him as she retired, expressing herself happy that the playmate of her youth would be restored to her. On that night I delayed my visit longer than usual, for I momentarily looked for his death. While seated on the balcony, I could not be but impressed with the prayer for each other's safety, in which, after "God preserve to health and usefulness our father and mother," the daughter added, "and Georgy too." The nurse came to me and tapped me on the shoulder. I followed her, and witnessed the gentle departure of the spirit of the favorite. I locked the door between the rooms. The nurse discovered the bureau of clothes, and, after washing the body, laid it out on the table. That tears were shed over innocence departed, and that sympathy would exhibit itself for the living by such expressions, were natural. He, as all children, looked the apotheosis of triumph over death, if I may so strain the sentiment. I cut off several locks of his yellow hair, which I wrapped in a paper, and placed behind the mirror on the mantle. My whole thoughts were now engaged in inventing stratagems to conceal his death. The mother would be on her feet in a day or two; but she, too, must be deceived, for fear of the consequences to her.

A carriage with a coffin followed me the next morning early, when I had Georgy's remains taken off without even the knowledge of neighbors. When we returned from the burial Ina was waiting on the gallery, and complained that she could not go in to see her brother. I reprimanded her for interrupting his deep sleep (she afterward reminded me of this expression), and required of her to keep to herself all that she knew of Georgy, unless she could say well of him to her parents. She did not understand my equivocation, and did tell of the circumstance to her parents. As the circumstance justified a deception, I concluded to play it out. Accordingly, I called Ina to me, and told her that I had sent Georgy away to a friend of mine at Spring Hill, where the fresh air would quickly recover him, and gave her permission to tell her parents of it.

"Georgy gone!" she exclaimed, and with that her little heart gave way, and her crying became so loud and long that it caused me serious apprehension for those in the next room. All this had been heard by the latter, for I spoke aloud on purpose. When I entered the chambers by the back door, the oldest girls, who were sitting up in bed, did not greet me as cordially as usual. One of them intimated that I was deceiving them with regard to Georgy, which I reproved with feigned anger.

As I met their anxious countenances, when I asserted again that Georgy "was doing well," my self-possession leaving me, convicted of the lie. Their wish, though, was so in consonance with my assertion that they did not criticise my awkwardness. Cheerful conversation on different subjects served still more to dispel suspicion. As they were convalesced sufficiently to indulge in conversation, I drew them out on their history prior to settling in Mobile. They also congratulated themselves that they were now free, as I told them, from many diseases hereafter.

When a yellow-fever patient has been properly cured (I mean without being drugged with mineral poisons, or his system abused by excessive bloodletting, and free from an organic disease previously), he rises with immunity not only from all fevers, but from rheumatisms and complaints generally of the nervous system. This is founded on observations of many years. I have only found it contradicted in a long absence from this latitude, intemperance, and, of course, old age.

To resume. My patients on the following day spoke cheerfully of, and counted the days to, the time when they would be restored to usefulness. The father remarked that he never knew, before this calamity, how much they were attached to each other; that they never before felt the strength of that reliance they had placed on their Maker; and that, with recovery, a new life, and the better appreciation of the end and aim of existence, was opened before them.

On that afternoon I had ordered the nurse to procure an assortment of groceries suitable for convalescents out of danger. As I remained later than usual, the nurse and Ina exhausted their ingenuity with the materials in several kinds of hot cakes, the fumes of which, mingling with the aroma of tea and coffee, provoked the appetites of the convalescents for their simple diet, and shadowed forth to them, by anticipation, the enjoyments they were. to indulge in as soon as the fiat of the physician was removed. Appetizing as were the dishes, the deceit I had used toward them respecting Georgy's death choked my indulgence.

After tea I offered my hand to each, saying that probably it would be the last time I should see them, as my services were at an end, and my time called for elsewhere. The hand was pressed with feeling by each. Compliments and thanks were fulsomely heaped upon me. I was promised to be remembered in their prayers that night and forever. Ina cried aloud as I kissed her farewell, and promised she should know of Georgy in a day or two. Grateful tears stood in the eyes of all, and I left, feeling as light of sin and earthliness in these acts of good as if I were above them.

Two days elapsed, when the nurse called upon me for a settlement. She reported them to be able to take care of each other, and to have sufficient provisions in the house to last them ten days. The day after I left one of the children spoke of going to see Georgy, without comment being made upon it. She believed the mother strongly suspected his death from one circumstance, that but one suit of his clothes had been taken. She had noticed whisperings between them which she supposed Georgy to be the subject of.

I determined to pay them a visit, and break to them the truth. I surprised the mother putting away clothing in a shelved recess. When she recognized me she approached to give me her hand. Her inflamed and swollen eyes, from bitterly weeping, revealed to me that she was confirmed in her fears. She was choked for utterance as she took from the corner of a shelf the pair of shoes Georgy had last worn, which had been concealed there by the nurse, and placed them on the mantle alongside of the parcel which inclosed the locks of his yellow hair. These were now sacred relics to her. "Be comforted, madam; 'tis God's will," was all that I could articulate. She, like Rachel over her children, would not be comforted. I saw I could not console her, and that her grief, as she rested her head upon the mantle-piece, would only increase with my presence. "You will pardon me for the deception?" I said to her. "Yes, yes," she replied; "I know you did it for the best."

I entered the next room, where I saw the father and four children seated around a fire. They had heard my voice in the next room. Instead of rising to bid me welcome, the children, on seeing me, buried their faces in their hands or handkerchiefs, relieving anew their bleeding hearts. The father remained firmly fixed in his chair, his body bent forward, each hand clasping a knee, while he gazed intently on the glowing embers. I gently touched his shoulder, which he responded to by throwing one hand back to me, and with the other to his forehead, he sobbed aloud, "My darling Georgy! gone! gone!" When Ina heard this she shrieked with grief and left the room. Apprehensive of danger to her from such excessive manifestation, I followed after her. I traced her to the shed, where she had been so useful. Her frequent ejaculations of "Oh, my brother Georgy! oh, my brother Georgy!" were painful to hear. She, too, would not be soothed. I told her I was about to leave them, perhaps forever, and, to please me, she must now check her grief. She became more passive. As I turned my back she ran after me, and in the simple innocence of heart asked me if I thought "Georgy had gone to heaven." "Do you not read it," said I, "in the Bible? 'Suffer little children to come unto me, for of such is the kingdom of heaven.'"

I returned to the group at the fireside. I was sure they appreciated the motive for concealing the death of

Georgy. Each seemed waiting on the other to address me. I had nothing to say, and was deferring from minute to minute the words of parting, for I felt as if their loss was mine also. They had not noticed that I was standing, so absorbed were they in their own reflections. At last I remarked that I intended to leave them for my home. All arose. Each pressed my hand feelingly, showering upon me the while words of gratitude and good wishes. I was to be remembered in their prayers; and the sick-cup which I had purchased for them to drink from when lying down was promised to be kept in a prominent place as a memento of their "stranger friend."

The mother awaited me in the next room. With both hands extended, as I entered she took mine, and drew them to her lips. "When you become a parent," she said, "you will feel the strength of my gratitude for your kindness to myself and family."

I hurried away, and drove rapidly to other patients, to shake off the load upon my heart.

Ten years afterward, on a visit to Mobile, I visited the spot, and made inquiries for this family. I was informed that two years after I left they set out for Texas.

To the thoughtful reflections of a wise and prosperous prince, whose sayings are studded with brilliants, I am indebted for one to convey my own conviction of its truth, " *That it is better to go to the house of mourning than to the house of feasting.*" Not in the ascetic sense, that the indulgence of mirth or the innocent enjoyments of life should be excluded; not that we should wrap ourselves in sackcloth to propitiate the Being of Beings, but " *the heart is made better by the sadness of the countenance,*" and in feeling for the distresses of others we are more prone to advance the sum of human happiness by relieving them.

CHAPTER IV.

Close of our Labors at Mobile.—Illness of the Members.—Pascagoula.
—Its Sick.—Ship and Typhoid Fever in New Orleans, 1847.—Hospitals crowded.—Liberality of the Citizens toward the Howard Association.—A Cholera Case.—Physic, Physicians, and Quacks.

WE had become so methodically organized for all purposes of relief, and in a short time so generally known to the inhabitants, that there was no instance of oversight or neglect to any in need of our services. During our sojourn in Mobile we had taxed our energies to their utmost tension. One by one of my associates were leaving, happily able to place their patients in the charge of the "Can't Get Away Club." As I had notified my intention of departing for home the next day, I paid my last visits with a member of this club. It is, I believe, a punishment of criminals in China to prevent them from sleeping until the excess of watchfulness produces insanity. · Those who have experienced the prostration to the nervous system consequent upon protracted loss of repose will at once admit the possibility of such a result; and, if added to this, irregularity of habit in eating, producing dyspepsia, and the necessity for the use of stimulants, it will reach the certainty, exemplified in the similar wanderings and imbecility of the pitiful sufferer from *delirium tremens*. At noon of this day I was sitting in our office at the hotel, when of a sudden a faintness came over me, succeeded by a blindness to all objects around, and a most painful nausea. I staggered to the sofa. Fortunately, our physician was near by. I was assisted up stairs and laid on a bed, feeling as weak and powerless as if just raised from a prolonged sickness. The doctor, who was no disciple of homœopathy, but believed in the simple principle that a greater will absorb a less, or that a burnt finger is relieved by being held to a flame, jocosely remarked to me something about the hair of the dog being the cure for its bite, and that, in my case, the excitement in my nervous system would rapidly succumb to a stimulating potion. This he directed me to continue every hour in moderation until I arrived at Pascagoula. At that time the mail-boat from New Orleans had ceased to run farther than Pascagoula, from whence the mails and passengers were conveyed over by land to Mobile.

For the first time since I had been away a host of fears sprung up within me. It can not properly be said that one fears death until the danger is immediate. Such a fear possessed me then, which was made more painful from the misery of being sick far from my family and friends. The hour for the stage-coach to depart at length arrived; with an adieu to all, I entered, and discovered that I was the only passenger. In an hour after I found myself obliged to hold vigorously to the strap which crossed the inside of the coach, and with difficulty maintaining my seat, while the horses were dashing furiously with their light load over a corduroy road, famous for being unsurpassed by any in the South for the irregularity of its construction. For fifteen minutes after I arrived at Pascagoula I was so debilitated as scarcely to be able to stand. My bones felt shattered and dislocated. Yet did the refreshing sea-breeze soon produce its invigorating effects.

My first impulse was to walk to the boat, which lay, with steam up, at the end of the long wharf. Afraid of the consequences of such an effort without support, I approached the hotel for assistance. To my surprise, not a moving soul was to be seen except a female form, that flitted from one door to the next on the upper balcony. As I reached the open doors in face of the steps, the story spoke for itself. On a square dining-table lay two coffins, with burning candles around, and a negro as watcher nodding in unconsciousness. He told me these were two of the dead of that day; that six had been buried the day before, and that fifteen or eighteen were "down with the yellow fever."

The visitors at the hotel consisted of Mobilians who had fled their city to escape its present calamity. The fullest reliance was counted upon an exemption from it here, as the location stands prominent in the Gulf, and is backed by the health-restoring pine forests. What, though, has been written of the plague at Constantinople, that no native of an infected town, though he was in a region distant from the infection, found any advantage in changing the climate, applies equally to this characteristic disease. It was noted that such a one was singled out as a sacrifice to the former distemper which raged among his countrymen, as if the seeds of the disease were latent for a long period back, and waited but the process of time any where to be developed.

The hotel had been so crowded that beds were placed in the passage-ways to accommodate all. Now death had reduced the number to one half of what the hotel generally received. Not encountering host or clerk, I unceremoniously walked up stairs, and into the rooms where were some unattended sick. Many a one, I have no doubt, sympathized with me in having fallen into Charybdis. I found myself, though, in my element, and at home.

An unexpected opening of a new field roused my dormant energies. I told several what I had done, what I could do, and found myself, while speaking of it, administering to their wants. Nurses were out of the question. The village, for miles back, had been ransacked for assistance, but terror of the fever, like the alarm of the rattlesnake, warned against approach. I restored much confidence to those not yet sick by the information that the epidemic was rapidly abating in Mobile, a frost having fallen, too, at Spring Hill, and that it had disappeared from New Orleans. Many took the suggestion, and departed immediately for the one or other city. The proprietor led me to the different sick-beds, where I inspired hopes which, I am sure, from the desire expressed that I should revisit them, was an element of good to them. To one I suggested a relief; to another I applied topical palliatives; and to all something. In this way I passed the time until after midnight.

All the boarders had the benefit of the successful experience of Dr. D., of Philadelphia repute, but long a resident practitioner of Mobile. Out of his family, who were with him, he had lost, the previous week, a lovely daughter. God knows what a miserable fate would have been that of the inmates had he not been present. Pascagoula, besides being famed in legendary lore for the self-immolation of the whole tribe of Indians so named, who preferred to plunge themselves in the adjoining river and be extinct rather than undergo the tortures of a pursuing enemy, would have had another reminiscence of distress and desolation, of which the mournful tones* that issue from the river at night would have been a fitting chant, had not this benevolent and able physician been present to stay the fury of the destroyer.

---

* All visitors at this fashionable summer resort have listened in the stillness of the night to these yet unaccounted-for sounds, imitative of the strumming of harps. Many have endeavored to explain them as produced by the undulation of gentle breezes through the bordering flags. Others have attributed them to the plaintive cries of the crocodile, or to a subdued sound common to the drum-fish. But, as all these vary in measure and intensity, and the former is uniform and inaudible when more than a ripple ruffles the surface of the water, superstition clings to the traditionary cause.

As I felt invigorated from the stay I made at this place, I deferred my departure until the next evening. The same routine of duties as elsewhere occupied me during the time. The succeeding day I was at home, and for five days was confined to the house with a severe bilious attack. By this time all my associates had returned, leaving some of the nurses and our physician. The latter had been prevailed upon to remain with the inducement of a profitable practice. He became much beloved for his courteous demeanor, social qualities, and professional skill, and remained there many years, finishing his career in New Orleans, where he died about ten years after.

All the funds given to us at our departure had been expended. Numerous bills were necessarily run up, involving us in a debt which it was well was assumed by the city of Mobile, for otherwise, as our authorities had withheld appropriations from the society, the members individually would have been taxed.

That season closed the existence and labors of the Samaritan Association, dispersing its members with valuable experience for the sick-room of their friends or families, or for future service in the ranks of the Howard Association, which still kept up its organization.

When our little party encountered each other from time to time after, we talked over the good we had done with so little injury to ourselves, though several deceived themselves; for, as one by one paid the forfeit of overtaxed powers, they traced their premature fate more or less to a sickness immediately consequent upon their return.

Four only of that delegation to Mobile survive.

From the year 1839 to 1847, the epidemics which prevailed in New Orleans were of a manageable type, bearing more the character of remittent, intermittent, and bilious in their symptoms, than of pure yellow fever.

Less fatality accompanying these, there was, of course, less distress. The hospitals being commodious enough to accommodate the poor sick, there was no need of the associations, except to relieve the wants of convalescents or their families, and to provide for the widows and orphans. In the month of April, 1847, the emigrant population exceeded that of any previous year. The anxiety to reach this country, after the severities of famine, forced them to take the first chance for passage, and, in almost every instance, ships arrived burdened with more than the number of passengers allowed by law. They were, of course, subject to the diseases consequent upon a corrupted and close atmosphere. Ship and typhoid fever owe their origin to this cause. The reports on every arrival gave a large proportion of deaths on the voyage. The survivors, debilitated by short rations of food and water, arriving in a climate so different from that they had left, under any circumstances should have exercised prudence in their food and cleanliness in their habits, to ward off the diseases of this latitude; instead of which, they indulged to excess in cheap fruits, and hoveled together in damp and unwholesome localities. It was not long before the hospital doors were shut to the reception of more patients. The Young Men's Howard Society, which had retained its organization, was called together to meet the emergency. A constitution and by-laws were adopted, and they became incorporated by an act of the Legislature under the style of the Howard Association.

Yellow fever was a specialty with us, and fraught with no danger. To linger in the infectious atmosphere of ship and typhoid fever, or brave the contact of cholera, *c'etoit toute autre chose.* The citizens, however, looked to us alone to avert or mitigate the suffering reported in every quarter. Proud of our selection in a forlorn hope, we set about it without thought of personal risk. The

fact that we were prepared for such duty was announced
in the daily papers; donations were called for, and in
ten hours after our office was opened $8000 had been
received in the treasury.

It is unfair to be invidious in remarks of the benevolence of any one people over another, yet I must say,
from experience, that the benevolence of the people of
New Orleans can not be exceeded by that of any community in the world. There may not be as frequent or
large bequests as elsewhere from flinty-hearted old fellows, who, while living, would thrust a suppliant tenant,
with her children, in the street for inability to pay a
monthly due, or, when they can no longer enjoy their
wealth, are suddenly possessed with the vanity of fame,
and, overlooking their poor kindred, make a forced heir
of charity in the endowment of religious institutions.
Whatever good may result from the latter, as Paddy
says, "there's no thanks to them;" no gratitude, as the
giver experienced no pleasure in his donation. But the
charity of our people is ever active. You may stop
nine men out of ten you meet in the street who will
lend a willing ear to an appeal for relief. Such charity
is true charity; spontaneous, not calculating; resembling
the gift of Abel—from the heart, pure and sincere. It
is, as I have said before, self-rewarding, as are other
virtues. Howard did not calculate for notoriety or compensation in his world-renowned active benevolence to
the poor and degraded of foreign climes. Massillon did
not claim heaven as a reward for his enthusiastic piety.
Nor did Washington bargain for fame with a patriotism
not vaunted to the public gaze. Men saw but the outer
expression, judged only the results, and envied their
fame without appreciating the inward satisfaction from
their acts; for, as stolen pleasures are said to be the
sweetest, great also is the charm of unseen charity,
whose worshipers nurse their acts with a miser's care,

and enjoy them in secret, "like a sweet morsel under the tongue."

The number of members of the Howard Association was limited to thirty. A due proportion was allotted to each municipality, who were again districted off. Placards at the corners of streets and advertisements in the daily papers gave the residence of each member. On the first evening of organization, an application was made, in full assembly, for a nurse, and for our supervision of a case of cholera in a boarding-house on Poydras Street. Few of us having seen a case of cholera, and none experienced in the treatment of it, there was diffidence, if not apprehension, in undertaking the charge of the first applicant. Another member and myself called at the residence of the patient.

The landlady, being much distressed at the stampede which occurred in her house immediately on its being known that the cholera was on her premises, was delighted to see us, and pointed to us the chamber wherein the patient lay. The room, which was barely large enough to hold a single bedstead, a table, and two chairs, had a window in dangerous proximity for an invalid left alone with a disease where insanity or delirium usually sets in. The sufferer was a man of large frame, and was stretched on the bed, stripped of covering. As we entered, he was imbibing from a bottle what we discovered afterward to be undiluted brandy. Several empty phials, the contents of which, from the labels on them, must have given him a distaste for life, were scattered on the table. We told him the object of our visit. His response was,

"Where is Dr. ——? where is Mr. ——, and Mr. ——?" repeating name after name of his friends; then turning to us, "Who told *you* to come here? What do you *want* here? *Clear out*, G—d d—n you! Are you going to take my measure before I'm dead?" These and many more remarks, rounded off with the vocabulary of oaths against his friends and the household who had deserted him, were uttered in such rapid succession as to give us no time "to edge a word in sideways." He finally exhausted himself, asked for "ice," then for "brandy." As I was about pouring the latter in a glass, he snatched the bottle from me and exhausted its contents. I had seen cholera treated in previous years, and did not count upon any ill results from this indulgence, as there is no perceptible effect on the brain from strong drink in this disease. On the contrary, it has been asserted that, where intoxication has been produced, the most favorable results have shown themselves. I put more faith, though, in the constrictive property of ice, and as long as it was agreeable I never checked the indulgence. We had ordered a mustard-bath to be prepared, and were engaged in the preparation of cataplasms for the cramps he complained of in his stomach, when of a sudden, in one volume, he threw up what he had been drinking, and shortly afterward the rice-water evacuations ran from him. Without a physician, and no instructions how to act, but knowing that something must be done to alleviate pain, if not to remove the cause of it, we applied a cataplasm to his epigastrium and wrists, rolled up our sleeves, and frictioned his limbs with our hands in a hot mustard-bath, when, in about fifteen minutes, we had the satisfaction of witnessing a genial warmth on the surface of his body, and arterial action established. We now wrapped him well in blankets. Overpowered by spasmodic and mental excitement, he lay composed, as if desirous to sleep. In a weak voice he directed us to give him a tablespoonful of a confection in a phial on the table, upon taking which he inclined his head in acknowledgment of our attentions, and quietly slept. When we first entered the room we were struck with the deathlike expression of

D

his sunken features; perspiration now stood upon his forehead, and a glow suffused his countenance. We remained by his side for more than an hour, while he slept. By that time his pulse had risen to sixty, and his whole frame was in profuse perspiration. After a little while he awoke, and asked for ice. He expressed himself free from pain, except from the blistering of the cataplasms, which we took off, substituting for them the usual oiled linen. A nausea set in, for which, at his suggestion, we administered several spoonfuls of brandy at intervals. As he now required only the attention of one of us, my associate left me to carry the patient through, or until relieved by his friends or the physician in the morning.

The patient proved himself to be a milder-mannered man than I judged on first acquaintance. Upon inquiry, he told me that he was on a business visit to the city; that he resided in Georgia, where he left a large family, whose injunctions against, and fears of, coming here he would not listen to.

"Now," said he, "when a man most wants the presence of family or friends, I am deserted by the latter to die like a dog."

"Not entirely," I replied.

"Far from it, my friend, if I may be allowed the expression; for I have found in you and your companion an instance of heroism which shall always endear me to you, and which will give me a better opinion than I have entertained of mankind. But, tell me, who sent you here, and why are you not afraid of the disease?"

I explained the objects of the association, adding that, independent of this consideration, on account of the fears that I really entertained of this disease, I thought the likeliest way to combat them was to face it, and familiarize myself with the danger.

It is a popular delusion that physicians and nurses are

providentially exempt from contagious diseases, while the danger to healthy persons in visiting the sick-rooms is much aggravated. Health is as repulsive of disease as disorganization is inviting to it. Unless there is a predisposition for a contagious disease from the latter, or, most of all, from fear, I have come to the conclusion, from observation, that a gradual familiarity to its influence lessens the liability to it, and dissipates the fear of it. How often do we notice that the scratch of a needle on an apparently healthy person has passed from the different stages of inflammation into gangrene and death, while another, of a temperament and frame more inviting from appearances to a fatal result, has recovered from a thousand-fold worse infliction!

My patient informed me of the names of his friends, and gave me such other information that, if an untoward event happened to him, his effects would be taken care of for his family.

At midnight he had a return of cramps and renewed purging. By manipulations, if I may use the term, I corrected the first, and by an enema checked the latter. During the whole time he was full of anecdotes bearing upon the nature of my duties and his sensations, and thus an hour glibly passed away.

In an unlucky moment, the duty presented itself to me to hasten home for a few minutes, and, by apprising my family where I was, to allay any anxiety which they properly had of me in remaining out so late in such troublous times, as well, also, to watch against any home-intrusion of the disease. I called the landlady to me, who promised that a servant should remain with the patient until my return, and that he should be properly cared for.

I had not been absent half an hour, when, hastily mounting the steps, I read in the lugubrious face of the landlady, with her upheld arms, my worst apprehensions. On entering the bedroom they were realized. The explanation was simple. One of his friends, whose compunctions of conscience for neglecting a stranger and a friend did not permit him to sleep, and whose fears allowed him to indulge no farther than to make inquiries at the door, had consulted with a physician, who impressed him with the belief that cholera succumbed alone to his mode of treatment. They entered the room a few minutes after I left. On diagnosing, or examining the patient, the physician pronounced the disease rapidly "resolving itself into a congestion"—such was reported to me by the landlady—and forthwith dragged the covering from him. The servant was sent for an additional quantity of ice, and, having made some water as cold as it could be made, he sprinkled it over the patient; then, with a sheet, which had likewise been saturated, he enveloped his body, overwrapped him with blankets, and, with arms folded, watched for that reaction in the sick man's system which was to prove his darling theory. In ten minutes collapse set in, and the Georgian was a corpse.

I did not select words to express my horror, contempt, and indignation at such barbarity and ignorance. Mind you, I do not say that the aforesaid treatment may not be in the books; for my experience has shown me that the imagination of man has not conceived or dreamed of such contradictions as an outsider like myself can not fail to be impressed of in the treatment by homœopathy and allopathy; but I had marked the progress of cure in the treatment which had been commenced with him, and which was successfully carried out in subsequent cases. When I reported the particulars of this case the next day to the association, the general response was to publish the name of the physician and the particulars; yet, as I have just said, to continue such a course would have involved us in as many controversies as there were theories of cure. Happily, pressed with engagements, we passed it over, and, as we grew more experienced, wisely concluded to follow a physician's treatment and his orders without feeling responsibility for consequences.

In this disease, as in all others of epidemic character, the unanimity of the faculty is akin to that harmony produced by each instrument in an orchestra going it on its own hook without regard to the score; yet never was a practice devised that has not been marked with some success, and which, in the opinion of its learned advocates, should not supersede all others; though, if the truth be known, the secret of success lies sometimes in the harmlessness of a supposed irritant, but oftener in the confidence of the patient in his physician, and the hope inspired by a reputation for professional skill; "for the prestige of success insures success."

The human stomach is the laboratory into which mineral and vegetable compounds, insulting, foreign, and nauseating to every sense, and sometimes antagonistic in their properties, are thrown by the scientific manipulator, to produce that *ignis fatuus* of alchemy, the philosopher's stone, or prolongation of life. It is a dispute whether a little more or a little less would have perfected the experiment. It is not the fault of the operator that he can not keep up the perpetual motion of life; it is the stubbornness of the compounds to assimilate to the necessity of the case; for it will not be yielded by the student of the Pharmacopœia that its principles are not applicable to every case, and as fixed and resultant as that light displaces darkness.

Unity in medicine, though, may as well be looked for as unity in religion; both intend the same result in their contradictions, and it is but charitable to infer that one is as useful to man as the other is acceptable in the eyes of God.

To listen to one physician expatiating upon the charming virtues of sulphate of quinine; to hear another pronounce it most poisonous in its uses; one as enthusiastic as the other is denunciatory, and both, in other respects, awarded by their peers the front rank of the profession, is, *messieurs les docteurs*, to us funny outsiders, a glaring eccentricity of genius, if not a positive conviction that you seek

> By your controversies to lessen
> The dignity of your profession.

The public cares little whether Dr. Sangrado is pitied by Dr. Bolus, or if Dr. Allopathy sneers at Dr. Homœopathy. Dr. Hydropathy and Dr. Raspail may excuse themselves by saying that it is the disease which kills, and not their treatment. This progressive age is opposed to the prejudices of education, and will always estimate and appreciate the pioneer in physic or in science, who, throwing books aside, without envy walks through the academic grove, culling by the wayside the flowers of new growth, and, well scanning the properties of a vaunted exotic, adapts the innovation, if useful.

Envy of talent is a step in progress, and, as such, is commendable. Every physician is ambitious to be in the van, and to invite notice by a startling theory. This he no sooner grasps than he is beset with unmitigated aspersions. Were the public capable of judging between the contestants, it would be well enough, but the effect of the warfare is to inspire a doubt of the capacity of both.

With all their animosities to *each other*, however, as a class and as a profession, "they are the noblest Romans of them all." Who as ready to give their hours of rest, without pay, to suffering humanity? It is the only profession or pursuit where brains, and time, and dear-bought skill are so disproportionately recompensed for the service given. The clergyman, who only points the way, and teaches how to reach heaven, is paid according to his talent to persuade rich men that it is as "facile as it is for a pig to whistle" to enter that abode, despite the allegory of the camel passing through the eye of a needle. The lawyer graduates his fee to the amount involved, play or pay. See, now, the surgeon, who by skillful hand saves a limb, which the possessor would give thousands to recover if lost; and the physician, who snatches, by a timely application, the patient from an inevitable death, which rather than meet, the last of his treasure would be promised; what is their pay—their recompense? A trifle compared to the service performed, and begrudgingly given. How seldom is that service so much estimated that the generosity of the relieved induces him to give more than in such cases "stipulated in the bond" of custom!

With all the drawbacks to advancement in wealth, the secret yet undeveloped is, wherefore the continual accession to their number, overspreading the land like the locusts in Egypt. Is it the fascination of good company, the love of "chimeras wild," in which there is more pleasure in the pursuit than in the possession? or is it for the respect, the esteem, and the confidence in which they are held by all men for the honorable and charitable character of its members?

In my commendation I allude not to charlatans or quacks, imitators of other men's stuffs with hydra-headed pretensions, their saddle-bags

> "Replete with strange hermetic powder,
> That wounds nine miles, point-blank, would solder,"

nor of the exceptionals alluded to by Yriarte in the moral to his fable of the ass and the flute:

> "Borroquitos hay
> Que una vez aciertan
> Por casualidad."

Such are those that wring the last dollar from suffering humanity in advance of every service performed, and, when no more can be exacted, abandon them for nature to do the rest. No greater enemies had we to contend with than this latter class. They thrust themselves upon our acceptance by a disinterested offer of their services. Their zeal and activity induced our confidence, and not until the close of an epidemic did we become fully apprised of the tricks they used to aggrandize themselves. If they did not succeed in obtaining money from our patients, they would divide with the apothecary the bill of expensive prescriptions.

Much of the mortality in our epidemics is due to the ignorance of the unparchmented pretenders in physic. The law does not allow every man to be his own lawyer, though no more than common sense may be required in ninety-nine cases out of a hundred; nor does it patent a man's capacity to make his own shoes, yet it paradoxically hangs for murder, and licenses unquestioned pretenders to deal out poisons by the grain or ounce. It is reasonable to hope from our legislators that, if life is valuable enough to be protected by penalties from the knife of the murderer or the carelessness of the engineer, it should be as well guarded by requiring a discrimination between a load that will effectually reach its object and a load that will explode. In other words, if laudanum, quinine, strychnine, veratrum viride, and such like counterirritants (poisons in multo, and curatives in parvo), are allowed to be used, the dose should be restricted by law, and heavy penalties enforced upon the experimental murderer.

CHAPTER V.

Pest-spots.—Treatment of the poor Sick.—Advantages of the Howard
Association.—The Scotch and Irish.

THE day following that of my first cholera case I
walked through the part of the municipality allotted to
me, to discover what progress the disease was making,
to note its localities, and the condition of the afflicted.
The apothecaries, who are always sure guides to neighboring sick, directed me to two nests of ship fever and
cholera, which of themselves I found sufficient to occupy my time and sympathies. One was amid the crowded divisions of the old German Theatre on Magazine
Street; the other in a row of one story attic brick tenements, built on one side of a lot fronting St. Thomas
Street, and running back 150 feet. The former was occupied by emigrant German and Scotch mechanics and
laborers, with the proverbial number of children; the
latter by Irish and English emigrants. In the one was
indigence, with quiet, and a show of order and cleanliness; in the other poverty, with disorder and dirt. Indeed, the selection of the places indicated the degree and
order of breeding of the occupants. What the former
habitation gained by its cleanlier surroundings and orderly keeping, it lost by the absence of ventilation; for
each room served the purpose to a family for eating,
sleeping, and cooking. The tenements in St. Thomas
Street were faced by an alley about six feet wide. In
this alley was daily thrown offal and refuse of every
description by the tenants, which waited for a rain alone
to carry off. In the mean time, the stench arising from
it added its influence in propagating disease. It was

D 2

my first effort to induce the inmates to correct this objection, but without success. Day by day I sent out
victims from both places to the hospitals as fast as they
would receive them. When the latter peremptorily refused farther admissions, we then established an infirmary of our own in a street between the two points of infection.

During epidemics our sick are attended to at their
homes, provided they are parents or children who have
parents to nurse them. Single men or women, having
no such attendants, were sent to the Charity or to the
hospitals established by us. Timely medical attention,
cleanliness, and ventilation were superior there to that
in their own homes. The police of the city had been
doing our service for weeks previous in sending off the
sick to the hospitals as fast as discovered. Although
disease had already decimated the inhabitants of both
places, I could not imagine where those remaining found
a place to lay their heads at night. Curiosity incited
me to a closer observation one night, under the excuse
of inquiring for a fictitious person. By the light of a
lantern I explored every room. As the door of each
was opened to me, the concentrated essence of breath
and animal effluvia nearly stunned my consciousness.
Somewhat used, however, to this, I manfully persevered,
and convinced myself that the annihilation of space was
as well provided against as if it had been surely anticipated. One mattress, in many instances, served the purpose of a pillow to six or eight adults, while the very
youngest occupied the middle of it. Yet soundly they
all slept, undisturbed, to all appearance, by fears of death
or starvation, one of which almost hourly dragged his
indifferent victim to eternity, while the other had already
impressed his seal upon their countenances. The greatest enemy the Germans and Scotch had to fear was starvation. They desired work, but could find none. The

Irish were no less inquiring for something to do; but, when they found it, the fear of the disease, and frequent attendance at wakes, led them to spend their wages for liquor, such indulgence the more exposing them to the certainty of a fatal attack. With both, where to sleep *to-night*, and what to eat or drink *to-day*, were the limit to desires. Commiseration for their companions in distress they could not have; self-preservation shut their eyes to all but themselves.

It is remarkable, as well as characteristic, with what sacred fidelity the Irishman perpetuates in this country his national custom of night-vigils, with intoxicating draughts and pipe, around the corpse of one of his countrymen. He will pawn his shirt but that the material should be forthcoming to wrap him in Elysian dreams, and do fitting honors to the spirit that hovers around its late tenement. This is not all. At a sacrifice of many home comforts, his family must be entailed with the expense of a carriage to increase the length of the mourning cortége. When one entirely destitute of friends or acquaintances is suddenly stricken down, the pride of nationality is awakened in the accidental visitor, who collects together some of his own friends to do this spirit reverence that now dwells with others gone before. Should an ancient belief be true that a man's heaven in after life is the indulgence of his master passion or propensity, well may it be ordained that a different planet be appropriated to Bacchus, Mercury, Venus, Pocahontas, and the rest; for, amid the excess of all, the disciples of neither could enjoy themselves, until confusion, becoming worse confounded, would bring all up to the conviction that this dream of heaven is now a sad reality of hell. But where am I roving to? An associate and myself relieved each other, and divided our attentions between the two infected places. Without entirely depriving any of stimulating drinks, we allowed near-

ly all indulgence at fixed times of the day. To those
not making wages we furnished groceries for themselves
and families. By such favors they were induced to set
about removing filth and objectionable matter from
around them, to cleanse and ventilate their apartments.
By a free use of chloride of lime the infecting vehicles
of disease were dissipated. From ten to fifteen in each
place were constantly on the sick-list, and from five to
ten died daily. Our physician instructed us that, when
he could not be found immediately, and in case of violent cramps, to give a salt and mustard emetic, to be followed by a dose of ten to twenty grains of calomel, aft-·
erward to keep the patient warmly covered in bed, and
equalize the temperature of his body by mustard-baths
or cataplasms on the extremities. When the cases admitted of delay, I administered a wine-glass of good
brandy dashed with a pinch of Cayenne. The latter I
found checked the disposition to vomit and diarrhœa,
and, at the same time, sent the blood tingling through
the veins. So rapid is the execution done by cholera
that it was important that one or other of us should
be in attendance night and day. This, though prostrat-
ing to our energies, was attended with so much self-
gratification at our continual successes, that we remained at our posts till cessation of disease gave us no more
patients. During the whole time their gratitude and reliance upon us was almost of the nature of deification.
It could not be explained to them that men would choose
to place themselves in the midst of a poverty and dis-
case that *they* execrated and even prayed to escape, nor
could they more understand that what they looked upon
as a mad folly we indulged in with eager earnestness.

The Howard Association, as now organized, is an institution inseparable from the prosperity of New Orleans,
and is suggestive in its results and benefits to the population of all large cities. Quarantine would no longer

occupy the Legislature and the medical world in learned and interminable disputes of its questionable utility
were associations like ours recognized by state patronage, with enlarged privileges. It is only imperfectly
fulfilling the objects of quarantine to keep off a diseased
or an infected subject, or to prevent the spread of malaria by fumigating a ship's hold, when the half-starved
or poorly-provisioned immigrant is either sent to the
city convalescent, without ability to work, or penniless,
and not equal to it. They then have to feed upon the
cheapest grub, huddle together in damp hovels, and form
of themselves a focus of infection for the whole city.
Were the money thus lavished upon quarantine laid out
in building and provisioning a commodious establishment, not distant from the city, where both sick and well
of steerage passengers should be forced to remain at least
a week, until they undergo a complete cleansing of their
persons, wholesome air and food would then dispel the
effects of ship confinement. In such an establishment labor would seek them, averting from them the evils arising from runners of low boarding-houses, who not only
rob them of their little store, but fatten on the premium
obtained from the sale of their time to contractors. Such
an establishment would be both politic and philanthrop-
ic. The mortuary statistics of all sea-port towns furnish
us with the fact that the poor immigrants introduce, or,
if not, generate and disseminate disease among assimilat-
ing elements in all of them. The cities, *per ipsis*, or
their inhabitants, are healthy. It is evident, then, that
the result of such a connection, as a prescribed attachment for state economy, to the Howard Association, or
like institutions, would be a falling off of admissions to
the hospitals, a gain to the general health, and in its
train increased wealth to the community and a saving
to the state.

With such a legislative attachment, the Howard Association would be shorn of much of its duties, for its objects of relief and care are almost entirely of the immigrant class. Every year more and more increases the importance of such an institution as ours. We can never again look for the extraordinary influx to our resources in 1853 ($225,000), which has afforded us, until now, the means of relieving widespread distress. When, however, one year of epidemic reigns without similar aid, and our organization becomes suspended, the pestilence would convert the city into a charnel-house.

A nos moutons. There are residents in New Orleans, as in other cities, not pestered with the itch of traveling. The intrusion of cholera snapped the cord to their hearths, and scattered them far and wide. Our streets were truly desolate. Where imperious necessity restrained some to remain, the closest attention to cleanliness and the nicest discrimination in food were studied by others able to leave the city. "What do you eat?" "What shall I eat?" were stereotyped phrases on meeting. The places of business resort were the scene of frequent merriment to some, who, knowing the strength of the imagination, would, upon the appearance of a visitor, joke him with the remark that he looked very pale, and, taking his hand, say that he was pulseless. It was invariably followed by a call for drinks all around. These jokes were carried at times to a cruel extent, as instances were reported where fear finished what a convalescent frame invited.

In 1847 our association attended to 1200 patients, losing 130. In the years 1849 and 1851, the Charity Hospital furnished room for all the indigent sick, making our duties light in the sustenance and support only of the convalescents and their families.

During these years I have many reminiscences of sickness and distress. Only to two shall I revert, not from superior interest, but that friends would be displeased with the reference to others. As a characteristic of disease, and the direction exercised by opposite forces, as well as to carry out the original intention of the publication, I shall dwell upon only the two following cases, leaving for scenes and labors of the more memorable year of 1853 to give a complete and close view of the workings of our association.

CHAPTER VI.

A stubborn Case.—The Selfishness of doing Good.—Eanes, the Cupper.—Predestination.

I HAD made the promise, frequently made by friend to friend, to Fred L., a native of Kentucky, that I would nurse him if he became attacked with yellow fever. We had been room-mates during years of clerkship, and had cultivated our intimacy since. The first intimation of his illness was about three hours after the disease developed itself. As was my wont, I bolted in up stairs, dispensing with any notice to the keeper of the *chambres garnies*. I was about handling the knob of his chamber door when the familiar face of a Creole nurse exhibited itself from the end of the passage with a cautionary gesture, at the same time beckoning me to her.

"Do you want to see Mr. L.?"

"That is my purpose."

"Well, you can't. The doctor has just left, and ordered me not even to let his father in."

"Tell the doctor I am father, mother, and all; and I promise you no harm."

With that I quietly opened the door, approached the bed, and found my friend lying with his back toward me, profusely and tightly covered with blankets, with a wet cloth concealing half his face. The act of passing my hand upon his forehead brought forth a grunt, with the exclamation,

"Will you leave me alone?"

"Not I, Fred," I replied. "I intend that you shall not be entertained with such disconsolate company. How are you, old fellow? Got it now well, eh? You're sure it's Yellow Jack you've got?"

"Oh! is it you? Indeed I have, or I have a touch rather of infernal fever. My brain is on fire, and I feel a weariness, without being able to sleep, which no position can relieve. Then these cursed blankets are adding fuel to the flame; and, by-the-by, I don't believe in this homœopathy of heat extracting heat; for, mind you, I feel as if I was digesting my entrails, and were going to be served up as boiled pork."

The comparison drew a simultaneous ha! ha! Of a lively, mercurial disposition, devil-may-care in every thing, and, as he was possessed of wit of the most companionable kind, I counted upon his playing upon his condition even *in extremis*. The physician attending him had been recommended to him by an old citizen, who for years had watched the success of his practice. I advised my friend to adhere strictly to the orders of the physician, with the assurance that he was now suffering the worst of the disease, and to comfort himself that, in bearing manfully what thousands had undergone, a successful issue was a safeguard against all other ills indigenous to a southern latitude.

"But I have no faith in a physician that has been torturing me from the start. First a dose of oil—a villainous potation, which I could not retain; then immersion in a hot bath, with cold water poured on my head, making me almost crazy; afterward God knows what in a powder, turning my head dizzy with an everlasting ringing in the ears. After all this, he whispers to the nurse to have every thing in readiness for the visit of a cupper. Do you think I intend to be tortured farther, with the doubtful chance of recovery? Not I—not I."

I enjoined upon him submission and quiet; assured him that he was what was termed by the faculty a *beautiful case, richly developed;* that every thing was in his favor, and by the morning he would be L. redivivus. He was about replying, when I threatened to leave if he did not discontinue talking.

L. was of a sanguine temperament and of robust frame, to whom disease or illness had been a stranger within his memory. In the evening I found him reposing, with a reduced pulse. The cupper had called in my absence, but my friend was stubborn in his objection to losing blood.

Late at night I had returned home, wearied from attending the poor unfortunates in my district. Immediately after performing ablutions, to rid myself of the fetid odor that seizes upon the body and clothes in a sick-room, a rap was given at my door. I was in the habit of answering night messages personally; exhausted as I was, I called the servant to receive the message for me, and ordered him, unless it was very pressing or a new case, to say that I was not at home. I soon lay down, in the sweet consciousness that a few hours of luxurious repose were mine, intending to go the round of my duties after midnight. Before I had shut out the world from my thoughts, the servant announced a message from L., desiring to see me immediately. In the contest between physical and mental indulgence, the latter prevailed. "What a hero!" exclaims the reader, in his imperfect experience of human nature. Listen while I destroy the delusion. There is a selfishness in every good act; the sacrifice of time, money, or health measures the degree of it. To act in conformity to the dictates of conscience is happiness. To be controlled by reason or interest, to the end "that the heavens may

fall and I perish not," is misery. I can not eulogize a
virtue so much as envy its disciple; for, as Plato says,
virtue is not acquired by human instruction or from
experience of its good so much as it is the gift of
Heaven. Again, with Milton,

> "Virtue could see to do what Virtue would,
> By her own radiant light, though sun and moon
> Were in the flat sea sunk."

The hypocrite with sinister motives, acting in repugnance to his feelings to gull the world into a conviction
of his excellence, is alone worthy of eulogy, for it is vice
paying tribute to virtue. Notoriety is his ephemeral
reward. We wonder at, while we commend, acts of
generosity and daring, because we do not know that the
impulse to them is perfectly natural, not feeling alike
ourselves. There are some endowed by nature with
the constitution and disposition to endure privations
and hardships, who sacrifice time and health in pursuits
resulting alone in the good of others, who are looked
upon by the world as martyrs; yet indulgence in their
favorite pursuit is more grateful to them than the world's
praise. There is a ruling passion in every man, which
is proportioned in intensity to education and physical
organization. (I exclude the consideration of vulgar
propensities.) I believe that he who is conformed to
doing good can not avoid his acts, and one less conformed is deserving of the more credit when he successfully
contends with his repugnance to charitable offices. In
the perilous enterprises of Franklin or of Kane—ay, in
the clashing of steel to steel in murderous array; in the
world-astounding privations and self-denials of the sister
of charity or pioneer priest, there is a selfishness—an
excitement in their soul-absorbing occupations, which
contemplates neither the blasts of fame from the trump-
ets of earth, nor the promised rewards of a future life.
When volunteer aid was called for in the Mexican war,

was it patriotism or love for excitement that moved tens of thousands of Americans under arms? It was certainly not for the pay. The world reads the thrilling narrative with the impression that the actors are heroes to themselves. Could the secret be revealed, the latter wonder in turn at the fascination with which other pursuits of less exciting character possess the majority of mankind.

A strange digression on the subject of my interrupted repose, but necessary, to dull the edge of censure for otherwise apparent vanity and egotism.

I dressed hastily, and was at my friend's bedside.

"You have been a long time coming," said he, "for in a few hours I have lived ages of pain and thought; all that is damnable rises before my imagination. My fancy fashions in the darkness a horrible panorama of the infernal regions. Can I be getting worse? and are these the precursors?"

"Of good results," I replied, "as every thing is by contraries in yellow fever."

A powder that was due at that time had to be taken.

"Another bee-hive!" he ejaculated, alluding to the singing effects of the quinine.

A mustard-bath was brought in, into which we gradually drew his feet from the side of the bed. As we were doing this, he groaned with pain. To laugh at his weakness only made him more unmanageable. We succeeded in a full immersion to his ankles, and commenced rubbing. No sooner did he feel a smarting between his toes, than with a sudden jerk of one leg he kicked over tub and chair.

"Enough of this; you're either *torturing* me, or I'm *dying;* so *leave* me alone. Tell the doctor I take no more stuff; that I want his services no longer; that I have *kicked the bucket.* Ha! ha! ha!" The sudden transition from the serious to the jocose caused me to join him in his winding-up laugh.

He turned himself around, we readjusted the bed-
clothes, and in a few minutes, to all appearance, he was
asleep.

The next morning the chances were even, although
the fever was not yet broken. The physician apprehended congestion of the brain, and was much chagrined
at the cupper being sent off, which was done during my
absence. I determined to use my influence, and for that
purpose set out for Eanes the cupper, who followed me
an hour afterward.

Eanes entered the room with me. With a blandness
of manner peculiarly his own, which, on first sight, dispelled the idea that any thing connected with him or
his profession was repulsive in its character, he bowed
to my friend, who had his eyes fixed upon him as if he
feared meditated murder; but, nothing daunted by the
inquisitiveness of the searching look, Eanes bowed, then
drew from his pocket a snow-white muslin kerchief,
which while passing over his face, he muttered an apology for his reintrusion, saying that "he knew now my
friend would not but submit to what would do him *so
much good.*"

"Your name is Eanes, eh? Well, my name is L.
Just as sure as there is truth in either proposition, if you
attempt by force or cunning to put your cursed intentions into execution, I'll make you swallow cups and
all—and you know I'll do it."

Eanes was a colored man, extremely neat in his person, gentlemanly in his address, and professionally discriminating in the use of his instruments. He believed
that cupping was a remedy for all the ills that flesh is
heir to, and most of those that accidentally endanger
life. In one instance, I remember the exultation he displayed upon his success in removing in a short time, by
his cups, an enlargement of the liver and its torpidity,
when the patient was assured that cure or relief would

not ensue except by a course of calomel, and confinement to bed for at least ten days. He was very communicative on the power of his cups to decrease any local inflammation or complaint without the use of medicine. His theory was that the system eliminated from food and atmosphere nothing but wholesome blood, and that the undue exercise of any one of its organs corrupted the blood in its passage by or through it, and from stagnation created pain and disease. "Send a healthy current through this," said he to me, "and nature is restored." He was, withal, a valuable acquisition to a sickroom. His conversation was replete with anecdote of professional experience, well timed to create a laugh, just as he was placing his cups on a delicate or tender part. He knew every thing about town *recherché* in the matter of scandal, and, when his memory failed, I had no doubt that he had the wit to invent many things, which I have heard him recount, that would have raised a laugh from the ribs of death. He had a steady hand, and was pronounced the most skillful that ever handled scarifier or leech. Many a physician owed to him their boasted success in wonderful cures; and, though he tampered not with their orders or prescriptions, he was consulted by them in the more delicate operations. His income was large, but he was wastefully extravagant, and liberal to his kind, and, I was told, died from chagrin that he had become too greatly involved in securities for others. Peace to his manes!

Eanes did not reply to my friend's remarks. With a look to me, he placed his box under his arm, and, as he put on his hat, on bowing himself through the door, his musical intonation of "Good-morning, gentlemen!" would have struck any one as a grateful acknowledgment for services fulfilled.

On that night I had no hopes of L. All that he asked for was a piece of ice occasionally. He permitted the

nurse to give him a mild foot-bath, and to apply sinapisms to his ankles. Again the doctor intimated his fear
of congestion, and told me, as his friend, that, as the patient was stubborn, he would leave him to his fate. I
entered the room to have a decisive talk with L.

"My dear L.," said I, "there are times which try the
best of friends, and I know none more trying than the
present occasion to me. You are, likely, not aware of
your condition. It is right that I should apprise you,
knowing that, if the worst happens, you have many
things to speak to me about, even if it is a dictation of
a letter to your mother."

At the last word, which struck a chord, he partly
raised himself from the bed, and, with intensely-inquir-
ing look, said,

"Are you serious?"

"On my honor, serious."

"And no hope?"

"But one—that you obey the order of the physician.
You must lose some of your sluggish blood, or you're a
dead man. There's no use mincing the truth—you're a
dead man!"

I said this with due solemnity, and he replied, "Do
as you will with me." I sent off for Eanes.

In the mean time a distinguished physician of my acquaintance was driving by, when I obtained the consent
of the one employed to stop him for a consultation.
After due examination of the patient, they entered the
adjoining room, shutting to the door after them. In a
low tone they exchanged opinions, and concluded that,
unless my friend submitted to the loss of eight or ten
ounces of blood by cupping, his chance was desperate.
They had not much hope of him, at any rate. I stepped
to the bedside, roused L., saw that he recognized me, but
with an indifferent air listened to what I spoke of. I
announced my intention of bringing back Eanes immediately.

Eanes had been fooled, as he said, twice, and showed
his chagrin in reservedness of manner. A table was
drawn by the bedside, and his box of implements was
opened in preparation. Having made his selection of
cups, set his scarifier, and honed a razor, he gently laid
his hand on the shoulder of the patient, and, in his soft,
persuasive voice, said, "Will you be so good, sir, as to incline your head to the edge of the pillow?" at the same
time assisting him to obtain the proper position. Lather
was now spread on the back of his neck, and in a trice
the field for operation was laid bare. A sponge dipped
in warm water was passed over the part, a cup rinsed
with its due quantity of alcohol set on fire, and instantly applied. I have never witnessed this operation for
the first time on any one that I have not made merry
over the surprise and exclamations of the patients. To
my astonishment, L. did not wince. In four or five
minutes the part was in good condition for scarifying.
As he was taking off the cups, my friend, heroic under
suffering, as he thought, exclaimed, "Thank God, this is
over; what next torture is in preparation?" He knew
not what portended the click of the scarifier; but no
sooner was it sprung upon its victim's tender flesh than
the latter fairly bellowed with pain; at the same moment, with a violent jerk of his body, he threw himself
crosswise on the bed, giving Eanes a look of defiance
and hate, accompanied by the quaintest oath in the vocabulary. So immoderate was my laughter, that tears
ran down my cheeks, while Eanes, with all his self-control, could not smother a chuckle. I rallied L. on his
puerile weakness. After much persuasion, mingled with
ridicule, he again put himself in position. A larger
quantity of alcohol than before was poured in a cup, a
flame set to it, and suddenly set upon the scarified part.
A whoop like an Indian's broke from him this time, his
body made a gyration of fifteen degrees more than be-

fore, and, rolling out this time an elephantine oath, he seized the cup, and, without caring where it went, dashed it against the bed-post, scattering the pieces in every direction.

Eanes saw now that expostulation was of no use. The patient had recovered his position in bed, was overpowered by his exertions, and covered himself up for repose. Eanes quietly and composedly wiped and put away his implements, not angry or surprised, as he told me, for such conduct was not new to him. "But, sir," said he to me, "did you ever hear such oaths in your life? That gentleman must be highly educated, or he could not have invented them." Taking his box by the handle, Eanes bowed himself out with his accustomed politeness of manner and language. My friend slept soundly, called for hot tea, which was given him, and when I left, after midnight, he was in the most profuse perspiration.

In the morning early I was at my post. To my surprise the fever had left him, and his skin and appearance were altogether favorable. The physician came in, pleased with the unexpected change, ordered pleasant and refreshing drinks, and was about leaving, when L. called him back.

"Doctor, I believe I should have been a gone case had I not overheard your consultation in the next room with Dr. ——, deciding on my fate. Every word was as a distinct whisper at my bedside. You opened a train of thought in me, bearing on necessity and predestination, which revived all that I had ever read on the subject. I convinced myself that, in defiance of mere physical cause and effect of your schools, I *would* live—*et me voici, Docteur!* I gave myself no concern for the consequences; on the contrary, I have the most pleasing associations connected with my fever; for, while my brain was whizzing under the influence of quinine, I forgot all pains in analyzing my sensations, and laughing within me at the strange physical phenomenon."

Touching the nice sense of hearing spoken of, it is remarkable that, when the attention is closely directed, it reaches an acuteness almost incredible. A perception as characteristic and as lively accompanies this, of the faintest expression of anxiety or doubt in the countenance of the physician or attendants.

In a few days afterward my friend was cracking jokes on the incidents of his sickness, denouncing physic and the paraphernalia of cure as humbugs, and was eloquent in his essays on the virtue of castor-oil, warm drinks, and nature, as a sovereign recipe for yellow fever.

Thinking that he had inflicted pain upon Eanes by his *brusque* behavior, he requested me to accompany him a few days after, for the purpose of settling his bill of cupping. Eanes met us at the door, and, pretending not to know my friend, for he loved a joke, asked me the result of L.'s illness. "Poor L!" moaned L., as he turned his back upon us. Catching the cue, I answered that L. died *very hard.* "I am *so sorry to hear of it,*" said Eanes. "The little I saw of him convinced me that he was a perfect gentleman; and, had he survived, I am sure he would have paid me handsomely. As it is, I can only look for my usual fee, and shall take that with reluctance." This was a sell, over the left, and not only drew down tears of laughter from all three, but caused the exchange of a triple fee from the pocket of L. to the hand of the facetious scarifier.

E

CHAPTER VII.

"Judge not, lest ye be judged."—The Secrecy of Immorality.—An enthusiastic Howard.—His Works.—His Sickness.—His desultory Remarks and dying Sentiment.

It is a common fault to test the sayings and doings of our friends and acquaintances by the conventional standard of honor and honesty, and to condemn without troubling ourselves to examine into the motives which impelled the censured. Society admits no excuse or palliation for offense to either. Men and women throng our path whose conscience convicts them of having, at one time or other, committed a heinous offense against morality, which flushes the cheek with shame when dwelt on; and a sense of horror seizes them when they reflect upon the precipice before them *from exposure*. We know that men commit offenses daily who escape the clutches of justice. With many of these there are no compunctions of conscience. The most pure and sensitive mind has its share of shame and self-reproach for neglected duties or for the imaginary wrong of idle words. But charge them with the fact, blazon to the world their sin or vice, they immediately sink in their own estimation proportionally to their fall in society. Each may justify his acts, or, if not, by penitential expiations and good works atone to God and their own conscience; but to the world no excuse is admitted—no reformation will place them above the malignant shafts of worse men. Accident discovers half the offenses against morality which occupy the tongue of slander. One has lived little in the world who has not been privy to the hushing up of peccadilloes and imprudences which, if exposed, would stamp the offender with lifelong shame, if it did not drive him to greater infamy, but, being kept secret, have enabled him to expiate the offense by a career of honor. In many such cases, the motives of the false step may be traced to a desire to escape a great evil and personal calamity. The offender, with the hope of timely concealment, resolves to make amends; indeed, the promise of ability to do so he thinks certain. He is disappointed, he is discovered, and the judgment of society is that he is a villain or rogue in principle, and that the willful love for the crime or passion alone drove him to the act.

If virtue has its own reward, vice has no less its certain punishment. Men suffer, in a moral penitentiary of their own, with tenfold greater severity to their sensitive minds than the hardened villain under penal infliction. Ever, in the court of their conscience, is their sin arraigned, and before them ever stands their stern accuser. The occupations and excitements of the world curtain it during the day, but in the lone watches of the night it is found clinging around the phantasy with Sinbad clutch.

Mark you well when you are listening to the details of another's shame, and study the character of the gossip and his hearers by their comments. He who *fears* exposure of much that is offensive to law or morality in his own life will be the loudest to condemn, as he will be the most active to disseminate the scandal and hasten the downfall of his fellow. Without pity or sympathy for the feelings of an already lacerated heart, with an expressive holy horror for the lesion, he stands beside the cross of his victim, and, by publishing the sin, pours vinegar in his wounds. Charity, in relieving the animal wants, is trifling in its good compared to that which may be exercised in society in healing dissensions in families and between friends, and showing encouragement and giving countenance to those who have but once offended against morality.

How many a man has suffered from wrongs in the home circle which society never dreams of, and which pride conceals even from a bosom friend, and, without a conceived or apparent reason to justify the course, places himself under the ban of proscription for giving loose to the worst propensities in order to drown his mortification, or to drive from his mind the injury inflicted. We are all given to vaunt our philosophical heroism in presumed positions. We count without our hosts. With the same cause operating, your course would have been similar, if not worse. *De te fabula narratur.* Therefore should we, when we see one suddenly degrade himself by a low indulgence, such as a resort to intemperance and its train of evils, qualify our censure by a charitable construction of the motives or cause, and thank God that we are not so tempted, so afflicted.

One man charms society with his social qualities, and is envied for his happiness and brilliant entertainments. Another, who has fallen from his own sense of propriety and become imbruted by intoxication, is pitied for his weakness and despised for his bestiality. The hidden cause of the extravagance and dissipation of the one, the motive for the degradation of the other, is never canvassed or investigated. Perhaps the motive in both is the same—to fly away from themselves. Let us look around. Before you is one whose only conscience is the law—who, by a *coup de finesse*, a financial roguery, has accumulated thousands, or perhaps has ridden to wealth over the broken hearts of widows and orphans. To conceal his humiliation—for depend upon it he despises himself—he flies to the atmosphere of festivity, and strives to keep down the upbraidings of conscience, and memory of the means whereby he was possessed of his ill-gotten treasure; at the same time he hopes to succeed, by his social gatherings and expensive *soirées*, to cast a Lethean pall over his antecedents, and to seem, if not to be, worthy of the company of the most honorable. In contrast, place him who has honorably struggled through life, combating with misfortunes and reverses perhaps caused by the rascality of the former. An additional event overflows the cup of his misfortune. Despair looks him in the face, blasted hopes half craze him, the future of his family and children finish his bewilderment. Can we less than pity? Can we not sympathize with the weakness of the sensitive mind which can not stoically stand up against accumulated ills, and will not stoop to crime or injustice to extricate himself from difficulties, but throws himself in the lap of intemperance? The world generally stamps such a course as the evidence of a lost sense of shame, or the existence of an innate love for intoxication, or for that which is low and degrading.

My experience has possessed me with many such instances, and perhaps none more explanatory of the preceding remarks than is attempted to be shown in the following:

Frank —— had been in successful business in New Orleans for several years. His social qualities, candor, and high-toned honor in all his transactions made him a favorite in society. His wife was as intelligent and domestic as she was beautiful. Their service was complete, and the chosen few that were admitted to his table have, years after, exchanged comparisons of, and referred to his house as the standard of elegant hospitality. In a season of financial difficulty, he became ruined by the villainy of a mutual endorser. Business now deserted him, and increased troubles forced him into court. Previous to the sale of his furniture, his wife and children left him to pass the summer in the North with her father, who was in affluent circumstances. He remained to complete the settlement with his creditors. With energies able to compete with any labors, he confidently hoped that those who had so often been assisted by him would give him a helping hand in another start. When the time approached, he was met by his quondam friends with all manner of excuses, and by his father-in-law with the observation that his extravagant habits had been such as to justify no hopes in his success, and no gratification on his part in advancing it. It was no doubt that, as the latter thought, so did the former. The professional friends and intimate associates of leisure hours—those by whom he was properly appreciated, and who deeply sympathized in his misfortunes, were unable to do any thing for him. Being deprived of the consolation and advice of his family, now most necessary to his happiness—left alone in his struggles—dark thoughts poignantly possessed him in his solitary chamber. The brooding anticipations of evil, which have at one time or other seized upon all men in the sleepless hours of night, and have been laughed at as visionary in the morning, painfully presented themselves to him during the livelong day. He wandered about listless for some days. His capacity for employment as any thing than a correspondent or manager of a business was defective, and in either he could not succeed in getting employment. Idleness and despair drove him to intoxication.

It is rare to witness an assisting hand extended to a bankrupt, however honorable, unless to secure a previous obligation. All pity; some excuse; but the instances are few where security is volunteered to place him in a condition to work through his difficulties, although many may have been largely indebted to him for their prosperity.

Frank's habits became now repulsive even to his friends and well-wishers. From morning until night, from night till morning, he might be seen haunting the resorts of intoxication, beastly repulsive to every one.

One day he entered the St. Charles, and, seeing me, approached. He seized me by the arm, drew me aside from my companions, saying he wished to speak to me.

"I want you to do me a favor."

"Out with it," I replied, as I put my hand in my pocket, expecting to be asked for small change.

He shook his head as if interpreting the action, and said, "It is not that. I am a poor dog, and miserable. I do not expect to live long—I pray not—and I wish to do some good before I die. Let me only go around with you in your visits to the sick. I will nurse them, and do any thing you bid."

A tear stood in the corner of his eyes as he suppliantly looked at me for a favorable reply. Believing him serious, yet supposing that the revel of that day or night would change his mind or make him forget his strange request of me, I made the appointment to meet him the next day at 10 o'clock at the post-office.

"And you will meet me at the post-office to-morrow, sure?" said he.

"I promise."

It was at this time that the cholera and ship-fever divided between them the mortality, the victim escaping from one dropping into the maw of the other an easy prey. Frank had not been acclimated, though a resident for three fourths of the year for several years. There was a report and a suspicion that yellow fever also existed, but the behavior of the cholera and ship-fever resembled so much the former, when black vomit did not certainly decide, that the faculty were divided.

At the hour appointed to meet Frank, to my surprise, I found him waiting. With an extended hand, entirely himself, he approached and said,

"Perhaps you did not think me serious yesterday. I have been sleeping on my resolve and your promise, and I am now ready for duty."

It was my hour for visiting the sick, and I led him forthwith to a locality most thickly infested with disease. It was a building on Constance Street. I had there then nearly twenty patients. I opened the door of one tenement, where the night previous I had left a mother and two children sick. On this visit I found her husband and two more children lying on the floor with cholera symptoms. The only exempt one was a child of over two years, who, frightened at our appearance, cried as it ran to its mother. I questioned those previously sick of the attendance of the physician, and learned that all the prescriptions had been procured and administered. Thus far all was satisfactory. On this occasion, as always, the able occupants of adjoining tenements followed us round to the sick, eager to do any service required.

"Frank," said I, "here is something worthy of your attention and solicitude. Do you think you're equal to it?"

"Indeed I am, and I thank you for the occasion."

I immediately selected a constant attendant or nurse from one of the neighbors, under an engagement of a dollar for twenty-four hours, and instructed both her and Frank what to do. I promised to see the physician, and send him in the course of an hour. The something to be done at the instant I came happily provided with. I carried about me always a half bottle of mixture famous for its efficiency in the incipient stage of cholera, and manipulated by an eminent druggist of the name of CANNON. On the first attack, and to be continued after every evacuation, I prescribed a dose proportionate to the age and strength of the patient. It was conceded that it not only checked diarrhœa and arrested cramps, but induced sleep and perspiration. I did not consult any physician as to this remedy. I had seen and known of its effectual use, and many have told me that they owe me their lives for persuading them to take this mixture with them, when they found themselves surprised by the disease in the country and on steam-boats. I do not believe that there is any secret in the principal ingredients used, and other successful prescriptions by other physicians have the same materials; but, being chiefly made use of by me, I owe this acknowledgment for the great service it did. What spoke volumes for it, too, was that I never heard a physician denounce it, which alone entitles it to class above the pale of other patent medicines.

On that afternoon, when I again stepped in, Frank was at the apothecary's. I found a change in the arrangement of the furniture and beds. The distribution of the sick in the latter was also different. Frank and the nurse had been at work in making something like order and propriety out of the articles of furniture and clothing scattered about the room. Their supply of tin-ware was neatly arranged on the mantle; the dirty-looking table was covered with a piece of white cotton purchased for bandages; the floor swept, and the mattresses, raised on planks, placed on the two sides of the room, out of the influence of currents of air. There being an insufficiency of blankets, old carpeting was wrapped round the feet after the mustard-baths had been taken. All looked comfortable, and spoke feelingly of the kind disposition and great interest Frank took in them.

"Ah! sir," said the old woman, "he is a gentleman, and may God Almighty bless him forever!"

Having seen my other patients in the neighborhood, I returned, and found Frank at his post.

I was agreeably surprised to mark the cheerful tone with which he greeted me. He looked a counterpart of his best days. He was clean shaved, and his cravat was tied with the care which he formerly bestowed upon it. The change was suggestive. The diversion of thoughts from himself by this occupation; abstinence from intoxicating influences; an absorbing interest in his patients, manifested themselves in his language and manners.

Hypocrites though there be who do homage to virtue by using her mask to reach nefarious ends, to the practiced eye nature speaks truthfully, and unveils the secrets and machinations lurking behind. Physiognomy is one of the most beautiful of natural sciences, and furnishes an infallible guide to a knowledge of the character of man. If the eye is the window to the soul, the human face is a hieroglyphic by which the student may interpret the words and actions of men; for as " a man thinketh in his heart, so is he," not as he does or as he says. It is rare that the predominant passion, characteristic, or general bent of a man's mind is not expressed in the truthful lineaments of the face. It is this written character of the soul which makes the beauty of ugliness in irregular features, and which causes, too, the finest-chiseled features to be repulsive. There is not a feature there that is not acted upon, and moved, and takes its peculiar expression from some passion. We know the thoughtful man from the frivolous; we distinguish the cunning man from the sincere and candid. Anger and lustful passions from frequent indulgence imbrute, and are stereotyped in the expression unmistakably. Each has its sign hung out for every intelligent passer-by; while love, devotion, benevolence, are no less signified than grief and joy.

A new epoch seemed to dawn upon Frank. He could not have looked better when sitting with former friends at his own hospitable table, and pleased was I at the change.

"I thought," said he, "that I was the most miserable creature alive, the most God-forsaken. Yet there is a dependency which in all my troubles I never dreamed of.

Do you know, ——, that I have actually shed tears over
these poor creatures, which I checked with difficulty;
that I have been patting and amusing the children with
all kinds of foolery, as I did my own, and as if they were
my own."

I was looking him full in the face, and noticed the
pleasing effect the recital made upon him, when at the
last words a watery film suffused his eyes, called up from
the emotions passing through his mind in alluding to
his own children. He suddenly turned his head, and
directed his attentions to the sick.

The next morning he met me at the door, looking
haggard and fatigued. He had overtaxed his strength
by sitting up with his patients all night, and was sickened by continual inhalations from the corrupted atmosphere around the patients. I rebuked him for his
imprudence. He replied that he was aware the nurse
was all-sufficient for the work, and that he had gone to
his room at eleven o'clock, when "his pets" were easy
and asleep, but that sleep fled his pillow from thoughts
of his wife and children, and he had returned to the invalids.

When Frank's dissolute habits became known to his
wife and her father, they ceased all correspondence. The
latter would not believe that Frank's failure, if honorable, would exclude him from the helping hand of his
business friends, and, on hearing of his dissipated habits, became confirmed that he was not worthy of countenance. The father's influence succeeded in destroying
the daughter's affection for him. The story of Frank,
and of malign influences upon those who should be the
last to receive them, is an "o'er true tale" of every-day
life. There is requisite no particular examples, for every village has its one or more instances of affections
stolen from the parent for his offspring by a stepmother,
to concentrate upon her offspring the accumulated wealth

of the former marriage, regardless that her husband's
legitimate heirs to that wealth go beggaring through the
world.   Such are an abomination; and for such there is
a retributive justice, if not in their conscience, in the
fading away of every happiness they hope to clasp or
have laid to their hearts.

Of all patients, those afflicted with the cholera are the
most repelling.   When the duties of a nurse or attendant are detailed, it is not to be wondered at that the disease spreads through a house or district, or even hangs
around the spot for weeks after, and insinuates its poison
in the new-comer.   We generally, on our visits, smoked
cigars, or kept in the mouth a camphor cigarette.   Coffee or sugar, burned on coals, was constantly used to
disinfect the atmosphere of the room, and where the bedding or floor was soiled, chloride of lime was sprinkled.
Even with all these the stomach became so nauseated
that only brandy or nature could relieve it.

I told Frank he must go home, eat a substantial breakfast, and walk or rest until evening.   The two children
and old woman were out of danger; the mother and a
boy were the only ones I had fears of.   The former insisted, also, upon Frank's going, saying that the old man
could serve when the nurse could not.   That night I
was full of engagements.   I left word at home of the
neighborhood I was visiting.   At ten o'clock a note
was sent to me thence.   It was from Frank, and almost
illegibly scrawled in pencil.   I read "cholera," and
"hasten."   I repaired to his room immediately, where
I found him surrounded by several of the lodgers, rubbing his limbs, while he was suffering from excruciating
cramps.

"Oh, you have come at last!" said he to me.   "Give
me laudanum or poison, if you are my friend, or take
the pitcher and dash out my brains.   *Where* is the
doctor?"

It is most painful for me to attend in sickness an acquaintance or a friend, for my usefulness is impaired by a want of decision consequent upon the enlistment of too much sympathy. When I witnessed the tears shed by his recent acquaintances from seeing so much suffering, I could scarcely master mine. Steadily they rubbed him, changing their positions as the cramps or parts affected were pointed out by him. Having previously used up the mixture of Cannon, I hastened to an apothecary, ordering hot water to be carried up as I passed out. On returning, I made a strong mustard-bath in a tub; in a basin I made a thick paste of mustard, with warm water, which, put on bandages torn from a shirt, we quickly enveloped his limbs with. Another sinapism on the epigastrium, and a wine-glass of raw brandy, largely dashed with Cayenne, given him to drink, in a few minutes drove away all pain, and prepared him for the visit of the physician. The suddenness of the change was owing to the sensitiveness of the skin, which had undergone severe rubbing. He yet lay dangerously low; the pulse imperceptible to the touch, and other symptoms as alarming. The physician's presence was a relief. Frequent doses of calomel were given, the effects of which were simultaneous with, or perhaps caused, a flow of perspiration, which now came from him. He slept, and in half an hour opened his eyes, which exhibited the dreamy expression indicating coma or stupor. Suddenly the eyes, which did not seem to convey to the retina the impression of what was before them, appeared to recognize us all.

"Doctor, I want brandy."

"Give him brandy, and whatever he wants, but continue the enema until effectual."

As the poultices now gave him pain, we took them off, and with feathers passed sweet oil over the blistered parts. The brandy continued to relieve him from pain,

without agitating his pulse. Later in the night he looked composed, and spoke as if in complete control of his
faculties. His eyes were sunken, but bright; the skin
of his forehead tense; his nose thin and pinched, and his
complexion clear as a child's, but all like the countenance of one lingering for years with the consumption.
Calling me to him, he said,

"How are my pets?" alluding to his Irish patients.

"Doing well, and out of danger," I replied.

"I am happy to hear it."

He spoke then of the real pleasure he experienced in
attending the sick; that it would have become a passion
with him had he undergone a probation in its duties
when prosperity beamed on him; that even now the
relief to his mind in doing good was so great that he
felt he had something to live for, and that it were cowardice to listen to the suggestions of despair. "As soon
as I get well," continued he, "count on me as one of
you."

"Get well first, and then we will talk it over."

"Do you mean by that that I will not get well? Except from weakness, I never felt better in my life."

As he said this he placed a finger on his wrist, and
held it there for a minute, looking at me.

"By Heaven! I have no pulse. Am I dying? Tell
me, for God's sake! and no considerate equivocation, for
I have much to prepare and to say. Do not deceive me,
for I have never seen a death, and can not tell."

"You are not dying, Frank, but you are in that critical stage where life hangs upon a hair. There is no
positive certainty that you will die, as there is none that
you will recover. It is always well to be prepared for
the worst in an insidious disease like this, if in doing so
it will not excite your mind. Be composed, and it may
be a relief to you to communicate to me your commands."

His voice faltered as he spoke catchingly: "In my *armoire* you will find a package—see if it is there—in the drawer—yes—that is it—hand it to me: if I die—send it to my wife—together with this letter. I wrote it when I thought death would shortly follow my dissipation. In it I have said every thing."

He opened the package, and exposed a daguerreotype of his wife, children, and himself in a group. With it open before him, his expression was the picture of grief in painful effort to be relieved by tears. He caught my eye, shook his head, saying, "Is it possible I shall see them no more?" then handed the parcel to me. He said his lawyer had his business in his hands, and that he had nothing to say on that score.

"Now, then, for a relief;" saying which his head sank on the pillow, murmuring a request that I would not leave him until he awoke. He did not sleep, however, but rolled from one side of the bed to the other. The physician having given me little hopes of him, with the order to give him what he called for, I gave him several drinks of brandy on ice. He was disposed to talk, but all my remonstrances were vain. "I am about dying," said he, "and it will be a greater comfort to me to speak than to think."

"Do you know, now, ——, that those poor devils with whom I spent happier hours than any convivial ones I can refer to, are uppermost in my thoughts. That short period seems crowded with more life, and with more that is worth living for, than all existence previous. I have been passing my days, like most of people, knowing or seeing no one but myself, or those that were a part of me. In the mean time, the dollar thrown away in idle luxury would have raised a smile of gratitude to God amid numberless objects within a stone's throw of my extravagance. Never before this have I felt as a man, or analyzed my feelings to know their virtue. As the future was almost a certainty of happiness and prosperity to me, I judged that it was equally so to all."

Frank had not studied that the world and all that therein is is balanced by the evenhanded justice of God. He had been led to believe, with Bias, "that the majority are wicked," from seeing inconsistencies which he deemed imperfections, and from drawing inferences from his isolated condition. In the constant excitement of antagonistic forces in organic as well as inorganic matter, the world is as the Creator wished it to be. "He made us, and not we ourselves." As virtue is hidden, and vice parades its shameless loathfulness, it is too frequently the conviction that the latter prevails. We have but to tempt or assail the former to see its strength. The display of the latter bristles up the former in armor, over which time, like decay, makes of it a germ of reproductive good. Nature's laws are never broken by mind or matter, though it *seems* otherwise. Each has its organization for necessity. Frank would have *pitied* his patients, and did think them miserable indeed; but he found them, under afflictions tenfold worse than his, happier than he, as they were, equally so with him, in their humble prosperity. This was an accommodation of nature to circumstances that never struck him before. He never perceived that true happiness consisted in being reconciled to one's lot, and true courage in not sinking under it.

In detailing the remarks of Frank with Boswellian precision—for my memory is extraordinarily tenacious where my attention has been enlisted—I desire to be understood by my readers that his opinions are given with no other view than to show the direction or turn of mind of one on the brink of eternity. At the same time, they would be shorn of their proportions if I thought them to conflict with, or suggestive of even a sneer at, morality.

As in yellow fever, so in cholera, it is not uncommon to find in patients, after mortification has commenced, and the brain has not been congested, a vigor of mind and a clearness of perception unnoticed before in intercourse with them. It has been often remarked, too, when artificial or external influences cease, as in a few hours before death, that the store-house of the memory is thrown open, and things buried since youth or college exercise strive for utterance. Rapid recitations from Horace or Virgil, the problems of Euclid, and other subjects which interested attention at one time, but were never called up since, are strangely mixed up with the phantasms of the wandering mind.

"My friends," continued Frank, "with all the denunciations against human nature instilled into us in early youth, with our own experience of wrongs which impress us for a time of the truthfulness of its corruption, we have no instance of other than bigots who have anathematized the world as bad. An extreme of goodness is constantly counteracting an extreme of vice. The constituents of true merit, which are a purity of morals and justness of sentiments, sweetness of manners, knowledge of one's self and the world, a solid and regular piety, seasoned with an attention to decency and a benevolent esteem of others, are as prominent in individuals as their opposites. Afflictions and sorrows, universal and frequent as they are, have a tendency to bring in question the goodness of God and the designs of creation; yet, in the face of this, we know of communities of men and women who, like the anchorites of old, continually punish the body, the better to prepare for and participate in the joys of a future life. As I believe in a spiritual existence after death, so do I believe that a man's capacity to enjoy it will greatly depend upon his afflictions and sorrows before it. Just as is the patient on arising from a bed of sickness, who en-

joys a renovated health more than he did before the
contrast presented itself; or, for a more homely illustration, in the case of a really temperate man, who does
not enjoy or appreciate sobriety so much as he who has
been an inebriate."

He paused for a few minutes.

"No, no," he continued, "I have never thought of
the moment coming upon me when I should have to
contemplate death, and I am now, for the first time,
awakened to a responsibility for my past life. I came
into life without knowing it, and without reflection of
its value as an educational stage for another. I now
find myself on the point of leaving it. Like the oars-
man, I have rowed one way and looked another. Still,
I am not so bad. When I have sinned against the propriety of God and man, it has been through impulse, not
premeditation. My sins were more of omission than
commission. Among the former, the gravest that chide
me are induced from the well-spent hours of the past
two days, for in that time was centred more of real
happiness than in all the excitements of years previous.
Accident, or rather Providence, has opened to me, I fear
too late to be enjoyed more, the mystery of life, sealed
to all else but those who love to do good for the good
it does them. I tell you I would rather do a kindness
and speak a word of hope to those Irish pets of mine,
than be restored to my former position in life, wanting
a sense of this gratification."

I thought myself enthusiastic, but he outstripped me.
His eulogy was no less a noble tribute to charity than
it was honorable to human nature, by showing that the
quality is instinctive, and only waits the opportunity
for exercise. Charity is as cardinal a principle of humanity as it is a cardinal virtue in all religions. Men
differ in nice points of sectarian belief with unmitigated
hate and persecution; yet the anomaly presents itself

of all religions making good works the test of worth, and charity the handmaid to faith.

"Now, my friends," he continued, "consider my words as those of a dying man. You will never have such a consequential opinion of yourselves as when you have done a favor or a benefit unasked and unexpected. Our claims upon society in certain cases are recognized and met from motives of mutual protection. What we do for each other has neither the grateful essence nor the generous disinterestedness of real charity. Strike into another path. Do as I have done. Go, if you will, sneakingly, in the obscurity of night, and enter a hovel or an humble dwelling, perhaps next door to your residence; inquire into the condition of its inmates—of people who can not make enough to lay by for a sick day or for old age. They have no claims on you; it is not their right to look to you. Relieve their wants, and encourage them in their despondency about the future. When you shall have closed the door between you and them, a feeling akin to affinity with angels will make the tear glisten in your eye with joy at the good you have done, and make you to know the existence of a chain of dependency through all nature, which to uphold is happiness—which to break is discord and misery. You all know what politeness will do. Heartless and hypocritical as are the idle words and ceremonies patented in good society, there is a fascination in the exercise that cheats the fancy into self-approbation. How much more satisfaction is received and given when the words and performances are sincere, and spring spontaneous to good-will. O God, I desire to live, if only for this. Do you not know that you have every day an opportunity of adding to your happiness by little acts of kindness? One thing strikes me now, in my own situation: some of my business acquaintances, who possessed more friendship for me than I had supposed, in-

formed others that, if they thought I would not have
been encouraged and set up by those whom I had a
claim on for assistance, they were satisfied of my honor,
and would have done it, but that my reckless life of late,
while it for the first time opened their eyes to my deserted condition, shut me out from all sympathy. But did
these last do their duty, as they would be done by?
Why did they not *see*, by asking, that I was abandoned
by all? Even—"

I saw that he was moved by a drift of thoughts to a
touching theme, and begged him not to talk so much.

"Oh, let me talk; I can not think merely; and if
no one will listen, I'll talk nevertheless. All that I have
been saying comes from my heart and from my experience. I should have no regrets for ill usage, for I did
not make my complaints in the right quarter. I will
not bear censure, for the neglect of one may have been
from the best of motives. Were I permitted to extend
my lease of life, rather than err by one refusal, I would
bestow alms on every beggar that crossed my path.
Like to the husbandman—"

Here a violent cramp seized him, from which, in a few
minutes, he felt relieved by a potion. As he felt again
inclined to speak, I asked if it would not be consoling to
him to have the attendance of a minister.

"I am afraid not," he replied. "My mind is so calmly and sweetly settled on the pleasures and joys of a future life, that I would not have it disturbed by the com-
monplaces of dying consolations. I have made but one
step in the scale of existence. When I shall place my
foot upon another, with the experiences of this world
and my present convictions to direct me, a vista of usefulness will open to me there too. Peace and good-will
must have their laborers as well there as here. A lower and more humble worker than I am may be met, to
whom comfort and assistance may be extended, to raise

him nearer to the throne of grace. It may be my lot to bear the cup of cold water to the parched lips of one more miserable than I. Death has never had the terrors for me that religion would impress us with. Religion fulfills its purpose in teaching control and subjugation of our passions. The mystery of another existence is vaguely shadowed forth in earthly comparisons. Every man forms his heaven or hell, his happiness or his misery, his good Father or his awful Judge, according to the tenor of his life, not from the teachings of the schools. The Indian and the Christian are alike in the eyes of their Maker, though their God be different. He opens an eternity to all, and to each for a design that is for the promotion and happiness of all."

Again he became uneasy. Occasional hiccoughs augured an early dissolution. We sat round his bed, offering him, by words and attentions, all the consolation and comfort in our power. Seeing us affected, he remarked,

"You do not sorrow for me, my friends; you should not. Rather rejoice and envy that, having passed man's estate, with faculties to appreciate goodness and virtue, I soar to my high destiny before you. Every day of farther existence, not passed as my latter ones were, might be with increased corruption. So do not weep for me—rather for yourselves."

I hinted to him that if there was any thing he desired to be done after death, he had better speak it now.

"But one: it is this. Fill up, all round, to the dying sentiment of a grateful heart, and deem it not blasphemy."

Glasses of brandy and water were handed to each. We held them in suspense for five minutes, all the while he gazing into the tumbler, apparently concentrating his thoughts upon what he was about to utter. In deeptoned, solemn voice, with eyes closed and uplifted glass clasped with both hands, he gave out,

"Here's to the ALMIGHTY GOD, whose dispensations are in wonderful contrast to our acknowledgments and appreciation; whose vast machinery of creation was set in motion for our use and good, and who gave us death, to strike from us the shackles of sinful flesh, that our spirit may soar free through the ever-regenerating stages of immortality. Here's to the ALMIGHTY GOD!"

Mechanically we carried, simultaneous with him, the glass to our lips, and drank in silent awe. No sooner had we drained the contents than he cast his glass on the hearth, shivering it to pieces; mechanically again we obeyed his impulse, all possessed with the same sentiment that it were sacrilege to put the glasses to a baser use afterward. He bowed his head approvingly, extended his hand to each of us, and gently pressed them a farewell. The opiates and excitement of thought were now sensibly affecting him: he was sinking fast. While we sat around his bed, each busy with his own reflections, Frank's eye was fixed on one or the other of us with a look expressive of weariness, as if to say, "I will not trouble you long; death is near." Silence was soon startled with a painful exclamation from him of "O God, hurry me away!" and instantly thereafter a violent spasm seized him. "There it is—there it is!" he exclaimed, as the convulsion ceased. "Oh, beautiful! Pardon them, and bring their hearts to Thee, my Maker. What! my Kate and son do not see their father? Speak to me again. One kiss—ah! it burns. Take her away."

His mind continued to wander, and vague expressions to escape from him—now plaintive, then angry—till the throes of death came upon him, and all consciousness ceased. While the limbs were flexible he was washed, dressed, and laid on the bed, preparatory to being coffined. Before the lid was put on, agreeably to his request, we placed within the coffin the daguerreotypes, and trinkets, and broken playthings that once belonged to his children. Six of his friends followed him to the grave: there one of us read the beautiful and impressive burial service of the Episcopal Church, and before the oven was closed threw in sprigs of cypress and our mourning badges. It is not uncommon, during an epidemic, for funerals to be unattended to the grave by the clergy. Their numerous engagements will not allow them more than to perform the service at the domicil of the deceased, especially if the latter be of the humbler portion of their congregation. It is held to be horrible by the Catholic poor to omit this service to one of their faith, and not an instance of neglect ever came to my notice. In the other denominations the ministers are from the North, or abroad, and, while instances of desertion from fear of the disease are numerous, there are noble examples of the soldiers of Christ who have battled through their duties, some falling victims to their zeal. During the long ride to and from the cemetery we were engaged in recapitulating the past life of the departed, and the incidents and sayings of his latter days.

From the only letter which was among his effects I became now informed of the principal cause of his self-abasement. She who should have comforted and supported him through affliction, upbraided him for his extravagance in ruining the prospects of his children, when, too, that extravagance was the incense of his idolatry to her love and beauty. His establishment and entertainments lost to her, he was no longer worthy of her affections. Her letter said, but in other words, that her pride could brook no diminution to her influence in fashionable circles, and that she saw in his bankruptcy nothing but the triumphant envy of her rivals and the sneers of the malicious. She wished him well, but to return to him was impossible, as it would make her unhappy to witness the humiliation of his employment by

another, while it would harass him by adding to his
expenses.

Two years afterward I received a letter from her, asking me for particulars of his death, having heard that I
had placed a trunk of his effects in his attorney's hands.
She reproached herself for deserting him, and said she
had retired from the world a changed and repentant
woman—that she lived only in the past, and for the
future of her children.   Later than this I heard that her
father fell into bankruptcy, hopelessly, helplessly broken,
and that she had become the wife of another for the
support of her offspring.

CHAPTER VIII.

Epidemic of 1853.—The aggravated Type of Fever.—The Howard Association commences Service.—Physicians volunteer.—Our Funds.—
Assume the Duties of a Board of Health.—Extraordinary Influx of
Relief.—Our Members.—Our Duties.—St. Philip Street Boarding-
houses.—Filth of Premises.—*Maison de Santé.*—A Swiss Family.—
Our paid Physicians.—Two Doctors destroy each other's Prescriptions.—The Patients recover.—Increase of Sick.—Members use Cabs
to visit.

> Quis dabit capiti meo
> Aquam?   Quis oculis meis
> Fontem lachrymarum dabit?
> Ut nocte fleam
> Ut luce fleam
> Sic tirtur—
> Heu miser, miser:
> O dolor, dolor.

THE summer of 1853 introduced to all benevolent institutions in New Orleans greater trials, with corresponding triumphs, than had ever presented themselves.   The
most fatal, because the most complicated, yellow fever
ever known to exist surprised the citizens this year.
Every questionable symptom of what is called simple

yellow fever had so engrossed the close attention of the faculty for some years previous, that the merest tyro in physic could not mistake the Simon Pure. The few cases, however, that ushered in this great epidemic raised a dispute among the faculty as to its genuineness. The diagnosis was far from being made with unanimity. With farther experience, they settled down in opinion that all were right and all were wrong. It was found that the disease was an aggravation of former ones; that phlebotomy, or cupping, indispensable to former treatment, was fatal in this. Before the disease became epidemic, the shining lights of the profession had adopted a practice which became general, because it proved successful. The pride of opinion and theory, natural to intense study, had to succumb to the practical effects of experience. Our Charity Hospital, which is the hygeiameter of this latitude, as it is the great school of medicine for tropical complaints, was daily visited to observe treatments and results. For once in the history of man or medicine, the general consultation resulted in the uniform opinion of the savans that the mode of treatment should be altered to meet the extraordinary symptoms that had invaded the diagnosis. The only questionable point at issue was the benefit to be derived from the administering of quinine. Prejudice still holds strong *pro* and *con.*, while practice and experience leaves it an open question. As I progress in the details of numerous interesting cases, without reflecting upon either practice, the reader may draw his own inference. Where quinine has been faithless to its purpose in extraordinary cases, it has been wonderfully curative in others.

Early in the month of July the Charity Hospital was filled even to its corridors with yellow-fever patients. The city council had adjourned after trying in vain to organize a Board of Health. The streets were in the most foul condition; the putrid water of the gutters was

F

covered with a thick green vegetable scum, from which
exhaled a sickening odor; showers of rain were frequent,
without thunder and lightning, and the temperature as
variable as the weathercock. Business being at its usual
periodical stagnancy, the knots of talkers at the corners
and elsewhere were occupied in giving the rumors and
circulating their experience. Alarm prevailed throughout the city. Before matters reached this point, the
Howard Association had gone quietly to work. We
were requested by editors and merchants to withhold
publication of our acts, as the report of an epidemic—
which might yet be checked—would entail severe loss
on merchants and shop-keepers. The apothecaries selected by us to fill prescriptions for our sick were supplied with slates, on which they directed applicants for
relief to write their names and residences. The members of their respective districts looked in at these places
twice a day, and when the patient could not be removed
to the hospital, he was furnished physician and nurse
under their superintendence. From the first intimation
of the presence of fever, we were offered the services of
twenty physicians gratis. Our treasury, not having over
$5000 in it, was too low to admit of paying for more
than medicine and sustenance for the poor. When we
became fairly under way, the accession of medical volunteers was greater than we could employ. The finance
committee of the council, with whom was delegated powers for emergencies, could not agree upon an appropriation to us. We determined to act independently; to
call upon the citizens for aid, and to assume the duties
of a Board of Health. We accordingly published in the
paper a proclamation that an epidemic was raging in our
midst, and furnished the daily returns of interments to
confirm it. We gave, also, the names and residences of
members, physicians, and apothecaries upon whom the
poor and destitute could call. We also announced that

certain members would call on the citizens for their contribution. Every body was prepared for what we stated,
and many the next day sent us liberally, with the promise of *more, if wanted.* On the first day of collection we
received fifteen thousand dollars. On that night we
counted but eighteen members, the most of them being
absent on business or for their health. All these did
us good service throughout the country where they
were by procuring subscriptions. Editors and report-
ers of papers could not but see the extent of distress in
their daily walks, and largely contributed to the influx
of means from wherever the printed sheet was read.
When the letters accompanying donations from every
hamlet, village, or town of the Union were read at our
nightly reunions, thrills of joy, like that which leaps
through the hearts of a shipwrecked crew on sight of a
sail coming to relief, pervaded us. Thankful were we
that Providence had favored us with being the medium
to dispense the hopes and comforts it was to produce.
The Israelites of old were not more dependent, not more
astonished or grateful, upon the rain of manna to ward
off death or starvation, than we were at the extraordinary manifestation of sympathy. How we have fulfilled the wishes or the hopes of the donors, these written
evidences can give but a trifling, faint idea. They are
an inconsiderable part of one member's labors—say,
rather, pleasures—and *his* services were far surpassed
by many of his associates. Many members, who had denied their patients many conveniences and comforts, for
fear that the fund collected here would soon be exhausted, now added comparative luxury to the hovels they
visited. The soiled mattresses and bed-clothes, seldom
washed or cleansed from indispensably constant use,
and reeking with the effluvia consequent thereon, were
thrown aside, and replaced with new. Habituated to
sleep upon the floor, they were now raised up on cots,

freed from a fatal dampness, and open to the ventilation
of a higher stratum of atmosphere.   Utensils accommo-
dating to their wants for cooking, or to prevent them
from rising from the bed, as well as many things which
even poverty calls for as indispensable, but which they
had not, were furnished to them.   The basket filled with
the daily quantum of provisions from the grocery, in addition to their order on the butcher for meat, with lem-
ons for their drinks; the daily supply of ice; the luxury of a fowl for the soup of the convalescent; the rich
man's privilege of bi-daily visit from a physician; the
attendance of a nurse, and our supervision of all, were
well calculated to awaken their astonishment, as they
did win their confidence, and inspire hope and gratitude.
It was not the abject poor that alone participated in the
bounty of our dispensations.   Those of a better class—
the mechanic, the small shop-keeper, and the widowed
family pinched to live upon a fixed pittance — these,
when disease would strike in their midst, were soon exhausted of means by the purchase of medicines; farther
wants drove them to sacrifice their furniture to the pawnbroker or at auction.   At the very last extremity, their
honest pride, to be independent of alms, yielded to the
suggestion, advice, and persuasions of kind neighbors to
claim from us what was their rights.   As the epidemic
drew to a close, our duties were chiefly of a relief character to this class.   Business had been suspended, and
not yet resumed.   A worse epidemic than even sickness
itself is want.   Such, whose delicacy forbade them to
ask, or would not come to us when advised, were sought
for, and their scruples overcome.   We were made the
confidants of distress which we did not communicate to
each other, and which to all intents and purposes we
have forgotten.   To a curiosity which would look to be
gratified by any developments in that respect in what I
am about to relate, there will be sure disappointment.

The duties of an association which commanded the patronage of the whole country, and which has, by its reputation, caused to be established and fostered similar ones elsewhere, are worthy of particular note. The constant call for our services, and the increased and extended field for operations, required a specification of duty and an equanimity of action which could in no other way be accomplished than by meeting together every night for at least half an hour, to provide for contingencies and exigencies which we had not foreseen. To supply the places of absentees, we selected from the numerous applicants to make up the number required by the Constitution—thirty members. These were termed assistants. Many who had the heart, but not the strength, resigned after a short probation. We became finally completely effective. The assistants exercised all the privileges of a member, except having a voice in our deliberations. Their services proved of incalculable benefit. Truly they worked *con amore*, and in their untiring and enthusiastic devotion to the patients they surpassed many of the members. Those who shared with me the portion of district under my charge far surpassed me. At our meetings each member gave a written report of the number of cases under his charge, whether convalescent, sick, or discharged, with the number of deaths. Some, from extraordinary duties, were frequently absent, and made their reports at convenience. Complaints from any quarter were also discussed and remedied. Night after night, as the work grew on our hands, different modes of relief were adopted. Due-bills or *bons*, printed on cards, for amounts of from fifty cents to one dollar, were distributed by the member endorsing them, as also tickets for a dime of ice and twenty cents of beef. All these passed as cash throughout the city, as they were promptly paid by the treasurer. Orders for groceries were given, of a week's duration, at from twenty-five to seventy-five cents per day; sometimes for a week's supply at once. Where the former, which was renewed from week to week, a pass-book was used, to show the member attending the quantity and quality of the provisions taken.

We strictly forbade the use of spirituous liquors. The French emigré, however, was allowed his accustomed bottle of *vin ordinaire*, and the German his potation of lager. We limited the pay of a nurse to two dollars for twenty-four hours, and by an additional sum obtained her services for other patients in the same building. When we were satisfied, from the respectability of the applicants, that our donations would not be abused, we gave to a family sums of money not exceeding fifteen dollars at one time. It was our duty to bring the physician to the patient, to visit the latter twice a day, to watch for any imposition toward him, to provide or see provided all his wants, so that the question asked, "Can I do any more for you?" should be responded negatively. Where they died, we either informed the public officer for that purpose, if there were no objections of the survivors to have their relative buried by the commissary, or furnished a plain coffin, hearse, and carriage.

The district in which I exercised my duties was inhabited by a different and better class of emigrants than any other. My patients were principally French or German. The latter language was a sealed one to me, but I was sure to find a willing interpreter in their devoted country-people always at hand. After noting the name, age, and parentage of the patient, I sent him a physician and nurse who could speak his own language. *Par parenthese,* I was now becoming good enough a judge of the requirements for the cure of simple yellow fever to justify treatment when the physician passed any in his rounds from misdirection, or neglect, or press of duties.

The stronghold at the commencement, in my district, was in St. Philip Street, near the Levee, where every other house has a beer-saloon, with lodging-rooms above. Isolated cases in private practice came to my knowledge at a distance from this spot. Here the service of our association commenced for this district. It is in the heart of the district. Having seen at the hospital that several cases had been brought from St. Philip Street, I repaired there, and, through an apothecary, was furnished with particulars. After telling the landlords of these houses of my mission, they permitted me to make a survey of their premises. The dormitories and out-houses were a fruitful source of disease. In rooms eighteen feet square there were at least twelve cots, so close together that one man could not pass another. In some the bedding was dirty, the musquito-netting filthy, the floors spotted with offensiveness, and an atmosphere correspondingly tainted. In most of them I found some ailing and some sick, the former complaining only of nervousness or headache, which a "little lager and a little sleep would drive off," they said. They would not be persuaded that there was any danger, nor would they take medicine, or any prescription I offered. I told them to wait till the morrow. My visit then obtained me the urgent solicitations of the landlord, as he saw that one death from yellow fever, likely now to occur from aggravated symptoms, would leave him without a lodger. Our association had made arrangements with the *Maison de Santé*, superintended by the Sisters of Charity, to receive the sick of this district. On the first day I sent off three, and every day thereafter as many or more. In the mean time, such as had families or friends to resort to asked for attendance at their houses, which, if single persons, was given them, provided they furnished their own nurse; otherwise to the hospital they were sent. We never separated families to send to the in-

firmaries or hospitals unless there was urgent necessity
for so doing, such as the foulness, etc., of the premises.
The greater part of these Germans had been working on
the Jackson Railroad, where, they said, they had been
for weeks drinking swamp water. St. Philip Street occupied my entire time for ten days, during which nearly fifty people had died of the disease. In no other
part of the district did I hear of any patients who called
for the attention of the association, yet the fever was
fearfully spreading in the other districts.

One morning my attention was drawn to the exposure
of three coffins in the entry of a house in which I had
heard there was some sickness. I had several times been
refused admission by the landlord on the ground that
there was nobody ill within. Upon requesting to know
the reason of his deceit, he replied that his boarders had
means to pay for a physician, and would not accept the
aid of the association. He told me that there were also
others sick. These I insisted upon seeing, and was shown
up stairs to their rooms. The same objection of cots
closely arranged existed here as elsewhere. The floors
were cleaner, the bed-linen appeared to be more frequently changed, and the occupants were also of a better class than in the other houses. Five or six sick refused positively to go to the *Maison de Santé*. They had
been strongly prejudiced against hospitals, and expressed themselves satisfied with the attentions of the proprietor and his wife. It did not require close examination to see that they had not the conveniences of a sick-
room, which, with the imperfect ventilation, diminished
the chances of recovery. I suggested a great deal, but
my remarks appeared to be received as impertinent, so I
left with the remark that I would call again that evening. As I was going out, I saw a man with his head
reclined upon a table in the bar-room. I aroused him,
and asked if he felt sick. His eyes were much infected,

and pulse high. He was only sick, he said, from an emetic which he took that morning, and thought he had caught a cold, as his limbs pained him. I used all manner of entreaties to persuade him to be put in a cab and be sent to the infirmary; but he, too, would not listen to me. That night he died in the most distressing paroxysms. When I called in the evening, one of the patients, whom I had told would not get well if he remained where he then was, entered the bar-room, supported by two men, and, stopping at the counter, left several gold coin, together with the key of his trunk, with the proprietor. He was much pleased to see me, and was now satisfied that his best hopes for recovery were in his removal to one of the hospitals. I gave him a card of admission to the infirmary, where I was pleased to see him convalesce in a few days, and be discharged.

All the vicinity now knew of the action of the association, and, on my appearance in the street, I was met by different people requesting my attention to new cases.

In one of these beer-houses I was shown by the proprietor to a basement room of the back building, occupied by a Swiss, his wife, and a child of four years. They were recently from New York by sea, on their way to St. Louis, and were ignorant of any language save their vernacular. They had been ill for three days, attended by a skillful German physician, but they had been neglectfully nursed by a woman they had employed. Their clothing, ornaments, and books on the mantle-piece made it manifest that they were as thrifty as intelligent. When the object of my visit was explained, they looked at each other, then at their child, and with a despairing look at me, as if to say, "It is too late now." I opened many complaints upon the nurse, and set about myself to remedy deficiencies. When I had restored comparative comfort, I went out for a few minutes, and returned with a watchful and experienced nurse. With all her assiduous care, and the frequent visits of the physician, the applications and remedies were ineffectual. Whether to attribute so marked a failure to previous neglect, the exceeding closeness of the room, or the despair which seizes on a family thus prostrated, were equally balanced in my mind. The nurse, who had obtained from them a recital of their condition, their sufferings and privations to reach New Orleans, and the hopeful anticipations held out to them on arriving at St. Louis among their relatives, wept as she repeated it to me. That night I spent several hours with them. Nothing we said could comfort them. The husband and wife frequently exchanged desponding glances after sorrowfully regarding their child, affectionately consoled each other as either would express pain, and thanked God that neither would survive to shed tears over the other. Natural enough was it that such a family, exulting in health and hopes, and suddenly finding themselves in the grasp of death and in a strange land—natural enough was it that, sharing such sudden affliction here, they should desire to be inseparable in their hereafter. When I returned in the morning they were all in the last stage, and at evening were removed to be buried together. Their effects of any value were put back in their trunks, and shipped to St. Louis to the address marked thereon.

In four or five days more the new cases increased in this locality, and occupied my sole attention. In a day more I was called to a case in the square below. The patient occupied one of about twenty-four rooms in a two-story building, which surrounded a large court. The building fronting the street was of ancient construction, roofed with tiles, and of one story and attic. Every room was tenanted by four or five persons. From day to day thereafter the majority of them had taken the fever, converting the place into a miniature hospital. Three nurses, with the assistance of the able occupants, divided their time among the sick. The fever had no sooner completed its work here than it passed from square to square below, gradually diverging from this point toward Rampart and Esplanade Streets. It was not until the epidemic had exhausted itself in the upper and lower districts that it showed itself in the rear of the city, toward the swamp, where the assistants so ably did their duty. It is a noted fact that, while in other districts the disease commenced in the swamps and gradually approached the river, when it had worn itself out every where else, it finished its relentless work with greater malignity in the rear of the first district than elsewhere. After our infirmaries were closed, patients claimed our attention here for many weeks.

At the end of my second week of labor I had sixty patients on my list. Besides these to visit, I had to look into the condition of those sent by me to the hospitals and infirmary. I was not sent for by many until the disease had had too long a hold to be manageable. These could not be removed, and were treated as well as circumstances would permit in their unhealthy localities. I had merely to follow closely the prescriptions of the physician, to strip death of its precursory agonies, and to hand in, a few hours after, the name of the deceased to the commissary for interment. Every day I found memoranda on the slate at my house: "A man dead at No. —— —— Street; please bury him." In many instances a corpse was deserted for more than a day, from the ignorance of the neighbors where to apply for aid, or their want of means to remove it. The suffocating stench in the neighborhood drew distant residents to the spot, who finally brought our attention to the cause.

Although almost every physician volunteered to attend the poor gratis, it was expecting too much to require constant attendance, to the exclusion of their pay-

patients, without some compensation. The largest prac-
titioners were relieved from this sacrifice of their time
as soon as we found ourselves able to pay for the services of others. In each district we engaged such physicians as had not much practice, and who we knew were
educated to their profession. These were generally
young men, who took our allowance of $100 to $300 per
month, with the use of a cab, more for the prospective
advantages, and for familiarizing themselves with the
disease, than for its compensatory return. Indeed, many
thus employed laid the foundation of a practice among
the thrifty and industrious population which has proved
a fortune to them. We adhered as close as possible to
the calling in to the sick a physician of their respective
nationalities. It would be invidious to particularize the
value of their services. Their modes of treatment differ-
ed widely, but, as the patient had faith, we did not de-
mur. We witnessed, equally without comment, the
Spanish physician, who gave to his patients, on the first
day of convalescence, the juice of fresh oysters; the
German, who, after the first course of medicine, when
the patient desired food, gave him successfully strong
fluid nourishment; another, who prescribed hard-boiled
eggs as the most nutritious and digestible in a more advanced stage of convalescence; the French physicians,
of equal success, with hot drinks and cold drinks, close
covering or no covering at all on the patient; him who
administered strychnine with reported success, etc., etc.
We took no liberties with their patients and prescriptions, but were always as happy as surprised at the results when they proved favorable.

I remember leaving an order for one of our physicians
to visit two German women lying in the same bed with
fever. They had both wisely taken a dose of oil and a
foot-bath, and when I entered they were beautifully-de-
veloped cases. The physician called shortly after, and

left them a prescription, to be sent for and "taken immediately." When I called at noon I questioned them with regard to their medicine. They informed me that another physician—one of ours, too, who had been attending in the immediate neighborhood, and who thought the visit of the other an impertinent intrusion—had just left, after throwing the mixtures of the other in the street, saying that *he* would send them the medicine they were to take. I read his prescription and obtained the medicines, directing them how they were to be taken, and retired. They, having more confidence in the first than the last physician, concluded to wait until the former returned, which he did that night, and, upon being informed of the cavalier manner in which his potions had been treated, sent those of the latter in the same direction, leaving again his former prescription. The patients now waited my return to obtain the order for the purchase of the medicines. I did not go there until midnight. I found the patients in a profuse perspiration, with a healthy pulse. Nature had been assisted in this change by frequent drinks of iced water. As I deemed it imprudent to decide between the prescriptions of the two physicians, and thought a continuance of the simple treatment as safe as any, I concluded to let well enough alone, at least until the next morning. I left word that if either physician called he should be requested to meet me at 9 o'clock. When I returned I found the favorite one in conversation with the sick, and in a few minutes afterward the other one entered. They had not been personally acquainted. My introduction of the one to the other was accompanied by a studied consequential bow from both. I opened with the complaint against the latter that, as the patients were under charge of the association, I had a right to call in the services of any physician, and that in doing so I meant no reflection upon the reputation of the other. The intrusive one, not satisfied with being thus discomfited, commenced a thundering rattling of words—all Dutch to me—which was responded to as volubly, until I thought my interference became necessary to prevent injury to the patients, telling them, at the same time, that the latter did not require the attention of either in their present excited state. At noon, until night, and thereafter, the patients continued to do better. They were provided with light sustenance on the fourth day, after which they rapidly convalesced. The above is, in one sense, illustrative of the Spanish proverb, "That one physician will cure of the colic, while two will cure of physic."

The number of patients increasing upon our hands, and their distance apart, required greater facility in our calling upon them. Accordingly, most of us used cabs for both day and night visits; indeed, they were indispensable, as miles had to be gone over every hour in looking up physicians, nurses, etc. Every morning I made up the list of patients on hand, with those whom I had to visit for relief purposes. The latter were increasing upon us in a greater ratio. Not only were the families of the convalescents to be taken care of, but we had demands upon us from the indigent class of the resident population. As our hours were fixed to be at our residences for the applicants for relief, it was no unusual sight to find as many as one hundred persons for successive mornings at those hours. It was our duty, before affording any relief in money or groceries, to visit the residence of the applicant, and judge for ourselves his worth and sincerity. Many who attempted imposition annoyed us much by most distressing representations, and sending for us, to the exclusion of previous engagements, to the outskirts of the city, to look in vain for their designated places of residence. The scene at our house or office on the occasions of such application was beyond description. There was the importunate beggar of all degrees, sexes, and ages; the worthy applicant, with his or her whispered plaint of distress; the kind neighbor, who asked our attention to some sick or needy; the nurse, to be paid or desiring employment— *cum multis aliis*—all of whom were either dismissed with their wants met, or promised an immediate and satisfactory visit. These gatherings took place at my house an hour before breakfast and before dinner, and for two months I was occupied, to the interference with my meals, in writing orders on the treasurer, giving bons to the grocery, approving bills, etc. The only time properly my own was after dinner, when an hour's repose compensated me for the absence of it the previous night. Having to hold colloquy with people of all nations, and imperfectly acquainted with two languages besides my own, I found little difficulty in understanding any except the German; for this language I invariably found an interpreter among some of the applicants.

My first occupation, after taking a cab, was to leave the names and residences of the new cases with the physicians; after this, to visit the old patients; then to notice the condition of those who had obtained or asked relief, and, before returning home, to visit the new cases, procure their medicines, engage nurses, etc., etc. After the third day of convalescence I left the patient with the nurse, who continued two or three days. Such cases were marked as discharged, and thus reported on our weekly returns to the association.

The night, which was the most fatal to the sick, was the most agreeable and less enervating to us. For many nights successively we did not sleep. Even were we so disposed, calls upon us would have prevented it. I say so disposed, because there was not one of us who was not so much enlisted in many cases that he knew his indulgence in repose would be fatal by the neglect of them.

Several members have told me that, with physical prostration calling imperatively for rest, they have frequently retired to bed, but found that their minds hovered around their particular sick, chiding them for desertion. Unable to sleep, they hurried out to visit their patients until daylight.

CHAPTER IX.

The Runaway restored.

UPON returning home late one evening, I read on the slate, "*Mary* ——, *No.* —— *Dauphin Street. Please call immediately.*" The proximity to my residence, as well as the sex of the applicant, induced me to give this the preference of a first call. Upon discovering the house by the number given, I was not a little surprised on finding myself accosted by several young females who were standing at the door, and who welcomed me as if I were an old acquaintance. The matron of the establishment next approached me, followed by the remainder of her household. She was a large, portly woman, of well-formed features, but with a leaden expression of the eye which chilled familiarity. Her "I am glad to see you" was delivered in the same tone as she would reply to a dun to "call to-morrow."

"You have some one sick with you?" I remarked.

"Yes," she replied; "there is one of the girls who has taken sick, and nothing would satisfy her but to send for you. I believe her nurse put the notion into her head. She wants for nothing, as I can take care of my own sick; but she has seen you visiting next door, and fancies you can do something for her. Let me show you to her room."

At the doorway of the room I was met by the nurse,

who had been frequently in our employ. I entered, followed by the matron and all the girls, seven or eight in number.

"Mary," said the matron, "here is Mr. ——."

"Oh, I am so glad you have come, sir; I did not expect it;" at the same time holding out her hand to me, and requesting all others present to retire for a few minutes. To examine into the condition of my patient the better, I brought the candle beside the bed. Her face was partially enveloped in the sheet, and her head sunk deep in a feather pillow. As I took hold of her wrist, she begged me to tell her the truth of her situation, for, she said, "I am not prepared to die, and least of all here." This was her fifth day. Physician and nurse had successfully done their office, and, to all appearances, the symptoms were favorable. On my assuring her to that effect, she raised her head, and leaning it upon her hand, ejaculated, "Thank God! thank God!" with great emphasis. "I did not send for you," she continued, "because I have no faith in my physician; but I wished to be assured, from another than him, that I should recover. I am tormented by day and night with thoughts and dreams that make me despise myself heartily, and I should die of despair did I not believe that I may yet live to repent and reform."

I reassured her of her favorable symptoms, and required of her to dwell only on the certainty of that future of reform and usefulness she hoped for. I was about leaving her with her nurse, who had just entered, when she asked me, imploringly, to call in on the morrow, as she had something to say which she felt she had not strength then to communicate.

When I entered her room the next morning she was awake, but did not notice my presence until I addressed her. It seemed I had driven away a pleasing reverie, for her recognition was followed by a formally-expressed "You are here?" To my different inquiries, she replied and remarked as follows: that she had slept for a few hours after I left; but since, until daylight, her wandering thoughts had raised visions of gloomy character; that she felt now that she was not so well as yesterday, and piteously besought me to do my utmost to save her.

"But you are doing well, Mary," I observed.

"Oh no, no, sir! I feel I am not. I dread that I am not." On saying this, she covered her eyes with her arm, and sobbed loudly.

"Mary!" said I, in as angry a tone as I could counterfeit, "I came here to relieve your suffering, and to cheer you under your affliction. If you continue to aggravate your sickness by these demonstrations, and in my presence too, the object will be better gained by my absence. You can not know upon what little your life depends. If you continue to despond thus, even though you were much better, you will die. You are now safe —I say, safe, wanting only obedience to all that is required of you. For you, a girl of sense, to anticipate your fate by harboring a suspicion of the worst, is unaccountable weakness. Cheer up! Had you the strength to stand up and look at yourself in the glass, you would wonder, as I do, that you are taken to be ill. Let me see you smile, nay, laugh, if it is not too great an effort."

The nurse handed me a potion for her. As I placed it to her lips, she made a sour grimace; then, with the remark, "Am I not brave?" swallowed the whole of it. "Now," said she, "I feel another person. Celeste, tell Emily I want to see her." In a few minutes the latter entered. "Give me your hand, Emily," she said. "Forgive me for what I said to you yesterday. I know I hurt your feelings. Am I forgiven?" "Certainly," was the reply from a young girl of melancholy sweetness of countenance, who appeared touched by the explanation, or the cause of it. They exchanged a few words, and I was left alone with Mary and the nurse.

Before leaving the room the shutters had been opened for some purpose, which gave me an opportunity of seeing particularly the features of my patient. Her face was oval, her eyes blue, and fringed by their almond-shaped line of lashes, a nose retroussée, her mouth large and well defined, and a chin wherein was seated a dimple that alone would beautify the entire expression of worse features. Her auburn hair yet retained the braids, though ruffled, which it had when she was taken sick. I judged her to be about twenty years of age. Yet how difficult is it to estimate by years a life which is crowded with events such as hers had recently experienced.

When I returned in the evening her symptoms were not so favorable. The physician had ordered her to be kept free from intrusion. It appears that she dreaded to be left alone, and, as soon as I was gone, she was surrounded by the other girls of the house. This could not be prevented by the nurse. I called the matron to me, and told her that, when I was called in to the sick, I made it a point to be second to the physician; that, from disobedience to his orders, in crowding the sick-room and talking to the patient, they were killing her. "She is convalescent," I continued. "All she now requires is repose and quiet. These she must have, if I have to put a guard at the door, or I do not return." Complete compliance was expressed to my wishes.

"Except Emily," said Mary. "She will not talk to me, and I have much comfort in her company."

To this I consented. With worse promise for herself, and with increased sympathy of her companions and attendants, her hope of recovery was yet stronger than it had been. With a "good-night," and advice to coax herself into sleep, for the prospect of repaying me for my visits by seeing her improvement on the morrow, I left.

On the morning following, at 10 o'clock, I again called. She had slept at intervals during the night, and was then in a slumber. In the evening, when I again called, to my horror and dismay I perceived her with her head over the side of the bed, supported by Celeste, in vain attempts to continue a retching which had been effective an hour before. The nurse had not, in the mean time, been able to prevail upon her to allow a sinapism to be reapplied to the sensitive skin of her abdomen. Having ordered it to be done as soon as I saw the state she was in, she made no objection. After her temples had been bathed, and the feeling of exhaustion had partially subsided, she noticed me drawing the attention of Celeste to a dark-colored fluid which she had thrown up on the linen; by candle-light it was scarcely discernible from black vomit. Catching at my suspicious, she searched my countenance for farther confirmation. As I was laying down the soiled linen, she seized it in her left hand, and, pointing to it with her other, gave out an hysteric laugh, followed by tears and sobs.

"Then it is all over," she said. "My dream of life—is finished. Just, too—when every thing of the future was so promising—so good. Oh, Mr.——, do you know —that last night—I dreamed of home? Father and brother were there" (here she sobbed so distressingly as to smother articulation). "Oh! it was a sweet meeting. Before I awoke this morning I was so happy. I tried to sleep again to continue the dream; but—now—it is all over; I must die—and here!"

"No, no, Mary," I replied, "not so quick. You have nothing to fear. You have not had the black vomit. On the contrary, your pulse—feel it yourself—is healthy; your skin moist, and every indication of convalescence. Your late exertions were entirely owing to the excessive

quantity of water you drank, from which you must restrain yourself hereafter; and the color of the vomit is
that of the medicine you have taken."

" Then I may hope, and will get well?"

I bowed affirmatively. The nurse again passed a cloth,
saturated in Cologne, over her face and neck, and in a
few minutes the luxurious sleep of the convalescent stole
over her.

To reassure myself of her condition, I remained for a
half hour to see the physician, engaged, in the mean
time, in looking at the books and ornaments of the room.

It is no small tribute to virtue that the greatest devotees to passion and debauchery desire to conceal from
themselves and others every thing likely to make them
dwell upon their particular failing. As much as a drunk-
ard revels in intoxication, or a *fille perdue* in sensuality,
they look with abomination upon any representation of
their sin in print. When they are whirled in a pool of
sensuality, reason becomes distracted; when lulled by
reaction, the intervals are a dreamy indifference to every thing, until the appetite for indulgence again over-
takes them. They would not be forced to think at all,
much less of their own degradation. Before now the
reader is aware that I have introduced him under the
shed where contamination breeds foulness, and where
the world has placed strong bars of resistance to its
charity. Even here, though, a lesson of purity may be
learned in the chasteness of taste characterized in the
ornaments and pictures of a room; and even here, too,
may be seen the well-thumbed BOOK, resorted to from
early association, or when desperate thoughts prevail,
which, in more virtuous ranks, clasped in rich binding,
is made merely ornamental to its owner's professions.

Our association is not frequently called in by this
class of females. They prefer each other's attendance in
sickness to the silent rebuke of a pitying Pharisee. I

should not provoke the blush of any one in drawing his sympathy to this instance but for the good the sequel develops.

The physician came in and pronounced Mary entirely out of danger. He gave her permission to sit up in bed the following day, and left orders for her future nourishment, saying he would not again call until sent for. This last remark had a telling effect. Mary's eyes beamed with hope and joy. I was taking my leave, when she called me back, and requested that I would call the next morning to listen to a recital that would be as strange to me as important to her that I should know it. I made the appointment.

Being detained by more pressing engagements, I deferred my visit until after noon, when, in passing home, a note was handed to me, with her name, and a "call immediately." I encountered Celeste in the corridor, who told me that she had been restless all night; wanted to walk the room; called for pen, ink, and paper to write a letter; and threatened, if force was used to keep her in bed, that she would seek an opportunity to jump into the yard from the window. I asked what occasioned this alarm. Celeste surmised that Mary had fears that she would be forced to remain in the house, when she had expressed herself determined to leave as soon as she got well.

As I entered the room I was surprised at seeing Mary sitting on the side of the bed, her legs hanging down, partly uncovered. I charged her more with indecency than imprudence; told her that I had done for her to the extent of my services, and that it grieved me, where there was so much promise, to see so early a departure from it. She threw herself in the bed, with her hands clasped together under the back of her head, while her arms protruded beyond and half concealed her face. She remained for a while silent; at length she looked

Celeste and I alternately in the face, to awaken in us some new development. Seeing we said nothing, she exclaimed,

"Mr. ——, you have seen me through the fever, but when I had it I did not foresee the dangers that waited on recovery. What shall I do? O God! why did I not die?"

I asked what new phantom troubled her.

"It is in remaining here—here, where I scorn myself, and from whence I have not the means to leave without submitting to a degradation that I loathe more now than ever. Though, if it is inevitable, it will not be long, and maybe my God will forgive me."

"Explain yourself, but without excitement to yourself."

She began: "I believe I am well, or out of danger. Now I seek a friend, such as I never knew the value of until now; but you have done so much, and I have so little in only a grateful heart, that I dare not ask you to continue your kind acts."

I replied that she was precisely in that situation of dependency that made our acts the more pleasing to ourselves.

"Then hear me through; I will tell you all. My father lives at ——. He sent me to a neigboring convent, where I was educated, and remained until I was 18 years of age. He is a wealthy farmer, and my brother, older than I am, is associated with him. My mother died before I knew that I had lost one. On my return home I found my brother engaged to be married to a young lady, the daughter of a neighboring farmer. It was settled upon by both families that I was to marry her brother, whether I would or not. I had before formed an attachment, which was warmly reciprocated, for a young man who was a clerk in a neighboring town. Without any dislike to my intended, I nursed

an affection for the other in a spirit of obstinacy and
wounded pride in having dictation in matters of affection.   My father noticed the coolness with which I received my intended, and threatened me with exclusion
from the world until I was of lawful age unless I complied with his commands.   Apprehensive of such an
event, I listened to the proposition of my lover to elope.
With the money he had saved we left home five weeks
ago, and took passage in a steam-boat for New Orleans,
determining to be married as soon as we landed here.
Not being acquainted with your laws, we were much
surprised that we could not fulfill our intentions; knowing no one to vouch for us, we could not obtain a license.
To each other, our pledge was as strong and binding,
and as sacred as parson or priest could make it : we
were man and wife.   Well, we put up at the —— Hotel.
After being there a week, Charles found his scanty fund
much diminished, and, with the hopelessness of obtaining a situation, certain misery ahead.   Another week of
board would exhaust our resources, and we had not
enough to return to our home.   The yellow fever, which
then was prevailing to a great extent, raised crazy fears
in both of us; night or day there was no consolation
for the horrible situation in which we found ourselves.
One night we were in agony from being kept awake by
the moans of a dying man in a room not far from ours.
We now acknowledged that we wandered away from
home like two foolish and guilty things, and that we
were justly harvesting the fruits.   One morning Charles
came in our room gloomy and dejected.   ' Mary,' said
he, ' we have made Judies of ourselves; let us retrace
our steps.   It is folly for us to be thinking of being le-
gally married when we have not the least prospect of
support before us.   It is of no use for one to be in the
other's way.   You are better off than I, for you can get
employment in a millinery; but I can get no employ-

ment, and must work my passage back. At any rate, I must leave you, for I can not pay this week's board.' I can not conceive what passion possessed me when he finished. I was so startled at the idea of his deserting me that I could not think for him, or for the causes that drove him to speak as he did. My first impulse was to spit in his face, but I only looked him full in the eye as I advanced to him and told him to 'Go!' I then took a chair by the window, thinking desperate things, not noticing Charles as he left with a bundle of his clothes, taken from our trunks. The dinner-hour passed; I was equally indifferent to the cravings of nature as to the world; had I known of poison I would have taken it. At night the chambermaid informed me that my apartment was engaged for the following day. Suspicions of my character, if not of my ability to pay, had been aroused. A hint was given me to leave. I replied, like a guilty thing, nothing, still indifferent to life. I wonder now at my feelings then. I could not excite myself at my situation, not being able to fully realize it. Suddenly a thought struck me. 'To the river,' I said aloud, and hastily throwing on my bonnet and shawl, I descended the stairway. Suddenly the hellish thought entered me, 'If I am lost,' I said, 'I will be still worse; I will go with the current.' It was after nine o'clock. Well, sir, I started off at a rapid pace on the streets, imagining that I should find Charles; not that I wanted to see him, but to have an object for my walk. I stared impudently into the faces of men, who took me, no doubt, to be crazy, in my fast gait, while I swung in my hand a kerchief violently by my side in walking. When nearly exhausted, ready for poison had I known how to purchase it, a cabman addressed me, and asked where I wanted to go. 'I do not know,' I replied; 'any where.' 'Jump in,' he cried, 'and I will show you a house.' Involuntarily I resigned myself to his assistance in put-

G

ting me in the cab. It rattled away for some squares, when it stopped at this house. After a short consultation between the cabman and the proprietress, I was invited to descend and enter the house. I was really beside myself; I mean, thoughtless of the danger I was running, but conscious of all I was doing, and felt as if a hand was pushing me from behind. My sense of propriety was dormant. Without a blush, as if it were the house of a friend, I familiarly entered the parlor. You have seen the parlors? They are splendidly furnished —much beyond the extravagance of the richest where I was born. The proprietress, as she is called, took off my bonnet, and, leading me through the rooms to a back gallery shaded by curtains, asked me to take some refreshment, which she handed from a cupboard. Then she showed me to this room, desiring me to give no thought of the morrow, as she would fix terms with me which would be satisfactory. Strange that I, brought up in the strict conduct of a convent, should find myself in parley with an enemy that I had been most educated to shun. I believe I thought I was in a dream; yet, in my destitution and despair, what hope had I then of bettering myself? I was not in the vein of sleeping, and, as the proprietress saw me transfixed in thought, she took me by the shoulder, saying she would let me see her company to drive away any unpleasant thoughts I had. I was led back to the parlor. Several of the girls whom you have seen in this room were seated there, talking with and familiarly sitting beside some well-dressed men. When I entered each girl closely scrutinized me; but two approached me as I took a seat, and proffered a welcome. One was Emily, who sat beside me, and seemed interested in me—as she told me afterward, because my conduct so reminded her of hers on a similar first step. I must have sat an hour. As I showed a diffidence and reluctance in moving with the others about the room, they shunned me. They were not encouraged to think that I was one of them, or perhaps they were, like Emily, too painfully reminded of their first step by my initiatory. At any rate, we were repulsive to each other. Shortly a gentleman of pleasing exterior approached me, and complimented me on my appearance and looks, at the same time placing his hand under my chin, which I repulsed without a word. Involuntarily tears coursed my cheek, yet I was not ashamed; they were more from a feeling of destitution and loneliness. I was not again disturbed. When they all left the room I was shown to this apartment. A few minutes elapsed when the proprietress entered, and in rather a brusque tone said, 'Well, my little miss, you have come to live with me, and I hope now you know where you are. But where is your baggage or clothes?' I informed her where my trunk was, and that not having paid my board was the reason it was left. I went to bed without saying my prayers; I could not pray: I thought it blasphemy. I thought the ear of my God was deaf to me. I locked my door, and in a few minutes the fatigue and excitement I had encountered induced a sound sleep. In the morning, on awakening, I was informed that my trunk was at hand, ready to be brought in my room.

"At breakfast, which was late, all the establishment was assembled. The girls were neatly dressed in blouses, most of them with their faces powdered, and took their seats without an exchange of salutation. There was no more attention to me, by word or look, that I noticed, than if I had been longer with them. Though all the furniture of the house is so elegant, the set-out of the table was meagre and slovenly, but not dirty. Broken cups and saucers, and dishes set without any regularity. Eggs, which were in a large bowl of hot water, and corn buttered cakes, seemed the most in request. Of these and some figs I made my first repast. Not a word was spoken loud during the meal. As each one finished, she left the table and joined a companion for a talk. How imitative of my convent life in one respect, how widely different in another! I thought I was the cause of this silence at meal, being a stranger, but I was since informed that it was always so. A perfect indifference to each other reigns throughout. As they change their names with their new life, they desire not confidants to remind them of that which they have left. I said a perfect indifference exists toward each other; I should except—yes, I do except—when one of them is sick; for never has been greater silent sympathy for any one than for me in their inquiries of the nurse, and their desire to sit by my bedside for hours in the day, musing in their own thoughts, anticipating my wishes, but giving me no verbal comfort, except, again, Emily. Well, I worried myself all day, thinking of my situation. I could not realize the reality. I was blind to the future, and desperate in meeting it. At noon I felt wearied, and lay upon my bed for repose. In the evening I was awoke to consciousness by the violent exertions of several to put me in a hot bath. I had a violent fever, with the strongest symptoms—cupping, nursing, and medicines; your visits, and you know the rest."

Exhausted by this recital, the interest of which enlisted my feelings to the exclusion of any regard for the imprudence of the indulgence, she rolled on her side with a sigh; then resumed her former position, gazing on vacancy, awaiting a reply from me to rouse her from the reverie that she was in. A thousand suggestions for her good passed one by one before me. She was not entirely lost, and here was a signal triumph within my reach. I felt her brow, then her pulse. There was a slight agitation to the latter, but a healthy glow to the former, albeit the intense thought had caused the per-

spiration to roll in torrents on her pillow. The poor
girl was now sensible of her situation, and looked to me,
as her only friend, to save her from the brink of destruction. As if in acknowledgment of the greatest boon I
could ask, I told her that I was grateful to this opportunity to meet her expectations in the fullest of mortal
ability, so far as supply means to send her home, and to
extricate her from her perilous situation. He who has
created the poison and the antidote flashed a ray of hope
through the heart of this unhappy one. She saw she
was not all lost to virtue from an indifference to vice.
The link to the latter was broken; the magnetic power
of good had not lost its binding and attractive power.

"Mary," I said, "you will be well enough to leave to-
morrow. I will, in the mean time, procure you a room
in a private house, where you will remain until you are
well enough to return to your home."

I begged her to be composed, and to place full reliance upon what I promised. I told her that the recital
of her past sufferings would be injurious if prolonged,
and that I would postpone what more she had to say until I returned the next day.

On the evening of the next day I called with a carriage to take her away. I now asked the proprietress,
who had not been apprised of this before, for her bill of
her board. At first she demurred; then supposing,
from a remark that I purposely made, that she would
be returned in a few days, sullenly acquiesced. As we
passed through the corridor several of the boarders nodded a good-by, while the girl called Emily came toward
Mary, and, with tears in her eyes, whispered some words,
the tenor of which can be imagined from perusal of the
account of her illness in the latter part of this work.
Four days after her release Mary was placed by me on
a steamer destined for her home. Upon acquainting the
captain with just enough of her history to awaken com-

passion for a deserted female, with the noble charity so often tested under similar circumstances, and characteristic of the commanders of our Western boats, he refunded her the passage-money. As I bade her adieu, I told her I intended one day to recur to the late incidents in her life as a romance of reality. She replied, "No one would believe it; for the subject, as well as the friend, never did nor could not again possibly meet under like circumstances."

Two months later I received a letter from her informing me of her reconciliation to her parent; her formal marriage to her repentant lover, who had satisfactorily, she said, excused his desertion, for, on the night he left her so insanely, he had taken the fever, recovered, and inquired every where in vain for her; and concluding with such lively expressions of gratitude that, had I opened the vista of heaven to her soul, I could be no less in her opinion.

Will Mary —— think this recital a breach of confidence if chance throws these pages in the way of her perusal? Perhaps they will stir up reverential feelings for that Providence that favored an humble individual in saving one soul from being lost to itself and usefulness, and may develop a corresponding gratitude in directing her to seek to do a like good and service to another as despairing as she was.

CHAPTER X.

Coup d'Œil of Distress.—Funerals.—Burying of the Dead.—Fright at the Grave-yard.—Frederika.—My Neighbors.

By the 10th of August the mortality had reached an appalling height. The whole city was a hospital, and every well man, woman, and child were instrumental, in one way or other, in relieving the sick. The streets were deserted save to the hasty pedestrian on an errand of mercy. The rattling of an omnibus and the swing of a doctor's gig, as either rapidly passed, were the only disturbing sounds. The vociferations of the coalman, the knife-grinder, and of other callings that enliven the thoroughfares, were silenced by disease or fear. The bar-rooms and club-houses were hurriedly visited, more for the purpose of exchanging calamitous news than from social impulses. As the announcement of the death of well-known citizens was made from day to day, a pitying look would follow him who had just left our company as likely to be the next victim. At the most frequented places a daily bulletin from the Board of Health was stuck up, announcing the number of interments for the day previous, and, as each individual walked to the spot to read it, the effect made upon him could be seen in the blanched cheek, while the downcast eye and absence of comment as he walked off spoke of the thrill of horror which passed through him. Such was Death's harvesting that, to keep pace with the call for interments, trenches of seven feet wide and one hundred long were being constantly dug, into which the coffins were closely packed, three to four deep, without intermediate earth. When one trench had received its complement, and a few feet of earth laid over all, a parallel one was made in close proximity. In the absence of labor to dig single graves, friends supplied themselves with spades for that purpose. Late in the night-hours I have had occasion to be present, and listened to the appeals of parents and others to assist in burying their dead, which were frequently left coffined in the bushes until morning. On a dark, cloudy night, when we had been detained later than usual, a rush of many people was made toward where I was engaged with their flambeaus in hand. Upon asking the cause for this alarm, I found them so paralyzed by fear that for some minutes they could not speak. With a hush! they directed us to moans and groans issuing, as it were, from the interior of the earth. As such things have happened, and to the ocular demonstration of many, as burials alive, our conclusions with regard to supernatural causes for this noise became more and more weakened. In a body we sought the inclosure, where a continuation of the sounds directed us to a new-dug grave. Our flambeaus exposed a man lying at the bottom, who, in his intoxication, accused a loving one of having thrown him there. Our closer examination satisfied us that John Barleycorn was the delusive *ignis fatuus*. We learned from this man afterward that he was the only one of six in his party who had survived the labors of digging graves, and that he attributed his escape from putrid or pernicious fever to his constant habit of going to sleep drunk and in the open air, while his companions, who were comparatively temperate, and lodged in a shanty near by, all sickened and died.

The morning train of funerals, as was the evening's, crowded the road to the cemeteries. It was an unbroken line of carriages and omnibuses for two miles and a half. The city commissary's wagon, and the carts of the different hospitals, with their loads of eight or ten coffins each, fell in with the cortége of citizens. Confusion and delay at the cemeteries were unavoidable. The sun's heat and putrid exhalations were sickening to the sense. All manner of experiments were used to diminish the aggravation to disease of the latter. Tar was set on fire around and in the cemeteries, and lime profusely thrown on the cracked and baked earth covering the coffins in the trenches. The Board of Health, in an unthoughtful moment, adopted a suggestion of firing cannon throughout the city to disturb the atmosphere. This was not continued beyond the first day, as it was attended with melancholy results upon the nervous systems of the sick and convalescent. Any expedient to escape a worse pestilence would have been admitted. The miasma from neglected streets, combined with continued diminution of the vital principle in the atmosphere, from even a short exposure to putrefaction before burial of 1186 dead the first week of August, 1526 the second, 1534 the third, and 1628 the fourth, may well excuse far-fetched theories of disinfection. The gas-works threw open to the use of the citizens their stores of tar. Besides those quantities used in the yards of private houses, drays were engaged to drop a half barrel of tar at distances of 150 feet in the middle of Canal, Rampart, and Esplanade Streets. At sunset, when all were simultaneously fired, a Pandemonium glare lighted up the city. Not a breath of air disturbed the dense smoke, which slowly ascended in curling columns until it had reached the height of about 500 feet. Here it seemed equipoised, festooning over our doomed city like a funeral pall, and there remaining until the shades of night disputed with it the reign of darkness. These experiments did not visibly diminish the ravages of the pestilence. Happy the theorists who could silence their own fears by the doctrine that filth and stench do not propagate disease, but, on the contrary, check it.

Adjoining my residence, in a house occupied by several tenants, there dwelt a German family, consisting of grandmother, her married daughter and son-in-law, with their four children, the latter from three to ten years old. The quiet that reigned throughout on my occasionally passing gave me no suspicions of any thing malign going on within. They were cleanly and industrious in habit. They had been informed, or knew, from the daily concourse of unfortunates at my door for the aid of the association, that their claims were equally presentable, if made. The oldest child had been a daily playmate of my children, and recommended herself to particular notice from the tastefulness of attire and sweetness of disposition. She was very observant and communicative, never, though, speaking of herself or parents, but fond in the evenings of making playful remarks of the neighbors, who all liked her, or in repeating, for the amusement of the children, legends and other tales which she had read or had been taught by her parents. From constant visits, she was allowed the privileges of one of the family. Frederika for several days had discontinued her visits. Upon sending to know the reason, my children were informed that she was too much engaged to be about. This drew complainings from them, and awakened in me a suspicion that all was not right within. As I opened the gate, I surprised Frederika busy over a wash-tub, where she appeared as handy as one of twice her age. Directly she espied me she appeared confused, and beckoned to her grandfather, who was sitting on the steps before the house. Seeing he arose with difficulty, I approached him, and commenced my interrogatories, but found I had to call in Frederika as interpreter. I asked, first, her reasons for discontinuing her visits. Without replying, she laid down the linen in her hand, and, pointing to an open doorway, led me to it, saying, with tears in her eyes, " My mother is sick. You see now, Mr. ——, that I could not leave here to see little ——. My mother was taken sick just after my grandfather got well. My father is now asleep from fatigue of last night's sitting up, and I must do all these things."

" And have no help ?" I asked.

She smiled at me when I asked the question, as if she thought I was ridiculing her.

" Help ?" she replied ; " what to do ? It is not very much. I work a little, wash a little, and get the medicines and drinks for mother. Dr. —— has been very kind, and sometimes brings things himself. If it was not for *him*, I don't know what we *should* have done. He would do more for us if he knew father had pawned and sold so many things; and, before mother gets well, every thing else will be gone, and I don't know what we shall do."

Her little heart had been charging itself during this recital. Not to be seen in utterance of her grief, she turned from me to the ascending steps, and at the turning dropped on them, giving full vent to her feelings. After seeing enough to know what was to be done immediately, I hurried out, and in a few minutes returned with a nurse who spoke their language. I checked a harsh reproach I had threatened them with for not applying to me under their necessities, and now, through Frederika, had arranged for their future comfort.

"I told my father," she said, "how good you were to the poor people. Richer than we are are some, I know, who call upon you; but he would not let me ask you for any thing, because your family were already so kind to me."

In my presence I told her to say to them that I was merely doing a duty imposed upon me; that it was not my own money that I gave; that it was intended for them, and they should not deprive me of the pleasure of bestowing it. Upon my taking leave the old man grasped my hand, and with his eyes to heaven whispered his heartfelt gratitude to his Maker for the timely succor. That day my children assisted in obtaining them comforts, making such duty an excuse for seeing Frederika for a few minutes. On the third day of my visits, the hopes that were all along entertained for the recovery of the mother were dissipated by a sudden change in the weather, to which she had been too much exposed. All attempts to re-establish her failed, and her life flickered away without apparent pain. Her death seemed to produce a more thoughtful effect upon her

daughter than is generally met with in girls of her age.
She had wept abundantly for a few hours after the
death, but the following day she was melancholy and
torpid, noticing nothing that was said or that passed before her.   That night I saw Frederika sitting on the
stoop of the door, from whence her childish laugh often
attracted to her her companions.   When I stopped before her she did not look up until I called her by name.
On inquiring how all within were—how she was—she
replied that they had been scolding her for not eating all
day, but that she could not, as she had no appetite, and
was afraid she should be sick.   At daylight the next
morning I was informed she was so.

When I took her hand I found it of burning heat;
the skin was spotted, as if from erysipelas; she was
drowsy, and answered only in monosyllables.   Her kind
physician had been to see her, and used all appliances
to moderate the symptoms, which were of the type pernicious, but in vain.   On that evening her playmates
heard of her calamity, and assembled together for a visit.
When five or six entered, her eye wandered listlessly
from one to the other, holding them alternately by the
hand, and beckoning them back as they stepped back
to leave her.   Not a word passed between them; their
hearts alone were communing through their eyes.   What
passed in Frederika's mind these little ones could conjecture better than I.   I withdrew, leaving her to the
consolation of their silent presence.

On the next morning a great change was visible.   Her
mind wandered in utterance of broken sentences of English and German.   The fever remained in full sway.
Constant watching was necessary to keep her in bed.
She did not appear to suffer pain.   The prognostic of a
hasty death was fearfully manifest.   The unsteady eye,
indifference to all around, and nervous twitchings of the
frame, assured this.   One of her playmates entered the

room—one who esteemed her of all others, because she was the joy of her playtime. Her demand of Frederika if she did not know her was this only time sensibly returned by the question, " Can I ever forget you, dear ——?" The effect of this reply upon her little visitor was heart-rending. The latter wept and sobbed over the hand held to her, begging her not to die; that if she did, she was sure God would receive her in heaven, as she was so good, etc., etc.

Later in the day every moment appeared to be her last. Several of the children lingered around the premises all day. There was a long interval of silence without the movement of a muscle, mortification now having set in. She looked as if communing with some invisible spirit by the motion of her lips and dreamy expression of the eye, in which the "rapt soul seemed setting." All at once she exclaimed, in a soft tone, "I see you, my mother, in heaven; I will come soon." The effect of these words heightened the impression made by her appearance; she even looked more angelic. I pictured to myself the sunshine of a spotless soul about bursting from its tenement of corruptible matter. In a few minutes more she glanced around her, and now, with recovered faculties and aware of her situation, as she saw her little friends and family wiping the tears from their eyes, she exclaimed, 'Do not weep for me. Good-by, father; good-by, grandpa." Good-by to each and every one was given, with their names, as she took their hands. No one proffered a word; the children were riveted to the spot, intent on their gaze. Their little Frederika closed her eyes for a minute, when, after one violent convulsion, she glided smoothly from life, through death, to that heaven which she did but dream of, and was there.

At night a harbor made of reeds was erected in the yard. Over this musquito netting was tastefully fes-

tooned, and on a table within, covered with white cloth,
lay the corpse.   A neighboring modiste, who was as
much interested in the child from her beauty and sweetness of disposition as from sympathy for the loss that
her own children felt by this death, assisted in dressing
the corpse.   The crown of white flowers, white satin
slippers and muslin dress, in which she had made her
first communion, were tastefully placed upon her.   Her
hands, clasped on her breast, held within them a crucifix, and her long auburn ringlets carelessly fell upon her
shoulders; artificial and natural flowers, the offerings of
her playmates, lay strewed about in profusion.   Here
lingered, late that night and all of the morning of the
next day, her mourning companions, attracting many a
passer-by to gaze upon loveliness in death.   Here, too,
fell the first tears for a severed friendship—here gushed
the first vintage of crushed and tender hearts.

With the greater part of those who die by black
vomit the skin becomes of a lemon-yellow tint a little
before or immediately after death.   It is not rare to
meet with exceptions, and then only from a short sickness.   The corpse of Frederika preserved until the next
morning its life-like fullness, expression, and color.
Waxlike as it was wont to be, it was difficult to believe
she was dead; the repulsiveness of death was not there
to affright the little ones.   To me her features recalled
the beautiful lines of Shelley on Ianthe:

> "Her dewy eyes are closed,
>   And on their lids, whose texture fine
>   Scarce hides the dark blue orbs beneath,
> The baby sleep is pillowed;
>   Her golden tresses shade
>   The bosom's stainless pride,
>   Curling like tendrils of the parasite
>   Around a marble column."

This was a fatal day in my neighborhood.   It did not
occur to me to notice the non-appearance of my neigh-

bors on the street or at their doors for two or three days at a time, nor would the circumstance of a store or shop being shut up infer more than business was slack, or that the tenant was busy with the sick. It accordingly surprised me to hear that a female opposite and a tailor two doors above me had both died that night. Both were in circumstances to be independent of relief from our association. The increase of the epidemic became now appalling. My associates and the assistants who had the charge with me of the second district began to experience great difficulty in procuring nurses for the sick. New cases constantly presenting themselves made it impossible for us to give but a few minutes to each patient. In the other districts the association found it both more beneficial and economical to establish infirmaries. The necessity of one in my district became urgent. The Board of Health, which had an appropriation of $50,000 from the city for charitable and relief purposes, appointed, from our association, superintendents to carry out their views also in the establishment of infirmaries.

CHAPTER XI.

Action of Board of Health.—The Globe Ball-room Infirmary.—Nurses. —Conveyances of Sick.—The Rag-picker's Family.—Admissions to the Infirmary.

ON Friday, the 12th of August, the Board ordered a suitable building to be rented in the second district. At an intimation from a friend that the Globe Ball-room, a building used for years past as the saturnalia of the depraved portion of our population, was complete in its arrangement of rooms and eligible on account of its locality for an infirmary, I made a successful application to the proprietor for its occupation. The promptness of its donation, at a mere nominal rent, for a use which was calculated to injure its future lease, is another instance of noble sacrifice that we are proud to point at. Citizens were ever ready to step forward to assuage the horrors of rumored or visible distress. "If it will do any good, although it do my property injury, the house is at your service." Such was the reply of the proprietor as he handed me the keys. I now hastened to make a close inspection of all parts of the building, preliminary to noting down the furniture required. Had the Globe Ball-room been built for a hospital, the rooms could not have been planned off with a better adaptation; nor could the quietness of the locality, nor the surroundings, be surpassed by any long-established infirmary.

The building is in outline an oblong square, of 130 feet by 40, occupying an islet of ground. On its longest side, south, it fronts the old Basin; on its northern side, the *Place d'Armes*, whose refreshing atmosphere, under the shade of thickly set trees, causes it to be a frequent evening resort. The only part of it that was occupied was divided between a bar-room and a feed-store, in the basement, having their entrances on the eastern front of the building. The remaining parts of the basement had been used as a restaurant, kitchen, and lumber-room when the balls were in season. The entrance was on the northern side, with circular steps leading to a corridor on the second story. The rooms now consisted of the ball-room, running the length of the building by 30 feet of its width, having on its side a bar-room and dressing-room for males and females. Every part of the house was freely open to ventilation from numerous windows and doors. A canvas cloth, twelve feet in height, was ordered to be fixed on a frame, to divide the ball-room equally for male and female patients; a similar one to partition off the bar-room, for the accommodation of male and female convalescents. A room alongside this was appropriated to patients *in extremis*, or when they became unmanageable in their cots or disturbing to others by frequent vomitings or ravings. Adjoining the building was a small two-story brick house, then vacant, but commonly occupied by the lessees of the ball-room, having communication from the second floor of the former, which we rented, and appropriated respectively to the store-room, office, and nurses' apartments. The ticket-office and hat-depository, at the foot of the steps, was admirably arranged to keep the clothing of the patients until they were discharged. Such as recovered had their clothing returned them cleansed or washed, and many went away better appareled than they entered, in the garments of those who had died.

Upon stepping off the room, it was found that one hundred cots could be conveniently ranged therein. Having made a complete list of every thing wanted, it did not take more than three hours' drive to the grocery, dry-goods, crockery, and hardware stores, to leave the orders, or to select the articles for a delivery the next morning. In the numerous streets to be passed through to visit a long list of patients, by purchasing here and there cots, mattresses, and musquito-bars, a sufficient quantity was that day obtained. It appeared that every thing favored completeness, even to the ready and willing hands who promised a delivery of cotton gowns for the sick, to be delivered as fast as required. While bargaining for these, I encountered a sprightly woman of about thirty-five years of age, who announced herself to me as just out of employment in the capacity of matron to an infirmary of long standing. With the understanding that I should be satisfied with her references, she was to meet me the next day at the Globe Ball-room. Her face was full of intelligence and good-humor, and it pleased me to learn, after strict inquiry, that her conduct

and capacity had gained her the reputation of the best
of nurses. She had left her late place on account of the
onerousness of its duties, and the monotony of a service
in one place for many years.

The following day she superintended the arrangements of the cots, and the tearing of cotton as sheets for
the beds. On returning at intervals of two or three
hours, I saw completeness rapidly approaching. The
sailmaker had spread the partition canvas. The numerous mirrors which studded the walls were covered
with cotton cloth, the beds blanketed and sheeted, the
musquito-bars suspended, and strips of coarse matting
put down on the main walks between the cots. A stool
placed aside of each cot was supplied with a cup and
small pitcher. In the orchestral part two cots had also
been placed. During that day engagements were also
made for a daily supply of ice, bread, milk, and meat.
Upon retiring that night, it was a great relief to know
that, by the morrow or the day after, many who were
suffering from want of proper attendance at their homes,
from the increased calls on physicians, or the difficulty
of obtaining nurses, could be removed here and be in
comparative luxury.

An advertisement for experienced male and female
nurses was answered by the application of three times
as many as were wanted. I was not aware until afterward of the preference given to hospital over private
nursing. A selection of twelve was made from their
physical appearance, and for their fluency in speaking
both French and German. A long colloquy was held
as each detailed his ability and practice. Their expressed earnestness for the amelioration of humanity would
have led a listener to believe they desired indulgence in
the good work beyond the pay. Those selected were engaged at $30 to $40 per month. The matron had never
seen any of them before, nor did I consult her opinion ;

but was much pleased with my selection, remarking that the less they knew the more serviceable she could make them. This I afterward perceived. Most of the applicants had been subjects in hospitals, where, during a long convalescence, they had acquired a passion for waiting on the sick, which became so strong as to be adopted as a pursuit for a livelihood in preference to a more lucrative employment. I learned afterward, though, that the peculiar fascination for it with some arose from the opportunities which they had of possessing themselves of valuables, which the sick are loth to give up on entering a hospital, but conceal about their persons in a belt, or cravat, or elsewhere. I had no sooner discovered this than I required the clerk of admissions to require of the sick to deliver their valuables on a receipt from him, with the admonition to the patient that, if he did not, there was a certainty of his being robbed.

The most important feature of the infirmary was delayed until the last — the engagement of two regular physicians. To make a selection from so many would be invidious, and would display arrogance on my part in assuming the ability to discriminate between talent. This responsibility I endeavored to throw upon the mayor or the Board of Health; they viewed it in the same light, and left me no alternative. At one swoop I could silence the complaints of my American friends, as it was indispensable that the visiting physicians should speak French and German, of which languages they are generally ignorant. More than twenty physicians, who had assiduously given their services without pay, were to be selected from—all equally successful, though of different practice; I could censure none; so I placed their names in a hat, and drew. The choice pleased me. I drew another; it was equally satisfactory. Upon calling on the first, he excused himself, owing to multiplicity of private practice. It was not until late at night, after frequent calls, that I found the other at home, who reluctantly consented, with the understanding that he was to select his confrère. On mentioning the pay—$250 per month—he refused to accept it, as he thought it no consideration, but allowed his generous impulses to sway the promise of remuneration in doing what he considered a charity, albeit an interference with the profitable pursuit of his private practice.

That night until three A.M. was occupied in going the rounds of my patients, which now summed up seventy-two. I prevailed upon many with fairy-like representations of comfort, of what was in store for them on the morrow, and noted the names of such as desired me to send wagons for their removal to the Globe Ball-room. These wagons were on springs, furnished with a mattress, and were stationed for this purpose before the different recorders' offices. Many of my patients, though in their second or third day, I was advised to move, as death hovered around with certainty of his victim so long as squalid misery and tainted atmosphere were present. So much was this their condition that nurses would fly at the sight of them, before even more repulsive things would offend the sense. To such, a change of linen and air was a medicine, and proved in many instances beneficial.

On Monday, the 15th of August, at break of day, I found nearly all of the engaged waiting for me at the infirmary. Notice had been given in the papers that patients would be received from this day. To the hour of eight no patient had presented himself. I returned home to dispense different kinds of relief to the fifty or sixty persons that I invariably met there at that hour. Among others was an applicant for the care of the association to a German family named Blaize, who occupied rooms over the dome of the Orleans Theatre. The same application had been made to me the day previous, but

I had been unsuccessful to meet information of their precise whereabouts after a tedious search through the premises. This time my guide led me up the stairs in the rear of the coffee-house, through a dark passage communicating with the dome; thence up a frail-constructed and movable stairway to a recess twelve feet square, with a small aperture on the roof for air and light. The protection of a recently-replenished camphor cigarette barely saved me from prostration from the effects of a concentrated odor of old clothes, rags, and perspiration. The heat alone was insufferable. By the assistance of a girl of fourteen years, whom we had aroused from a repose, we distinguished the sick. They were her father and two sisters, lying on an old mattress and old clothes spread upon the floor. There was no furniture in the room; a few trunks supplied the place of chairs and tables. A small tin bucket, nearly drained of water, was within their reach. They had had no physician, and taken no medicine. A negro, employed in the bar-room below, had discovered their condition from a curiosity to know what had become of Christine, the eldest daughter, whom, he said, he had missed for a day past from her daily work near the hydrant. They were rag-pickers, and had lived in these quarters for several months, quiet and uncomplaining. I determined upon their removal at once, satisfied that, if left here, with even the best attention they would perish. With the labor of three men they were carefully carried down the rickety steps, and through the dark passages, and laid in the sick-wagon on mattresses *en route* for the infirmary. They were my first visitors. On my return at noon they had been cleanly sponged, bathed, and garmented, and signified to me the happiness they experienced in the comparative luxury of clean sheets, and the anxious attendance of so many to their wants. On reference to the register, I find the father died five days after admission, and all the children were discharged well on the 18th and 20th.

Here was a signal instance of the remedial force of change of atmosphere. The three children first named had been seized with the fever from twenty-four to thirty-six hours before I removed them. The commonly practiced injunction to preserve the temperature of a room at all hazards is unreasonable. Dr. Priestley has clearly shown that one great and indispensable use of respiration is to carry off or lessen a certain quality in the blood known by name of phlogiston. This can only be done by pure air, which is returned from the lungs with the poisonous qualities of paint or lighted charcoal fumes. My observations in this particular, among patients found in unventilated or filthy places, when removed to the purer air of the infirmary at a progressed stage of the fever, or even immediately after the crisis, have been confirmatory of the beneficial advantages.

Before night seventeen admissions were recorded, ten of which were German, two French, two Swiss, and two Irish, and nine of these females. Nearly all of these had been treated before they entered, and the majority of them in a progressed stage. Out of these first seventeen eight died. This day and night the establishment was drilled to proper working order. The physicians paid regular visits at eight A.M. and five P.M., and at intermediate hours when sent for. The cook had always ready a large supply of hot water for baths, together with abundance of nourishing drinks or gruel. Adele, as matron, had nothing that the daintiest could complain of, while she required of the nurses strict and ready obedience. The male nurses were excluded from the female division. A cupper was lodged in the house, to be ready at a moment's notice. Every thing offensive to the patients was removed instantly. Indeed, so well ventilated were the rooms, and so cleanly kept, that during the whole occupation of them as a hospital the peculiar odor of yellow fever atmosphere was not more remarkable than would be found in the room of a patient of a better class. The patients were notified that a rap on the stool beside them would bring the attendant to them, and if not answered to complain to the matron or to me. To each nurse was allotted a certain number of sick, while they were to assist each other in removing the convalescent or dying, or taking below the corpse. When they failed in duty they were discharged without mercy. The nurses had appointed to them their regular day and night watches.

CHAPTER XII.

Eliza ——.—Female Courage.—Black Vomit.—Recoveries.—Italian Exiles.

AMONG the names of early patients to the infirmary that of Eliza —— is associated with a melancholy reminiscence. She was of Irish parentage, and gave her age as twenty-one years. She was accompanied by several women and a young man, whose interest in her was shown by the proffer of pay for a private room, and by more than ordinary solicitude. Making no distinction in the treatment or comfort of our sick, the cot designated to her had to be occupied or none. Fortunately for her aversion to a hospital, the one assigned to her stood before the door leading to a small balcony on the eastern side, more out of the way of passing attendants than others, and commanding a view of the Place d'Armes. Here what was revolting to the sense from neighboring sick could be relieved by the aspect of nature in changing clouds and green trees, in which are pictured pleasing groups to the dreamy, imaginative eye of the fevered sick. My attention was particularly drawn to her the day after her admission by the cupper, who told me that she resisted his endeavors to carry out the orders of the physician. She had just before witnessed the operation of cupping on another, and became so horrified at its cruelty that, when I approached, she arose and implored me with tears to let her die rather than undergo the infliction.

"Do not murder me with such barbarity," she said; "I could not survive it." Her language and intonation were remarkably impressive. Her choice of words denoted an educated and sensitive mind. We finally persuaded her of the happy results, drawing her attention to the heroism of the one who had just been cupped, and the fatal consequence to the neglect of it in another, who was expiring at some distance from her. As much as she was before repugnant she was now womanly brave.

I do not say manly brave to express my full meaning for voluntary physical suffering. It would not convey the fullness of meaning I desire to. To designate the weakness or cowardice of men as effeminacy is a reproach to women not supported by experience or facts. Women are far superior to men in moral courage and physical endurance. Physicians will tell you that she does not so often shrink as man does from surgical operations, while we have the voice of history that, wherever they have braved the public eye, their self-possession has been so unwavering as to instill courage and confidence to their hearers and followers of the other sex.

In this instance, with all the horror she felt, she submitted throughout the scarifying and cupping without a movement of the frame, without even a shudder; while I have seen men of athletic proportions, inured to hazards and to danger, not only writhe at every stage of its application, but fairly roar out like wounded bears. The cupping, to her, had its usual composing and somnolent effect. I left her in full faith of its efficacy. Until the evening of the next day her symptoms were promising, and she became even cheerful in the anticipation of leaving her bed in two or three days. She was disposed to be talkative with the sick near her, and offered consolation to them during their sufferings. She had frequent conversations with Father L. when he made his rounds of the sick, but, being a Protestant, she did not participate in rites he was constantly administering to others. For some days she had complained of the stringent rules of the infirmary, which forbade admission to friends to see patients until the latter were certainly convalescent. As I was passing her one morning, she called me by name and said,

"A few words to you, sir, in private; and do not blame me for being complaining when you have all been so kind to me, neither deceive me in your answer. The reason of all you will know hereafter."

"I am all ear," I replied.

"Well, then, sir, the identical heaviness of heart, which I never felt before, nor since I left my parents, now possesses me. Be candid with me. Does it prognosticate ill, or am I really getting well?"

I told her the crisis was passed, and her symptoms were of the most promising; in support of which, I referred to the description of nourishment ordered for her by the physician.

"But why, if it be so," she continued, "do you forbid my friends to see me now? The nurse has just told me that my cousin was sent away this morning. I sincerely wish to see him."

I left her with the comfortable assurance that she should, and gave directions to retain him until my arrival when he should come on the morrow. The next day she held her hand to me and said,

"I have been so happy; but what misery, after the dreams of friends and home, to awake to the reality of

II

being here. You remember your promise to admit my cousin to me to-day?" As she said this, her blue eyes beamed with hope and anticipated joy, which explained to me the nature of her attachment for her cousin.

"I feel well—very well to-day," she continued, "though I was somewhat sick last night, and could not retain the gruel given me; but that is nothing, for I am out of danger. Oh! if I could only see him."

As she threw her head aside with a sigh, a slight convulsive movement of the throat was followed by a small quantity of the dreaded, unmistakable black vomit oozing from the corner of her mouth. She saw it, but her thoughts were elsewhere, and did not notice the surprise it gave me. I hastily wiped it from her mouth and neck as she lay with contracted brow drawing up some reminiscence deep from the recess of thought.

On directing the attention of the physician to her, she was removed, with her cot, to the room in which we placed those like her, who were apt, in a little more advanced stage, to disturb the repose of the other sick. Adele interested herself in the different appliances to counteract the sudden turn which the disease had taken in her. At noon her cousin was admitted to see her. She was in a stupor. He begged us not to arouse her if it were likely to prove injurious, asking permission to be admitted again in the morning. During the night she was one of the most unmanageable of our patients, alternately crying out names, quoting snatches of poetry, waving her hands, and speaking to imaginary objects, while at intervals she would calmly make a reasonable request of the nurse.

As with her, so with others; whatever was called for in this stage of the disease was permitted to be given. After the Pharmacopœia had been exhausted of its known virtues—after artful experience had failed, nature was desperately called in for a suggestion:

"For, where one's case can be no worse,
  The desperat'st is the wisest course."

I have had as many as twelve patients with black vomit
at one time in the same room. Some asked for toddies;
others for coffee, milk, tea, whisky, and brandy, all of
which we had of superior quality. On asking some if
they would have claret or Champagne, it was freely bestowed. By an oversight, or rather from the confusion
attending the diversified wants of such as were given up
to the indulgence of any appetite—as they were to hope
—no memorandum was kept of the beverage drunk by
many, who, with this frightful symptom of dissolution,
were found afterward in a natural sleep, with a healthy
pulse and skin, and, upon being replaced on their cots,
recovered. The most potent agent in arresting the
black vomit, and restoring the tone of the stomach so
as to induce digestion with corresponding appetite, was
brandy toddy or milk punch. I have noticed two recoveries through these means, and witnessed successful
results from weaker mixtures given as the constant drink
of the patient after the crisis.

Eliza —— demanded coffee and milk. She appeared
to relish it much, and drank copiously of it, I was told,
all night. Sponging and sinapisms had been duly applied to her. Early the next morning the curiosity of
a wonderful change presented itself to us. Many hopes
were long entertained of her, and she was carefully
watched in her diet. The physician assured us she was
now safe. There was no symptom to lead us to suspect
that this promise was but the deceit previous to a last
fatal convulsion. We had her cot taken back to its former position. She had not shown that she was conscious of having been removed. Her first words on recognition were, "Has James been here?" On being informed of the circumstances attending his visit the day
before, she continued, "I know I am well; I feel I am

well; but why this ever to-morrow to my hopes? I
dreamed you took me in that room among the dead people. I know I was dreaming, for I saw myself here,
and that my cousin stood beside me."

Such are the unaccountable hallucinations in the fevered sick.

At noon her cousin called. I met him on the stairs,
and gave him joy on her recovery. He would not be
satisfied without seeing her, although I told him her situation was more critical than ever. With the understanding, however, that he should not hold a conversation with her, I listened to his urgent appeal. I went in
advance of him, and prepared her for the meeting with
a like caution. Her face, at the agreeable information,
became slightly flushed, and her eye sparkled with joy.
I brought him to her bedside, again enjoining him to be
prudent, and stood apart to witness the meeting of the
lovers. Fondly, yet delicately she grasped his hand,
throwing a piercing gaze upon him, as if to read the effect her appearance made on him, and by that to read
her hopes of safety. "Eliza!" "James!" were simultaneous. Thus they looked at each other for several minutes, while their hands were pressing tighter, and a smile
was stamped on her face. Both were tenacious to the
promise not to exchange words, albeit their hearts were
surcharged for utterance. A little while, and his face
expressed despondency at her situation. He relaxed her
hand, and, raising both of his to his eyes as he turned
away his head, uttered a sob that fell like a death-knell
on her ear. She read his thoughts and his fears with
lightning rapidity, and from them portrayed her own
fate. She read that he despaired of her—that there was
a parting of heaven and earth—and, with a look accusing
me of deceit, her head sunk with leaden weight in her
pillow, uttering a guttural sound and obscuring her face
with her arms.

I saw the deed was done. I blamed myself for trusting to his firmness. In my anger I reproached him for hastening, if not causing her death, which I soon regretted, as he keenly felt all I said, and left the infirmary speechless as if an arrow had transfixed his heart.

Her fever returned. In half an hour her pulse sank. Violent heavings of the breast succeeded, accompanied by incoherent ravings. In a few hours she was a corpse. After this I was cruel in excluding relatives or friends when there was the least danger to be apprehended from the interview.

Her friends came that evening and sat up with the corpse in an adjoining room until the morning, when they followed her to the grave. I have never encountered any of the party since to recognize them, and I presume that this simple recital, to show the importance of caution in keeping off excitements of any kind from a patient, will not have the effect to open afresh their wounds.

On the 16th of August the admissions were twenty-four, divided about equally between French, Germans, and Italians. Those of the latter were recently-arrived exiles. They had all occupied one room in a back building of a house on St. Philip Street, where I had many patients. On my first visit to this locality I had several times observed this room tenanted by one of them with his wife. The latter was soon after taken sick. Upon offering service and aid, I was repulsed with the remark that he had a specific for the malaria of Italy which he deemed efficacious for the yellow fever. As near as I could conjecture, he was treating her *à la Raspail*. She shortly died. A few days after they held me in conversation, in French, on the subject of the great mortality around them, and showed fears for their own safety. I recommended them, when ill, to seek the infirmary. One of them, by name Hercule, gained something of a livelihood by teaching sword-exercise, of which many yet remember his proficiency. His companions, exiled like him for participation in insurrectionary movements at home, and only acquainted with the routine of military life, had yet no ostensible means of support. They were a vivacious trio, and seemed to laugh at the court of death around them as they quaffed their sour wine to a frugal repast. They promised to seek more agreeable quarters when sickness should prostrate them. In walking through the wards a few days afterward to look at the new-comers of the day, I no sooner recognized them than they exchanged words in Italian, and stretched out their hands to me. They spoke of the room, its queer conversion to its present use, and disturbed the otherwise sober and quiet by witty comparisons of their situation now and when they had once visited it. I did not encourage this, though I was glad to see in their dauntlessness and good spirits a hopeful prognostic of convalescence. At night I again passed them. Hercule was the spirit of the party, and kept his companions in good-humor by his soldier-philosophy. He talked of life as if it were "to lose a thing which none but fools would keep." I told him he must sleep and be quiet, and retain his fun until his fever was allayed. "Sleep!" said he; "have we not all eternity to sleep in?" I passed on to others.

The next day there was a marked change for the worse in Hercule. The other two were in doubtful condition. The tendency of the disease in the former was cephalistic. He bore cupping and blisters as playthings, throwing off remarks, in the mean while, which brought laughter from his companions. At night the disease had not been manageable, and he was in a stupor. On the next morning, to my regret, I found he had been removed to the dying-room, and there I saw him rolling and writhing in convulsive agony, but insensible to any thing addressed to him. I offered different drinks, which he cast off with force, accompanied by what I thought an apologetic look toward me for my perseverance. Victor and Michaud were wanting in their usual welcome to me. I sat between their cots, asked how they felt, and inquired if all their wants had been met. Despondency at the loss of their merry friend, and, I believe, their sole dependence in health, seemed to have overpowered them. They merely answered to the squeeze of my hand. The nurse told me that they did not converse with each other afterward. The day following they were restless, with the full complexion of a wasting fever. At night I was present when Father L. was in long converse with them, and we received from them an expression of gratitude for all that had been done to them, "in a world," they said, "in which they never had occasion to offer it before to man." Thus died two men, who, I inferred from their conversations, were educated to the monotonous servility of a soldier's life, where all sense of what is noble in immortality had been deadened within them until their last moments. Their mere duty as puppets absorbed all higher considerations. They did not perish, however, without one draught of religious hope, repentance, and reliance on the mercy of their God for their ignorance and neglect of another duty and service, which makes the poor man's exit the rich man's envy.

CHAPTER XIII.

A Family from Metz.—Admissions.—Convalescent Infirmary.—Little
Billy.—A Drive through the Cemeteries at Midnight.

I HAD been active from day to day in removing to the
infirmary all new patients, as nurses could not be found
for them, and for the convenience of concentrating my
labors in one place. While thus engaged, I was accosted by Dr. ——, who urged me to visit immediately a
family dwelling in —— Street, whom he represented as
being very worthy, and reduced to claim our charity.
To the attic of a one-story house I was shown by a slave,
who had descended to let me in. Three rooms were
scantily though cleanly furnished. One was used as a
sitting-room, and the other two as bedrooms. In the
first of the latter that I entered I saw that the bedding
had been taken from the bedsteads; in the second, which
was the smallest room, I found two mattresses on the
floor beside a trundle-bed. In the latter lay a young
woman and a boy, and on the former a young man. The
heat from the roof was intolerable. When the mother
of these children was apprised of my visit by the slave,
she pictured in her manner the wildest distress as she
flung up her arms and pointed despondingly toward her
children. Her children then were constantly ejaculat-
ing comfort to her. I saw that all stood equally in need
of it, and told her she must now command me. "I will
tell you all in a few words," she said: "*I am poor*. The
papers in that tin box will tell you what we have been.
Save them—save us—all of us, or leave us all to die."
My sympathies or feelings had never yet been excited
to such a pitch. I was determined to do every thing

that suggested itself, and if they could not be moved to the infirmary, to triumph in saving them by a change to better-furnished rooms in the same building. The physician had followed me, and just entered. Philomene, aged sixteen, and her brother Charles, aged nine, were in the trundle-bed. Philias, aged eighteen, was the name of the young man on the mattress. The latter was suffering from a relapse of a fever cured some weeks previous; the other two had been taken the night previous. The physician advised me to move the first to the infirmary, and, if possible, furnish a nurse for the latter. Both I consented to do, and started to procure the wagon for the sick. On my return, another daughter, by name Euphemie, aged eleven years, entered with a parcel from the apothecary. She cried piteously when she learned that they were to be separated, and almost wrought her mother to a phrensy. What to do for a nurse for Philias troubled me. I had been inquiring for several daily without success. I expected to be no more successful now. I told him I would spend half of the night with him, and, if no other assistance offered, I would spare a nurse from the infirmary.

"You can do nothing for me," said Philias. "Rather give your time to my brother and sister; save them; and support my poor mother until her relations in France answer to the letters we have written them. For me there is no hope, for I was cautioned against a relapse."

And, noble soul! how did he thus brave such fatality? He had not fairly stepped from the influence of the danger himself, than, upon learning of a friend's prostration, he devoted himself to the enervating cares of the night-watcher at the bedside. This unadvised and imprudent step, before twenty-four hours' service, canonized him a martyr to friendship.

I noticed the feeble frame of Euphemie as she was preparing a sinapism for her brother. Continued atten-

H 2

tions to the sick would be fatal to her, and I requested
the mother to allow her to sleep that night. The latter
looked at me, and signified her dissent by shaking her
head. Philomene and Charles were now ready to be
carried to the wagon.

The parting of friends in health, though sorrowful,
bears with it the consolatory pleasure of meeting again;
but to gaze upon a brother or sister in the embraces of
death, with no such hope, is an experience replete with
bitter reflections. The endearing words exchanged are
not to be written: it is a sacrilege of the heart to repeat
them when they are not felt. Philomene and Charles
were assisted to the side of Philias, and as they murmured their affection, sympathies, and hopes, but, most
of all, their prayers to God that he would be pleased to
assemble them all near to him, a heart of stone would
have melted. Each kissed the crucifix suspended from
the neck of Philomene. The mother the meanwhile
rested her head despairingly on the back of a chair. My
assurance that every thing should be provided for their
comfort and her necessities brought no reply. Philomene and Charles were carried to the wagon. Euphemie and I accompanied them. On arrival at the "Globe"
I had them carefully taken up stairs and placed in cots
aside each other. Father L. happened to be there, and
on his approach and conversation they became more reconciled to the change. Euphemie was provided with a
cot in the nurse's apartment, where I insisted upon her
retiring for repose, after she had taken some refreshment. In an hour afterward I found both patients more
hopeful, and improved in appearance and in spirits. I
took with me a nurse from the infirmary for Philias, and
provided every thing requisite for the comfort of the
mother. In the morning early, on my way to the infirmary, I stopped to see how she was. I found her in
the ante-room, packing away papers, and books, and

clothing in boxes and trunks as methodically as if she was preparing to set out on a journey. When she beheld me she made no sign of recognition, but continued her occupation, leaving me to infer that her son was deceased. Advancing to the next room, I saw, too, that Philias was not there. She now told me that he did not wish to die apart from his brother and sister, and he prevailed upon a friend to take him to the infirmary in a cab an hour previous to my arrival. The mother expressed her intention to follow as soon as she finished packing up. As we were placing the trunks and boxes in a corner, she directed my attention to one trunk, in which was a tin box of papers explaining who and what they were. "Should I not live to satisfy you on that point," she said, "the papers there will tell you of the hardships we have undergone and the respectability of my family." After locking the doors, she descended with me to the cab for the infirmary.

She appeared self-possessed, and nerved for the worst. From the first sight of her I had been struck with her easy manners, indicative of one who had seen better days. There was a delicacy in accepting my services or aid, as well as in mentioning her wants, that commiseration or charity shown to such a one causes the offerer unhappiness for the sense of dependence he has created. Her gratitude for being saved from the sight of her children perishing in misery was couched in the most feeling language. I told her there were many like her, and enumerated instances of worse distress as we rode along.

"I have not words, sir," she said, "to thank you for this disinterested kindness, for it is bestowed upon one whose recent life has been a succession of misfortunes and hardships, without a friend able to give us more than their pity or sympathy. From the time I fled from penury in France, after the death of my husband, until

I reached New York, and thence to New Orleans by land, I was subjected to all kinds of impositions and privations. Until I reached here I had not known an assisting hand. When we landed at Peoria, out of money to proceed farther, we thought that even in a wilderness our honest industry would support us; but ignorance of your language, added to a hostility to our religion, shut us out from employment there. By pawning jewelry and clothing we were enabled to pay the debts we had incurred, and to obtain deck-passage on a steamer to New Orleans. The sight of our country people here opened a new life to us. By the assistance of Father ―― we obtained recommendations to families who gave us work. Philias shortly obtained a situation at $40 per month, and we actually found, at the end of the month, that we were supporting ourselves. How happy were we in our retired rooms, when we talked over all we had passed through, and contemplated the happiness of the present and the future! You can not, sir, appreciate the feelings of a weak woman who at last saw her children cheerful in a new home. The fever came. Philias was one of the first victims. As our chief reliance was on him, you may imagine the anxiety and care with which we tended him. Our thanks were daily made to God for his deliverance. He thought himself so well, a few days after he was permitted to walk out, that he could nurse a friend who was then taken sick. The exertion was too much, and he was again ill. On the same night his brother and sister also were taken. What little we had saved was exhausted on him before this. You know and see the rest."

She then offered me her keys, which I refused to take, with the remark that she acted as if she never would have use for them. "I shall not," she replied, "if Philias dies. None of us could survive him; I know I can not."

Upon entering the infirmary, she found Father L. at the bedside of Philias. For some minutes she bent over him, while burning tears coursed down her cheeks, but not a sob. She asked me what I thought of him now. I was too much affected to reply. She read my doubts, and hastened from him to Philomene and Charles in the next division. Here the joy of meeting was affectingly mingled with sympathy. Euphemie had not yet arisen. When we sought her in the nurse's apartment, her pulse was unpromising. Upon inquiry, the nurse told me that she was restless and feverish during the night, and, apprehensive of her being worse, she had given her a footbath. The mother now saw that she was the only one able to move about. We used persuasions to make her retire for repose, but she would not listen to them.

I returned at one o'clock. Philias was now sinking fast, and was delirious. It was deemed proper to place him with others like' afflicted. He recognized no one, nor was he aware of being moved. His mother, who saw me enter, followed me to the other division where she had left her son. Upon finding his cot empty, she begged to know where he had been taken. There she fell upon his body with disheveled hair, kissing him, and pouring forth expressions that only a mother can utter over a dying, well-beloved son. The effort was so overpowering that she had fainted, and had to be carried to her bed. When she recovered she piteously related to her two daughters and son, who were near her in cots, the dying condition of Philias; begged them to recommend themselves to God, and pray that He should take them too. Thus they lay the entire night, the nurse told me, wailing over their fate and misfortunes.

In the morning all were worse from the loss of repose and excitement. Euphemie was in tears all the time. Father L. was assiduous in his ministrations to them. In sight of each other, extreme unction was administered, and there they now lay resigned and quiet. The mother refused nourishment or farther repose. She alternately sat by her children, comforting and weeping with them, and praying for a like visitation upon herself. She said her brain was on fire, and wondered she could not get the fever. The symptoms of Euphemie were promising. I begged the mother to desist from exciting her; that she, at least, would be saved to her; and that it was unchristian and selfish to wish all dead because she was tired of life and worn down by its cares. I promised that I would see to her future provision.

"Euphemie," she said, "can you live without your mother? Can you live without Philias, Charles, and Philomene?"

"Oh no! my dear mother, I want to die too."

Expostulation was out of the question when such despair had set in. All we could do was to make them as comfortable as possible.

The next morning I found Charles had died at daylight. Philomene was in a stupor, life flickering away slowly; while Euphemie had thrown up black vomit in the night, accompanied with great hemorrhage from the gums and nose. Madam C., the mother, had not risen. I drew her musquito-bar, which attracted her attention toward me. I at once saw that the disease she courted was strongly fixed in her. Her eyes were infected, her skin hot and dry, with a quick but feeble pulse. She was passive as a child in our hands, but frequently shook her head as we administered drinks, or applied cups to her, as much as to say all your efforts are vain, for I will die. As the servants wrapped the sheet around the corpse of Euphemie, she looked intently upon them. When they passed her, she entreated a kiss. The last pent-up tear was not proof against this. The attendants almost dropped their charge as they were lowering it, with the face uncovered, to receive a mother's sad, parting kiss. She had partially raised herself, and when the corpse was taken away, she exclaimed, "Now, my God, permit me to follow my children." Extreme unction was administered to her. She lay resigned, calm, and asked for nothing. I asked if she had no commission for me to perform, no letter to write. She searched for her keys, handed them to me without saying a word, took my hand in hers, and, gently pressing it to her lips, whispered a few words I did not catch. The next day she followed her children.

After the epidemic had ceased, I visited the rooms they had occupied. Their bedding and clothing were delivered to the landlady for the rent due to her. The trunk with books, and tin box of papers, were put away until sent for by their relations in Metz. I saw by the letters of the bishop of that town to them, and by other letters, that the family was one of distinction, and that they were in easy circumstances during the lifetime of their father. Certificates of his professional ability from the Minister of Education, as well as printed diplomas, and appointments to high station in the educationary department, were scattered through the papers. The few books they had were of the purest morality, and inscribed with the names of one or other of the family. Four or five weeks after their death, I was told by a lodger in the house they occupied, a gentleman called to pay them 1000 francs, which had been remitted to him for their relief.

On the third day from the opening of the infirmary the number of admissions reached sixty-nine; on the 19th, ninety-three; and to the morning of the 22d of August, only one week, we had under treatment 160 patients, of which forty-six died and forty were discharged. A number of the latter insisted upon leaving the infirmary as soon as the nourishment which they had taken during convalescence strengthened them sufficiently to walk. Many paid with their lives for their too great haste. To each we gave an amount sufficient to pay two weeks' board, or an order on a boarding-house. A little later we sent the convalescents from all our infirmaries to a well-suggested establishment, under the charge of two of our members, called the "*Convalescent Infirmary.*" The building used for this purpose was the present lodge-rooms of the Polar Star Order, which fraternity charitably gave us the use of it free. It stands in the middle of a large lot of ground, surrounded by shrubbery. The rooms were lofty and well ventilated. The basement was appropriated to males, the first floor to females. Here they were treated with wholesome and strengthening food, watched in their exercise, and in the course of a week or ten days were able to resume their occupations. Many left in better health than they had enjoyed for years before. It is such an institution as is wanted in all large cities, particularly during epidemics, as the hospitals do not count upon more than just putting a patient upon his legs, then to give place for another. It is only one half the danger overcome to snatch from death; security against a relapse, and a provision for sustenance, should be considered.

Included among the admissions to date were eleven orphan children, most of them of too tender years to communicate their own name or age. They had been left by citizens as the offspring of such as had died of the fever in their neighborhoods, or humanely picked up in the streets. They were all chubby, healthy infants, without any peculiarity in their garments or marked physiognomy to trace their nationality. For these we found no difficulty in obtaining nurses, as many women were left childless by the epidemic, and sought this opportunity of relief. A room was set apart exclusively for these youngsters. It was counted as a relaxation from severer duties by the other female nurses to amuse

themselves in this room. After several days many of
the children showed symptoms of sickness. It was proposed that they should be all baptized. As nearly all
of the destitute poor in our midst are of foreign birth,
and Catholic, it was not amiss to baptize them in the
rites of that Church. An entertainment of cakes and
innocent confections for the oldest was therefore obtained, they were clothed in their best, and the ceremony
performed by Father L. They were named after several of the donors to our fund, each of the children having the surname of Howard. The half hour thus passed that morning, and the scenes that transpired, are
treasured as saintly relics by all who attended. Com-
passion for the motherless, and joy upon seeing them so
happy with each other, amusing themselves with noisy
glee, were in strange contrast with scenes transpiring in
adjoining apartments. One of them, who entered later
—a lad who gave his name as Billy—was a source of constant entertainment to the nurses, as well as amusement
to the convalescent. He was the pet of the infirmary,
but the most unpromising of all the children. A neglected sore on the leg had eaten to the bone, and produced lameness. It was in its nature scorbutic, and required patient care, spare diet, and denial of every thing
stimulating. Billy, however, thought he was the best
judge of the treatment for himself, and, whether from in-
herent love of the ardent, or in having shared the bottle
of his parents, he acquired such a liking for the wine
sangarees and brandy toddies surreptitiously taken from
the tables of the patients, that his demand was constantly for them. The physician of the hospital, noticing that
Billy became stronger from indulgence, with increased
appetite, and that when it was restrained he became enfeebled, put him on a weak allowance of brandy toddy.
He was ordered to be watched, and kept from farther indulgence. As he made his usual sly walks among the

patients, the nurses amused themselves by twitting him with the question of "What will you have, Billy?" in order to obtain from him the few words he spoke, and then so quaintly, in a high key, of "a little bran—dy tod—dy." He remained in the infirmary until it was closed, and became entirely re-established in health. With other children he was then sent to the orphan asylum, where, six months after, when I saw him, he had lost the desire for his favorite beverage from being kept from its temptation.

In ten days after this christening our joys were turned to wormwood as seven of these infants dropped off one by one. This was in the most fatal week of the epidemic, and characterized by sudden and extreme changes of temperature. A girl and boy, presumed to be of Spanish descent from their swarthy complexion, were adopted by a wealthy lady of the third district. The remainder, and all others afterward sent to us, were conveyed to the asylums then instituted by the Howard Association and the Board of Health for the reception of orphans during the epidemic.

After having visited my outside patients on the night of the 20th, and left all quiet at the infirmary, after midnight I started in a cab with a friend to the lake to breathe a fresher air. The moon threw a melancholy light over the city. Our cab alone disturbed the quiet of the night. Even the canine species, noted in the suburbs for their watchful noise, were silent; nor was that howl heard from them which superstition interprets as a prophetic vision of a coming death. Perhaps they were affected by the malaria, as were cattle and poultry, wherever the fever appeared. In the suburbs and in the country, the poultry, horses, and mules fell dead in the fields. As we passed the cemeteries, we saw coffins piled up beside the gate and in the walks, and laborers at work digging trenches in preparation for the morrow's dead. We did not stop. A fog, which hung over the moss-enveloped oaks, prevented the egress of the dense and putrid exhalations. The atmosphere was nauseating to a degree that I have never noticed in a sick-room. We hastened our speed to get beyond its influence. When we had refreshed ourselves with the purer atmosphere of a north wind that just rippled the lake, we were still more impressed with the stifling pestilential odors on our return.

CHAPTER XIV.

The deaf and dumb Printer.

AT home I found an urgent request to call at No. — St. Peter Street, to see a deaf and dumb man, just attacked. Having detained my cab, I drove there, and seeing it a hopeful case, I drove to the infirmary to bring with me Dr. ——, who told me he intended to remain there to watch the result of a particular treatment for black vomit. The patient occupied a little room in the attic, and was lying upon a cot with his back toward us. Dr. —— touched his shoulder. The patient reached to a slate that was suspended to the wall, and wrote, in French, "Who are you?" "Dr. ——, of the Howard Association," was the written reply. Upon reading this he lowered the slate upon his breast, and after looking at us for a few seconds intently, tears of grateful acknowledgment filled his eyes. As he extended one hand to Dr. ——, with the other he designated the pains in his limbs. A prescription was immediately written. Being too late to procure a nurse, I determined to remain to administer to his wants. On my return with the medicine I found him sitting up in bed. If expansion of brain and deep-traced lines on the brow are indicative of intellect, he had no common share. When I had mixed the potion, he desired to know the ingredients. When informed of its being quinine, he signified by gesture that he had not much faith in it, but drank it, and turned over on his side. On scanning the room by the dim candlelight, I was struck with the appearance given to it by the numerous colored pictures of historical subjects that were tacked on the walls nearly to the ceiling. On the table were several volumes of miscellaneous literature and a Latin breviary. Hot water for a bath was brought in after half an hour's delay, when he was again aroused. When he recognized me making preparations with the servant to give him the bath, he beckoned me to him, and after written questions, being informed of the duty that devolved on us, he was fulsome in his expressions of gratitude. At daylight his fever had abated, and the most hopeful anticipations were entertained of his recovery. The proprietress of the rooms promised to see to his wants during my absence of a few hours. On my return I found a woman and two men sitting round his bed, talking loud to each other during intervals of his written responses to them. They had been thus occupied for an hour. No wonder that his eyes were strongly injected and his pulse feverish, for they had been entertaining him, as I saw by the slate, with exaggerated accounts of the epidemic, and enumeration of friends deceased. Without ceremony, I took the nearest one by the shoulder, and told him to leave the room. He showed belligerence, until I quietly informed him that I acted under extraordinary authority, and that I had privilege to use force upon any interference with my patients. They thought they had been doing a kindness to the patient, and muttered as they went down stairs something of the "strange country they were in." My patient, who witnessed all this, expressed his great gratification at my conduct, and wrote that he could make nothing out of their laughing and talking but indifference to his fate; that they annoyed him exceedingly. He knew so little of them that he did not remember their names.

There is a prurient curiosity which infects some people that is as difficult to be accounted for as any idiosyncracy, and which no censure or ridicule can shame. It exhibits itself in gloating the eye on corpses, and lingering about the sick-bed, to witness the agony of the patient, or console him by preaching resignation and preparing him for the worst. With those of better feelings it is mistaken for sympathy, but not a particle of such virtue exists in it. So long as it is exercised as a pastime, and is not offensive to mourning friends or relatives in the one instance, or injurious to the sick in the other, it is a creditable manifestation. There is something forbidding in the appearance of a corpse even of a relative; but when it is that of a stranger, the sight of it, in most people, calls up the ejaculation of a pah! This contemptible curiosity is akin to the character of the gadabout who peers into your market-basket, and gossips on your domestic troubles or business difficulties. Whenever I have discovered such in a sick-room, I have no patience with them; their presence is ever a mortal injury to the fevered sick. There is another class, who enter the sick-room with the best of motives and intentions, but who have a natural aversion to its atmosphere, and are permitted to sit up with their friend during the night. When you can say nothing to promote the cheerfulness of the patient, or raise his hopes of convalescence, you are doing him a charity to keep away. When you are not practically serviceable, your air of sympathy only makes every thing more lugubrious. "Save me from my friends" is an apophthegm better applied in this connection than in any other.

Upon reading the different questions and remarks

written by these intruders to my patient's room, I found
reference made to the great mortality in the city, and
requests that, as life was very uncertain, bequests or last
words, if he had any, had better be made at once. They
actually placed him in fascinating contemplation of
death when he was most desirous of casting off thoughts
of it by hopeful prospects. The effects upon him of
such reflections were to make him despond, and to be
stubborn in the belief that he could not survive the fever. Thousands have died from no other cause than
this. When the sweet hope of convalescence is banish-
ed from the pillow, by his resignation the patient invites
dissolution.

Dr. —— came in while I was there. He saw that
something had gone wrong, and inquired particulars.
He wrote, "You must keep your mind quiet; you will
not get well if you think you will not. I will leave you
a potion to give you repose." In reply he wrote, "I
have changed my mind with my hopes; I now wish to
die. I have suffered in this sickness a hundred deaths
—*veniat mors.*"

"Here is a stubborn fellow," exclaimed Dr. ——. He
wrote on the slate, "You shall live, and there is every
hope of early convalescence; so do not torment yourself farther." In a few minutes the potion was brought
in. The doctor handed it to him in a glass. He struck
his head with his hand several times in support of his
determination to take no more medicine; then, seizing
the slate, wrote, "My brother, a priest, who has been
written for, will arrive to-day to perform the last rites
over me. He will thank you for your noble charity
toward me. My last prayer will be for your salvation,
my friends." His frequent sighs, or long breathings,
occasionally met with in patients treated with quinine,
were unfavorable prognostics. As he did not court
communion with any of us we left him, with directions

for farther treatment. On that night he became delirious, and had ejected black vomit. He refused now any thing but ice, which was crushed between his teeth and swallowed as fast as put in. At midnight he recovered his senses. I had been absent on other visits, and, upon making my appearance, he took his slate and wrote, with tremulous hand, in large letters, "I have been waiting for you. Be patient with me." On my writing "Go on," he wrote as follows, as near as a good memory and ability of translating permit me to give it: "As there is but one God, so there is but one salvation, and that is through the Redeemer. Would you die happy, as I do now, learn to contemplate futurity through Him, and its value will be so enhanced to you that the waters of separation will bear you kindly to your wished-for home. I am your friend."

In the morning I was stopped on the stairway with the announcement of his death. On entering the room to make arrangements for his interment, I attracted the notice of a priest who was kneeling by the bedside weeping. Seeing that he was absorbed in prayer, and did not recall me when leaving the room a few minutes afterward, I concluded my farther services were dispensed with. In the next room the proprietress handed me the slate, on which he had written, almost illegibly, scraps of the Psalms and Liturgy in the Latin language. He was a printer by profession, and, I was told, highly educated; of an amiable and sociable disposition, ever entertaining his company with sententious remarks which evinced depth of learning and acuteness of observation.

CHAPTER XV.

Nurses on a Frolic.—Volunteer Nurses.—Desultory Remarks.—Sisters
of Charity.—Nurses repent.—Exposure of Thefts.—The Barber.—
Fire!—Effect of a wrong Prescription on two Patients.

SEVEN days had elapsed.   The infirmary had now its
complement of patients.   From fifteen to twenty-five
were received daily, taking the place of the discharged
or dead.   The nurses were beginning to show carelessness in their duties, and required constant supervision.
They were allowed rations of wine or spirits, but they
contrived to get more, from the facility of access to the
pantry, or by appropriating such stimulants as were intended for the patients.   It was a regular thing, by midnight, to have five or six patients *in extremis*, who were
restless and noisy, and were removed to the dying-room.
As these had stimulants *ad libitum*, it was no difficult
matter for the nurses so disposed to be liberal toward
themselves.   On the night of the 27th the matron had
retired at her usual hour, after having given her directions and placed the watches.   The doors of the infirmary were also closed, the lights about the house reduced,
and proper care taken in the adjustment of the windows
against an inlet of night air.   An associate and myself
being out late on visits, I proposed to him to accompany
me, and see how things worked at the infirmary after
midnight.   We drove to the door, and, after repeated
raps, brought the matron to the window.   She admitted
us and retired.   On entering the wards, our surprise was
great to hear calls made upon us in every direction for
ice-water, drinks, etc., while, at the same time, the foul
offensiveness of neglected matter in the room was sickening in the extreme.   With the exception of an old col-

ored nurse, who had been sent gratis to us by a Creole lady, none others were to be seen. On searching, we discovered two male nurses snoring beside the dead and dying in the room appointed to them, and empty bottles strewed on the floor. Several others were asleep on the vacated cots, while the females were asleep in their rooms. We aroused them all, but they were of no service. The intoxication from a three-gallon demijohn of brandy required a longer time to be dissipated. It was so general that I could not but think it habitual, and this time preconcerted. My associate and I, with the matron, remained up the remainder of the night doing their duty. A few days before this I had abolished the system at first adopted of alternate four hours' watching at night for one of service the whole night, allowing all to sleep during the day as much as they pleased. This was done because I was daily offered the services of female nurses gratis. Ladies of mature age, and young ladies, in many instances, of respectable Creole families, with quadroons in easy circumstances, presented themselves all of the day, begging permission to nurse the sick. I found the number too great to admit all. Some came at the first visits of the physicians, and made themselves useful in carrying out prescriptions and doing menial service to the sick. After a stay of two or three hours they would leave, and be replaced by others. Some came daily, others at intervals of a few days, as if the duties were repugnant, and they were doing them from a sense of charity or for a penance. There were those with strong will and of tender frames, whose hearts were ready to burst with pity and sympathy for their suffering fellow-creatures, who bravely stood the ordeal for an hour or less, and might be seen hurrying to gain the door with countenances of livid hue, from being placed in the midst of so much despair, despondency, and suffering. Nearly all, upon taking off their bon-

I

nets, threw a veil over the head, which partly or entirely concealed the face.   Whether this was in imitation
of the first comers or a conventional type of volunteers
to the sick, I could not learn.   I rarely saw their faces.
They passed me without a word or a look of recognition,
for they seemed desirous to destroy all identity with
those "acts of goodness which themselves requite."

Allowing that a controlling power is over us which
necessitates the will and bends us to His views, and that
every character is the necessary consequence of its physical organization, it is no less beautiful to dwell upon
the extreme of self-denial exhibited in females who dangerously expose their health by ministrations to the sick,
in contrast to the cold mediocrity of passion and feeling
which distinguishes the mass.   Who is not proud of human nature, and of the perfection it is susceptible of, after
having witnessed and watched the devotions and privations for others' good of the "Sisters of Charity," or "*Les
dames de la Providence?*"   The latter body is composed
of ladies of wealth and respectability, who may be seen
in winter the foremost and gayest of our fashionable
soirées; in summer, or during epidemics, untiring in good
deeds by day and night.   In bodies of three or four, they
perambulate the streets from house to house; they notice absence of comforts which the sterner sex are regardless of, and by their presence impart a sustaining joy
and hope to the destitute of their own sex.

Chief above all, though, do I record the praise of the
Sisters of Charity.   I have been long a witness to their
modest yet active charity.   I have seen the fruits of
their watchings, and wondered at the charm which sprung
from their ministering.   In no place can they reap such
harvest of good as New Orleans, the consciousnes of doing which is their sweet reward during their devoted
pilgrimage on earth.   They do good by stealth.   The
light of publicity is no stimulant to them, for virtue like

theirs rather shuns the more the more observed it is.
They triumph over the flesh, and live outside the body,
as we do in dreams. They stand on the pedestal of the
Vestal virgins of old, who had charge of the ever-living
fire, which was the principle of all things and the emblem of purity. Fanaticism, which would mar a divinity not cast in its own mould, points to them sneeringly
as instruments of a selfish sectarianism—as an institution maintained to conceal glaring imperfections, and to
make proselytes to their religion. Be they so; the poor,
disconsolate, miserable, or expiring mortal cares not to
know or discover their seeming; he feels the solace from
the presence of those who have no trumpeter in this
world except the meek and lowly, whose voices are not
heard, like his own, beyond the hovel or the hospital.
We should be above the ungenerous reflections that are
ingrafted on young hearts against this order of charity.
With the admission that they do much good, let us of a
different sect institute a like order for the same objects
with the same purpose (*nosce ab hostibus*). The world
would then be better; religion will be loved for this
great feature, while each sect will find it the brightest
jewel in its coronet of faith and profession. The religion of the Sisters, though, should be no prejudice to their
acts. Were they Hindoos, their mission would be no
less divine, their self-denial no less admirable. There
are many Florence Nightingales in the dissenting religions who only wait the door of opportunity to be opened
by authority of their *custos animarum* to associate together and rival these privileged few in the good they
dispense throughout the world. Charity is the main-
stay of religion; without a prominent exercise of it, all
faith is emptiness. It is also the foundation of justice,
epitomized in the words, "Do unto others as you would
they should do unto you." Begin the good work at
once. The institution of the Sisters of Charity is the

triumph of the Catholic religion. It is practical. It has in it nothing of the dreamings or enthusiasm for African or heathen regeneration, the fruits of which are not visible. What is sympathy with the heathen to doing good to a neighbor spiritually or physically? I have seen the Sisters of Charity in the silent rounds of duty, in the infirmaries, hospitals, and rickety tenements of the poor, comforting their own sex of all religions, castes, and conditions, fearless of contamination, dressing loathsome wounds, and inhaling the most nauseating odors. Sinner as I am, I hold them too holy and sacred to disturb them by any remarks from me. They knew my mission, I reverenced theirs; and never has a word passed between us that was not in reference to a duty to be performed. In fact, the rules of their order enjoin a silent tongue to all. The world may be bad in the main, but a redeeming feature is this institution, which is as a golden connecting link between heaven and earth. Their hearts are mediums through which angels visit humanity, and humanity pleads to God. Theirs is the seed which, planted here, blooms in heaven; they are the purest on earth;

> "Their every day is Sabbath; only free
> From hours of prayer for hours of charity."

The morning following the intoxication of the nurses, I summoned all of them at the office for the purpose of discharging and paying them off. Several were repentant, and begged to be retained, having, they said, been misled by the others. The remainder made an excuse, which, though natural, I would not admit. They urged that the duties of attending the patients through sickness, to carrying the corpse to the dead-room, was so sickening that they could not continue without an extra allowance of stimulant. I sent off all but two: one, who had been the most useful, to whom I promised an additional ration; and the other, an old man, as an act of charity; "for," said he, "if you turn me out from here I shall starve." There is nothing like a dismission or a threat of dismission to find out the past conduct of a body of servants or employés. The guilty ones break the *enteinte cordiale*, and expose the faults of the others so soon as they are made examples of. All kinds of abuses were hinted at as having been general. In this adventure, as in all others, one must pay for experience. One of the nurses was a barber, and assisted the regular cupper in his duties. It was with great reluctance I dismissed him. He, however, expressed no desire to remain. From those retained I afterward learned a reason for his submission with quiet grace. As previously remarked, our patients at the Globe of late were of a better class than those who were earlier admitted. They were single men, of more or less means, who, when taken sick, and finding it impossible to obtain proper attendance at their lodgings, gave the preference to the Globe Infirmary. Some, having money in sums of over five dollars, from apprehension, perhaps, that it would be lost to them if they deposited it with the clerk, kept it about their persons. The barber, who had before served in a hospital, was quick in discovering this hidden treasure. I shall not convict him of cruelty in his duties to secure impunity for his crime; but, from the various sums of money and jewelry he was said to purloin from the pockets or belts of the patients, there is room for suspicion that he was indifferent to their recovery. The location of the concealed money became exposed to him from the anxiety of the owner to watch or retain it. In stripping a patient to be habited in the gown of the infirmary, his unwillingness to part with any piece of his clothing generally indicated the value of its contents. This piece of clothing would be carefully placed under the mattress or pillow of the patient. When the patient became delirious and his case hopeless, the booty would be secured by the attendant. No complaints were made by those who recovered of being robbed. On one occasion, a Frenchman, well dressed, was brought by several of his countrymen to the infirmary. He denied having any thing valuable on his person. He died two days after admission; and upon examination of a pocket-book which he had managed to conceal from every one and to place under his pillow, we found in it $175. Having learned he was a Protestant, we purchased for him an oven in the Girard Street Cemetery, and expended the remainder in the coffin and hearse. His friends were afterward advised of what we had done.

Many patients who were now admitted requested to have the attendance of their own physician, and to pay for the privilege of a selected place in the wards. When not objected to by the regular-appointed physician to the infirmary, I could make no objection, but placed them without choice in the numbered cot.

A week had not elapsed since the discharge of the nurses when the barber was brought in, suffering under pernicious fever. He had had the yellow fever, and was supposed to have induced this present attack by dissipation. His ill-gotten treasure had proved his ruin. He was cognizant of nothing, and wild and unmanageable from delirium. The same process which he had introduced of securing such patients to their cot was exercised upon him. A rope was passed under his arms and across his back, the ends secured under the cot; his feet were separately tied to the corners. We tried all in our power to subdue the symptoms. At night his case was hopeless. On my return at eleven o'clock he was insensible, and literally burning out. I had left him for a few minutes, and was making arrangements for the next day's services, when suddenly a cry of "Fire! fire! fire!" startled us. It was cried in the methodical cadence of a fireman. Supposing the voice to emanate from the

rear of the building, we hurried there, and as quickly
hurried back to the wards to meet a scene that beggars
description. The moans of the sick, the shrieks of the
dying, accompanied with the sounds of tables turned
over and broken crockery, preceded a rustling and disorder through all the wards. The women, who had
caught the alarm from the male patients entering their
division, jumped from their beds, and *en masse* made for
the head of the stairway. Had we not by main force
stemmed this mass of ghost-like people, clad in long
white gowns, the city would have been rife the next
morning with horrible reports of crazy people running
the streets in the middle of the night to avoid an imaginary evil. After we had somewhat quieted their fears,
some clung to the walls for support, while others sunk
on the floor from exhaustion. All was now confusion.
Many were speechless from fright, and blunders were
necessarily committed in placing back the invalids to
their proper cots, for the nurses were doubtful of the
identity of many of them. Such as we found lying beside the cots we were certain of. We did the best under the circumstances, until, by degrees, the patients became sensible enough to point out their original positions. But what a check to its usefulness did the infirmary receive that night! The physicians, on the next
morning, estimated the certain fatality from this accident
to over ten cases. Many of these had been convalescent.
Upon inquiring the cause, we were informed that the
cry was started by the barber, under delirium. At the
extreme corner from him a patient became excited by
it, and suddenly leaped from his bed, turning over his
table and breaking the crockery on it. The rush of
nurses to the spot alarmed the sick, who in their turn
halloed for help, some passing the nurses, through the
canvas division, to the female wards. The women, confirmed by the appearance of the men of the reality of

the danger, now made their desperate effort to escape. The cause of this unfortunate disturbance died that night.

A day or two afterward, a circumstance grew out of this confusion which was food for comment to lookers-on. It appears that two patients, who had arisen from their cots, had returned and changed places. The physician attending had ordered a treatment for each, according to his number on the cot, until his return the next morning. One was turning convalescent from nine days' illness; the other had been ill but thirty-six hours. The condition of each continued to improve, and it was not until two days after that the physician discovered that he had been successful under an error by accidentally noticing the medicines which were mixed in glasses on the table. Both finally recovered. It was a question for amusing deliberation at the time, that, had any other course of treatment been pursued to either, would there have been a recovery at all?

CHAPTER XVI.

The Pole and his Wife.—A Case of Confidence.

As an illustration of the many uses we were put to, and of the singular convenience or advantage in being sick, I have extracted from my dairy the following morceau.

On leaving the house of a pay-patient with Dr. ——, who was also engaged by our association, I was addressed by a servant by name, requesting me to call upon a lady opposite, who was convalescent of fever, but fearful of relapse. Being informed that she had been visited by another physician, Dr. —— jumped in his cab and drove off. It was scarcely seven o'clock, and I was surprised, upon entering the room, to find the numerous articles in it all orderly arranged, the bed-clothes smoothed,

and the musquito-bar drawn. The patient was a bru-
nette, of Jewish features, pretty withal, and delivered her
French with a patois accent. She complained to me of
having been deserted by her nurse, and begged that I
would procure another for her.

When I glanced my eye around the room as she was
speaking, and beheld the walls hung with handsomely-
framed prints and two crayon portraits, the furniture of
costly French patterns, the several tables crowded with
articles of taste, the mantle-piece with a bronze clock,
candelabras, and statuettes, and the delicate odor of gera-
niums floating in the atmosphere from an opened window, I fancied myself to be in the chamber of a fashionable milliner or a *fille perdue.* Wondering that, with
such a display of luxury, she should seek our charity, I
remarked to her that we confined our attentions solely
to the destitute poor. With a smile at my ignorance,
she gave me very decidedly to understand that she had
not fallen so low, but contemplated to pay for the nurse
which I might send to her. She at the same time intimated that my visits would be agreeable until her fears
were quieted, as her physician would not call unless sent
for, and she would like me to say how she progressed in
health from day to day.

"And bring with you," she added, in a lively tone,
"the physician I see visiting with you my opposite
neighbor."

"Then," I replied, "I shall have to enroll you as one
of our patients, and take your age and place of nativity."

"As for that," said she, "it is nothing. My name is
——; aged ——; born at ——; but I wish you distinctly to understand that I desire no relief from you, or to
occupy the time of the physician, without remuneration."

I did not, of course, take any more notice of her name
and nativity than to remark that it resembled in sound

that of a countryman of hers opposite, where she had seen me visit.

"You are right, sir. Now sit down for a moment, and I will tell you more."

With that she beckoned to the servant, who brought her to the opposite side of the bed a bowl of water, into which she had dashed several jets of a perfume. Her face and neck being well sponged, her hair thrown back from her forehead with her hands, she laid herself back, quite refreshed, upon two large pillows, which had been, in the mean time, beaten and turned for her. "Now for a development," thought I, "in keeping with many that I am subjected to."

"You must know, sir," she began, "that the Pole opposite is my husband. To tell you the truth, you must be a partner in my designs, and interest yourself for the good that will result to both. I am not so sick as I pretend to be, though I am not really well. I must confess to you that my pretended illness, and desire for the regular attendance of yourself and the physician, is to gain a point in which you will sympathize with me. As I have said, the Pole opposite is my husband, with whom I have lived on confiding and affectionate terms until the announcement of the epidemic. Then he became alarmed and querulous. He remained home the greater part of the day, and seemed to delight in recapitulating to me all the horrors of the disease which he had picked up at the cafés or the corners. The consequence was, the constant dread of the thing invited itself. I took the fever. When the physician announced the fact to him, he became so excited and tremulous that he could not sleep. The second morning after my illness he kept in bed, and told the doctor that he also was a subject. The doctor laughed at him, and ordered a toddy to bring repose to him. Thus he lay one day. The next day he could not be persuaded that he was not under the influ-

ence of the epidemic, and asked for, but did not obtain,
the prescription for cupping and for medicines ordered
for me. I thought him really sick; he knew I was. I
broached to him the necessity to prepare for the worst,
and suggested that we each make a will, leaving the other the effects. He has always been jealous of me; and
from the visits of several who had courted my hand, to
inquire of my health, he interpreted much to my prejudice. When I still farther aroused his suspicions by
thus anticipating his death—for he did not consider mine
—he thought there was a conspiracy to end him. He
would not trust himself to my keeping, he said, and,
with an excuse to his friends that there was not room to
accommodate two, he was removed to the house opposite. When I became convalescent my solicitude for
him made me very uneasy, the more so when I learned
that your physician was visiting him three and four
times a day. I sent over my servant to inquire into his
condition. For some time she reported to me what I
supposed to be true, which she had learned from a woman who was attending him, who did not know that the
information was for me. When she found this out, the
servant was answered indignantly that it was none of
her business, and that it was a pretty thing for a wife to
pretend to an interest in a husband she had thrust out
of doors sick. Hearing he was convalescent, through
another servant I sent to him broth which I had made
for him. This was admitted twice; then, upon suspicion,
I suppose, of the source from whence it came, it was afterward refused. I was well enough the other day to
have my bed moved nearer the window, whence I commanded a view of his room. I saw you and the physician enter, and, when you were about to leave, hold a
conversation with a woman at the door. Now, sir, her
presence explains many things. She is a vile character,
who pretended much love for him before I married, when

she was only attracted by his money. She has privately abused me, and her venom has reached me through my husband. She is the cause of all his jealousy of me, and I have no doubt that she has continued to calumniate me until she has obtained complete control of him. I saw my husband sitting at the window yesterday. Directly he saw he was observed by me he drew the curtain, and ever since has been invisible. I thought of an expedient to bring him back to me, and to see if he any longer loved me. I thought that I would feign sickness; that I would employ you as physician, and, in a day or so, have conveyed to him the intelligence of my dangerous condition, to see if the power of that woman, who flaunts in ill-gotten goods, is as strong as I suspect. I have hopes of accomplishing my object, for he has a proper heart if only seasonably touched. I am a seamstress, and can make my own living; he is a jeweler, and equally independent of me."

She breathed a while. I found the whole narrative funny, and only wished for the presence of Dr. —— to have enjoyed it in its raciness of delivery. I told her that I would consult with him on her novel complaint, and had no doubt we could manage, by some means or other, to disperse all manner of misunderstandings. She directed the servant to hand me a glass of cordial from a handsomely-carved buffet, bidding me to act with discretion, so to deserve her lasting gratitude.

To deserve a woman's gratitude or to receive her acknowledgments after acting as her tool to heal the wounds between herself and lover is as unlikely as obtaining thanks from a combative married pair whom you have separated. Kindness like this is more frequently followed by a complete ignoring of the rash adventurer, as the last one wished to be encountered is he who presents himself a mocking witness of another's weakness. Indifferent, though, to the result, so far as we were concerned, the doctor and I set our heads together to accomplish her wishes. It was a pleasant episode in our melancholy round of duties. At ten in the morning we dropped in on the jealous Pole, after having paid two visits to his wife. Before entering we had fixed upon no certain plan, but left all to the inspiration of the moment.

"Mr. ——," said the doctor on entering, "you are getting quite well now, and I do not think it will be necessary to visit you again. Your wife here can safely assume farther responsibility of you."

"My wife, sir, did you say?" as he looked inquiringly at us.

"Your wife—is she not such whom I always see with you here? The lady opposite tells me she is, and I presume, from her having the same name with you, that she is a relation or connection who knows."

"The lady opposite?" He was on the point of saying more, but checked himself.

"Yes, sir, the lady opposite, who has been confined to her bed for some time, and is now dangerously ill. I hardly think she would have told me an untruth. If she is wrong, it is not my intention to intrude upon your private affairs."

"Do you say, sir, she is very low?"

"I have my greatest fears for her," replied the doctor.

Just then the woman in question entered—no beauty, by-the-by—who, after some whispering between herself and the Pole, left the room.

"Doctor," said the Pole, in Dutch gutturals, "I am a miserable man. That lady opposite is my wife. She drove me almost mad. She drove me into this fever. With all that, I love her. I am willing to forgive her. To bring her to her senses, and make her repentant, I invited this woman to stay with me in my sickness. I thought by doing so, as she was jealous of her before and after my marriage, that it would bring out some demonstration from my wife. But no! not once has my wife sent to know if I was sick; she has, though, abused me to the whole neighborhood, and sent me messages to worry out my life."

The mist vanished. We assured him he was doing his wife a great injustice and laboring under a mistake; that we attended her, and that she constantly asked after him; and we supposed her to be only a relative. Also, that we knew, in several instances, that things had been prepared for him and sent by her servant. The Pole seemed pleased to be convinced that he was wrong, and was profuse in thanks for the interest we took in him. He begged we would intercede for him, and placed his happiness in our hands.

Before noon I dropped in and advised his wife of the progress we had made. Two hours after, the doctor and I again entered the husband's room, where we found his female friend sitting. They had been in loud conversation, and stopped abruptly when they saw us. She had apparently an inkling of the *dénouement* in contemplation, and looked daggers at us, but used not even a sententious arrow from the quiver of her lips. Now for our *coup de main*.

"Mr. ——, there is a relation of yours opposite," said the doctor, "who says she longs to see you. You are strong enough to cross over with us. Will you go?"

The Pole arose doggedly, as if he had some terrible forebodings that he was to be made a jest of. He thus wavered in resolution as we approached the door. Perhaps, thought we, the woman has poisoned him anew by inductions in respect to the interest we took in his wife. Be it what it might, he did not move cheerfully, but as if about to undergo some punishment. An infliction, for which we were not prepared to witness, but which he may have foreseen, visited him directly I placed my hand on the knob of the door, in the form of a tirade of abuse, which only a woman's imagination can lend to language when her self-esteem is stung by disdain or disappointment. Her tongue flashed its lightning through his brain, striking him dumb, with an occasional fling of scorn at us and our "disinterested interference," as she sneeringly termed it.

When we led him to his room, she cunningly received him lying in her bed in morning dress. We saw him take her outstretched hand, and hurriedly left without hearing a word or giving them time for their acknowledgments to us.

Before the doctor had presented his bill, he received a check to his order for a liberal amount, inclosed by itself in an envelope. This was fair warning to both of us that farther acquaintance would be disagreeable, which was fully confirmed by a blank stare the two gave me when I encountered them a month afterward. Thus, by accomplishing a good, we created two *ingrates*.

CHAPTER XVII.

Similarity to the Plague.—Physician treats himself.—The helpless Family.—A Cold-water Enthusiast.

To the 27th of August the admissions reached 237, of which sixty-four were discharged well, and seventy-one died. The difficulty in managing the type the epidemic had now assumed grew greater. Analysts of the atmosphere said there was an absence of ozone, which, being the result of electricity, is continually more or less floating in it. Others said it was an aggravated form of the disease, said to prevail in Rio Janeiro with similar symptoms, and introduced lately among us. It was thus marked. After the patient had been some days convalescing, his appetite or strength did not increase. An irregular pulse was noticeable; boils appeared in the upper parts of the body, principally in the region of the head in men, and on the breast of women. These boils were deeply seated, gave excessive pain, without fever, accompanied with loss of sleep. When coaxed by blistering to a large and ripe excrescence, the lancet was applied, and a copious flow of yellow matter followed, offensive to the smell. Suppuration continued several days after. In some instances anæsthetics were applied to the spot before the patient would submit to an operation. I noticed that almost all cases attended with these symptoms recovered. Another characteristic was in some patients who on the second day of their admission presented on their bodies round purple spots the size of a dime, with the edges darker than the centre. If they survived the third day, the side on which they lay for a few hours became of the same color, as if mortification had set in from interruption to a free circulation through the laggard veins. In nearly all these cases hemorrhage of the gums and nostrils was present, and a cold, clammy perspiration preceded their fatal result. Some physicians conjectured the boils to proceed from an intemperate administration of quinine, and the spots nothing less than a modified type of the famous plague which infected Athens, and which Lucretius describes so graphically that in its precision, *mutato nomine*, it daguerreotypes our visitation. I use the translation:

> "The head first flamed with inward heat; the eyes
> Reddened with fire suffused; the purple jaws
> Sweated with purple ichor; ulcers foul—
> *　　*　　*　　*　　*　　*　　*
> Yet ne'er too hot the system couldst thou mark
> Outward, but rather tepid to the touch;
> Tinged still with purple dye, and brandish'd o'er
> With trails of caustic ulcers, like the blaze
> Of erysipelas.　　*　　*　　*　　*
> For the broad eyeballs, burning with disease,
> Roll'd in full stare, forever void of sleep;

The mind's pure spirit, all despondent, raved;
The brow severe; the visage fierce and wild;
The ears distracted, fill'd with ceaseless sounds;
Scanty the spittle, thin, of saffron dye,
Salt, with hoarse cough, scarce labor'd from the throat.
The limbs each trembled; every tendon twitch'd.
Spread over the hands; and from the foot extreme
O'er all the frame a gradual coldness crept.
Then, toward the last, the nostrils close collapsed;
The nose acute; eyes hollow; temples scoop'd;
Frigid the skin, retracted; o'er the mouth
A ghastly grin; the shrivel'd forehead tense;
The limbs outstretched, for instant death prepared,
Till, with the eighth descending sun—for few
Reach'd his ninth lustre—life forever ceased."

To every one who has diagnosed the yellow fever, this book of Lucretius is interesting in a high degree, and deserves a thorough perusal. In the second book of Thucydides, the behavior of the plague, as there described, likewise presents a striking similarity to our complicated yellow fever. Our city, like Athens, was one vast charnel-house. Many who were able to pay for the interment of relatives or friends were worse off than the poor, whose corpses were regularly removed by the commissioners. From the excessive demand for hearses and carriages, many a corpse poisoned a neighborhood for hours with its peculiar stifling effluvia; or, what was equally offensive to many, a sickening odor from burning pastiles, scented principally with musk, greeted the nostrils in every direction. At the infirmary we trusted entirely to ventilation, cleanliness, and occasional use of chloride of soda or lime. The air was sweeter there than in the streets.

——, a very gentlemanly-looking man, who left with us his diploma from the College of Medicine at Paris, entered as a patient a few days before this, with the request that he be allowed the permission to direct the treatment of his disease. The well-known courtesy between gen-

tlemen of the profession justified me in granting what I
knew our appointed physicians would not object to, and
I was not mistaken. He ordered for himself cupping
and foot-baths, and heroically took his own prescriptions.
The nurse attending counted for him his pulsations. All
went well until the third day, when he did not show
signs of mending. He ordered himself to be cupped
again, and increased the number of ounces previously
drawn. I do not remember exactly, but this second infliction so exhausted him that he was from that time a
willing patient in the hands of our physician. He, like
most people sick of any disease, was more ignorant of
the diagnosis in his own case than in others. I did not
note the nature of the curatives he employed, but recol-
lect that our physician expressed a surprise at the strange
treatment he had subjected himself to. He sank gradually, having prostrated his strength too much for reaction.

Though the treatment in his case may have been out
of all reason, it is well known that a practice is followed
by some physicians successfully, the secret of which is
as surprising as startling. We all know that, without
confidence in our physician, the odds of getting well are
against us. His faith in his own remedy had the advantage of confidence over that of any other. His judgment was strongly favored by his will. Were it to be
told to a patient that the hieroglyphics of a doctor's prescription could be figured into strychnine or corrosive
sublimate, which were actually used and partially successful during this year in yellow fever, he would throw
physic to the dogs. We heard of such ingredients in a
potion, and, fearing censure from countenancing such a
bold innovation, we directed the physician to discontinue
them. We deemed it on a par with the treatment of
some of the faculty at Mobile in 1839, in applying a blis-
ter to the shaved head, an invention of cruelty not to be

surpassed in the records of torture for producing raving madness.

——, a woman in delicate health, called at my house, and requested me to follow her to her home to see what she would not describe. "We are not sick," she said; "but if I would see, I could judge if they were proper objects for relief." In half an hour I visited the place of her address. It was the basement-room of a back building, next to a kitchen, about eighteen feet square.

"Walk in, Mr. ——," she said. "Here is my husband; here are our four children. He is suffering from acute rheumatism of long standing, taken by exposure on the Levee at his business, and has been entirely disabled from work for six months. In the mean time, I have been occupied day and night in sewing for the Repository, but the little gain from that barely enables me to buy bread for my children. As for flesh-meat, we have not tasted it for a month. We occupied for years a house up town, which we had to give up when we could not pay the rent, and to sell a great portion of furniture to pay our debts in the neighborhood. From thence we came here, and had this room and another in the main building, both at seventeen dollars per month. From that time to this I have had to sacrifice furniture and dresses to pay the rent and buy clothing for my children, until, not being able to pay for both rooms, we removed our remnant of furniture to this. If we are not worthy the assistance of the association, who are?"

All this was said in an earnest tone, feelingly and despairingly. When she had concluded she threw forward both arms, and directed my attention, by their movement around the room, to the living and fixed objects in it. Then she gave way to a bitter, prolonged grief, which the youngest children not understanding, joined in with her. I saw enough without questioning—without doubting—and sickened at heart at such misery.

"Why, madam, did you not call on me before? You have been cruel to your children to let them suffer as you have done."

"I did think to do so several times, but waited until the very last extremity—until I could work no more—until I saw the starvation of my family staring me in the face. I have been educated to despise a beggar, and the better days I have seen makes this humiliation as poignant as it is necessary."

I was struck with the sense of her remarks, and as I was engaged in writing an order for a pecuniary relief upon the treasurer, I made it now threefold what I had intended. The smile of joy that lit up her countenance when she saw the amount written pictured too ineffable happiness in prospect, and she was speechless from emotion. At last she recovered herself, and, running toward her husband, who was lying in the bed with his clothes on, cried out, "William, look here! look here! Look here, too, Johnny, what this gentleman has given your ma—five dollars!" Could the little girls of Tennessee, who contributed their picayunes "to help poor children," mark the joy that beamed on these children's countenances, and believe that it was their contribution that saved these children from starvation, it were an enviable enjoyment for them.

I approached the husband. His frame was reduced to a skeleton. By describing his employment he brought me to a faint recollection of him. The picture of hopelessness and helplessness was complete by a brilliancy of the eye noticeable in men of acute suffering from nervous disease or long privation. The four children grouped themselves together, each with one or two garments, shoeless, thin, emaciated, and cheerless. I walked toward them, and asked if they would not like to have some cakes. Instead of a joyful reply, they looked at me as if I mocked them, or was the dreaded landlord.

I left them, promising that I considered them under our charge; that I should first meet their pressing necessities, and return in a few moments to listen to other wants. At an adjoining grocery I purchased every thing that was indispensable to comfortable subsistence for one week, including cakes, and was followed with them to the house. First distributing the cakes, which were greedily munched, I left the packages for their private examination and enjoyment. That first night's feast for many months must have made them feel that virtue is not dead in this world, since a Providence had furnished the instruments to dispense the goods of others to the poor and needy.

At dusk I returned; a candle was burning, and the children playing about the room. When they perceived me, they stood still. Upon my beckoning them to me, they all approached with confidence, the largest ones smiling and glad from the effects of a satisfied appetite.

"Are *you* the gentleman that sent ma the coffee?" said one.

"Didn't *you* give us the cakes?" said another.

"It was the grocer," I replied.

"No, it was *you;* and you do not know how happy our dinner made us. *Didn't* it, Jane?"

"Yes," said Jane; "I ate a *heap.* I wish I could have such good things *every day.*"

The mother stood by in the mean time, watching the expression of her children, and smiling with kindred feelings of relief. Then rolled the unbidden tears from her eyes. "Oh God!" she exclaimed, "what have poor people to do in this world!"

I told her she should not want during the summer; that we had plenty of money, and all for such as she was. I requested her now to tell me, and for once without delicacy, of what more she wanted, and, if possible, she should be relieved.

She said she had three days before had an advance on some furniture sent to auction, among which was a cradle, of little value in itself, but endeared to her from having rocked all her children in their infancy; also a work-box, which she had presented her eldest daughter in better days. She knew they would not bring more than the advance, and she thought the auctioneer, who spoke kindly to her, had given their full value for these times. They were to be sold on the morrow.

The next day, at twelve o'clock, I went to the auction, and had pointed out to me the articles by one of the children whom I recognized there. I was afterward joined by the other three, who stood beside me, silently waiting for their things to be put up for sale.

"That's my work-box," said the eldest, as it was handed to the auctioneer. I bought it, and handed it to her. She bent her head over it as she took it; she wept, while the others smiled with joy. The other articles were successively put up and bought in. They went home, the box in front, to announce to their parents the recovery of their cherished lares.

I rented the adjoining room they had vacated, and set them to work in putting in the furniture. Every day for a week I dropped in to see these worthy recipients of the charity of our donors. I sent the husband to the *maison de santé*, whence he departed two months after, sufficiently relieved to resume his calling and support his family. The mother occupied herself with her needle, while the children were tidy in their appearance, and since have enjoyed the advantages of our public schools.

Of all the good I had agency in, none pleased me in the result more than this. Years have passed; they still remain together in comfortable circumstances. They will instantly recognize this sketch, but, as no one was in the least privy to the circumstances, the liberty I have thus taken with the circumstances can not humiliate them.

In its place I should have noted that the mother called at my house six months afterward, and presented an elaborate and beautifully-worked child's jacket, which she begged me to accept. My patients had many ways of expressing their gratitude after they had recovered health and occupation. One never approached me without the extravagant demonstration of falling on her knees. Some seized my hand and kissed it. A pair of white doves was the present of a young German, whose husband and herself were saved from the epidemic, and who could not express in intelligible language to me her appreciation of my agency. To deal with others at their little shops was equivalent to being presented with what I called for, for they would take no pay, and thus drove me elsewhere. Many requested me to name some article of their handicraft, which they wished to make for me; but, foolish things! if they knew how much I had the advantage of them in the pleasure of bestowing, my debt would ceaselessly remain unpaid.

On the 29th, a genuine New Englander, who said he was not acclimated, and was of that thin habit of body which generally goes through an epidemic of yellow fever, but not cholera, unscathed, presented himself to me, and asked permission to introduce a system of cure for yellow fever that he had tried on several of his friends successfully, the certainty of which he would demonstrate in twenty-four hours if I would allow him some patients. The certain cure for yellow fever may never yet be discovered. All practices have a like ratio of cure, and knowing their partial success, adopted, too, by professional men, I was naturally enough opposed to a new-fangled theory from an amateur which might have cost the life of one patient. In this year one of our most eminent physicians, who is now always called in on consultation of important cases, left the city early, not having saved one patient, and determined not to experiment when his knowledge and experience had failed to produce expected results. I remember being at the hospital one day when a practitioner from another state was accompanied through the wards by the visiting physicians, all acknowledged men of talent, for the purpose of seeing yellow fever. After he had satisfied himself on the diagnostic points, he said, "Gentlemen, being satisfied with an inspection of the article, will you now tell me of the treatment you adopt toward it?" The four M.D.'s were silent, neither assuming that he was addressed. The question was again put without personal direction. At last the boldest of them said, "Do you address yourself, Dr. ——, to me, or to Dr. A., B., or C.; for we each differ in treatment, though, I believe, with average success?"

The year of the great epidemic, a sanitary commission was established to obtain from all tropical points within the yellow fever zone the most eminent testimony respecting the origin and behavior of the disease. A voluminous treatise was the result; but the most important object of the commission was lost sight of in not propounding interrogatories respecting the nature and the success of the different modes of treatment. The book is simply designed to prove that the evil may be prevented, when a trifling addition would enhance its value to the student and general reader by valuable information for its cure.

'A nos moutons. My Yankee enthusiastic, whom I had referred to the physicians, conversed a long time with them, but did not prevail over them. He went off with a leer of disappointment on his hatchet face, as if he had failed in a mighty speculation through the stupidity of others. When he left I was told that he designed to cure the fever by the cold-water system—to plunge in

cold water, cause reaction under blankets, and for ene-
mas and drink nothing but, and plentifully of, cold
water, which, *entre nous*, might be as successful as any
treatment, and is very plausible. From his language
and gait I took him to be a sea-captain ; his manner was
pleasant, while good-humor and shrewdness gleamed in
his countenance. I do not doubt now that the purest
motives of benevolence actuated him, and I regret that
the physicians had not consented to his request. Some
of the most famous cures have been introduced into professional practice by charlatans and quacks who were
ignorant of the specific qualities of their agents, and
why should we be surprised more than the diplomated
when we know that science is built upon nature and experiments?

CHAPTER XVIII.

The Italian Restaurateur.—An afflicted Female.—A Physician and a
Friend.

A SINGULAR complaint was made to me by a patient
in the male ward against an old man, who was one of
the nurses I retained, by his urgent appeals to do so, as
an act of charity, even without pay, and by the promise
not to be caught near where the liquors were stored.
The patient told me that the old man sat on the bench
at the head of the walk between two rows of cots, from
whence, oblivious to every thing else, he watched intently the motions of eight or ten nearest to him, so
much so that he was frequently deaf to raps or calls.
When, however, he discovered any of the sick express
agony in the lineaments of their face or contortions of
limb, he would chuckle audibly, to the great annoyance
of the sufferer and the patient-complainant. Shocked at
such an outrage upon decency, and such desecration of
his service, I stepped aside, unobserved, to watch him.

K.

In a few moments I noticed the old man swiftly sweep with his eyes the range of the cots, when, fixing them upon a frame twitching under convulsions, a smile lit up his face, as if chewing the cud of some sweet fancy. When, in another, black vomit exhibited its fatal prestige, or prostration of muscular force was shown by a patient in attempts to move or to pull the bed-clothes over himself, a grin, sometimes accompanied by a chuckle, was visible in him. I noticed that when he caught the eye of any who was affording this strange delight to him, he would throw his gaze upon another. While he continued abstracted in this idiosyncrasy, I placed myself before him. His countenance immediately exhibited its usual quiet and benevolent expression. I beckoned him to follow me, and, when outside of the room, demanded what he meant by such infamous display of unfeelingness—such contempt for human sympathy.

"I beg your pardon, sir," said he. "I am an old man, and have suffered much in the body and mind. I would not hurt any one's feelings for the world; but, when I reflect upon what poor creatures we are, and what funny objects we make of ourselves when dying and suffering, I can not help laughing at the exhibition I must have made of myself, and what I shall make of myself."

I did not exactly appreciate the philosophy of his indulgence, and told him that I would not discharge him, but would change him to duties where he might enjoy his passion to his heart's content. Accordingly, I put him in the corps of those intrusted with the removal of the dead bodies, giving him exclusive charge of their delivery to the commissary for burying. He proved a willing worker, with grim-visaged death itself to confront. The summer after this, on a visit to the Charity Hospital, I saw him resting his back against one of the bed-posts. He accosted me, saying he had no employment, and, feeling sick, he was admitted, saving to him thereby the expense of board. "Look, Mr. ——, at that man there!" chuckling as formerly, as he drew my attention to a man of about forty years, emaciated by disease, and scarcely able to sit in his chair. "Still at your old vice," I rejoined, and passed on. If ruined hopes and a seared heart are any palliation for such conduct, we should pity rather than execrate him. He applied to me months afterward to recommend him to a situation that he was equal to, and in his garrulity was led to speak of himself and his past life. To me only, he said, he had ever revealed as much; but, as I had done something for him, he wished to show how he had suffered, and wherefore he was worthy of my assistance. He had kept a restaurant at Washington City twenty-six years ago, which was resorted to by Webster, Clay, Calhoun, and Jackson, with whom he pretended intimacy. Like all Italians, industrious and frugal, he accumulated a large fortune. An only daughter of his, who had received an accomplished schooling—his only pride—"his eyes," as he expressed it—was run off and seduced by a villain. Humbled and disheartened, he forthwith retired from business. To suppress grief and mortification, he gambled. In a short time all his wealth was gone. He removed from Washington, and wandered through the larger cities of the Union, officiating as cook, waiter, and nurse ever since. He concluded by saying, "You reprimanded me for laughing at dying people; I laugh at death now, but he does not take his revenge." He has now, though, conquered him, he having passed its portals some years since.

Though business required but little attention, the time I gave to it I desired to be undisturbed, and gave positive orders that no applicant for relief should be directed to my office. It was with some surprise, then, that I learned from those in contiguity to it that a lady had re-

peatedly called to see me within the previous twenty-
four hours, and had refused to seek me at my house. I
remained, awaiting another call from her. Several friends
were chatting with me, when I heard a rap at the door.
It was she. On being informed of my name, she remarked, in French, "I wish to see you, sir, for a few minutes
in private."

"Speak out, madam," I replied; "the gentlemen here
will not understand a word you say."

"What I have to say to you, sir, can not be said now
or here."

By retreating through the doorway she invited me
after her. I closed the door, and told her she might
now, safely and unheard, tell me what I could do for
her. As I approached she continued to retreat, until she
had descended several stairs.

"Pardon me, sir. I can not tell you here what I have
to communicate. Pray oblige me by calling at my
house."

"Is any of your family sick? or perhaps, madam, you
wish to convince me you are in need. Be not over-del-
icate in mentioning your wants. *Is* your family sick or
in distress?"

"No, sir, neither. You can relieve me, though, from
much misery. I again pray you to call on me. My
name is Mad. ——, in —— Street."

"Enough, madam. I do not know your motive for
all this mystery, but I see you are earnest. As your
residence is far off, I will take it in my round of visits
this afternoon."

She begged me to be punctual, and left.

Her appearance and language indicated the woman of
good-breeding and active intelligence. Her brow was
alternately knit and relaxed. The restless eye spoke to
me of intense mental suffering, endeavoring to be relieved
by something to divert the agonizing thought from her-

self. Had I been told she was insane, I should have been confirmed in the belief. Her frame was *en bon point*, her complexion ruddy with the glow of health. It was remarkable in her that she did not remain still or quiet an instant, either moving her limbs as though with an uneasy-fitting dress, or engaged with her hands in arranging her cape, or pressing a handkerchief to her neck and bosom. As it was an exceeding warm day, this restlessness I attributed to no other cause, but is explained otherwise in the sequel.

I was later to my appointment than I had fixed upon. Indeed, I thought some play was intended upon my sympathies by a home manifestation of want which did not really exist. A faint suspicion at one time possessed me that, from the obscurity of the place, an evil design was in waiting. "*Jacta est alea,*" as an apophthegm, has always sustained me under apprehension; so, trusting to the guidance of the cab-driver, I was ready for the *dénouement*. To my knock at the gate a lad of twelve years made his appearance. He said his mother was near by, and if I would wait a while he would go for her. On the side to the entrance of the house was a plateau of Bermuda and cocoa grass in beautiful luxuriance, flanked by rose-bushes and spreading fig-trees. Vines of different kinds were intermixed, and formed a complete shade to the gallery, the steps to which, and the floor, showed habitual handiwork from the polish thereon. The door was shortly opened, and a servant invited me within. I endeavored to learn something of my mysterious applicant by scanning the furniture and ornaments of the rooms. They were neatly furnished with what every one considers merely necessary to mediocrity of pursuit. An escritoire with shelves contained a select library of miscellaneous and historical works, while some pendent shelves were filled with lighter reading, all in French. On the walls were hung several

large engravings, which, by the twilight of the room, I
judged were more prized for the subject illustrated than
for their linear excellence. I had not time to pursue
investigation farther, as a rustling in the passage announced the approach of my applicant.

"Madam, you are a mystery; please now unravel
yourself;" on saying which, I advanced toward her and
extended my hand. Of this she took no notice, but,
stepping back to a rocking-chair, pointed to me a seat
near where I was standing. I advanced the chair toward her, and again stretched out my hand. To my
surprise and chagrin, she not only held hers back, but,
to make the rejection of any such familiarity more pointed, placed both of hers behind her back. A little miffed,
I remarked that perhaps she had changed her mind with
regard to seeing me. "Oh no, sir," said she; "first hear
all, and my conduct will explain itself."

First shutting the door, she resumed her seat in the
rocking-chair; then, bending over her hands, sighed as
if she strove to master her feelings for the proposed development. I again arose from my chair to advance,
and urge her to unburden herself of this strange affliction. No sooner did she see me again erect, than, apprehensive of my approach, she sprang from her seat, and
with fearful gestures, as if keeping off some monster of
the brain, extended her arms, and in a solemn theatrical
and decisive tone cautioned me not to move a step farther. Immediately the thought electrically flashed upon
me that she was insane, and that, knowing the periodical visit of the paroxysm, she had invited me to see it
and meet the consequences. My first impulse was that
of the cat, which instinctively fixes upon an outlet for
retreat before a threatened danger is encountered. Beside me was an open window. In my mind I had meas-
ured the facility of clearing it, and awaited the least
demonstration of approach on her part. She maintained

her ground, I mine. I can not compute the time by minutes when there were hours of nightmare horrors presented to me in an encounter with a woman under such influence, and in her own house. At length she sat down, and bade me do the same, saying if I remained still she would explain all.

I now found myself at comparative ease, but, for fear of awakening some latent feeling, or touching some chord which would reproduce the excitement in a more startling form, I was as dumb and fixed as a statue. She began:

"Mr. ——, when I determined to see you, I knew of you from many whom you have attended during their sickness. I saw that your goodness of heart was such that you can sympathize as well as pity. I will now tell you of my peculiar distress; but first, sir, excuse me if, with the great horror that I have for my complaint, and exposure of it to others, I think proper to require of you a solemn promise not to divulge to any one what I am about to relate to you."

The mystery thickened with the confidence and flattery. I could not rid myself of the impression that she was laboring under some hallucination. I concluded that, as I was in the play, I must take the cue accordingly, and emphatically and without reservation gave her my word of honor that I would forget all she told me as soon as I left her house.

"Then, sir, we understand each other. If you look around at the appointments of this house, your inference would be that its mistress is endowed with a taste for and a habit of cleanliness. Indeed, sir, the luxury of cleanliness is no less attractive to me personally than the necessity of it, as one of my parents died from a cutaneous disease, and I always feared to inherit it. I determined, when it should show itself upon me, that if I did not succeed in destroying it in its incipiency, I would swallow laudanum, and thus conceal my shame from the world and my husband. Last week my husband left town, to be absent on business for two or three weeks. On the night before last I could not sleep on account of a pricking sensation over my whole body. In the morning I found I had so tortured my flesh that hard lumps appeared here and there, which later in the day became of a bruised color, with increased and continued irritability. Ashamed to see a physician, I consulted a medical work which I bought, and have dosed myself until I am feverish from the effects. From feeling no relief, I thought I must be mistaken in the disease, and determined to see you and ask you to devise some way that a physician could examine into the symptoms so that I should not be identified by him or any one else. No one sees me—no one shall see me until this dreaded disease is destroyed. I have to keep my son at a distance from me, for fear of giving to him the disease by contact. This is unhappiness to me, as he has but a short time of vacation to remain with me. What is more dreadful than any thing is meeting with my husband, who can but repel me as a mass of corruption. Am I not miserable? am I not to be pitied?" She threw herself in a posture of distress, and sobbed and wept.

A thousand reflections passed through my brain. When I saw before me a robust frame, and cheeks flushed with health, complaining of a loathsome disease, I was disposed to think her hypochondriac. Pretending to treat her statement with levity, as proceeding from a disordered brain, I again advanced, with a determination to put an end to the farce and my farther apprehensions, and said I would send her a physician on whom she might rely with the fullest confidence, at the same time again offering my hand, hoping that, as I persisted in taking her by the hand, she would be impressed with the folly of her suspicion that she was afflicted with a contagious disease. Upon her again repelling this act of politeness, I took up my hat and was about leaving the room, when she hurried between me and the door, and, with her back against it, begged me "not to leave her to despair."

At the agonizing tone of the words I halted, and, obedient to the significant motion of her hand, again seated myself. In my experience of distressed humanity I have seen much madness, and its twin-sister delirium. Being acquainted with the form or nature of it, whether proceeding from complete derangement of the mind or temporal, as in fever or dissipation, I could be sufficiently guarded against its freaks. This case presented no clew to divine the seat or cause of it. I saw she was determined to have a disease whether or no. Her position at the door satisfied me that she would use force to convince me; and, if I did not expect to survive to record this adventure, it was because the atmosphere of her presence was electric and subduing, as are said to be the vapors that reach the sense within the hissing sound of the rattlesnake. I again seated myself, when she resumed her confidence in a calmer tone.

"A few words, and I am done," she said. "I must apologize to you for this display of feeling, but I could not help it. I will check myself hereafter. Approach to the window with me and look at these blotches on my arms; as they are here, so are they over all my body. Oh! sir, what will cure them? Can you not bring your physician to your office in the course of an hour? I shall there be unknown, as I shall be completely veiled; and, for the sake of a woman's happiness, think not of me afterward."

During the whole time she was speaking she was writhing with pain, as she had commenced to scratch one part affected, which gave her an itching for irritating her whole body in the same way. I thought her com-

K 2

plaint was a very common one, though in a progressed
stage, and asked her if she was not in the habit of lying
down on the inviting grass before her gallery. Mistak-
ing my question for insult or derision, she turned upon
me a scornful look, remarking that she took me for a
gentleman, and that she would have her husband cowhide me when he came to town. She was about leaving by the door opposite the one I entered, when I followed, acting her part over again by placing myself
against the door, with the remark that she must be as
patient with me as I with her. "Sir, you can add no
more to the mean, ungentlemanly insinuations you have
made; so what more have you to say?"

"This, madam, that there is an insect which is termed the *bête rouge*, which infests grasses in this country,
the bite or entrance of which into the skin will produce
precisely the same marks from irritation which you have
now on your body. It was for this I asked you if you
were in the habit of sitting on the grass."

She studied a while, and then said, "Are you certain?"

I told her it was in my experience, and that, if she
would produce me some sweet-oil, I would charm away
all sensations of itching and pain. She looked rather
credulous, passed me, and returned with a bottle of sweet-
oil. With her handkerchief she applied it to her arms.
In the mean time I was looking upon the horizon, rev-
eling in the anticipation of immoderate laughter should
it turn out as I expected. In a few minutes she said
she thought she felt so much relieved that she must abruptly leave me to make the application on her body,
and, if successful, nothing would prevent an early acknowledgment of her gratitude, and ample amends for
the harsh language she had applied to me.

Has it ever been one's *good* luck to be shot at and
missed, or to be singled out in safety from an explosion

or shipwreck? Such a one may properly appreciate my feelings in escaping the dreadful suspense I was in while confronting a woman whom I supposed mad, to which may be added the comfortable assurance that her husband would cowhide me for a supposed insult. I resolved thereafter not to be led into such slippery places; that yellow fever and cholera were specialties of wide enough range for relief; and that, if any more confidence cases presented themselves to me likely to invite scenes as in the foregoing, I would at once refer them to the physician or the priest. I took French leave, jumped into my cab, and threw myself back with a long breath, revolving all the circumstances in my mind, a feeling of mortification at being misapprehended overcoming every other, until I saw our physician's gig standing before a house a little ahead. Then I prepared myself for a treat in disclosing the whole of this eventful evening. Without mentioning her name to him, I thought myself fully justified by the suffering I had undergone, and by the extinction of her fears of the supposed disease, to waive the solemnity of my promise of secrecy. It was replete with scenes too rich to be chuckled over in private or without the zest of companionship. Sending my cab ahead, I took a seat with him; and, what with his interruptions by laughter and comments, before the *dénouement* was closed I was fully repaid for the mental suffering I had experienced.

About three weeks after this, curiosity prompted me to drive out of my way some squares to pass the house of my *bête rouge* afflictant. She was sitting by a window, and beckoned me to stop. With the liveliest emotions of joy and expressions of gratitude upon seeing me, she recapitulated the adventure of that evening, portraying more minutely and amusingly my embarrassment than I have her hallucination. She said that, when she became satisfied that I had correctly stated the cause of

her annoyance and its remedy, she was bold in communicating her fears and her cure to her neighbors.   In one
thing I had presumed upon, she said, which gave her
then excitable mind a suspicion of my frivolity or disposition to insult her, I was mistaken.   The *bêtes rouges* had
not invaded her person from sitting or lying on the
grass, but from the bed-linen, which she was in the habit of having daily aired upon it.

A melancholy connection hangs to this reminiscence.
The same physician who had enjoyed with me its relation met me on the same night at a late hour at the club.
When it lay in my way, I generally resorted there to
pick up the news of the day.   One was always sure to
find three or more habitués, who lingered out the early
watches of the night in social talk in preference to being
tossed on a sleepless pillow in a solitary room, disturbed
by sad thoughts on the devastation the epidemic was
making among their friends.   It was a pleasant relaxation from my duties, and time flew, as did the Champagne, as each would add his quota of talk for its enjoyment.   Aside from all, Dr. —— and I again brought up
the night's adventure and similar professional ones.   It
was the only night during a long reign of gloom that
joy held entire sway over me, not to the prejudice of
my patients, for I had left nothing unattended to either
at the infirmary or outside.   It was a night, though, as I
have intimated, pregnant to me of mournful result and
of bitter memories, as I believe the indulgence to an
early hour hastened the development of the seeds of yellow fever in our estimable physician.   He was counseled by myself and others not to overtax his energies in
his duties, as it was his first season among us.   His ar-
dor, quickened by more than proportionate success, knew
no relaxation.   He was indefatigable in acquainting himself with every phase of the disease in every patient, and
even visited the infirmary between times to mark the

progress of cure there. Having at his command a ve-
hicle for his visits, it can not be said that physical exertion hastened his attack. It rather resulted from exposure to the night air and the unwholesome odors that
hung around the patients. On the morning after our
chat I received a note from a relative of his advising of
his illness. From day to day, the reports of him being
favorable, I looked for his return to usefulness. To the
surprise of the patient himself—for he and his physician
coincided in early convalescence—the disease assumed
suddenly a dangerous type. His natural cheerfulness
of disposition overcame the fear of death. He knew his
end was near, and became resigned to his fate. On the
fourth day of his illness he rapidly passed away.

The storied urn and high-capped monument mark to
gazing gossipers the renown of the son of Mars or of
Minerva. A far more precious emblem of worth is pictured in the quivering tear that tells of the full soul
brimming over with sadness for the loss of one dearly
cherished. It is of thought and feeling eternal. The
painful regrets from those whom our physician had been
so sedulous to save bordered on canonization. Their
hearts were full of gratitude and love for one who blend-
ed the graces of a polished exterior with professional
skill and a sympathizing heart, which identified him
with the family whose threshold he crossed.

Like the best of his profession, he was unassuming in
his manners, proud of success, and grateful for the acknowledgment. He was too young a practitioner to be
known among the old population; but time, which
eventually discovers talent in any profession, promised
in him the full fruits of renown. The humble and the
poor would have pushed him to enviable notoriety, as a
successful practice among them has always proved to be
its harbinger. Talent is at such a high premium now-
adays that the measure of it in any one is his practice.

The world will not allow the light to be hid under the bushel. Parlor influence may give an ephemeral fashionable notoriety to a lawyer or physician, but one can hardly go astray in his selection of either if he notices well the docket of the court or the constant employment of the physician.

The rich materials of a soul like our friend's, at once so manly and so kind, were gradually developed as he gained the confidence of his patients. As they received him, so did he conduct himself. His reservedness would relax with their opening confidence, and, as they became convalescent, a jest or joke, uttered with a laughter-provocative spirit, caused them to look eagerly for future visits. We lingered around the sick-bed together, where I witnessed the good cheer his company imparted. I here regret that, in the exclusion of all names from my narrative, I can not mention his in testimony of the regard in which he was held, and as a tribute due to his name and his services.

CHAPTER XIX.

The Dead-house.—The wrong Corpse.—Our Clerk.—Music for the Sick.—Frightened to Death.—The Maskers.

THE commissary charged with the removal of the dead bodies from the infirmary was in the habit of throwing wide open the doors between the street and the room where they were kept, for the purpose of obtaining both air and light. Morning after morning I noticed a gradual increase to a curious crowd, waiting to see the dead coffined, until it numbered over thirty persons. From the balcony above I overheard mutterings among them against the men employed for their want of humanity and decency in their careless way of slinging the corpse into the coffin, and in putting others in regardless of the falling off of a sheet, which was always wrapped around each when carried below. One morning, when the carts drove off with twelve or fourteen corpses, hootings of disapprobation were made. The morning following at least fifty persons assembled, who were excited by the rumor that disrespect was shown the dead. There are some occupations in their nature repulsive, which require a peculiar organization. To reason with men whose feelings are blunted by such pursuits, or to expect them to conform to our ideas of propriety, is preposterous. They could see nothing wrong or shameful in what they had done. Fearing a demonstration thereafter, which would reflect alike upon all, I had the bodies put into coffins immediately after death.

While on the subject of corpses, I am reminded of an incident about this time which, though some may smile upon as a solemn joke, irritated and annoyed me exceedingly. It was the duty of the clerk, when so required by the friends of a patient, to give them written notice of the latter's death, that they might assemble for his interment. To guard against oversight in such an important matter, he noted opposite the name of the patient the residence of the friend applying, which he was sure to observe on entering the death. One day the clerk, feeling sick, had gone home, leaving the cupper to attend to his duty for him until the next morning. That evening a patient died who was noted " to be buried by his friends." The attendant not being instructed in this particular, the corpse was coffined and taken away with others by the commissary early on the morrow. At 8 o'clock the clerk returned to duty, and saw the error which had been committed. He informed me of it, and asked my advice in the premises. I could give him none, but told him he must get out of the scrape the best way he could, and notified him that, if a complaint was made of this unfeeling negligence, I should be forced,

though reluctantly, to discharge him.   The day after I
learned that he had notified the friends of the deceased
that the corpse awaited their disposition.   A mahogany
coffin was sent by them to hold the respected remains.
At 5 o'clock P.M. fifteen or twenty persons attended,
with a hearse and carriages, to pay the last tribute of respect to their friend.   The clerk in the mean while had
placed in the coffin the corpse of some stranger, and well
secured it down to prevent the gaze of any who might
be curious to look for the last time on him they bewail-
ed.   The name of the dead who was thus treated with
funeral rites, while the proper one lies roughly coffined
in a ditch, the register saith not.

Ever after this occurrence the clerk was faithfully
particular in all he had to do.   When the infirmary was
opened he was employed on the recommendation of an
associate, under whose nursing and care himself, wife,
and four children had been safely carried through the
epidemic.   He was born on the Rhine, fluently spoke
French and German, and was proficient in the dead languages.   His knowledge of English was confined to a
few phrases which we taught him, such as to ask the patient's name, age, and place of nativity.   As nearly all
visitors and sick spoke either French or German, he had
seldom occasion to speak any other language.   When,
however, he did not understand the English spoken to
him, he pointed to written notices hung in the entry,
such as "No admittance to any but city officials except
between the hours of 12 and 1."   The forty dollars per
month he received was a God-send to his delighted family.   Though he kept the register in a beautiful German
text, and studied to be correct, he made laughable errors
in Germanizing English or Irish names.   Curran was
Kerchen, and Smith Schmidt.   Here and there he showed his Latinity by writing after the names of some admitted, "*in articulo mortis*," of which, by-the-by, there

were eleven who died before they were placed in their cots; and when an applicant was too low to give his real or assumed name, he was entered pedantically as *nomen ignotum.*

A company of firemen, headed by a band of music which discoursed lively airs, passed the infirmary on their return from a funeral. I marked the effect upon the patients. Those at all susceptible of appreciation from convalescence drank in the sweet sounds with evident delight. One patient, who had an incorrigible habit of sitting up in bed, to his ultimate injury, lifted himself on his elbows and bowed his head in unison with the time, and expressed his entertainment by a ghastly grin. To many, whose only perfect senses were sight and hearing, the music must have called up associations of health and better days, thus breaking the gloom of fatal presentiments. As music not only promotes cheerfulness and elasticity of spirits, but, according as the chord is struck, is soothing in its effects, it is worthy of suggestion in the treatment of mental hallucination, and of all conditions where the nervous system is deranged.

The peculiar bent of the mind toward habitual pursuits or ruling passion is singularly exhibited by some in a state of delirium. A man who had been a cobbler employed his last moments in going through the motions of sewing an imaginary shoe between his knees, drawing out his arms to the full length where the thread should have been adjusted. Another rapidly quoted verses from a language foreign to his own, while others manifested the extremes of fear or anger at imaginary objects, using most pitiful lamentations or impious and indecent oaths. The former were tractable; the latter required to be closely watched against violence to themselves or others.

A young Frenchman of genteel appearance and address, who was convalescent, determined, against all re-

monstrance, to leave the infirmary a day or two before
it was prudent for him to do so. He had shaken hands
with us at the door, and was about getting into a cab,
when a lady entered on a visit of inquiry for some acquaintance within. Having recognized her, he saluted
her. She looked intently at him for a while to revive
her recollection of him. He mentioned his name. Upon
hearing which, she stepped back with a theatrical gesture, placing both hands upon his shoulders to scrutinize
him still closer. Astonishment was classically depicted
on her countenance. "What! Charles ——? Is it really *you*, Charles? Oh! my *dear* friend, you look like a
corpse." The young man was exceedingly feeble. Her
pressure upon his shoulders, and the confirmation of
what we had endeavored to persuade him, clothed in
such frightful sympathy, overpowered his remaining
strength. He sought a chair near to him, and, without
replying to her, sank upon it, gasping from agitation.
The female was likewise shocked when she was informed of the likely effects of such imprudent language, and,
in continuous accents of self-reproach and commiseration
for his state, walked up and down the entry until she
saw him carried up stairs to be replaced in the cot he
had left. So finely strung is the organization in convalescence that any sudden excitement of mind is attended with fatal results. He rapidly sank that night,
and was carried away by his friends in the morning for
interment.

   In the female division were two women near to each
other who had been acquaintances before admission.
They were often checked by the nurses for their frequent conversation. While engaged near them one day
I overheard them commenting upon the feelings which
possessed them when they visited this house for a dance,
and those different ones necessarily imposed upon them
in their present condition. Their remarks were pithy,

and were not immediately replied to, the long pause between implying to me that many more thoughts were passing through their minds than they gave utterance to.

"Any how, Mary," said one, "I'll bet you'll come to a ball here if you once get out."

"Ah! Jane, how could you think so of me? Could I ever forget the dead people I have seen here, and wouldn't their ghosts haunt me if I break my vow to Father L.?"

There is no such reformer as contrast. The painful moans and sighs that filled the hours of the night; the sight of disease in every gradation from the furious onslaught to quiet convalescence or complete prostration; the devotional preparations for another sphere of existence, naturally enough made the visitor or invalid shrink within himself when he dwelt upon the midnight dissipations which he witnessed in the same spot on former occasions; for here had been held the orgies of ribald wassailers, whose actions and language mocked every sense of virtue or decency, disfiguring humanity with the loathsomeness of hell. Here, where fiends gloated over their harvest of impurity, could now be found the tearful aspirations of the dying soul in communion with its God. The invocation of saints and angels, which now dispensed its sweet influence in establishing hope, was in strange contrast to the imprecations and hate which possessed the desperate fallen ones who once whirled through the room in a mad show of merriment.

This hall of revelry had always been the resort of the lowest class in bestial indulgence. The common antipathies to amalgamation with people of color, which, in broad day, would bring a blush of shame to the hardest cheek in this latitude, were, perhaps from that fact, more fiercely hugged here. It was the crowning pleasure to the day's infamy of the low gambler, the loafer, and the thief; and, if police reports speak truthfully, it was a

trap to catch the villain, as well as a rendezvous to plot
mischief and murder. There are some men who are not
content to learn human nature in all its phases through
the anathemas pronounced upon crime, or from the written experiences of others. These, fearless of losing reputation or life for a sometimes dangerous as well as
censurable curiosity, push their inquiries and observations through every haunt of vice; but, clad in the armor
of self-control and virtue, pass all unscathed, and leave
with confirmed disgust. With an earlier insight of such
resorts, it was not with this intent that I proposed to an
associate member a visit to a dance which took place in
the Globe three months after the epidemic had disappeared, and when the town was full of eager harpies
and hungry harlots. It was a visit to contrast the extremes of wild life with the associations of past misery.
Being known to the proprietor, and guided by him
through the apartments, which were now filled with a
tumultuous sound of voices, suffocating fumes of heated
liquor, and an atmosphere that dimmed the view, from
the dust which the rapid waltz raised from the floor, we
felt assured of our safety. Without such a protector,
respectability unmasked would be the certain forerun-
ner of disturbance and danger. We would have been
hustled out as spies or dumb reproachers of excesses we
would not indulge in. We had not promenaded half
the length of the room when we were surrounded by a
motley crew of female maskers, addressing us by name,
who joked on the use made of certain parts of it and
other localities, which convinced me that some, if not
all, had their experience to prompt them. Passing from
these, we walked to the bar, which was kept in the room
that had been appropriated by us to those in the last
stage of black vomit or of delirium. Here we were followed by many others, with quick ears to catch our comments or remarks. As we complied with the politeness

of the proprietor to drink with him, the women continued their jests, and inquired if we remembered who lay in such and such a part of the room.

"Do you remember who lay in a cot *just there?*" said one, as I again entered the ball-room, and pointing to the spot.

"Indeed I do not," I replied.

"You do not remember the girl who had one side of her head shaved to have a poultice put upon a boil?"

"I have now a faint recollection, if she remained long sick. Was it you?"

"It was, and I am now entirely well. I used to come to these balls frequently years back; but I resolved, after being sick here, never to enter the place again. I came, though, to-night, not to dance or to amuse myself, but to see the place I suffered so much in; to see people dancing where I have prayed, and where I have seen so much misery; and I came here to confirm me stronger in my reform and in my hate."

"You are, then, the girl who made a vow on leaving the infirmary never to enter this room again?"

"No, sir; but I expect it is the one who lay in a cot beside me—the one whom you heard bet that she would not come here again."

"Has she?"

"I fear she has, for we were to have seen each other frequently; but, being unable to find a place, as I have done, she suspended her visits to me, and intimated on parting that, to pay her board, she had but one resort. But come, sir. The sight of you to-night is to me as if God sent you to keep me in the right path. Come, sir, and let me thank you, and drink to your health in a glass of wine. Do me this favor; come."

We all returned to the bar. By this time the scowling looks of men who knew not of us or of our intents, and who could not conjecture the extraordinary attention paid to us by the female maskers, gave us some apprehensions of a disturbance from a prolonged stay. Quietly complying with the grateful compliment of the reformed one, we passed rapidly through the crowd of dancers.

The dark stains of black vomit were yet perceptible on the floors. I missed, though, the marks of spittle which blackened the walls, and which nothing short of frequent whitewashing could entirely obliterate, when we vacated the house.

As is my wont, I do not intrude myself upon the notice or acknowledgment of a patient after the relief has been complete. Jane or others may assume it to be haughtiness, or contradictory to the interest previously taken in them. Their convictions do not trouble me so much as would be the annoyance to me of reiterated thanks for a service which I have enjoyed more in fulfilling than they can possibly feel in receiving. I passed Jane weekly, for several months after the epidemic, in company with children she had in charge, when a look of recognition —nothing more—was exchanged. One Sunday morning she met me in the market, and, stopping me, introduced me to a young man, whose arm she had, as her husband, at the same time making a complimentary remark of me. I have no doubt she was much surprised afterward to meet with an averted look whenever we met. The recent epidemic of 1858 again brought me to her rescue from want, which service may have altered her previous conclusions, but leaves her still in ignorance of the cause of my indifference to her when established in health.

CHAPTER XX.

Les Gardes Malades.—The C. Family.—Gamblers and Gambling.

WITH all the remedial agents which wealth can command for the comfort of the yellow-fever patient, directed by the most skillful practitioner, the issue hangs by a thread unless a discreet and experienced nurse is in attendance. The faultless administering of the physician's prescriptions; a watchful attention to the apparently simple wants and necessities of the patient; the studied corrective resistance to a sudden change in the atmosphere or to a fluctuation of pulse, are among the most prominent reliant assurances of success. A slight omission or disregard of either has baffled the calculation of the most experienced physician, and diverted him in his after remedial appliances. For many years, during epidemics, I have had at my bidding several colored nurses, whose assiduous care of the sick has been markedly successful. When my sympathies were strongly roused to save for society the useful or intelligent, I have invariably employed one of these either to nurse the case through or superintend a less experienced one. In fact, so much more is required of a nurse in yellow fever than in other diseases, that the attendance of an experienced one is a better guarantee of early convalescence than even the frequent visits of the physician. Their services are properly estimated by the handsome remuneration of as high as ten dollars per day.

Their passion for usefulness is accompanied, too, with a love for gossip and anecdote, which, timely indulged in, is extremely agreeable to the convalescent. Their knowledge of the condition and standing of the resident pop-

ulation is always reliable.   Their suspicion of the status
of any is the shadow of coming developments.   The
greater number of these are free and intelligent, rarely
associating with slaves—indeed, heartily despising those
who are not "smart enough," like themselves, to purchase their freedom.   Though they are exorbitant in
their demands as nurses, when their feelings are enlisted by the respectability of an applicant unable to
pay, their services are given gratuitously.   To every
confidence they are faithful.   To me they have been of
especial service in preventing and discovering impositions on the association which otherwise would have
succeeded with specious grace.   I found, on close examination of their reports, that their assembled wisdom
rarely failed to fathom the truth from more than manifest inferences.

At noon on the 20th of August, one of these, whom I
shall present as Eugenia, called upon me to say that in
an adjoining house to that of a patient she was attending lived a lady with a very sick child, who requested
her to carry a message to me to visit her.   She said the
lady had two slaves, appeared to be in good circumstances, and was married, she supposed, to a gentleman
who left the house every day at noon, not returning
during the day.   She did not know what the lady wanted, but cautioned me against imposition in the matter,
for she had diligently sought for particular information
of them, but could elicit nothing, either from the servants or neighbors, to form an opinion of their character,
and judged that the former had been properly cautioned to keep their counsel.   Having nothing imperative
at that moment to attend to, I followed her to the house.
As it were by instruction, Eugenia opened the door
which fronted on the street and ushered me into the parlor, when she went to the back room to announce my
presence to the mistress.

The apartment I was in indicated comfort and competency. The furniture was of a tasteful selection, without being extravagant or pretentious. On the centre-table lay gilt-edged books, surrounding a vase of magnolias and roses, which filled the atmosphere with their delicious fragrancy. The caution of Eugenia, though considerate, was unkind, as here none could be convinced or suspect that pecuniary relief was desired by the mistress of such elegant taste and expensive gratifications. While the mantle-clock was vociferously ticking the fleeting seconds, and I was conjecturing for what purpose I was called in, Eugenia appeared at the door and beckoned me to the next room. The side of a bed, with the musquito-bar drawn, was within a few steps of me. A table at the foot was covered with phials, mixtures, and the paraphernalia of a sick-room. My first impulse was to lift the bar. As I did so, I saw a lady on the other side of the bed, bending over a child. When she recognized me, "Ah!" said she, "you are Mr. ——? I am so glad to see you. How kind in you to call! This way," she continued, as she left the bedside to meet me. Upon taking her outstretched hand, I remarked that she could command my service, but that I feared little would be accomplished by me, as I learned she had a physician, and as I saw that she was in a condition entirely above the ordinary objects of our care.

"I know you attend exclusively to the poor sick," she said. "You may be of as much service to me, though, as to them. I have all, as you say, for comfort apparently, yet I am poor in being alone in the world, knowing nobody here, and suffering the anguish of a mother with an only child at the point of death. Let me not entirely despair. Dr. —— says he can not live. Give me some better assurance. For God's sake, save him—save me. Come and look at him."

The curtain of the window was drawn aside that a

L

better view of the little sufferer could be had. He was
about five years old, with long yellow hair, sedulously
curled. His skin was hot and dry, and his breath felt
upon my cheeks as if charged with volcanic heat. I do
not remember an adult whose breath was more impregnated with acidity. He was not asleep, but in a stupor,
regarding us through his half-closed eyelids as if he
doubted our presence. His mother aroused him by
smoothing across his forehead a cloth saturated with
cold scented water, saying,

"Horace, my dear son, don't you feel better now?"

"Oh, ma, I feel *so* sick. Won't you give me something, ma?"

"My dear child, what *can* I give you? another spoon-
ful of your sirup?"

"Oh no, it is *so* nasty. Won't pa come home soon?"

If the reader has witnessed Miss Heron, as Camille,
depict the agony of a contemplated separation from Ar-
mand at the entreaty of his father, he can better imagine
than I can describe the effort to suppress emotions which
seemed to tap the very heart of its life-blood. The painful contraction of the brow, the closed eyes, the compressed lips, and hands clasped on the forehead as if she
feared her reason would be unseated, told of some mystery hidden under these last words of her child which
tears might relieve if they could be bidden. With a
convulsive quivering of the head and a long, deep sigh,
she struggled with her feelings, and, turning suddenly
from me, dropped on a cushioned stool by the bedside.
I seated myself and waited several minutes for her to
break the silence. I at last remarked to her that Eugenia should divide her time between the patient next
door and her boy. She replied that a nurse would be
in her way, as she would not leave the side of her son
while he was sick. "I am distressed, sir," she continued, "for him, to be sure; but this is not all. There is

yet something, which is almost as great as this affliction, which oppresses me. I ask a relief which will be strange to you to grant, and which is as important to my poor boy's recovery as it is to my future peace and happiness. Will you please to listen to me?"

I nodded acquiescence. After again cooling the feverish brow of her child, she thus delivered herself, hesitating between each sentence as if to secure attention and to make her revelations more distinct.

"I shall be brief, sir, and explicit. I am the *wife* of one whose whole soul is enlisted in the idle indulgence of play. We are both of respectable parentage in Tennessee. I had pledged my affections to my husband long before I knew of his habits, and, when I surprised him by questioning the fact, in the true nobleness of his nature he begged me not to think of him more—to strive to forget him; for, as sure as he knew himself, he was certain that the inveteracy of his passion for play would ruin both him and me. My woman's nature for an early love, my devotion to a man who was otherwise honorable before the world, my appreciation of sentiments which had often fallen from his lips and made me proud of the soul that gave them birth, overcame all consequences from being the companion of his fate. Ay, as I loved him, my fancy pictured the joy of recovering him. We married. As an earnest of reformation, after a bridal tour of a few months he opened an office for the pursuit of his profession. His impatient spirit could not brook the tardy patronage of the law, and in a village where oppression and strife had no foothold. He determined to accept my father's proposition to engage in farming. The means he could command, with mine, would purchase us just such a farm as we wanted. Day after day it was talked over, but nothing conclusive. In the mean time, I gloried in being able to wean him from his old habit. One evening I was anxiously awaiting his return, as he had been absent for the first time so long after dinner, when my father entered my room, and, seeing me in tears, inquired the cause. He misinterpreted my fears of my husband's old passion into an alarm for his safety, and forthwith set out to engage a neighbor to hunt up the absent one. They traced my husband to a tavern some miles distant, where, unobserved, they perceived him, surrounded by strange faces, betting on cards. They returned, and my father sorrowfully informed me of the fact. He had known, however, so little of my husband's habits that he expressed himself satisfied that it could only be a frolic, of which he would repent at leisure. After a harrowing watchfulness until midnight, I heard his footsteps as he approached the room. I had made up my mind to refrain from reproaches. I knew him so well that I was satisfied that submission to his pleasure was the greatest earnest I had for a reformation in him.

"When he entered the room he threw down his coat in a careless manner, and feelingly reprimanded me for sitting up so late for him, while he, as he said, was merely enjoying himself with some old friends. I inferred that, at any rate, he was not a loser by his indulgence. After breakfast the next morning he proposed a walk in the grove near the house. There he confessed to me that he had heard of the arrival of some gamblers, and, full of his former infatuation, he stifled all better reflections and hurried to meet them. They loaned him money to bet, and closed the game only when they thought he was so much involved that he could pay no more. On that night one half of my dowry had been pledged and lost. When all this was confessed, as much as I might have dreaded poverty, so much was I wrapped in his fate, his happiness and honor were uppermost. I had yet hopes of his reformation, and was glad to show him my magnanimity. I did not upbraid, but told him

we could easily spare the amount. That day he informed my father that he would part from him the next, and
settle in New Orleans, where he intended to establish
himself. My dowry was paid over, the gamblers satisfied, and we started for this city. All this may be necessary to state to you, that I may command your confidence and assistance."

She arose from her seat, and, after arranging the bed-
clothes around her restless child, she relieved herself
from the exhaustion of this hurried narrative by a glass
of iced water. For a few moments she stood before me,
with intent gaze upon the floor, as if combating with
some reproachful idea that possessed her, when she continued:

"I may as well go on now and tell the whole. You
are a gentleman, and will too well appreciate my motives for such disclosure to despise me for the act. And
now for what I mainly desired your counsel and assistance. You have concluded that my husband is hopelessly lost in gambling. I feel it and I know it. This,
though, to his credit, I must tell you, that if he hugs the
vice, he despises the rude association with gamblers as
he does his own infatuation by it. To its alluring hopes
through their ministry he daily bewails his loss of self-
respect. He found himself in the Maëlstrom of its bitter end, but preserved intact all other ennobling traits;
among these, a devotion and love to myself and child
that more than divided his thoughts with his passion.
Some incidents lately, however, have made me suspicious
that the world in which I live—for this my house is the
limit of it—is invaded. When he comes home he is not
as communicable as he was wont. His endearing expressions have subsided into commonplace. Our little
boy, who was the life of every hour that he spared at
home from his play, ceased to make his prattle forgetful
of our bitter existence; and now, that our child is pros-

trated by a fatal sickness, when I should most expect
that a sacrifice of other objects should bring him home,
his stay with us has diminished. I can come to no other conclusion than that some one else possesses his affections, or that I have lost them. To be sure, he shows
anxiety for our son by inquiries of the physician, whom
he meets elsewhere, and reports to me the conference.
He even sits by his bedside with the hand of Horace
clasped in his, but not a word to me—not one word.
As he was about to depart this morning, not to return
again until midnight, I remarked to him how miserable
we should surely be if Horace were to die. With an
oath, accompanied by a stamp of his foot, and such a
look of despair or hate, I dare not say which, he muttered through his teeth, 'It were better, then, that you follow him,' and left the room precipitately. Now, sir, if it
is not impertinent in one who feels she stands almost
alone, can I rest on your confidence and advice? Can
you *say* or *do* any thing to relieve me, either to dispel
my suspicions or to bring my husband home to my affections?"

I saw she had finished, and hazarded to withdraw my
eyes from the wall, upon which they were fixed during
the recital. Tears happily came to her relief, and rolled
from her eyes unaccompanied by a sob or moan. Perhaps she was mastering herself for some comfort she expected from me in reply. My conclusions were rapidly
drawn. Had I not been in a sick-room, the smile of in-
credulity that partially displayed itself on my countenance would have swelled into a loud laugh, and would
have better convinced her of the sincerity of my conviction than I could by reasoning with her. As it was, I
told her that imaginary evils alone possessed her; that
she must allow her husband to be affected by such a
prospect as she had depicted to him of her son's death
in a different manner from her. I concluded by saying

that her long experience of his heart, their mutual ardent affection, their fixedness of interest in one fate, and entire exclusion of participants in feeling or friendship for so long a period, forbade any such suspicions, that, like bats, brooded through the darkness of her sad visitation. "Besides," I continued, "how much good soever may be produced by my investigation, you are proposing to me a dangerous and disgraceful service. To be a spy upon your husband in such a research would be infamous."

"I do not desire you," she said, "to do any thing which will compromise your honor or your safety. I merely want to be relieved from suspicions which rack my brain by night and by day, and which sometimes even make me forget that I am in the presence of my sick child. The result of your simple observation of him—a few carelessly spoken words from his lips—may remove them all. I wish to believe my suspicions unfounded, for I could not survive his infidelity. I will tell you where he frequents. He tells me it is not a public gambling-house, but a club resorted to by gentlemen high in the esteem of the world. You could easily make his acquaintance, and could, without suspicion, inquire if those hours of stay from home are passed there. If he could be drawn out in a conversation to satisfy you that his affections are not elsewhere, you will afford me a happiness that I shall never too highly appreciate. Do not refuse me. My life hangs upon my peace of mind in this respect."

My resolve was made, and, having learned the locality of the club, I took her hand and assured her that I would do my best. As I was leaving the room she cautioned me to visit her in the afternoon only, and then to open the street door without knocking, so that her husband should know nothing from the servants of my visit to raise his suspicion of her honesty.

Here was a pretty commission—to hunt out a gambler's amours. "Well," thought I, "this is making of us physicians to the mind diseased with a vengeance." The more I reflected upon the novelty of the application, the more I reasoned myself into its consistency with honor and propriety. Besides, the adventure promised an agreeable relief from other duties.

The frequent indulgence in any sin or vice grows into a passion which absorbs the entire thoughts of its victim. Like to the willing sojourner under the upas shade of filthy and criminal infatuations, who becomes dead to all sense of nobility and decency, the devotee of gambling stifles within him every corrective impulse. Her handmaid intemperance is not now indispensable to palliate the insanity of rushing to ruin, or to excuse the forgetfulness of virtue. Though the victim has suffered in estate and mind, and would fain withdraw, by the extinction of every other passion he is forced back to his confirmed habit. To its indulgence he now even sacrifices his wife and children to the inheritance of shame, and, with an infatuation like to the holy zeal of the worshipers of Juggernaut, he lays down his broken spirit and ruined fortunes in despair under the chariot-wheels of his pitiless and false god. Examples are around us of many such, and you might as well essay to change the spots on a leopard's skin as to eradicate the desire or dispel the vice that is in them by reason. Chiding is insult. The reformation must come from some providential interference—from some unexpected turn in their affairs.

From all I could understand, he whom I now sought was in this category. He was the willing slave to gambling—he was not of its priesthood. Some great calamity, or the prospect of it—his utter ruin, perhaps—would alone change the direction of his bent. I knew of a man, an honest, hard-working mechanic, whose only weakness was an occasional investment in lottery-tickets. He had the fortune to win a prize of several thousand dollars. Having lived to maturity with all his wants satisfied by his manual labor, his head became turned with the excitement of sudden independence. For months his shop was deserted. In the mean time, he fell in with associates who helped him to pass the days and nights fleetingly and agreeably. He shortly sickened of dissipation, and tried again to work; but the money which was acquired so easily burned in his hands. He again flung down his work, and in a rapid succession of extravagances got rid of all. Labor was again sweet in its return to him. Again he invested in a lottery, and with a similar fortunate result. This time he gave it all away to his poorer relations, and avoided ever after the temptation of Fortune's wheel, that he might better enjoy the fruits of honest labor. Thus it is that extremes meet. There are as many who lack philosophy to bear adversity as there are those wanting in common sense to keep them within propriety under a sudden elevation of fortune. On my way to the club-house I fell in with an acquaintance, who happily possessed information of its rules and visitors. I ventured to ask him if he knew Mr. C. He gave me the most prepossessing account of him. He said that he was recognized as a perfect gentleman by all who had intercourse with him; that he lost, to be sure, but with the grace of a man of fortune. Cheerfulness and an easy wit were his marked characteristics. Furnished with this information and an unmistakable description of his person, I ventured to demand admission at the club door. This club was not organized as are the present ones, which deny admission to all except subscribers or their stranger guests. The proprietor exercised the privilege of dismissing any one from his doors of whom he had any suspicion of ability to meet their obligations or disposition to create a disturbance. He particularly excluded the professional gambler. It seems that he I sought was not considered as such. The proprietor in welcome tones ushered me into the rooms. My presence did not disturb any of the parties that surrounded the five or six round tables. It was only after some minutes of observation of the game at one table that my name was called aloud by an acquaintance, and I found, as a new-comer, that all eyes, for the nonce, were upon me. At one table a seat was vacant, which I was requested to take. Seeing there several acquaintances, I sat down, and, being supplied with the customary counters for the game, in a short time I found myself in the vortex of its excitement and interest. I discovered after a few deals, by the description of Mr. C., that he sat at my side. As no introduction was given to me, I ventured an occasional remark to him. Card-playing, like cock-fighting or racing, is a leveler of distinction. Community of interest in a special vice places all the sinners on an equality and loving brotherhood. This, I suppose, naturally proceeds from the ignoring, for the time being, of every principle of virtue, morality, and good-breeding, that the vice which is uppermost may be enjoyed with *abandon* and without shame. I remained at the game, holding my own, as the phrase is, until supper was announced. There the company mixed. I took particular care to be seated beside Mr. C. Every variety of conversation was introduced except on the topic of gambling. Appetite was satiated with the choicest viands, while excellent claret and Champagne made the winners witty and the losers relax the severity of their brows. It was at the close of this prolonged feast—for no hurry was manifested— that I caught Mr. C. giving some account of his early life and experience at play in the form of anecdote. Had I not known that he was entirely and ruinously addicted to his passion, I should have mistaken him for a satirist on human frailty, or an incurable searcher after the bitter experiences of life, for the sake of the consolation they gave him by discovering in others what he thanked God he did not possess. Something in connection with the subject brought a remark from me. We touched glasses, and he addressed himself to me exclusively. Learning who I was, and having also heard of my visits to the sick, the conversation took the turn upon the epidemic. He had been fortunate to escape from it, and attributed the fact to the excitements which engaged him. He had a confirmed belief that the mind can prevent the susceptibility to an epidemic disease, as that it invited it. He pronounced yellow fever and cholera to be nothing more than the effects of nervous fever, something on the principle that, if you don't know a danger, there is none. Playful remarks were more in keeping at a supper like this than argument, so that, without combating his assumption, I asked him if he had not a family. At once he eyed me inquiringly. I excused myself by saying that, if he had, his doctrine would be confirmed by none of them getting sick. His eyes, at this remark, dropped. Slowly he advanced his glass to his lips, and appeared in deep thought. "Do you know," said he, "any thing of the reputation of Dr. —— ?" I assured him it was good. "Is he successful with children?" "More so," I replied, "than the majority; but why do you ask?" "To tell you the truth, sir, I *have* a child who is sick—very sick. He is the life of my thoughts, and it so maddens me, the idea of losing him, that I fly from home to avoid dwelling upon it. I should be pleased if you would call before ten to-morrow to give me *your* opinion of him." This I promised to do. I was now fully satisfied that I could convey the most cheering satisfaction to the wife of her husband's fidelity.

The next afternoon I called to see the jealous wife. She met me with a smile, and said her husband was dis-

appointed that I did not call in the morning, as I had
promised. I told her I was afraid of a contretemps
which would have exposed my agency in discovering
what I had now to announce. I detailed our whole
conversation and his manner. I assured her that future
developments would prove that the strong love she bore
him and the child was the only cause for her suspicions.
I took the liberty, though, to tell her that she had a more
formidable rival than a woman—a rival that it is difficult to be divorced from when once it surrounds its victim. I told her that the excitement of play is of such
soul-engrossing character that its devotee loses thought
of every thing else. Wife and children, health, friendship, and honor, are sacrificed at its shrine.

"But," said she, "he is not a professional gambler.
He does not live by it. On the contrary, his losses are
greater than his gains. Play is his passion and his pastime, but he would scorn to inveigle another to play, or
to be called a gambler. I yet hope for his reformation
through the agency of that silent, yet correcting and
maddening monitor, the loss of all whereby to support
his indulgence. Then the necessity to provide for the
sustenance of myself and child will stare him forcibly in
the face. We will begin the world for ourselves. We
are both young, and the hard earnings of industry will
be sweetened by domestic happiness. I thank you for
the kindness of your interposition—for the peace of
mind which you have given me by your observations."

To say that the tear which glistened in her eye met
not full sympathy from me would dash the joy that a
simple act created. Volumes of thought bearing on her
condition engrossed my mind for many days after, and
the interest created for the fulfillment of her hope retained me an unobserved watcher of their future. On
my way home, the reflection intruded itself of how many
in our community are and have been thus situated.

Some, pursuing successfully a like career as his, under the guise of a profession or business, when, if the society that harbored them knew that neither law, medicine, or business supported the gay and expensive habits—that they have prostituted their honor to the sacrifice of the happiness of many associates, who concealed from the world the cause of their ruin, they would be thrust from its portals with a howl of shame and execration. It is a known fact that the impulsive character is the most susceptible of imposition and temptation. Excitement is wedded to such characteristically. The cold and impassible look of the professional gambler—of him who cheats or uses superior skill to entrap his victim, is a reflex of his heart's callousness. He presumes upon the credulity of his victim, whose experience of play is confined to the social circle, where no suspicion of unfairness exists. He knows his victim is ignorant; that in playing against him the game is not one of chance, but of a certainty so skillfully arranged as to delude the dupe into the belief that, if he had bet on the card turned up, he would have won his venture. It has been known of gamblers that, after having won all of an individual, they have proffered their sincere advice on the folly of persevering, but their disinterestedness never leads them to return even a portion of that which has ruined the latter. Sympathy, says he, love, friendship, and the world's distinctions, are the pastimes of fools. The evil eye of the gambler sees in all animate or inanimate creation merely objects of aggrandizement and spoil. The argument is advanced that they dissipate the money gained from the rich, and are thus useful to society in one respect. What the rich lose, and which the former distribute in their extravagance, in measure of good to society, is in no comparison to the hellish and headstrong destruction of every hope and virtue caused to the more numerous class of victims. With all engaged, priests

and pimps, they live without God in the world, forget-
ting the end and aim of existence, and with brazen face
defying shame in their pursuit.   There is not in them a
single redeeming quality to make good citizens.   They
class lower than the *"fruges consumere nati"* of Virgil.

The hydra heads of corruption, lust, gambling, and intemperance, are the criminal perversions of God's gifts
for man's happiness and solace upon earth.   The first
sin is the brutalizing of the love which nature has planted in the hearts of all its creatures for their happiness;
the vices of gambling and intemperance are desecrations
of the pastime and solace which society countenances for
the promotion of cheerfulness and sociability.   The
temptation to excess is not natural or innate, but is fostered with a serpent's hiss from such as have already
fallen, and he is strong in resistance who, after the se-
duction of the first step, is not blind to the next.   Happy are such, yet should they not be vainglorious in their
strength, nor reproving in their triumph and exemption.
They have to thank God that they are not thus tempted, and, instead of harshly judging the dereliction, advise and help the fallen one from the slough in which he
is being lost.   Many are brought to their senses by a
respectful and considerate advice, as many are saved
from suicide by a timely proffered assistance.   Then are
the uses of adversity sweet to the sufferer, by making
life appreciated for "the precious jewel" of sympathy and
friendship—for the humanity it stirs in his bosom.

It is no justification of gambling that, if it were put
down by the severe hand of laws such as existed in the
days of Mohammed, and subsequently, to a late period,
throughout Christendom, private gambling would be
more ruinously engaged in.   The severity of the punishment would brand it as ignominious.   It is the winking
of justice; it is the facility of indulgence; it is the con-
secration of its necessity and existence by the counte-

nance of respectable devotees, and their undisguised familiarity with its priests, that make gambling now and increasingly dangerous. No one denies it to be an evil of threatening consequences to the happiness of families; no one doubts that an acme of outrage to the laws and society will soon be reached by it; that a terrible vengeance will fall upon its abettors. It is a melancholy prospect to draw the future of our American youth. Already the accumulated wealth of the sweat of the brow of fond parents, anxiously garnered for the certain security from poverty of their offspring, is lavished upon the strumpet and the gambler. The *far niente* of the Italian, succeeded by all his vices and effeminacy; the desperate passions of the Frenchman, which are at the bottom of his instability of character and indifference to the fireside virtues, have found a home in our simplicity. Progress in all that becomes a man and independence of character are wilting away under the shameless pretense of foreign refinement and adoption of foreign vices. To such an extent does it now range, that he who can philosophically contemplate the chances of happiness by entering matrimony with antiquated notions of domestic bliss, and an old age of proud satisfaction in the progeny around him, flatters himself into the possession of a rare prize in the lottery of life.

Revenons à nos moutons. I gave it as my impression to Mrs. C. that her husband would only be brought to a show of affection by extraordinary gains or by complete bankruptcy. She was satisfied that he was deeply pained at the illness of their child; and, as I said before, I watched and looked into the progress of affairs between them.

Having occasion to visit frequently the sick in her neighborhood, one morning as I passed I met C. as he was coming from his dwelling. "Ah ha!" he exclaimed. "Opportunely met. Come in and see now what a fine fellow you interested yourself for."

Mrs. C. met me at the door, but as different in manner and spirits as the gloom of a funeral is from the joy of a wedding. What I saw in her before—care-worn expression and timid confidence—was now a picture of beaming intelligence and the liveliest self-possession. The change in her dress from that required during her bedside duties was charmingly shown in the graceful contour of her figure under a well-fitted corsage and a tasteful arrangement of her hair. Her boy reclined upon the sofa, for he had not yet strength to venture at will; and, as he recognized the return of his father, in a ringing, healthy tone, so different from the plaintive one I had heard before, cried out, " Pa, you did not forget my marbles and my drum?"

Simultaneously the parents' hands pointed me to their son. They exchanged looks. Delight suffused their countenances. A thrill of joy seemed to pervade them, for I felt it as if electrically. To enjoy such happiness is frequent; to witness and sympathize with it is rare. I magnified my own agency in producing it, and felt a bliss I would not have exchanged with theirs. And who may not? To create a happiness where none existed before; to dispel the weariness of a life by placing within grasp some of its enjoyments, long yearned for; to well up from the heart smiles to a face which has been stereotyped by sadness; to force into play a sympathy and an affection where all was bitterness against God and creation; to induce by all these a foretaste of another and a better life, and make the creature sensitive to the divinity within it—all these are luxuries in private which the widest applause of publicity can not compensate for in its hollow honors of commendation.

When I retired with C. he opened to me his heart and intentions. With the little, he said, that was left of his means, he intended to economize, and forswear the tyrant that had kept him in a whirl of dangerous and unhappy excitement. I had no comments to make, but saw that he spoke feelingly and resolutely.

Two months after this, on a Sunday afternoon, I was strolling through the *Place d'Armes*, when I was accosted by a little fellow, gayly dressed, and holding in his hand a bouquet, which he presented to me, saying, " Ma sent this to you, and says Thank you." He hastily ran back to his mother, who was standing within the palisade of orange bushes. A simple recognition from her intimated her reluctance to encourage an interview which might be discovered and misinterpreted by her jealous husband. The fragrance from that bouquet had not entirely departed from the drawer in which it had been placed, when one morning I met Eugenia, who told me she had been several days engaged in packing up their effects, to depart the evening previous. She farther informed me that for months Mr. C. was daily at home, and that a thorough reformation had taken place in him. A letter from her parent, inviting them to the possession of a farm which he had purchased, was the immediate cause of their departure. Three years later I encountered the subject of this on the street, who assured me that he had kept his resolution, and now found sufficient excitement in his profession of law at home.

It seems like fiction that a man so deeply imbued with a passion from long indulgence should have suddenly halted, when he had the means yet to gratify himself, and no one to chide him. The secret lay in the wonderful power and foresight of that woman, who endured the silence of solitariness, submitting herself entirely to the will and pleasure of her husband, indifferent to the loss of her dowry, perhaps praying for its rapid exhaustion, so rapt was she in his happiness and fate, and confident that a time would come when the sentiments he had instilled into her mind of honor and purity of character would before long develop themselves in him.

As a sensible man, the moment reflection was induced of his suffering wife, and of the misery that hung over him, like the sword of Damocles, from the possibility of his child's death, shame overpowered his passion. Pride whispered to him, "Will you hurl affections that approach the divine into the selfish flames that are consuming you?" Honor reproached him for entailing upon the offspring of such a mother the disgrace of having his sins visited upon his son ; and will it be pushing the point too far to conclude that holier emotions, outside of the impulse of worldly considerations, consummated the result?

CHAPTER XXI.

Inoculation for Yellow Fever.—The Clergy.—The veteran Chiffonier.
—Supposed Causes of Yellow Fever.—Cecile.

I BELIEVE that there is no idea that ever started up in the mind of a reasonable reflecting man that is not susceptible of development in nature and reality. It is the whispering of truth which thus casts its shadow before. Some inventions and discoveries are accidental to all appearances, yet we daily meet with passages in old authors that remained of hidden meaning until a later invention or discovery explained them. Many truths that are now patent to every school-boy were the cherished monomania for years of men who died laboring to persuade their fellows that they were not proper subjects of lunacy. In the closet, by the slow research of another, a future generation is indebted to the successful development of the so-called lunatic's idea. In medicine it is generally known with what pertinacity the faculty over the world resisted the innovation of vaccination and anæsthetics. They are now the staple, *par excellence*, of the good and of the certainties of practice.

Among the numerous modes for curing the inexplicably caused yellow fever offered by studious enthusiasts for adoption to the association was one which struck us with its singularity. Of course, no physician would advocate it, but rather declared it absurd than jeopardize his reputation by countenancing what was diametrically opposed to his practice. It proposed no less than to inoculate the unacclimated, and thus bring their blood to the condition of the acclimated without submitting to the dangerous course of nature from external influences or natural causes. The Italian who presented this produced certificates of successful practice in the West Indies, and indulged us with an elaborate, and to us reasonable exposition of its principles. The stamp of authority had not, however, been placed upon it by any medical review or college, and we could not, consequently, take the responsibility of encouraging it. Finding no encouragement, he left the city with the heavy heart of Him who lamented over Jerusalem that she would not be saved.

The clergy of all denominations did honor to their calling during the epidemics, and seemed proud of their service, so willing and assiduous were they. The exceptions were rare of desertion from their post; the examples were numerous of martyrdom to their excess of zeal. So much were they in request that it was impossible to meet every demand on their time. Some of the dead were buried without a priestly service; others were interred with the funeral prayers read by a layman. It was no unfrequent occurrence for a minister or priest to be called upon every hour of the day and night to smooth the last hours of the dying, or by kind sympathy to reconcile the survivors to their bereavement, and comfort them with the assurance that what has been done is by the will of God, "who doeth nothing wrong." The dead were rarely attended to the grave by the minister.

The service on the part of the Catholics was commonly
performed in their chapels.   The one contiguous to the
grave-yard on Rampart Street was a thronged receptacle
of the dead and their mourners during the day until after dark.   Thence arose the mournful *Miserere*, filling the
air with its melancholy influence, and heightening still
more the universal despondency and sadness.   In the
district I attended the poor sick consisted chiefly of the
emigrant class, who were generally of the Catholic persuasion.   My information, therefore, of the doings of any
other than the clergy of that denomination is only from
hearsay.   Poor people are generally religious, if not ob-
servantly so, for religion with them is hope and dependence on Providence.   They live by the sweat of the
brow, while the rich feast by the sweat of their gold.
When an emigrant places his foot on his adopted soil,
the first impulse is to thank God for his safe arrival, the
second to purge his soul of sin at the confessional.   The
priest, next to his God, is his staff in adversity and
trouble.   His wants and weaknesses are laid bare to his
confessor.   It is the province of the latter to comfort,
encourage, and advise ; and, where the obedience is perfect, an interest in the penitent is created, which is un-
relaxed, which increases, until the last rites of religion
are administered.   Herein consists the power of the
Catholic clergy in a superior degree to that of other
sects.   The poor of the latter are not approached by
their pastor unless solicited.   They dare not send for
him.   Too humble they think themselves to trespass
upon the time or patience of one whose profound skill
in analysis and metaphor echoed through the high-vault-
ed cupola to the ears of such as are alone educated to
appreciate them.   The democracy of the Catholic Church,
on the other hand, secures the humblest member from
feeling his insignificance.   This fact is patent to every
observer.   I am not a Catholic, nor yet a complaining

Protestant. I can not refrain withal from demonstrating a feature in one religion which possesses such binding force between its members and its priests.

The soldiers of Christ, of whatever denomination, in this memorable epidemic of 1853, accomplished in a short period pleasures in their labors that a lifetime elsewhere would not have gathered. The zealous Jesuit, fired with the love of serving his God by bringing to redemption the untutored Red Man, ventured across the seas, and, under many privations and risks, blistered his feet in ceaseless journeys through the wilds of America. The holy emblem of the Crucifixion, which glittered in the sun, was only gazed upon by the savages as the white man's idol, and, though for the time respected, was as soon forgotten as it was removed from sight. The benefits were never tangible; they existed only in the enthusiast's brain. Not so the results of this year's labors at death's harvesting. The sympathy of the priest and dying penitent was complete. Every hour of the day and night the former heard the last prayers of the wanderer to the shoreless sea, whispering hope to the timid, and pressing the outstretched hand of the speechless dying. His duties were more akin to those of one of an intermediate state than to common humanity. Confirmed scoffers at religion, even the leading cheats of atheism and infidelity, have confirmed the divinity that is within us in their dying moments. There is a sweet consciousness of a coming good induced by faith in Christian promises that causes the sufferer, once so fearful of death and loving of life, to pray for the moment of separation from earthly objects. Those who have observed the expression of the eye and features when the spirit is thus possessed have noticed an ecstasy, a calmness and serenity common only to the innocent young; and after Death has grappled his victim, the triumph of hope is no less beautifully fixed in the expression. Then it is that the priest feels his reward for his patient watchings, and for his instrumentality in the spiritual conversion. With less of sorrow now than envy, he hastens away to fulfill like offices to another, and another, and another.

Almost every resident on the great thoroughfares of the city—on Chartres, Royal, and Camp Streets—have noticed an old man of the rag-picking fraternity, wearing a precisely-cut gray and black beard—the former color preponderating—and a well-defined mustache. A tattered cloak, thrown artistically over his shoulders, fell over his left arm, which was akimbo; in his right hand he held a barbed pointed stick, which crossed his breast, having the last piece of rag that he had picked up dangling from the end thereof. He walked erect and theatrically, as if he were on parade, or the cynosure of all eyes in a triumphal entry. To observers who would stop to look at him he would give a glance from sprightly, dark, small eyes, while a cynical or conceited smile played on his countenance. His head was a study for a Flemish artist. His physiognomy indicated more of the savant than the stolid and filthy rag-picker. He was the bugbear of children, whose attention was drawn toward him by his drum-major antics, but who as rapidly retreated when they met the glance of that lustrous black eye from under its shaggy brow. He was discriminating in his search for rags, and rarely lost his time by inserting his stick into the box of offals thrown from a poor man's door. I had several times accosted him, but received no reply. He taught me my place; in turn I was bound to respect his.

In a dilapidated house on Ursuline Street I visited several patients, when one day I was informed that an old man was lying sick in a small basement room in the rear of the building. I went to the door, rapped, and, after a few minutes' delay, the door was unbolted, and I was confronted on its threshold by my *chiffonier*. I told him I heard he was sick, and if in distress too, I should like to be of service to him. He looked at me with surprise, and, belying his appearance, said, "I am not ill, sir; though, if I were, I could take care of myself. I thank you, nevertheless, for your condescension." Such were his words, delivered with emphasis and a courtly elegance of manner. He still held to the door, covering with his body an insight to his dark and damp chamber. I remarked that I hoped I had not offended. "By no means, sir; you do me honor—*Je vous salue, Monsieur.*"

This was decisive. On giving the result of my visit to my informers, they said he had been sick for several days. An old colored woman who washed in the yard had given him baths and made ptisans for him. They also told me that he had several thousand dollars in bank, which was known by the landlord of the premises. He had occupied that room for three years, never leaving it except at sunrise, and returning at noon with a piece of meat and some vegetables, which he cooked himself.

In the summer of 1854 I was promenading the Levee near the shipping, when I exchanged looks with a man that I thought I had met previously. On turning round I again met his eye. He stopped, as if inviting an interview. I approached toward him. With a grace not to be excelled by a Brummel, he bowed and lifted his cap. I immediately recognized him. He was now in search of a French vessel for Havre, giving it the preference, as he could not speak English. To my questioning, he informed me that he was tired of this country. The social distinction was too great for him. "In France," said he, "so that I live honestly by my business, I am the companion of all I care to know. My countrymen here become changed. They look upon my pursuit as you Americans do; besides, it is a (*vilain*) rascally place to live in. Every one strives with his life to make money, and before, or soon after he thinks himself rich, he is fattening the soil of your swamps. I came to make money at the instigation of a confrère, who is now enjoying in France the fruits of a few years' labor here. I am frank to tell you that I have accumulated in five years francs enough to retain me in comfort and respectability at home." To my question as to the amount he had amassed, he answered 20,000 francs. "I have not," he continued, "denied myself any thing in my pursuit; I lived as well as I wished for the present, being sustained with the prospect of better enjoyment hereafter. When I return home, my success will induce others to emigrate. There is a large field for them. You Americans, unlike the French, daily throw out fortunes on the street. Were I younger, I would not take 100,000 francs for a ten years' residence among you." As he offered me his hand, he raised his cap from his head with more of an air of "high consideration" than of equality, and feelingly thanked me for the considerateness of my visit to him during his sickness. Vale! my peripatetic philosopher.

From the 1st of September, 1853, patients were more successfully treated. Not that there was any change in the curative process, but perhaps owing to a noted circumstance, that the force of the wind from the west and north had become greater. I say *perhaps*, because there is no certain deduction to be made in any thing that concerns the cause or existence of yellow fever. Physicians have been so long confounded to find one, that they allow themselves to be tossed upon every theory that is floated before them. Every epidemic initiates a new cure and a new theory, which experience explodes. Great reliance had been placed in a rainy season and a dry season, a low stage of water and a high stage of water. By comparison of years of epidemics, we will see the fallacy of any fixed theory. The year 1858 sprung a new theory upon a recently-discovered substance, said to be oxygen electrified, produced from lightning passing through the air, and called ozone. The property of vitality attributed to this principle is so great that where it is created epidemics can not exist. Yet, if we compare the two great epidemic years of 1853 and 1858, we shall see that during one there was abundance of rain, with frequent and heavy thunder-storms; and in the other a remarkably dry season, and not a single thunder-storm until the close of the epidemic in October. By the same comparison, in the two years, the disturbance of the earth, as a cause, in digging canals and making rail-roads contiguous to the city, falls to the ground. The exciting cause of yellow fever in a locality, no less than a fixed cure or preventive of it, will exhaust conjecture for some time to come. The suddenness of its attack upon an organization free from lassitude, loss of appetite, or any inviting predisposition, is as wonderful as its mysterious agency in the economy of nature.

For several days every cot in the Globe Infirmary was tenanted. The few discharged were more than replaced by new applicants for admission. The consequence was, that when the surplus was rejected by the Charity Hospital, I was obliged to do the best that circumstances would permit for them at their own homes. I had much to contend with in obtaining nurses, and was kept constantly driving from one to the other to administer medicines, replenish their drinks, and perform the necessary and all-important duties of a nurse. In one square on Main Street I had over twenty patients, all of French or Swiss nativity. Two of the former were man and wife, both young, and taken ill the same day. On the second day I removed the man to an adjoining room. There was nothing remarkable in their symptoms or conduct until the fourth day. Then the

M

man appeared to be doing well, while his wife was continually moaning and restless from excruciating pains.
Sufficient was revealed to me to hurry off for an accoucheuse. The heart-rending moans, succeeded by
burning tears, are yet alive in my memory. I despaired
of seeing one saved in her situation. When I returned
with the accoucheuse, her suffering seemed yet more intense. Having other duties to perform, I left, and about
midnight went home to rest. Although fatigued in
body, I found I could not sleep. A stimulant even failed to induce it. The cries of that woman were ringing
in my ears to the exclusion of the composure necessary
for repose. I dressed and went out again. Not a sound
was to be heard, not a moving thing to be seen. Even
the occupation of the watchman seemed to be gone, from
the absence of the baton-raps on the pavement. The
moon shone in unclouded grandeur, and gave the lie in
its serenity to the misery it overlooked. I had arrived
within a square of my destination, when a succession of
piercing cries, like death shrieks, curdled the blood in my
veins. I soon divined the cause. I hastened my steps,
and, on ascending to the gallery which fronted the rooms
of my patients, I encountered four ladies who had been
attracted to the spot by the cries. Seeing the attendance
complete, I stood aside, awaiting the result. One of them
appeared to know me, for she excused her visit by saying that they were of the society of *Les dames de la
Providence,* which is composed of married ladies belong-
ing to the most respectable class of our Creole population. They confine their attentions to their own sex,
and are liberally provided with funds from private contributions. I had frequently before heard of them making nocturnal visits in couples, but met them for the first
time now. While they were engaged with the wife, I
stepped into the room to see the husband. The door
was open, through which he could distinctly hear the
plaints and implorations of his suffering wife.

"In the name of God, come to me, Alphonse. Oh, come to me! Come to your poor Cecile."

Prostrated from the weakness of repulsed attempts to leave his bed to go to her, he returned her endearing exclamations with the constant entreaties of "Do not cry, my Cecile. Do not moan. Have courage, Cecile," and the like, all the while sobbing and weeping like a child.

The crisis of her suffering was soon past. After an infliction of such startling sounds upon the dull ear of night, that can compare with nothing less than the wail of ghouls, Cecile had now swooned into insensibility or death, none could tell me which. The child was premature, but healthy, and pronounced likely to live. Quiet was established. Alphonse was silenced, and his alarms for his wife dissipated, and there was no occasion for my longer stay. When I stepped on the gallery, a peacock, the annoyance of any neighborhood, voiced its hideous notes in a lengthened strain, as if in mockery of man's weakness, or in triumph of its own exemption from the suffering and death around. Those Ladies of Providence must recur to the events of that night as one fit to commemorate a feast of horrors, for silence and the perspiration of their brows showed how their frames were unnerved and powerless to move, as if under the influence of a terrible dream.

On the next morning I was an early attendant. Cecile was composed, held out her hand to me, but said nothing. A slow but significant movement of her head told me how much she had suffered, and that she had no hope. Hearing of the urgent entreaty of Alphonse to be brought to her bedside, which was delayed until my arrival, we carried him in his cot and placed him beside her. Involuntary tears simultaneously coursed their cheeks as their eyes met. She beckoned for her infant, placed her hand on its chubby cheek, and drew it toward her lips. The anguish that was expressed in her countenance after this embrace feelingly depicted the mother's pangs at parting with her offspring, though heaven, with all its allurements, were held out as a choice. As it was taken from her, she muttered, "Alphonse, my child, may the Holy Virgin guard you!"

For fear of exciting her dangerously, Alphonse had been cautioned against speaking to her, and was now carried back to his room. Undisturbed repose and quiet were her only safety. On my return two hours later, her strength was gradually failing her. Her confessor, who attended, received but monosyllables in reply to his whisperings. Hope had fled, and disconsolate she died, with the hand of her infant pressed to her lips.

My stay at her bedside was unusually long, but I was there retained by the chord of sympathy which held the others to the spot. Before she had breathed her last, one of her friends, too poor to contribute enough, and unwilling to see her remains interred with the poor and unknown in St. Vincent de Paul's, solicited subscriptions from her husband's acquaintances near the French market. A sufficient amount was collected to defray the expense of a cherry coffin, hearse, and a distinct place of interment.

In this instance I was not asked to contribute the funds of the Association for her burial. From former deaths, all knew that our rules allowed us to make no distinction in our dead. The exceptional cases were when the late condition of the deceased or his relations in life were of that character that he should not be confounded with emigrants and unknown persons. This charity was due to the surviving families of old residents. I do not know how I should have acted in the present case. Any question in my mind was anticipated by the early action of friends.

The husband recovered. For months afterward I was saluted as I walked through the market by a man whom I could not place in my recollection. Having stopped at his stall to purchase some article, he asked me if I did not remember Alphonse. The bitter memories of those days opened the fountain of his heart, and he could not conceal his emotions as he thanked me for my sympathy and aid.

CHAPTER XXII.

Mortality at the Globe. — Some of the Patients. — Impositions. — The deserted one.

UNTO the 12th of September, 338 cases of fever had been admitted into the Globe Infirmary, of which 156 died, and 182 were discharged cured. This was not below the average of cure, considering the cases under treatment. More than one half of those admitted had been treated for several days by physicians at their residences, or were entered in a desperate condition. Many were sent from boarding-houses in the last stage, to get rid of the expenses of the burial; while unfeeling cabmen, to obtain the fare of transportation to the infirmary, hunted up cases at the beer-shops and on the Levee. Speaking of the average of deaths by yellow fever, it was laughable to hear of the boasts of some physicians in referring to the number of yellow-fever patients who died under their hands. The proportion of one was sure to be diminished in the statement of another. Our records and our testimony would have settled the question between them, but the result could not be arrived at from the certificates of death handed to the sextons. Reputation was too dear to the physician, and the sexton's record too conclusive, to commit one's self by assigning the cause of every death to yellow fever. Hence many flattered their consciences with fixing on the dead some other disease, such as typhoid, congestive fever, cholera, etc. This will account for the large number of deaths reported in a sparse population of other diseases than of the epidemic.

As I have previously remarked, for some weeks before the closing of the infirmary the applicants were of a better order than at the opening. A French gentleman, of middle age, dressed in a frock-coat ornamented with frogs on the breast, presented himself, and gave his initial as Mons. D——. He offered to pay for the attendance, which we, of course, refused. He could not be persuaded to put on one of the infirmary bed-gowns. He recovered, and again proffered pay ; and, upon again being refused, passed a feeling eulogium on this singular institution of our country.

Another was brought in during my absence, whose companions informed the clerk they would bury him if he died. He gave a fictitious name to the clerk for entry on the books, but confided to him his real one. From day to day, as was my wont, I stopped at his cot and inquired of his condition. At first he was very taciturn. Hearing one day from him that he had left the St. Charles Hotel for the infirmary, I asked how it came that he gave us the preference.

"Dog it," said he, "I prefer a hospital to the solitude and gloom of every thing around me at the hotel. Misery loves company, and I would rather see it than hear of it or imagine it, as I did there. If I die here, I shall, at least, have an opportunity of diverting my thoughts from myself." He wished nothing added to what was prescribed or administered. With the exception of a monosyllabic answer to my usual questions as I passed the cots of the sick, he took no notice of me or invited conversation. He died on his third day of a congestive type. Besides notifying his friends, I examined the papers he had left with the clerk. From them I learned that he was the dissolute son of an eminent London banker. On inquiring of the house to the care of which his letters were addressed, I was shown a bill of exchange for £500, which had been sent to the house for him by his father, accompanied by a letter. This letter, together with his papers, bill of exchange, and certificate of death, were sent back to the latter.

The constant surveillance of every member in his district was not complete security against imposition. So far as determining the condition of the sick, we had the infallible test of the pulse or appearance to govern us. Importuned as we were for relief of destitution, we gave money and groceries to many whose sincerity we did not in the least question. Women appealed to us, certified to by credulous neighbors of the dreadful penury of their large family of children. Personal observation of the five or more children assembled in one room, with scarcely bedding for half of them, opened our hearts to the maximum of relief; strict inquiry would have exposed to us that the children were borrowed for the occasion. Once successful with one member, the same woman was encouraged to play off a like deception upon another by changing her residence and her name. To the credit of our country, I must add that all such discovered belonged to the class of alien professional beggars. Among other impositions were the bills of apothecaries. Though we had regular appointed and paid physicians for each district, we did not deny a patient the attendance of one of his selection, provided we had nothing to pay for his services; neither did we show an exclusive preference for any apothecary, choosing rather that the physician should have his prescriptions put up where his hieroglyphics were best understood. Thus did we become subsidized to almost every apothecary shop in the city. In some of these the physician was entirely interested; in others a partnership existed to the extent of patronage given. In both cases the temptation was strong to put up prescriptions of the most extravagant character. Neither member or nurse questioned the contents of the six-ounce phial, of which a few teaspoonfuls would be given on the first day, to be substituted the next and every day after for other mixtures—perhaps all innocent in effect, though the color of the liquid might be changed. Sponging the body with the expensive solution of quinine, a frequent repetition of fly-blisters, never on long enough to irritate the skin, and the like, rapidly footed up a large bill of expense on a case. As the accounts were only presented monthly for settlement, the patient was very likely to be too far out of the way to be inquired of if he had taken or submitted to the enormous quantities of mixtures and topical applications. When we endeavored to convince such apothecaries that it was impossible for any man, sick or well, to swallow so much stuff or to undergo a succession of such expensive applications to his body without rapid dissolution, and suggested to submit the bill to the inspection of another apothecary and physician, we rarely failed to obtain a large reduction on the claim. Some apothecaries refused to give up the prescriptions of physicians, which we were entitled to as vouchers for the correctness of the bill. These were either unpaid or compromised. The accounts of old and reputable apothecaries, made on prescriptions of our paid physicians, were not questioned. They rarely averaged over five dollars to each patient. As much, though, as we might be disposed to question the latter, we were entirely ignorant of the scale of prices, as a mixture of a few grains (say of quinine) in a six-ounce phial of water becomes doubled or quadrupled in price, according to the number of other ingredients and the time taken in its preparation.

After ten o'clock at night I was met by a colored woman, who informed me that in St. Anne Street a fe-

male was sick of yellow fever, and in the greatest destitution. Following her to the house, we entered the al-
ley-way, which led to a small room in the basement of
the back building, and in the rear of a kitchen. A dull
light from a tallow candle exposed to me a woman lying
on a cot before the window. There was not another
piece of furniture in the room—not even a chair. On
the mantle-piece were several bottles and phials. I was
shocked at the utter misery and desolation around.
There was a chair in the yard near the door, which I
suppose had been occupied by some watcher during the
day. But how was it that she was thus alone? My in-
formant had been by accident in the yard, and came to
me without the suggestion of any one. Was the patient
to lie thus hopeless and unattended during the night?
Without addressing the sufferer, who looked curiously
and inquringly at me, I went outside to the main building to seek the proprietor of the house. I was not in
the humor of mincing words at the sight of such barbar-
ous neglect, and in this spirit I rapped violently at a
door opening on the back gallery. I was replied to in
a woman's voice.

"What do you want?"

"The proprietor of the house."

"I am she."

"Then come out; I must see you immediately." This
decisive language was followed by the unbolting of a
side window and the appearance of a female head.

"Madam," said I, "there is a woman in that room lying dangerously ill. Do you know it, and intend that
she shall die like a dog?"

"In one moment," she replied. "Wait." When she
again showed herself, half robed, she said, "Are you the
doctor? No, you are not. Poor girl! she has suffered
much. I have been nursing her and sitting with her
night and day. She insisted yesterday upon my remov-

M 2

ing her from this room here to the one she now occu-
pies, so that I could rent this one. I am poor, sir; she
knows it; but, poor as I am, I would not have removed
her if it had not been at her urgent request. She owes
me three months' board; I owe my landlord, and I must
have money for my own sustenance as well as hers. All
that I have I have spent upon her; I only left her for a
few minutes of sleep. The neighbors have assisted me
in nursing her. I am now so weak that I am sick myself. I have her child in my bed. Can I do more than
I have done?"

"Why did you not send to the Howard Association
for assistance?"

"I did think of that, sir, but she said she would not
die in a hospital."

Upon my informing her that we did not always send
our patients to the hospital, she reproved herself for not
taking the advice given to her.

I returned to the sick woman, and remarked to her
that, as she appeared so miserable and badly treated, I
had been expressing my indignation to the proprietress;
but, now that I learned that she was from choice in this
apartment, I would make her as comfortable as possible.

"She told you truly," she replied, at the same time
turning her head around with pain and difficulty, as if
looking for a chair for me. I interpreted it thus, and
sought one on the outside. When I first arrived I experienced great exhaustion; the excitement of so great
misery before me dissipated it, and nerved me to continued exertion.

"You say, sir, you belong to the Howard Association; you visit and relieve sick poor people. We have
nothing of this kind in France. You are an American?
Is it not so?"

"Madam," replied I, "I am entirely at your service.
I am recompensed for that I do at your command. I

can not turn your chamber into a palace, but I will have
for you all that you can desire under the circumstances."

"Do you say so?"

She pressed two fingers on her eyes to assure them of
greater strength, while she looked at me and inquired,

"Can I recover?"

"There is every possibility of it," I replied. "You
look robust; and, since you have survived the critical
days, I think, with nursing and composure on your part,
you will get well."

"Oh, thanks! thanks!" she ejaculated.

I promised that, if I did not succeed in engaging a
nurse, which it was difficult to do at that hour of the
night, I would return and sit up with her myself.

Her voice, accent, and language in the remarks that
followed impressed me so favorably that, with the excuse of looking at her tongue, I brought forward the dim
candle from the mantle, that I might learn more of her
character by seeing her face. It is irreverent, I know,
to expatiate upon the physiognomy of a sick person,
when sympathy should be exclusively wrapped in her
sufferings; but in this case it was so irresistibly impressive that, for a moment, I forgot that the poor creature
was at the point of death. Praxiteles, in his conception
of perfection in feature and expression, would have turned in disgust from his creations for this charming original. Her complexion was slightly flushed from fever;
disease had left its handprints on her sunken cheeks;
care had moulded its thoughtfulness upon her brow; the
expanded blue eye reflected the fever's internal fire; the
well-defined nose and lips were thin from suffering; the
dimpled chin alone preserved its healthy contour; yet,
with all these defects, each enough to mar the beauty of
a blonde, the *tout ensemble* was so graceful that I imagined the sight of her in health would madden an an-
chorite. Rarely do I allow myself to be disturbed by

such reflections during the sickness of any, be they rich or poor. I study to be indifferent to the piece of mortality, be it repulsive in form and feature, or partaking of angelic attributes. In this instance it may be that, as the misery was so deep, pity magnified her claims to my greater exertion. Despite weariness and fatigue, I felt nerved to save this praying anxious woman.

Being without a cab, I hurried on foot from place to place to seek a nurse. In half an hour I had persuaded one to follow me, who had been broken down by frequent watching, and had counted upon being undisturbed this night. My patient seemed cheered by her presence, and I abruptly left her with the sick one.

In the morning early I met the physician, who pronounced her condition hopeless. This did not make me despair or relax attentions, for I have frequently seen nature strangely overcome the disease when the physician, friends, and even hope have abandoned the sufferer. The nurse was one of the best. In my absence she had curtained the door and window, and furnished the room with chairs and a covered table. On the latter was spread every convenience and comfort for the patient. As I entered the room the invalid held out her hand to me, and pointed to her lips, which appeared so parched that she could not articulate. Small pieces of ice, instead of liquids, placed in her mouth from time to time, greatly comforted her, and enabled her to speak. She spoke to me of fatal precursors—a burning sensation in her breast and dimness of vision.

At noon I again called. She was scarcely conscious of my presence, and kept her eyes fixed upon the ceiling.

At ten o'clock that night she recognized me, and called me by name. She had been restless and delirious, and now writhed under the irritability of the stomach. The mere pressing down of a cataplasm caused her to

scream with pain. Feeling relieved a few minutes afterward, she stretched her hand to me, saying,

"I am dying, and want to speak to you alone."

The nurse retired. I drew my chair by the side of
her bed, and placed my ear so close to her that she
might not fatigue herself in talking aloud, and that I
might better understand her broken sentences. She
spoke between breaths, uttering but few words at a
time.

"I desire to tell you—what has been a secret—in my
own heart. My father—is a jeweler—in Paris. Mr.
———, in ——— Street—knew him well. He has been
—at his house. He came out in the ship—with me—
but did not know—who I was. Without the knowledge
of my parents—I married Mr. ———. He is an ———.
He will come here this fall—my child is his. He promised to write—he has not. In the name of God—preserve my child for him—tell him I die blessing him—
and when I am dead—take this ring—and give it to
him."

Her utterance was so incoherent that many things escaped me. She said something of having left France
without a passport, and alluded to certain debts she had.
She had evidently exerted herself beyond her strength,
for her breathing became much faster, and her eyes rolled as if she was approaching unconsciousness. Her
hand wandered about her neck and breast apparently
searching for something; when it encountered a cross,
which was suspended by a small gold chain, she rapidly
drew it to her lips, kissed it frequently, and called aloud
for her child. The nurse hastened to fetch it. When
she returned with it she was entirely unconscious of its
presence. Her writhing and trembling shook the cot
incessantly for an hour; and, as a sudden paroxysm
seized her, a guttural "ha!" was loudly ejaculated.
When, to all appearance, pain had ceased, and her breath

would scarcely dim the face of a mirror, she straightened her limbs, closed her eyes, and passed gently away.

There was in this death nothing of the repulsiveness which commonly results from yellow fever. The hemorrhage of the gums and nostrils was slight, and she had been free from black vomit. Although the saffron dye rapidly possessed her skin, when she had breathed her last, her complexion was transparent, and resembled much that of one from a sudden death.

The proprietress of the rooms informed me she had rented a room of her for five months past. She gave her name as Madame ———, which was not the same as she told me. She had her meals from the restaurant; and when not promenading, she was at home reading or writing. She had no visitors, and was very reserved on being addressed. A month previous to her death she had given birth to a daughter. "Disappointed in not receiving remittances from France," said the proprietress, "she went with me to a pawnbroker, to whom she at several times pledged several articles of dress and jewelry. You know, sir, how little one gets when they are thrown upon this resort. When she took the fever, her anxiety for the fate of her child, from inability to hire a nurse, made her uncontrollable in the physician's hands. She would have her child sleep with her, and insisted upon nursing it. This was enough to produce the worst consequences to both. The third day of her attack the danger of her condition dawned upon her, and she concluded to be obedient to advice. Knowing how much I was distressed in circumstances, she grieved to owe me for rent; and on hearing that I had an applicant for the room she occupied, she entreated and insisted to be moved to the room in which she died."

After this explanation the proprietress led me to the room in which was her armoire. The clothing and dresses that were there were of the finest quality. A silk dress and a Cashmere shawl, unsoiled by wear, had been wrapped in a paper to be the next sacrifice to the pawnbroker. Two shelves were packed close with made-up linen of the best description. In a drawer was a writing-desk which contained a few pieces of jewelry and a package of letters. The latter had the endorsement of her name as given to me. As she owed for her rent, and some time would yet elapse before I could safely send the infant to the asylum, I directed the proprietress to take possession of the clothing, and appropriate the proceeds to the debts and future expenses. The jewelry and letters were wrapped together, to be kept until claimed by her husband or relations. The next day she was decently buried in the St. Vincent de Paul's.

The next day I procured a wet-nurse for the child. As a necessary consequence of imbibing the feverish milk of its mother, it drooped away, and in two days after was buried by her side. I wrote to her husband in Paris, and also addressed a letter to a relation with whom she had correspondence. Neither was answered. On the arrival of the ship in which she expected her husband, my inquiry was also fruitless.

I concluded, then, that she was deceived—then deserted.

Some years after this an acquaintance recalled this case to my mind, having been requested to see me by her husband. I detailed to him all the circumstances. Whether from shame or not, the husband never sought for me, or claimed the ring she had given me for him, nor her letters.

It was ever regretted by me that I had not been called in to her at the commencement of attack, that she might have lived to frown upon the heartless father of her child.

CHAPTER XXIII.

Orphans and temporary Asylums.—A Countess.

THE duties of a member of the Howard Association were only partially fulfilled by attendance during sickness. The care and sustenance of families afterward was a source of constant anxiety. The homes made desolate by a mother's or father's death, frequently by both, relied upon our guardianship until some disposition could be made of the children. Before the close of the epidemic the instituted asylums had received their full complement. We were thus driven to the necessity of disposing of the grown children to any respectable applicant who would promise to bring them up properly to some trade or service. The extremely young were put out to nurses, whom we paid at the rate of $12 to $15 per month. The numbers soon became so large that it became difficult to provide for all by these means. This led to the establishment of temporary asylums in each district. These became rapidly filled with from forty to seventy in each, as were also the two asylums established by the Board of Health, placed under our surveillance.

In each asylum were a matron, six or ten nurses in proportion to the number of infants, and three or four servants. No expense was spared in fitting up the establishment, in the provisioning or attention to the cleanliness and comfort of the children. Shameful omissions of duty on the part of the employés were frequent, but corrected so soon as discovered. Every citizen had the privilege of sending orphans to the asylum of his respective district. It was required that, upon entering

one, the names of the child and its parents should be
given, to be recorded in a book for that purpose. This
was not strictly followed. The names were frequently
forgotten by or unknown to the person bringing the
children, and they too young to give them. This was
dreadful, and one of the worst features of the epidemic.
Many children are now growing up who are ignorant
not only of the names of their parents, but of their nationality. It was, indeed, a sight to make the heart
bleed. No visitor could behold without tears these woebegone children, who looked upon every new face that
presented itself with a curious gaze, as if to recognize in
them the ma or the pa that they continually cried for.
Some there were, brothers and sisters, who found a
compensating comfort in each other's company, and never allowed themselves to be separated for a minute.
There was an epidemic sadness portrayed in their countenances; there was none of the joyousness or glee of
children. They cared not to play, but seemed weighed
down with the apprehensions of something worse in reserve for them. Not more exempt from disease than
their parents, they were daily frightened by a death in
an adjoining cot; and heavy must have been their little
hearts, when dreams of home, or father and mother, left
them in the morning, to gaze upon such sights and to
feel their desolateness.

When the epidemic had partially subsided, a number
of ladies of the Catholic persuasion, who had witnessed
the ignorance and inability of men to take care of young
children, petitioned the Board of Health for funds to enable them to assume the entire charge of the unfortunates until a final disposition was made of them. Conscious that it was their peculiar province, the proposition
was favorably met. A committee of conference, consisting of three members, was appointed. To avoid the censure of the religious community, it was enjoined upon

the committee, as a *sine qua non*, that the faith of the children should not be tampered with. These ladies were of known respectability. Their society was represented by five or six, who met us on the following day. After explaining our wishes and accepting our proposition, a memorandum of agreement was drawn up, to be submitted to and confirmed by the board. From a rough sketch in pencil which I find among my papers, it read, in substance, as follows:

"The police committee of the Board of Health, to whom was referred the communication from the ladies of St. Vincent de Paul's Association, in respect to their offer to take charge of the orphans now under the care and protection of the board, report,

"That in their conference with these ladies an agreement was concluded to give them the entire management and control of an asylum to be established by them in the spacious buildings known as the school of the 'Christian Brothers,' to which all the children supported by this board are to be immediately removed.

"The ladies aforesaid also agree that, in case any other Christian denomination offers its services for a similar purpose, the board shall exercise its discretion therein, and make a division of the children agreeably to the religious belief of the orphans.

"The ladies of St. Vincent de Paul farther engage themselves to submit to the board a weekly report of the number of children in their charge, with names, age, nativity, and religion, as near as can be ascertained; the names of such children as shall be given away for adoption by citizens, of those sick and dead, and whatever else may refer to the interest of the institution.

"It is farther understood that, at the expiration of the term of this board, the children shall be subject to the disposal of the City Council. In the mean time, all the expenses of the asylum are to be borne by the board;

the bills for all expenses to be signed and approved by
the lady president of the association."

I doubt if any measure of so much importance was
ever so rapidly passed to completion as this; for on the
day the memorandum of agreement was accepted by the
board, the ladies were promptly notified of it, and by
midnight they had assiduously engaged themselves in
having the proposed building cleansed, whitewashed, and
furnished with bedding and provisions. On the following day I was one of three who undertook to remove
the children from one of the asylums. Three omnibuses, containing each over twenty-five children, and one or
two grown persons, left for their new home at ten o'clock
in the morning. The prospect of a change had a merry
effect upon the children; they felt that any place was
better than their former quarters, which was exposed to
dust and the effluvia from surrounding gutters. A basket of cakes, presented and passed around to them by a
gentleman, completed their joy. As they jostled each
other during their ride in the omnibus, they became wild
with laughter. On reaching the asylum, they spoke of
the amusement and play in wait for them in the large
yard, with its swing and seesaws. They fairly tumbled
out of the omnibus in their haste to enter the premises;
and no sooner were they in than they dispersed themselves in every direction, screaming with delight, and mingling with the children brought from other asylums. The
ladies were all assembled to receive them, and I thought
they began to feel the responsibility they had assumed,
for they had not yet determined upon a code of discipline.
I handed the president a list of over eighty children, sixteen of which had only their Christian names. The inces-
sant glee of the little ones, as in groups they pried through
the buildings or raced in the yard, stifled in all, for a
time, the sad reflections touching their condition and their
fate. The ladies freely mingled among the children. To

the neglect of their own homes, they by turns remained during the days at the asylum to instruct and overlook the nurses. A week had not elapsed when all the orphans were clothed alike in dresses made by the members of the society. In fact, the children now had but one thing to grieve for—that they were without father, without mother. So strong was this feeling in some of them, that they looked searchingly at every face in hopes of finding their parents; and sometimes, being in doubt, ran up to one or other of the ladies, calling them their mas. On the second day of their admission I surprised a lad of ten years writing with a pen on the torn leaf of a book. It is before me, and I copy it *verbatim literatimque.*

My fathers grave
My dear father I love you of all my hearth. And you did
Died so quick. And I think that I see you always.
And I which that you would live. You was so good.
Our hole famely were—

Here followed four names. I asked him what became of those. "They all died too," said he, mournfully; and, dropping his head upon the table, gave vent to his feelings in tears.

The providence of the Creator is beautifully exemplified in nature by the contiguous existence of an antidote to every poison. It is no less markedly present in the fountains of charity that gush from the human heart in periods of pestilential visitation. The greater the misery to be relieved, the more blessed are the chosen ones whom He calls to relieve them. I venture to say that not one of these ladies felt less than heroines, and revert to their self-sacrificing and enthusiastic duties as the happiest epoch of their lives. Their souls were then possessed of a sympathy which raised them in feeling to the scale of angels. At that time,

> "Their life was in deeds, not days ; in thoughts, not breaths ;
>   In feelings, not in figures on a dial :
>   They counted time by heart-throbs."

A few days after the opening of this asylum some Protestant ladies urged their claims for a similar patronage. They established an institution called the Orphans' Home, which was largely endowed by the Howard Association, and exists to the present day, a monument to their zeal and virtues.

At the close of the epidemic lists of the orphans were called for by the Board of Health, for the purpose of making a final distribution among the asylums agreeably to their religious belief. There were upward of sixty orphans whose religion we had no clew of ascertaining. Our chief guide with the greater part of the others in determining if they were Catholics was the presence of an AGNUS DEI or a cross suspended from the neck. A delegation from the Catholic and Protestant Asylums divided between them, by alternate choice, those whose religion was unknown.

Besides donating over $30,000 to the incorporated orphan asylums, and taking care of many of the orphans at the infirmaries, the Howard Association appropriated $100 for each orphan. In the temporary asylums boys and girls were promiscuously sustained. After the separation agreeably to their religion, it became necessary to separate the sexes. I was present on this occasion. An interesting-looking girl of ten years old was informed that her brother, who was two years younger, would be now separated from her, but that she would be permitted to visit him at the Boys' Asylum. "*No!* *no!* NO!" she cried out, with the firmness of desperation. "I promised my mother on her death-bed never to leave my brother Sammy, and, if you take him away from me, I will kill myself." In the mean time she closely clasped him to her, and, dropping her head upon his, cried out hysterically. They were both fine-look-ing children, of American parentage. This touching in-cident so much affected all present that none had the heart to allude to them until the other children were be-ing conveyed away. It was then concluded upon to keep them inseparable, to meet applications for adoption, which were frequently made by citizens. A few days afterward I heard they were both thus disposed of to a rich couple, who engaged themselves to the committee not only to furnish them with a good education, but, as they were childless, to make them their heirs.

At each of the temporary asylums the closing was celebrated by a collation gotten up by the ladies, to which all of our members were invited. I was present at them all, and can compare the entertainment with nothing that I had ever witnessed before or since. La-dies, whose tears were but yesterday mingling in sym-pathy for the helpless ones under their protection, now that their usefulness had ceased, and their little ones were amply provided for, gave way to their expressions of joy upon the disappearance of the epidemic and its heart-rending associations. Toasts and sentiments were boldly spoken, and wine circulated freely, until the ex-treme of merriment chased away from every heart the last shades of sadness which had so long hung over it.

An old Creole lady "who had seen better days," now reduced to the necessity of providing for her children by keeping furnished rooms on Royal Street, called upon me to help her in the expense of attending to the only one remaining of all her lodgers. She remarked that, so long as Mr. ——, her landlord, gave her rent free during the epidemic, she would spend the last dol-lar on the unfortunate under her roof. An hour after this visit I waited upon her. The parlor and bed-room occupied by the invalid, who was then asleep, were fur-nished with articles of the most costly make and patterns, somewhat the worse from time, but not impaired by use. The colors of the satin curtains and damask-covered chairs harmonized with the rosewood and mahogany, which had lost their polish. Every thing was in its place and free from dust. After shutting the door between the two rooms, Madame gave me the history of her own reverses, and then acquainted me with the secret history of her lodger friend.

"She is a countess," said she, "who left France to free herself from family persecutions. I could show you her correspondence to convince you of her rank, but I hope you will be satisfied with my mere assertion."

I replied that it made little difference to me whether she was a countess or a peasant; it would be equally agreeable to me to see her get well. It struck me at the moment that it was strange that a charitable association should be sought for relief where there are hundreds who would pride themselves on the honor of such acquaintance and the anticipation of her wants. Having learned that the immediate requirements were the hire of a nurse and an order for groceries, I consented to continue the one who had been attending, and sat down to write an order for the latter. Having to affix the name of the relieved to all orders, I now asked for that of the countess. "You must excuse me from giving you this," she said, "as I have promised not to reveal her name except under the most extreme necessity." I urged no farther, and filled the order with the name of her landlady.

On the next morning I called to see how she was. Before the patient knew I was in the room I had passed softly on the carpet to her bedside. She was lying on her back, with an arm thrown across her eyes. Gently I felt her pulse, which I found natural, with a healthy skin. As this did not disturb her, I turned to depart, when I was called back by "Is it you, doctor?" When she saw it was not, she raised herself on her elbows and said, "Are you here, Adolph, to upbraid me in my dying hour? Leave me to die in the misery that I am in, rather than force upon me the thoughts that your presence brings." I told her she was mistaken in the person she was addressing. The landlady, who that moment had entered, explained my mission. "Sir, your hand," she replied. I sat beside her, told her I sympathized with her in her separation from home and friends, and that nothing should be left undone for her comfort or safety. "I am very weak now," she said; "pray call this evening; I shall have much to say to you." Before leaving, I was informed that, from imprudence on her part, or improper treatment, she had been kept in bed for five weeks. From being a robust woman, she was reduced to a skeleton. Her digestive powers were gone, and she had been sustained for two weeks by light stimulants. Her sleep was irregular, and broken by dreams that caused her to cry, sob, and laugh alternately. When she was awake she frequently called to her landlady to prop up pieces of her music before her, in which she became enrapt, her fingers the while running over the bedclothes as on the keys of a piano. In the evening I was again present. In the corridor I met the physician and the landlady, and was informed that she could not survive the night. I left them to step into the sick-room. When she recognized me, she said, "Are you a father? and your wife is alive? Do you love your child? Do you love your wife?" I bowed responsive. "See what creatures we make of ourselves. Is it not infamous? My God has placed me here with the best heart to appreciate all his works; I am now leaving life in disgust with every thing. Every thing human has disappointed me, and served to crush me. When I die I hope to forget the earth. Oh! that my spirit could be embodied in some sweet air, like this (showing me a piece of music folded in her hand), that I might ever reach the ears of angels, and forget that I was mortal."

I reprimanded her for giving way to any excitement, and cautioned her against the effects of it.

"You do not know me, sir," she said. "You will never know who I am; yet you should, for your disinterested, conduct has almost balanced a lifetime of wrongs. I am not long of this world, and I shall quit it with but one regret, which is, that I leave an infant, perhaps to inherit its mother's bad fortune, and most surely to feel the misery of loneliness and dependence. I have requested madame to see that she is placed in an asylum; to be watchful for remittances addressed to me, and to preserve all letters, that my child may one day know who she is. If it will be no trouble to you, I should like you to see that my requests are carried out."

The effort to speak so much weakened her sensibly. She breathed quickly, with periodical checks, as if holding her breath for the long moans which followed. I left her with the madame and nurse. On the morning following I entered the chamber, and saw the two sitting beside the bed on which the corpse of the countess lay. She had died at midnight, after a single convulsion. They told me that she had completely prepared herself for a Christian's death. She had the daily visit of her confessor, and injuriously occupied the hours for repose in reading prayers, or having them read to her.

Two days after her death I called to see that the promised disposition was made of the child. The madame informed me that she did not intend to put it in the asylum, but would take care of it herself for the present. I endeavored to change her intention by repeating the instructions given to me by the deceased, and by appeals to the sacredness of the promise she had

N

made. She still persisted in her determination, and I concluded to let the matter rest for the present.

It was frequently the case that neighbors or acquaintances rapaciously took the children of deceased persons, sometimes with the laudable purpose of adopting and educating them, but more frequently to bring them up as apprentices, servants, or worse. We became very jealous of our rights, and could not watch too closely these children-snatchers. During and since the epidemic, it has pained and mortified us that we had no clew to the whereabouts of children whose parents have died under our care, when distant relatives wrote to us that they wished to give them a home. In several instances relatives have passed many days in visiting the asylums and questioning the children as to their identity. It particularly chagrined us when requests from abroad reached us for certificates of a death, and to be unable to give information of the survivors.

Intending to act authoritatively in the case, I called upon madame about a month subsequent. I was fortunate enough to meet at her house a man of family, whom I knew, who said he had been acquainted with the deceased, and would defray the expense of raising the child until it was claimed by her relatives. For future reference, his name was entered upon my report.

CHAPTER XXIV.

Convalescent Infirmary.—Closing Feast of the Globe Infirmary.

THE crowning benefit of the Howard Association, and, for its novelty, a most attractive feature of benevolence, was the separate infirmary for the convalescent of yellow fever. The excellent suggestion was admirably carried out in all its usefulness by its enthusiastic originator, an old member of the association. An edifice known as the Polar Star Lodge, at the corner of St. Anne and Claude Streets, was charitably placed at our service for that purpose. The building was an oblong square, thirty-five feet by ninety, which stood in the centre of a lot of 120 feet square. Trees of thick foliage, and fragrant shrubs and bushes, overspread and lined the walks, imparting the deliciousness and purity of a country atmosphere. Being away from the great thoroughfares of business favored yet more the deceit. The building contained a basement and first story, having each a large hall and a vestibule. Numerous windows afforded complete ventilation. Each room was fitted up to accommodate forty persons. The basement was appropriated to the males, and above it to the females. Meals were cooked in a neighboring house, occupied by the warden of the lodge, whose family devoted themselves to further the objects of the institution. The nicest discretion and the most watchful care were required in the due apportionment of exercise, and of the quality and quantity of food, for the convalescent. The virtue of personal cleanliness was enforced by daily ablutions and frequent change of garments. The fetid odor which hangs about the wards of a fever hospital was not present here; consequently the convalescence was rapid. The inmates were required to do more or less of the domestic duties, and were encouraged to pass their leisure moments in reading instructing or religious books. The master spirit of this establishment was almost worshiped by them. When prepared to resume their various pursuits in life, the unbidden tear gracefully interpreted the full heart, which could not by words express its gratitude. Many of them, who may have been of an abandoned character before sickness, doubtless were moved to a sense of moral dignity, and left with firm resolves to become useful members of society. The degraded female, who, under such circumstances, feels strongly the shame of her past life, and never discloses the truth respecting it, may have been gradually brought to contemplate the horror of lustful insanity, and insensibly incline to a life of labor and propriety; for it is when the body is enfeebled by disease that the passions which have degraded the past life are as indifferent to temptation as to indulgence, and the mind susceptible to wholesome impressions, which, if ceaselessly held up to contemplation, with encouragement and assistance to procure an honest livelihood, the effects are lasting. As a school for moral reform, it presents itself as the only theatre for completeness of design. With such results, as likely in reason to flow from such an institution, the advantage of creating a similar one wherever there is a public hospital forces itself suggestively upon the philanthropist.

During an epidemic infirmaries and hospitals are exclusively devoted to curing the disease, and not to the complete restoration of health. As soon as the patient gains strength to walk, he is discharged. On such occasions he is directed to our association for board and lodging until he is able to resume his avocation. The due-bill which is given to him for two weeks' expenses is generally sufficient; when it has proved otherwise, we have extended it. So numerous was this class before the establishment of the Convalescent Infirmary that, with our other engagements, it was impossible for us to watch the result, or guard the patient from excess in his indulgence. Imprudence frequently followed license, and, from absence of proper restraint, the mortality was considerably augmented. The difficulty of obtaining a simple diet, the temptation to indulge in rich and seasoned dishes, and the indifference of the landlords to their fate, provoked the convalescents to an untimely end. I had occasion to inquire into the condition of several who I found had disappointed the watchful cares of a protracted illness by one or other of the above causes. When I brought to my recollection the earnest desire to live which some had exhibited, enlisting a sympathy in their future that gladdened the heart to see that the hope was to be realized; then to have it announced that the anxious one had, for lack of an advising friend, suddenly lapsed into eternity before the good he contemplated had begun to be accomplished, a mortification at the untoward result dimmed the pleasure of a whole day's work. Often, as I passed the cot in which they lay at the hospital, or the house of their fatal relapse, a rehearsal of past events associated vividly presented themselves. So frequent and impressive was this the case that, in the waking hours of the night, my mind seemed to be more engaged in sympathy for the lost hopes of the dead than in the cares for the distressed living.

In the month of October it was announced that the remaining convalescents would, on a certain day, be in a condition to be discharged, and that the day after a collation would be spread in joy thereof. About twenty-five sat down to a table which was furnished by the warden's family with all the nice essentials of Creole cookery. What was solemn in our past duties was turned into ridicule, and each one endeavored by such means to destroy sad recollections, even to the extent of disparaging the service rendered. Compliments or commendations would have been received as insults. We toasted each other, sneeringly, of duties rendered; we toasted the remarkable ones that survived after long sickness, and we toasted the dead. The latter alone commanded our silent respect. As a finale, each man filled his glass; standing up, he jingled his with others in his reach, and drank "Thanks to God for the exit of this pestilence."

On the 18th of September all the employés of the Globe were engaged in removing to a basement room such unsoiled beds, bedding, and furniture as we intended to do-

nate to the insane and other asylums. What was unfit
for use, and likely to breed infection, it was thought, at
any future time, was sent, together with a cart-load of
old clothes, to the swamp to be burned. The cotton
cloths which overhung the mirrors, to prevent the sick
from being frighted at the reflection of their ghastly
features, were taken down. The canvas partitions were
dropped. The windows and floors were washed and
scrubbed. Burned coffee and sugar filled the rooms with
a perfume that dispossessed the curtains of their infectious quality, and on the next morning the atmosphere
of the building had recovered its former purity. Barring
the lines of black vomit which marked the position of
the cots, and so stained the floor that nothing short of
the plane could obliterate them, the entire building was
in as good order and condition as we received it.

To conform to the custom in closing other infirmaries,
we prepared for our feast of joy at the end of our labors.

Being, from observation and experience, satisfied that
the chemistry of cooking has virtues in it more inviting
in hygiene than the medical manipulations of minerals
and medicines, it was an important requisite that a cook
of the first class should be had. The one I obtained
was not only skilled in extracting the nourishing qualities from meat or vegetables, and in the due seasoning
of gruel and food for the different stages of convalescence, but also sustained her reputation for appetizing
entremets and provoking pastries. I did not hesitate to
give her the highest wages; and I justified my extravagance to the mayor and other officials, who sometimes
visited us at night, by submitting to their judgment and
gout her dainty cooking. Having sufficient quantity of
the best wines left, I was sure to bear off the laurel for
giving the completest feast.

The number of guests was limited to thirty, which in-

cluded the privileged visitors and the physicians. The
funeral of one of nature's noblemen, R. W. Hill, prevented the attendance of more than fifteen. From those who
had never visited the rooms when filled with the sick
and dying, I expected no show or feeling of repugnance.
Of these were several whom I had invited, no less from
esteem than from an experience of their entertaining
talents. It was, above all, necessary that scenes which
had raised our sympathies to a painful degree should
not be recalled without being combated by care-dispel-
ling wit. We were for the time to rejoice that grim-
visaged death had here met a repulse, albeit his victims
were numerous; to exchange congratulations that it had
fallen to our lot to smooth the pillow of the sad and disconsolate waning spirit, and to return to usefulness many
grateful subjects. Excepting the hated death-stains on
the floor, naught else to the eye invited mournful memories. One of our guests, whom I principally counted
upon for his well-known convivial qualities, was the first
to arrive. His face wore its wonted wreath of smiles,
and indexed a generous liver. He entered the room
with the conscious air of one who defied rivalry in gibes
and jests. The appearance of the ball-room, with a table in the centre covered with borrowed silver and
glass, and bouquets of fragrant flowers, over the whole
of which fell variegated rays reflected by the setting
sun from prisms pendent from the chandeliers, while the
latter imitated clusters of precious stones, was likely to
impress a guest of the admirable fitness of the room for
a festive entertainment. By way of pastime, I thought
to introduce my guest to a knowledge of the various
uses to which we had put the several apartments. No
man knows the strength of his nerves, or the force with
which imagination can elevate or depress him, until he
has undergone a practical test. Knowing our friend
was gifted with wit, I should have remembered, in kind-

ness to him, that he was proportionally endowed with its twin faculty, imagination. As I walked him throughout the building, I explained the arrangement of the cots, and thoughtlessly directed his attention to their exact position by the lines of black vomit on the floor. I showed the spot where the dying were placed on mattresses on the floor, and pointed out spittle ejected by them, which disfigured the walls to the ceiling. Meeting with no interruption, I thought his interest in my discourse kept him silent, until he surprised me in the middle of a sentence by turning full upon me, and asking if "I had a design upon his life." I saw by the livid hue of his countenance and settled features that I had entertained him *ad nauseam*, and instantly set about retrieving my error. My first impulse was to lead him on the gallery near by, where the fresh air could percolate his thin locks, and his eye could be refreshed with the green of the adjoining park; my next, to hasten for a glass of sovereign balm in cholera. He was shortly himself again, and now braved complete explanation. Thenceforward I was corrected in intruding my experience of the horrors of the pestilence uninvited. When urged to do so, the truthful details have blanched the cheek of many a listener. Even the most pleasing cases which I have briefly chronicled in these pages have to be shorn of much that would make them repulsive.

Our party sat down at six o'clock. The soups, viands, entremets, and dessert were artistically served before us. Every adjunct to satisfy the appetite and to raise the spirits was at hand, yet a gloom hung over every one of us unlike we had ever before experienced under similar circumstances. Attempts were made to poke fun at each other, but the results were stillborn. We finally fell into an argumentative conversation, which frequent libations could not turn. In less than an hour and a half, the feast, which in every respect was fashioned to eclipse all preceding it of similar character, was ended. The studiously-prepared dishes were merely tasted; the wines alone received a complimentary attention. Before parting we responded to several general toasts, and closed our sad failure by dashing the floor with Champagne, thus formally resigning to Terpsichore the apartments of joy which Pluto and his kindred spirits had invaded.

CHAPTER XXV.

Disappearance of the Epidemic.—The last Cases.—La Ceinture Dorée.

MORE than two months had elapsed since I sent home to her family the runaway whom I had snatched from certain perdition. The month of October imperatively called many to the scene of their business, regardless of risk from the subtle poison that yet lingered in the atmosphere. A frost, which commonly destroys its effect, had not yet made its appearance. Those who had so far escaped the disease had strong assurance that they would pass the season unscathed. Should they be drawn into its influence, the chances were that the result would prove fatal, as the latest attacks have always been so. A more invigorating atmosphere by day, exhibiting little of thermometrical difference between sunshine and shade, rendered the visit of the unacclimated comparatively safer from attack than the summer resident, whose system was more or less impregnated with the disease. The epidemic of 1853 had outrun its predecessors in duration. Sixty days was its allotted course. It had not spent all its force until after ninety days. The busy note of preparation for the fall business was apparent in heavy arrivals of produce and goods. The streets became enlivened with gay and thoughtful promenaders.

N 2

Families, which had waited patiently and in sufferance for encouragement to leave their now uncomfortable sea-shore residences, dashed gayly through the streets in their carriages or phaetons, thronging the fashionable resorts of Olympe and Fryer for fall novelties.   The congratulations of new-comers and the joy of the residents dissipated every reminiscence of heart-rending scenes. Yellow fever was avoided as a topic by those who had suffered from it or by it.   The members of the association in many districts had long since made their last calls to the convalescent, and furnished complete records of their work to the secretary.   Each went his way to his respective vocation: some to meet thenceforth, and at long intervals, on the levee or street, with a hurried nod of recognition; others so confined to their peculiar pursuits that they were not seen again until a like occasion or a meeting of the association brought them together.   Our advertisement had gone forth that no new cases would be taken by us; yet, if any presented themselves, we were charged with sending them to the *Maison de Santé*, or Charity Hospital, where a per diem was paid for our sick in wards exclusively appropriated to them.   After the epidemic had exhausted itself in other parts of the city, the rear of my district, on the borders of the Swamp, suddenly became the theatre of its virulence and exodus.   One would have judged, from the miserable tenements and their occupants, and the filth that generally accumulates there, that the poison would have first generated amid them.   It was certainly more fatal.   As our labors were closed elsewhere, the greater part were sent to the hospital.   When resistance was made to this, we consented to furnish physician, medicines, and support, provided the relatives or inmates would act as nurses.   The objection on the part of the poor to be treated in hospitals, constructed as they are now, with wards containing twenty or more cots, is natural and reasonable. It is assuming too much for the richer and better educated class to say that they alone are sensitive to extraneous influences. Imagination magnifies terrors during sickness, and the shock on witnessing suffering and death agonies is as strong and as prejudicial to recovery alike to all mankind. I have not wondered that the patient who only required a composed mind and undisturbed repose at proper times has relapsed, and been himself the provoking cause of death in another. At all hours of the day and night these twenty-four patients in a ward call for attention to their wants. They are commonly such wants as are offensive to the sense. When this is unabated, and the death-rattles and vomit are loudly manifested, it is almost a miracle that any within sight or hearing recover. The effects of all these might, in a measure, be repelled by hanging curtains between the cots. The offensiveness that then arose from each patient would pass above, instead of spreading around, and more quickly escape through the let-down windows. The eye, not attracted to the sufferings of others, would close to necessary repose in spite of the wonted sounds in the room. As I have before remarked, I believe the effort of thinking, the indulgence in conversation, or any exciting cause for the imagination to take hold of, are dangerous to convalescence. Attention to these is the secret of cure in private practice, and they should be studiously enforced in our public hospitals.

On the 6th of October, in the afternoon, the following note, written in pencil, in a neat but tremulous hand, was given at my door:

"I beg Mr. ——— to remember the promise he made me, that if I should be taken sick he would attend me. Please come soon, if only for a minute.

"EMILY ———, No. —— ——— Street."

I did remember, and called to me the bearer of the note. I was pleased to find that it was an experienced Creole nurse, whose attendance rarely failed to place the patient on his feet. After I had given my promise to call upon Emily immediately, the nurse desired to know if I would be responsible for the payment of her services, as she feared the patient had nothing to give her. Knowing her price to be exorbitant, more than twice as much as we paid generally, I proposed to engage her at two dollars and a half for the twenty-four hours. The pleasant expression that I had always seen in her countenance suddenly gave way to a haughty surprise. "Do you think," she said, "that I would level myself to ordinary nurses? If you can not pay my fixed rates, please say so; but you hurt my feelings by knowing so little of me." I gave her to understand that it was not a matter of feeling, but of business, and that I would be responsible for no more than I had mentioned. "Then," said she, "I will look to Heaven for my reward, for I have taken an interest in the girl, and should never distress her for pay."

I called to see Emily at dusk. The front door was open. Facilis descensus. I walked into the front parlor, and rapping with my cane on the table, I soon raised the sounds of approaching footsteps. I found I was addressed by the same mistress of the house who was here when the "runaway" was visited by me. When she was told of the purpose of my visit, and recognized in me the same person who had called previously on a similar errand, she gathered herself up with dignity, and assumed an expression of danger and resistance, forcibly reminding me, in her rotundity of figure and arms akimbo, of the alarm and watchfulness of the hen who guards her progeny from the hawk soaring overhead.

"You can not see Emily, sir—you *can not* see her.

We are not beggars here, and seek not your visits or your charity. I can take care of my own sick. You should be satisfied with having once insulted me by entering my house. You shall not have another chance of making a hospital of my house, and decoying my boarders away from me."

I read Emily's note.

"Note or no note—and a fig for her permission—I tell you I shall exercise my rights in my own house, and you shall not see her."

Upon this her bulky figure removed from the doorway, by insinuation inviting my exit. Here was a rebuff that set me for the moment *hors de combat.* I knew she had the right to refuse me admission, and was about leaving, when it occurred to me to bring the fear of the recorder before her eyes. In an authoritative tone I explained to her that we were an incorporated body, and had privileges higher than the law, and that, if she attempted to interfere with the prosecution of my duties, I would bring an officer to enforce my demands at her expense. This expedient soothed her into an ungraceful acquiescence. Our loud talking had in the mean time gathered several of the inmates at the door, some of whom, having seen me on my previous visit, addressed me by name, and directed me to the room occupied by Emily. I opened the door, shut it behind me, and found myself alone with her. As she held her hand to me, with the imploring and anxious gaze of the fevered, I strove to bring her to my recollection. The flushed face and disheveled hair would have disguised one even more familiar to me; but when I heard her note of welcome in the familiar voice that recalled to me "Mary's friend," I recognized her fully. She had been sick for thirty-six hours, and was not apparently a hopeless case. The physician who attended her was more than ordinarily successful in his practice. This I told her, as also that

I was glad to see she had secured so excellent a nurse.
When I regarded her again, tears rolled down her cheeks.
This was no period for desultory conversation. What
little was to be said must be cheering to the spirits.

"So I have you at last, Emily," said I. "I thank
you for the opportunity of serving you. You shall get
well quickly. Every thing betokens it. Why, you look
now as rosy as the Goddess of Health herself!"

A mournful attempt at a smile flickered around her
mouth. She looked intently upon me as I felt her pulse
and forehead, as if to read her fate in my tutored countenance. Her pulse reached only 90, and the skin at
her wrist was moist. The tongue indicated the inflam-
matory nature of the attack. Her eye was yet injected,
and more distrait or anxious in expression than is common to the accompanying symptoms. The latter may
have been aggravated by grief. As I dropped a few
words of comfort and hope, tears bubbled again from
the corners of her eyes. She pointed to her heart, saying, "I do not want relief to this miserable body so
much as here. 'Tis here that I am sick." I turned on
my heel and laughed at what I deemed a misplaced
avowal. "If that is all," I replied, "your case is not a
desperate one; a few days more, and you will be permitted to see this troubler of your peace. You must
love him mightily." "Oh! no, sir, you do not understand me; I thought better of you; and it is cruel in
you to mock me thus."

She relapsed into a thoughtful silence, and appeared
wounded at my levity.

Society entertains the opinion that when a woman
lapses in chastity, and scandalizes the public ear or
eye with her sin, all the properties of her soul partake
of its corruption. A *fille perdue* must necessarily be a
creature of mere sense, of animal propensities, to whom
love, benevolence, religion, and even hope exist but in

name, and are as sealed things. Society so judges, and it must be so. As many as are made desperate from their loss of self-respect, and rapidly course through their career in drunkenness and bestial indulgence, yet there are many in whom the same cause creates a hate of the sin by which they fell, and a repentant spirit in the exercise of other virtues. There is no sin in man that engulfs in such misery as the loss of virtue in woman. The charity of the world provides nothing for her redemption from the first step. Instead of being dragged from the flames that threaten to consume her, its harsh edict forces her within their annihilating influence. The car of God is deemed inaccessible to her, though, were the sore hidden from public ken, and the powder of the Church sprinkled over it, the contamination from contact would be destroyed, and she might yet be what she seems. There is a sentiment in the human breast of faith in promises instilled in early youth, and a goodness instinctively its own, that the mere indulgence in one sin can not eradicate. The whirl of licentious passions may deaden its sense in its earthly tabernacle for years, but this germ of the soul's reproduction in a future life "still lives." Kindness and sympathy, when the body is prostrated by disease, revivify it; neglect, reproaches, and ridicule depress it with leaden influence.

I felt that such a one lay before me.

"Emily," said I, "if you have any thing that weighs upon your mind, out with it, and relieve yourself and me. I am disposed to serve you, but must know how. If you would make my services agreeable to me, I must be met with smiles, not tears and despondency. Be brief, then, and tell me how I can serve you. If your story is long, I would prefer postponing it."

"Hear me now," she said; "I can not defer. I came to the city last fall; from whence or why, I wish to forget. I have run through all the dissipations of the miserable life I have been leading. I am forgotten by all that ever knew good of me, and I hate myself. I have ever had the presentiment that if I had the yellow fever I should die. I do not want to live longer, but I want to die good and repentant, and this desire possessed me ever since your attendance here on Mary. We spoke confidently to each other. I thwarted designs upon her the night she arrived, and counseled her against the step she was about to take. Since she left I have lived an altered life. My heart was my own, though my body was prostituted for a support. I hoped to save enough to follow Mary, who promised that she would place me where I could conceal my shame and live a better woman."

"Had you," I asked, "no friend to assist you immediately?"

"Me? me? Do such as we have friends?" she replied. "Oh no! I believe the more a man sees of us unhappy creatures, the more he despises us and our sex."

Seeing she was excited, I interrupted her, saying that I would listen to a continuation of what she had to say some other time, as to prolong the conversation would certainly make her worse. At that moment the mistress of the house entered. I took my leave, and encountered the nurse in the hall, who gave me assurance that the patient was a manageable one, and the result promising.

As I descended the stairs I saw several of her fellow-boarders in the corridor. They invited me into the parlor. On the centre-table was a bottle of Champagne, of which they insisted upon my partaking. "Now tell us how Emily is," was the simultaneous ejaculation of several. "Doing well," said I; "very well; but be cautious in disturbing or talking to her." "Talking to her!" said one; "why, she will not even notice us with a reply, which is strange in her, for she always was the happiest and gayest girl of us all."

"Happiest?" said I, as I looked at the speaker and touched her glass with mine. She made no reply. I saw I had touched a chord of mournful note. Emily's health was given and drunk. All seemed awed by my presence into a respect which was not agreeable to me. By restraining their indulgence in the customary jollity of Champagne-drinking, they set me an example of deference paid to the presence of a sick person in the house. On finishing the wine I took my leave.

I shall not assume the mock modesty of most men in feigning ignorance of the character and manners of such women. They force themselves upon our observation in the highways of fashion, ever presenting a contrast of some kind or other to respectable people. They are the first to herald a new fashion, for it brings them more prominently to notice. Coquetry and studied arts, applied with an acute intuitive perception of the weak points in a man; in many, a refinement of language, ease of manners, and grace which elevates the exceptional beauty in power to a level with her superiors in virtue, make them as inviting to admiration as they are dangerous to encounter. The estimation these held me in caused them to manifest a naturalness of behavior which would deceive a novice, but gave me an insight to their real character. Though jealous and envious of each other to an extreme—though they find no friendly ear to receive the secret thoughts which ask for sympathy, but each goes independently through her avocations, yet, when sickness hovers around one of them, or the hand of Death threatens to snatch her away, all fly to the relief of the sufferer with their last dollar, and present a wonderful contrast of feeling and humanity to lost virtue and the character given them in the world. There exists a Puritanical sense of delicacy which would shut us from the Scriptures because of the Song of Solomon—a sense that is shocked at the sight of Power's Greek Slave, because there are developed the graceful outlines of the body which are conventionally hid. "To the pure all things are pure." In a civilized age such as ours, where research and investigation in morals and physics know no barrier to progress, I require no apology to write freely my observations. I introduce the subject as well to hold up the vice to detestation as to agitate suggestive remedies for an evil that is fearfully invading the peace of families. If it can not be arrested in its inception, measures at least should be taken to assist the fallen one from a hopeless misery. These women have souls which one sin can not shear of all redeeming qualities. They have feeling which is sufficiently sensitive to the shame of their condition without the scorn and persecution of their kind. They have a right to be considered and treated as human beings. Laws should be instituted applicable to their case to improve and to redeem them. As they barter their love, they should pay a license to the state for indulgence. When they have sunk so low by debauchery that they become dangerous to society and are incapable of supporting themselves, they should be placed in establishments which, in providing a home for them, might be made the means of bringing them to repentance and usefulness.

Men pride themselves on their chivalry; they can exhibit their championship in nothing more beneficial and exemplary than in alleviating the misery of those whom they have been mainly instrumental in ruining by their encouragement of the vice. Women must feel deeply humiliated in dwelling upon the degradation that a portion of their sex is reduced to, and should not be silent spectators in efforts to elevate their fallen sisters. Strong in virtue themselves, they need have no fear from contact with the latter, while their counsel and encouragement would possess tenfold the force of men. A work of this nature is begun in this country in the establishment of the "Order of the Good Shepherd." It has proved its virtue in France; it has produced its good fruits in New Orleans. Here women whose thoughts even are unruffled by sin shut themselves from the world, and are exclusively devoted to the object of redeeming the penitent fallen one. Habits of industry are gently enforced, which, after several months' exclusion from temptation, with daily devotional exercise, enable them to make a living, and lead a decent life in some place distant from the scene of their guilt. There is a wide distinction in these fallen ones. One half owe their degradation to very early indulgence; their associations up to girlhood, the education of their thoughts, are selfish and sensual. Advice is thrown away upon them; sympathy is ridiculed by them. They are reckless of the future, and die in dirt and disease, scarcely conscious of an existence beyond animal indulgence. The other half have been raised in virtue. There is an intensity of expression in the language of the best class of the latter that strikingly exhibits the strength and peculiarities of the sex at large, for they do not restrain themselves in freely speaking their thoughts on men and things. They know the low fellow from the well-bred at a glance. Mustache and jewelry do not inspire favor, having paid too dear for their experience to be foiled by such bawbles. The want of good manners in entering their presence with covered head, with tooth-pick between the teeth, or with cigar in mouth, is a fatal prestige of disgust. They are sensitive to any insult which society declares such, and feel the compliment of a respectful manner. They know what is thought of them without being reminded of it by rude words or acts. When they undertake by intrigue, open or covert, to play upon the weakness of man, their wits never fail to bring to their feet the young, the mature, or old, "by well-placed words of glozing courtesy;" these wiles are their vocation and study. Could but the history of one day in a large city be disclosed, the Machiavelian plots of these women and their conquests would be as mortifying to our pride as I have no doubt they are a source of laughter to them. We may extract an arrow from the sententious quiver of the Bible for confirmation of their superior cunning, which, after declaring that "her house is the way of hell, going down to the chambers of death," it tells us "that her mouth is smoother than oil, but her end is as bitter as wormwood." Volumes might be written upon this.

Let us view their condition and influence a little closer. The street is like to a masquerade. The contest for effect between libertinism and respectability is displayed to the height of absurdity. Perhaps the latter would doff its parade of the duchess if it were aware of its proximity to the *ceinture dorée*, whose modest gait and more studied taste in dress eclipse her in the eyes of spectators. Perhaps it would advance morality if a marked distinction was assumed between the two in style and extravagance of dress. Respectability would lose nothing of its charms by relapsing into plainness and decency, leaving the other extreme as the distinctive characteristic of vice and lewdness. It would do more: it would remove from the eye of the virtuous the chief incentive to vice, for the first fatal step in many is induced by the passion for display and dress.

The "daughters of joy" in this country differ essentially in education and habits from corresponding grades in Europe. Ours possess superior education and intelligence. They are more dissipated and extravagant. Having little regard for their health, the attraction of their charms is sooner gone. They have more sensitiveness and feeling, with less selfishness. They kindle

a passion more furiously, but command less permanence
of affection. They are toiling slaves to short-lived indulgence of their passions, while the foreign class curb
theirs that they may enjoy them the longer. It is an
exception in the American to resort to prostitution for
the support of her parents or family. In Europe it is
common. One follows the vice from necessity, the other from interest. One courts pleasure for its Lethean
virtues, the other seeks it for its real gratification of the
senses. Far from adopting any pursuit as a pastime
and employment, to them also a fixed passion for any
elegant enjoyment is a paradox. They pass through
life within a wild maze of uncertainty, and symbol, in
their gaudiness and being, the butterfly sipping from
the chance flowers to which it is tossed by the winds,
and subject to be destroyed by the least change in the
elements. "Vivimus læti" is their motto; "procul ab
angustia, vivimus læti." Yet, as before remarked, there
is a spark of divinity, a trace of early virtue in these
reckless, heedless ephemerals, which develops itself especially on occasions of sickness—which is susceptible of
being fanned by sympathy, advice, and encouragement
to a shining light, to lead them from a path dark and
thorny to the forsaken one, which they will gladly pursue. Who is to heal their lacerated hearts when repentance and remorse then overtake them? Shall they
wait for the heavens to open and an angel to minister,
or may they not more properly and certainly look to the
exemplars of their own sex for consolation? The wel-
fare of society, though, forbids it! They are prejudged
without trial, without mercy. The most distressing picture of humanity is to be seen in the wards of our Charity Hospital appropriated to the sick of this class. The
first degree of repentance is shown by the shame they
manifest in concealing their faces on the entrance of a
stranger. Perhaps the attendance and constant presence

of the Sisters of Charity have their influence. To be permitted to say "sister" must have the effect to human- ize them. It is now and here that reformation, repent- ance, and good resolutions spring. But who steps forth to encourage, to sympathize, or to save? Say that the poor sufferer, enfeebled by sickness, and the attractions of her charms destroyed, leaves the hospital cured; she is penniless. Where is she to go? She can not ask employment, for she has learned none, and, without rec- ommendation, would be hooted from our doors if she ap- plied for menial service and told her o'er true tale of misfortune. She can not, even with repentance on her lips, seek welcome, like the prodigal son, of the parents she has dishonored. She is forced back to her former companions, who shut their purses until *she can earn her bread.* If she has not this resource, with hunger and starvation staring her in the face, without a friendly shel- ter from the elements, enfeebled in body, broken-heart- ed, despair gives her resolution. She seeks the lowest of her class. The excitement of desire is supplanted by the bestiality of intoxication, madness and death ensue, and society is avenged!

Numerous have been such instances in my experience.

Success, then, to the "ORDER OF THE GOOD SHEP- HERD." It is a home mission worthy of more of the re- generating care of Christians, with more useful and tangi- ble benefit to society than all real or prospective advan- tages in the conversion of the heathen; for they are flesh of our flesh, and bone of our bone; a humiliating pic- ture of ourselves, not of savage nature, whom we should be eager to save, and when the cry is for help! help!

I have no apology to make for my earnestness when- ever I have been called upon to bestow the charities of the association upon this class. My sympathies and strivings have not been so much to save as to smooth the raven down of their despair. If ever words of kindness were medicine to the soul—if ever attention was appreciated in the physician or the watcher, it is by them. An interest shown toward them awakens a fervent gratitude bordering on adoration.

I shall pass over the particulars of a surprise which was gotten up for me on my second visit to Emily. She had been removed from the room she occupied, by order of the physician, because of its too great exposure to the north winds. Learning that she was asleep, I left to return in the evening. I ascended the steps at about nine o'clock that night, without meeting or being seen by any one. Gently opening the door, my sudden appearance startled the nurse with an exclamation that aroused Emily. The dim light of the taper obscured me from recognition until I spoke. I was expected earlier, and reproached for my delay. Seeing a large bouquet on the window-sill, I remarked that she had not been entirely neglected.

"That," said she, "is the joint offering of Jane and Clara. I know you think us girls a heartless set, as I always did until now. Had I been a sister instead of the miserable companion of their shame, I could not have been shown more kindness. You can not imagine how kind they have all been to me. Each anxiously waits her turn to sit at my bedside. They do not say much, but from my own heart I read their thoughts. Well, we are outcasts, and have no one else to think of us; why should we not be kind to each other? Not one of my male friends has inquired of me, much less visited me. I am rightly served. It is a sad thing, though, to die without being regretted by any to whom we have once afforded pleasure."

In this strain she continued to talk for some time. My injunctions to silence were disregarded. She only ceased when I threatened to leave if she continued. Were I to relate all that she spoke of in this interview, the noble sentiments to which she gave utterance, and the poetry she aptly quoted, the reader would suspect that they were creations of my fancy. While I recur to them, the scene and my feelings at the time vividly rise before my mind as the shades traced by a painter on his favorite study. Emily was a girl of good education, and had been morally and religiously trained. She was not an exception in her class. She necessarily felt the more deeply her humiliation. Her contrition for her past life was sincere and poignant. She blamed, however, none but herself. When she spoke of the home that she had left, and mentioned the names of her brothers and sisters, who dreamed not of the sorrowful end of their once-attached Emily, and when she appealed to God to save them from a like temptation, her bosom heaved convulsively from anguish and remorse. On the side of her pillow I discovered a book, and stretched my arm to take it. She handed it to me with the remark, "You may look at it, and I know you will be surprised."

It was the "Catholic Manual," which she had procured from the nurse. I remarked "that I was glad to see that her thoughts were so inclined, and hoped she was benefited thereby."

"Yes," said she, "I have been reading the prayers which I once knew by heart. At first I found no consolation in them. They were a reproach. I thought myself too wicked; but every time I read them I feel more assured that I may hope. And why should I not? Is my Maker's hand against me for my weakness? I never stole or wronged any one except my poor parents. If I can make peace with my God—"

The sobs and tears that now welled up from the heart of this penitent creature arrested farther utterance.

"This is well, Emily," I said; "you have made your peace when your desire becomes thus strong. Cheer up and compose yourself. You are now getting well, but if you continue in this indulgence it will be fatal to you."

"I do not wish to recover," she replied, with firmness. "I hope never to recover now. My presentiment is strong that I shall not. I feel happier with this feeling than I have for many years. This book has instilled into me hopes which living might destroy. One thing I desire above all things, but I fear it is impossible. It can not be."

"It may be; speak."

She looked imploring and anxious, as if her life depended upon an affirmative, when she asked "if I could persuade a priest to visit her."

"Most assuredly," I answered.

"But will he be admitted?"

"I will see to that. Before to-morrow night I will console you with the visit of one."

"Without a doubt?"

"Without a doubt," I responded; and, bidding her a hasty adieu, I left. In the multiplicity of cases visited by me during the epidemic, my mind was not seized upon by any particular patient to the exclusion of others. Each had its periodical interest for me successively. The present case of fever was the only one that called for my attention, and naturally enough engrossed my mind more completely. I could not but dwell upon the reflection that, while a Christian exhibits in his last moments a cold mediocrity, the repentant sinner rapidly passes between the extremes of vice and virtue, and is more enthusiastic in expression, and more confident in the promises of a future life. The heart possessed of the most sinful thoughts is suddenly vacated for its purest joys.

On the following day I called upon Father ——. The devotion of this truly good man to the poorest class dur-

O

ing the epidemic was unceasing. He was singular in
this respect, that he did not wait to be called upon when
he knew that one of his persuasion was sick. Upon my
mentioning the condition of life in which the patient
lived, expecting an objection, his reply was, "Such as
you speak of have my readiest service, for truly do they
stand in need of the consolations of religion," a sentiment
which I shall ever treasure as an epitome of his life. He
wished to accompany me at once. I postponed the visit until after dark. As a member of the association, I
felt no reserve during the epidemic in walking into such
houses in broad day, for my object could not be misinterpreted. I doubt if any of us would be so independent of public opinion as to be seen doing so at other
times. To avoid the scoffing of some malicious passer-
by, I concluded to take him at night.

This was Emily's fourth day. I learned that she had
been regardless of the advice of her physician; refusing
to take the potions prescribed, and indulging immod-
erately in other drinks. Upon entering with the priest,
I motioned to the nurse to leave the room.

"Here," said I to Emily, "is Father ——."

In a tone tempered with deep feeling, which must
have throbbed her bosom with a holy sentiment, he remarked, "I hope you are not very ill." I saw that I
was one too many, and left them together. I waited in
the hall for half an hour, when I descended with Father
—— to the street. He told me that in all his life he had
not heard such expressions of contrition—had never witnessed such an appreciative sense of shame and horror
of guilty hours as in her; that her devotional complaints
and her prayer for mercy affected him beyond his wont.
In short, it was the most signal triumph of latent virtue
over worldly corruption. Was resolution so firm in her
that she should never be led or driven to a relapse? We
thought so. Yet exposure to temptation was dangerous

in one whose conversion was so rapid, and my unex-
pressed wish was that she would not survive her sickness.

On the next morning she told me of the happy sleep
she had fallen into; that, in contemplating holy things,
she experienced a joy of innocence she had never before
felt. She knew she had been forgiven. She only now
desired to live long enough to make her peace with her
Maker more sure. "The life I have led," she continued,
"appears to me so horrible that I dare not trust myself
to its dangers. I want to die. I never was happier in
my life than now. It is a pleasant dream to the awful
reality that is past, and all this under the sway of one
sin. I thank you for the attendance of Father ——.
How unreprovingly he received my confession! Every word of hope and comfort that he uttered confirmed
me that I was not entirely lost. I told him all. I told
him how I was encouraged—yes, driven to my first
step. I told him of my flight from home to conceal my
shame and lessen my father's mortification. I told him
of three years of licentious pleasures—not pleasures even,
for they wanted the enjoyment to make them such. Oh,
sir, could you look into the hearts of such as I was
when we appear most gay, you would see us striving to
keep down remorse and shame. Our thoughtful brows
show the intense workings of the mind. When we are
cheerful, the peal of laughter has nothing in it of the
ring of innocent mirth. All our study is to run away
from ourselves, to drown the reproving conscience. The
intoxicating revel finished, another must be commenced.
As we hate ourselves, we despise each other. We know
that we could be justly called a name that is the greatest insult that could be inflicted upon us. We know
what we are, but will not permit it to be told us. I have
never seen one of my companions die, nor do I believe
any in the house have. I hope my example will benefit

them. Indeed, I think several only want a helping hand to reform entirely. I judge them from myself."

Having learned from the nurse that the physician would not again call unless sent for, her indulgence in conversation I did think prejudicial to her. Her fever was subdued, and nourishing drinks were ordered to be administered. Every dangerous symptom had been allayed. Her soul, too, which had been clotted with the sins of sense, was now washed of their baneful influence by the tears of repentance. Its dross of indurated earthliness had crumbled before the spirit of holiness, exposing the lustrous diamond-purity of sanctification and grace, and raising her from the hell of burning passion. Her countenance glowed with a triumphant smile, and an ecstatic expression beamed from her eyes.

I left, saying I should not call again unless sent for.

Often since, when I encountered any of her frail sisters, the sincerity of her manner—the truthfulness of the picture she drew of them, arose before me. But for the sometime gaudiness of attire, a stranger will not suspect that the thoughtful countenance he has just passed was of one of these so-called "daughters of joy."

On the next morning I was surprised to learn from the nurse that Emily had been very imprudent, and had a dangerous relapse of fever. She had dismissed the nurse at midnight, saying that she would attend to her own wants from the necessary articles placed within her reach. At dawn the latter entered the room, and was horror-struck upon finding Emily on the floor beside her bed. She had, to all appearance, in her fall, dragged with her some of the bedclothes and the pillow, on which her head then rested. A raging fever was upon her, and she gave no explanation to the questions which were put to her. I went after the physician, who repaired immediately to her. That night she recognized my voice, and called me to her. She mumbled something,

and then closed her eyes, as if the effort to speak was
too great. A little later, on expressing my surprise at
her imprudence, she explained to me that she had sent
the nurse from the room purposely to manifest her repentance in form as in spirit. As her knees had not
bent to her Maker for years, she thought her contrition
incomplete without the position. Too weak to stand,
she had gradually let down her body to the floor; she
had then drawn herself to a chair, over which she bent
in prayer until she felt a faintness come over her. She
had scarcely time to pull to her some of the bedclothes
and the pillow before she was totally unconscious.

I now beheld in full display the fatal relapse. The
pupil of her eye dilated and contracted alternately; a
jumping pulse indicated its diminished strength; breathing was rapid. Her restlessness called for continued
watching, while every now and then she gasped for
breath or ejaculated an "ugh!" To the sound of her
name no response was given. Her gaze was wandering;
small pieces of ice were eagerly swallowed. Her tongue
appeared paralyzed, for she motioned with her hands, as
if she wanted to speak. Her hand was held to ours in
token of a farewell. She drew them to her bosom, nodding her head in acknowledgment of our attendance.
Consciousness soon ceased. Paroxysm on paroxysm
shook her frame, and while the Angelus was ringing at
the dead-church, all semblance of vitality ceased. I remained aside until the nurse and a servant had washed
her body and dressed her cold limbs in clean linen. Her
features pictured forth a happy expression. With a
heavy heart I descended to the parlor, where her frightened companions were seated in silence. Tears were in
all eyes. How bitter was their grief in comparison with
others, if we could read their thoughts ! Sorrow for her
death was made more poignant from the anguish they
felt for their own fate when the Destroyer should appear

for them. They had arranged among themselves to bury her. Each bade me an affectionate farewell, and thanked me from their hearts for the simple service I had performed.

The open air was a relief to me. On the following morning I stood near by to witness the cortége of her weeping sisterhood, and as it disappeared in the distance my prayer arose that the spirit of Him "who could drive out the seven devils of Mary Magdalene" had so purged her of her seven senses that she may awake to immortality the embodiment of virtue, and that "her sins, which are many, were forgiven, for she loved much." Who dares to say that a thousand liveried angels do not attend the awakening spirit of one whose sincere repentance was as "bitter as wormwood," and whose life and death so forcibly illustrated the truth of the proverb, *Une bonne renommée vaut mieux qu'une ceinture dorée?*

Here, for the present, I arrest my pen. Materials for yet more interesting recitals fill my diary for 1858, which, if encouragement invites and leisure permits, may be shortly forthcoming in another volume.

APPENDIX.

REPORT

OF

THE HOWARD ASSOCIATION

OF NEW ORLEANS.

EPIDEMIC OF 1858.

APPENDIX.

EPIDEMIC OF 1858.

OFFICE OF THE HOWARD ASSOCIATION OF NEW ORLEANS. }
New Orleans, 20th November, 1858. }

THE following exhibits the transactions of the Association during the late epidemic of yellow fever in this city, as reported by the undersigned, who were specially appointed to prepare the same for publication.

CASES OF YELLOW FEVER.

Natives of United States	409		Natives of Ireland	1485
" Germany	1069		" France	250
" England	69		" Scotland	12
" Switzerland	10		" Italy	59
" Sweden	6		" Norway	7
" Denmark	10		" Portugal	3
" Poland	6		" Holland	2
" West Indies	1		" Canada	2
" Belgium	1		" Malta	1
" Bavaria	3			1830
	1584			1584
				*3414

Died 771
Discharged cured 2643
   Total cases 3414

E. F. SCHMIDT, President.

D. I. RICARDO, Secretary.

Treasurer's Report.

ASSETS.

Cash balance on June 1, 1858		$ 4,774.87
Contributions acknowledged in daily papers		10,422.33
Obligations of Odd Fellows' Hall Association	$31,000.00	
Less amount paid to negotiate the same	932.67	30,067.33
Total		$45,264.53

DISBURSEMENTS.

Paid physicians	$ 4,865.00
Paid apothecaries and cuppers	10,498.16
Paid Maison de Santó and Touro Infirmary	6,130.50
Paid general relief—cash to our convalescents and to the destitute applicants at the office; also for the weekly board of convalescents discharged from Charity Hospital, and for expense of sending destitute ones to their friends	8,007.15
Carried forward	$29,500.81

---

* The number of patients are exclusively the sick of yellow fever attended to. From motives which the recipients of our charities will appreciate, we have not recorded the names of the destitute who have applied to us for sustenance; the number thus relieved are several hundred.

Brought forward.....................................	$29,500.81
Paid expense account—rent of office, stationery, etc.	720.00
Paid groceries—supplies furnished for the support of the families of the sick..	3,369.37
Paid nurses	7,885.70
Paid printing—advertising, cards, etc.	860.31
Paid cabs for the use of our physicians and members, and for the conveyance of sick to hospitals	1,038.25
Paid cemeteries...	1,200.00
Balance, cash on hand	670.09
	$45,264.53
November 2. To balance cash	$ 670.09
To investments secured by mortgage	1,250.00
Total assets this day.......................................	$1,920.09

John Livingston,
J. J. Brown,   Finance Committee.
Henry Bier,

WM. L. ROBINSON, Treasurer.

The Howard Association presents herewith the result of its operations during the prevalence of the epidemic of this year. It assumed, on the 14th of August, the responsibility of declaring the yellow fever epidemic, and on the 1st of November of announcing that it had ceased to be epidemic. It commenced with a fund considered adequate to give relief to all the destitute sick, and which would have answered the purpose, had the epidemic continued only its usual length of time. Its extraordinary duration compelled it to appeal to the *citizens* for voluntary contributions. It acted upon the principle that *"Charity should begin at home,"* and it sent forth no circulars, public or private. It made no appeals to foreign aid. It discountenanced every attempt to accumulate a fund which might not be wanted during the present season. But when it found that assistance would be required, it appealed to its own citizens, and the appeal was promptly responded to without personal solicitation; and when *enough* was sent in that *appeal* was withdrawn.

It has, it is believed, fulfilled its mission. Three thousand four hundred and fourteen cases of yellow fever have been treated, with a result, considering the malignant type of the fever, very gratifying—the deaths averaging about twenty-two per cent. Those cases, it must be recollected, were among the destitute alone—those who were outside of public or private charity, and who were not connected with the various charitable institutions. They were treated under every disadvantage, in hovels and rooms without comforts or conveniences, and many only administered to after the fever had gained a firm hold upon its victim.

Besides these, the Association gave relief to several hundred convalescents—those discharged from the hospitals, and those suffering from want. The average expenditure is about eleven dollars for each person treated and relieved.

It is most gratifying to the Association to know that its warmest friends are among its own citizens; in the place where it was first organized; where it has labored, and where it intends to labor while it has supporters at home.

Abroad, the Association has the honor to acknowledge that it has numerous friends; that offers were made to collect funds, and that funds, equal to any emergency, could have been collected, if even an intimation had been given that funds would be wanted. To those non-resident friends it returns its sincerest thanks, and it hopes that no future epidemic will ever appear in our city in so aggravated a form as to tax their benevolence; but should such a calamity come, it will then unhesitatingly appeal to them, with a firm conviction that its appeal will not be made in vain. It hopes that its services may never be wanted in the future, but it will keep up its organization, and will be ever ready to act its part.

List of active Members.

E. F. Schmidt,	F. Moreno, jr.,
D. I. Ricardo,	H. St. Paul,
C. H. Nobles,	J. M. Vandergriff,
J. F. Caldwell,	R. L. Robertson,
H. H. Dentzel,	A. J. Vandergriff,
H. Bier,	J. J. Brown,
G. W. Shaw,	A. Duquercron,
John Livingston,	J. Willis,

W. L. Robinson.

CONTRIBUTIONS.

Joseph W. Allen, of Mississippi	$50.00	Twitchell, on part of visitors at	
E. H. Wailes, of New Albany	50.00	Dr. Tegarden's, Mississippi City.	$50.00
A Lady	5.00	Anonymous, to "Dear Bill"	20.00
John Watt	100.00	Payne & Harrison	100.00
A Lady of St. James	25.00	Fellows & Co.	100.00
Fort Hamilton Relief Society, N. Y.	433.28	Phillips, Nixon & Co.	100.00
H. O. Colombe, of St. James	50.00	J. B. Murrison & Co.	100.00
B. Stuart, of Fayette, Miss.	50.00	Cuthbert Slocomb	50.00
Michael O'Brien	10.00	J. D. Denegre	100.00
Paul Tulane	50.00	Officers of the Citizens' Bank	100.00
T. & Co.	100.00	Union Street, No. 2	25.00
T. Mallard & Co.	50.00	Peschier & Forstall	50.00
Ruliff & Co.	50.00	A Friend, Atty. D——	30.00
J. Felt, of Boston	10.00	S. & C.	25.00
R. S.	20.00	J. F. Rub	25.00
John Watt & Co.	50.00	Slark, Stauffer & Co.	100.00
Lewis & Oglesby	25.00	Cash, A. N. O.	15.00
Edmund Goldman	25.00	Bradley, Wilson & Co.	50.00
Herwitt, Norton & Co.	100.00	J. W. J.	2.00
W. & D. Urquhart	50.00	E. B.	20.00
A Friend	100.00	N. N.	10.00
W. E. Stark	50.00	Buckner, Stanton & Newman	150.00
Hughes, Hyllestedt & Co.	100.00	Rugely, Blair & Co.	100.00
Watt & Noble	25.00	Carroll, Hoy & Co.	100.00
Cotton Factor	50.00	T. M'Cluskey	20.00
Capt. Geo. Kirk	10.00	Chas. A. Hensler	50.00
Hewitt, Murphy & Co.	50.00	Officers Branch La. State Bank	60.00
W. H. Letchford & Co.	50.00	A. & M. Heine	100.00
F. W. Coeler	25.00	L. Spangenberg	50.00
Haggerty & Bros.	100.00	Thos. Murray	30.00
B. O'Connell	20.00	Luskins	5.00
Misses Jane M'Cerran and Jane		Mrs. Turner, 109 Canal Street	25.00

D. M.	$5.00
Peet, Simms & Co.	50.00
Palfrey & Co.	30.00
S. O. Nelson & Co.	50.00
Check No. 124.	25.00
Check No. 123.	25.00
Check No. 1399.	25.00
G. N. M. & Co.	25.00
County Cork	2.00
Place & Brennan	25.00
Edward Davis	50.00
Geo. W. Parker	50.00
P. & E. Reilly	50.00
Wright, Allen & Co.	100.00
M. J. Bujac	50.00
Spalding & Rogers	50.00
D. Bidwell	25.00
D.	10.00
Proctor's "Woods House"	125.00
Thompson & Barnes	25.00
A. L.	50.00
R. Geddes.	50.00
Knoxville, " A Mite"	1.00
W. Chambers.	25.00
Bowman & De Lee.	20.00
C. B. Payne.	50.00
John Stroud & Co.	50.00
Oakford & Ferriday	25.00
Freret Brothers.	50.00
J. & J. C. Davidson.	50.00
John M. Chilton.	25.00
Richard Aldige & Co.	50.00
A. A. Nevins & Co.	50.00
C. S., Cotton Factor.	100.00
B. Piffet & Sons	50.00
Frank Piffet.	20.00
Employés of Piffet & Sons	10.00
Gillis, Ferguson & Co.	50.00
H. J. Ranney.	50.00
Webfoot	5.00
Clason & Co.	100.00
West, Renshaw & Cammack.	100.00
In a drop-letter.	25.00
Bogart, Foley & Avery.	100.00
Coleman, Britton & Withers.	100.00
Augustin & Thibaut	50.00
Warren, Gilmore & Co.	50.00
A Friend.	50.00
German Volksfest Committee.	500.00
Miller's Billiard Saloon.	32.00
Chas. E. Leverich	25.00
Queyrouse & Langsdorff.	50.00
Mrs. Samuel J. Peters.	50.00
Samuel J. Peters, jr.	25.00
Frank Peters.	25.00
Penn & Shortridge.	50.00
Samuel Nicholson & Co.	100.00
C. G. Gaines & Co.	50.00
J. D. Lang.	10.00
M. N.	25.00
Bellocq, Noblom & Co.	125.00
Le Ronde & Co.	20.00
Check No. 169.	50.00
Mrs. T. B. Heirn, from the Ladies at Pass Christian.	170.00
H. M. Bassett.	10.00
Judge R. H. Dennis.	10.00
T. B. Heirn.	10.00
Carroll, Holmes & Co.	$50.00
Samuel M'Cutcheon, St. Charles.	25.00
C. N. Pasteur & Co.	25.00
Cash, Pascagoula, through W. Hyllestedt.	100.00
Employés of Turpin's Confectionery	30.10
Officers of the Louisiana State Bank	100.00
S. S. Littlefield	20.00
Voigts, Jenrenaud & Co.	50.00
H. Lee, grocery bill,	10.60
A. Dubuc.	25.00
O. Talamon & Dessoumes	50.00
C. M.	10.00
Menard & Vigneaud	50.00
G. M. Bailey & Co.	50.00
Stanley & Wright	50.00
S., Pass Christian	5.00
" Widow's Mite," Pass Christian.	1.00
J. L. Gubernator	25.00
G. W. Dunbar & Co.	50.00
T. F. Murray (pr'ds rec'pts 26 Oct.)	44.00
Townsend, Tompkins & Co.	50.00
C. A. Townsend, New York	50.00
Moore and Simmons	50.00
Chas. M'Guire, New York.	25.00
Mary, Bella, and Florence.	10.00
J. Y. de Egana.	100.00
M. Weber.	10.00
Abat, Generes & Co.	100.00
Gothschalk & Magner.	25.00
Anonymous, per steamer Capitol.	15.00
Metropolitan Club	40.00
M. W. B. & Co., Philadelphia.	250.00
Dr. E. Borland.	25.00
H.	20.00
Blache & Leaumont.	50.00
Joachim Kohn	50.00
Check No. 270.	25.00
Dr. G. W. Campbell	50.00
H. T., Bay St. Louis	10.00
Miss S. S. Hull	50.00
Rives, Battles & Noble	50.00
Unknown Friends, thro' the Mayor	150.00
P. Mallard.	10.00
J. H., 3d District.	2.00
Braud & Landry.	50.00
Jules Belly (Treasurer Classic Music Society).	50.00
Farley, Jury & Co.	75.00
B. De Bar.	100.00
The Groves of Blarney.	25.00
Donations left at True Delta Office	6.50
A Friend.	25.00
J. R., Port Hudson	20.00
Eliza M'Grall	10.00
Dramatic Association	30.45
J. J. Roman and others, Tibodeauxville.	90.00
J. C. Kline, St. Joseph, La.	50.00
Citizens of Montgomery, through Farley, Jury & Co.	350.35
W. P. Converse & Co., New York.	100.00
E. R. Stevens & Co.	50.00
R. W. Montgomery, New York.	100.00
Drop Letter.	50
Gas Co.'s bill.	22.05
W. & D. Urquhart, for——.	100.00
George Barnsleny, Liverpool.	24.70